SPIRIT OF THE MOUNTAIN

"Do you want me to shave you or not?"

Folding his hands in his lap, Nathan pretended to get serious. "I want you to shave me."

"Very well," Spirit of the Mountain said, lathering his chin and cheeks liberally with soap. Slowly, carefully, she began to scrape the remnants of his beard away, revealing soft, slick skin.

"Maybe this wasn't such a good idea," he groaned in the seconds she paused between strokes.

She pulled away. "Why? I have not even nicked you."

Nathan swallowed hard, then wrapped his fingers around the wrist of the hand that held the razor. He drew her closer to him. "I suddenly have other things in mind. To hell with the shave."

"What of your wounds? Libby would be—"

"To hell with my cuts. To hell with Libby." He kissed her deeply.

Spirit of the Mountain wanted him, desperately. But she twisted away. "No," she cried out, stepping away from his arms as he tried to pull her back....

Other *Leisure Books* by Fela Dawson Scott:
BLACK WOLF
THE TIGER SLEEPS
GHOST DANCER

FELA DAWSON SCOTT

LEISURE BOOKS **NEW YORK CITY**

This book is for everyone who dares to dream...but even more, for everyone who dares to make his dreams come true.

And a very special thanks to artist Rick Cain, for letting me use his poem.

A LEISURE BOOK®

July 1995

Published by

Dorchester Publishing Co., Inc.
276 Fifth Avenue
New York, NY 10001

The name "Leisure Books" and the stylized "L" with design are trademarks of Dorchester Publishing Co., Inc.

Printed in the United States of America.

"Spirit of the Mountain"
by
Rick Cain©

You see me.
But I see not
Your great form
Draped in furry stone.
With such tact and patience
You watch as I pass you.
Posed and still as the mountain
The mountain
Gives its presence away
But relinquishes not
Its secret.

Chapter One

North Carolina Wilderness—Spring 1772
Shaconage, *Place of Blue Smoke*

Spirit of the Mountain stopped, then stood at the shallow edge of the pool. She heard no unusual sound, yet she sensed danger. She moved to the riverbank and stepped from the water. The gentle sway of the maple trees, the soft rustle of its leaves, and the chatter of a gray squirrel made all seem right in the world. Spirit of the Mountain sniffed the air heavily perfumed by the pink-and-white blooms of the mountain laurel, studied the river's edge crowded with flowering dogwood.

Every evening she came to this spot, where the gentle bend in the river's course created the deep, still pool of water in which she bathed and swam. A good distance from the camp, the quiet solitude here was her haven after a day of hard work. But now, despite all the assurance of her surroundings, the hair on her neck stood on end, warning her something was amiss. She grabbed her dress and raced for the village, pulling the doeskin garment over her head as she ran. Fear crawled in her mind, fierce and strong. Spirit of the Mountain ran as fast as she could.

Out of breath, Spirit of the Mountain paused on a knoll just above the camp. The sight below horrified her. Shawnee warriors lay waste her home, their weapons dark with her peoples' blood. Women and children ran from their attackers. Acrid smoke and dust stung her nostrils as the bark-covered lodges were put under the torch, the fields of newly planted crops destroyed. But the smell of blood and death and the screams of her people assaulted her senses most strongly.

Spirit of the Mountain's feet barely touched the earth as she charged into the nightmare. A cry of anguish passed her lips, but it fell unheard upon the dead. She stumbled past one body after another—too many to count. When Spirit of the Mountain came upon her own mother and father, she dropped to her knees. Tears blurred her vision. They were all dead.

The outcry of a warrior made her look up, his gaze meeting hers through the haze of smoke. She did not move as he raised his weapon and lunged at her. In a numbed daze, she watched him fly toward her. Her brother, Running Deer, stepped between them. His right arm dangled uselessly at his side and blood stained his bronze flesh. With his left hand, Running Deer struck the warrior a deadly blow to the head.

As Spirit of the Mountain stood, another warrior grabbed her from behind, jerked her head back with a handful of her hair, and pressed his knife to her throat. She felt the blade dig into her skin, blood squeezing from the cut, running down her neck. She could see the despair on her brother's face, his proud, strong features distorted into an ugly, hate-filled grimace. His cry echoed in her mind, ending suddenly as a lance pierced his back and protruded through his chest. He stood for a long moment staring at her, surprise and dismay on his face. He fell to the ground and did not move again.

Spirit of the Mountain heard the warrior chuckle in her ear and felt his hold on her tightening. She struggled against him as he kept the blade firm at her throat. The cutting edge sliced deeper.

With a slow, deliberate movement, he eased the knife away, then pulled it across her flesh, cutting only a little. He stopped. He wanted to enjoy her death. Spirit of the Mountain understood his deliberate actions.

Anger pushed her pain away, and she brought her elbow back into his ribs. The slight discomfort she caused him made him loosen his hold on her. She twisted free before his knife could do further damage. Feeling him grab for her, Spirit of the Mountain stumbled to the ground. When he reached to pick her up, she flung dirt into his eyes and scrambled away.

She managed to get back onto her feet, but found her way blocked by another warrior. She turned, only to meet the gaze of another, then yet another. The men surrounded her, their taunts and jeers ringing in her ears. She tried to get past them, but they used the handles of their weapons to prod her back. The circle tightened. Like a pack of wolves descending upon a wounded deer, the warriors moved in. Like a wounded deer, she fought for her life.

Suddenly, the wall was broken, and one warrior stepped to her side. Her legs no longer able to support her, her lungs burning, Spirit of the Mountain fell to the ground, panting. She stared up as the fierce-visaged man approached her, and she wondered if he would be the one to deal the final blow. He raised his arm, his tomahawk red with blood. She did not flinch; her gaze never left his.

Finally, he spoke, his voice raised for everyone to hear. She couldn't understand his words, but his intent became clear. He turned and faced each of his brother warriors, silencing their outcries and argument. Only one dared step forward, the one who had started to cut her throat. He looked angry.

The man who stood over Spirit of the Mountain grabbed her by the hair and jerked her to her feet. He pulled her arm next to his, the white of her skin stark next to the brown of his. Grasping her face by the chin, he pointed at her blue eyes and yelled again.

His point made, the warriors dispersed, leaving Spirit of the Mountain to him. Because she was white, she would not be killed. A new fear grabbed her, twisting into a knot in the pit of her stomach.

The fierce-visaged warrior tied a leather tether about her neck, making it tight enough to prevent her from slipping free, yet loose enough for her to breathe. He bound her hands, then dragged her along behind him. Only four of the other men followed. The remainder of the war party had gathered together the women and children they had spared, and they headed north, most likely back to their own camp.

Spirit of the Mountain twisted about to watch the last of her people disappear into the thick growth of hardwoods that surrounded what had been their mountain village. She whispered a prayer for them and for the dead left behind.

Dusk darkened the late evening sky. Night came quickly as the sun disappeared behind tall granite crags poking like fingers through the veil of green. The rocks, strong and straight, reached for the sky, the tallest snagging clouds that passed by.

Spirit of the Mountain's small group continued northeast, following a faint trail through the wilderness along the ridge of mountains, moving into the lush pine and fir forest. Little moonlight filtered through the foliage, but the dimness did not hinder her captors. They walked deeper into the dense woods, blackness closing in like a blanket folding about them. Her only thoughts were to put one foot in front of the other so she would not stumble and fall.

They were well away from her village before they finally stopped to rest. She collapsed to the ground in exhaustion. The noose had tightened about her neck; the cut had become swollen and painful. Quietly, Spirit of the Mountain gathered needles of white pine and the soft pink-and-yellow lady's slipper that thrust through the mulched earth. Her captor watched her closely, but made no objections as she made a poultice to treat her wound.

He was tall and muscular, his obvious strength keeping the other warriors from crossing him. Though he kept his face void of any expression, the black war paint alone gave him a fierce look. Spirit of the Mountain looked beyond his physical appearance, and deep in the brown of his eyes, she saw a small flicker of warmth.

When she was done, he offered her food and water. Spirit of the Mountain accepted. She needed to keep up her strength. Then she curled up on the ground to sleep, the damp, musky scent of fallen leaves and earth cleansing her nostrils of the odors of smoke and blood that still lingered.

Her mind's eye replayed the horror: her adopted family slaughtered, her blood brother giving his life to save hers. Spirit of the Mountain brushed her tears away. With grim determination she willed her mind to blankness. She could not afford to grieve now. She must concentrate solely on surviving. She drifted off to a dreamless sleep, accepting the quiet rest she desperately needed.

When Spirit of the Mountain awakened, the sun barely touched the morning sky and stars were still showing. Slowly, the heavens turned from black to deep blue, then lightened to purple. A soft spray of light touched the frilly blossoms of the rhododendrons, their glossy, teardrop leaves stark against delicate pink blooms. A lacy canopy of green hung over Spirit of the Mountain, reminding her of the patterns

14

her mother used to crochet. Stray streams of golden light filtered through the leaves, warming away the mist that clung to the earth.

It was the same as any other morning in the mountains the Cherokee called *Shaconage*, Place of Blue Smoke. The swirling cloak came in the night. Like a living animal, it walked on silent feet, casting the ground in its mysterious, blue-tinged fog, only to disappear in the light of day.

Soon Spirit of the Mountain's captors were ready to move on. The day passed in a tiring march, beginning in darkness and ending the same. The small party had left the familiar mountains where Spirit of the Mountain had been born Samantha Jacoby. That night, Spirit of the Mountain put herself to sleep with memories of earlier times.

Over 20 years had passed since her parents had traveled to this vast wilderness to start their life together. The death of her mother from fever when Spirit of the Mountain was ten was the first sadness she had known; her father's accident and death a year later was the second.

Even then, she had faced being left alone to survive in the wilderness with little fear. Her father had taught her well, training her, as if she were a son, to survive in the wilds of the Great Smoky Mountains. She spent over a year on her own with little difficulty, the mountain and its thick, overgrown woodlands her home, the wild animals her friends.

Spirit of the Mountain felt a surge of pleasure as her thoughts turned to one friend in particular, a female cougar she had called Mama Cat. The spring before her mother died, Spirit of the Mountain had found the cougar struggling to move her kittens from the den high spring runoff had threatened to flood. Watching as the animal gently carried each kitten to a new site, Spirit of the Mountain had seen the mama cat would be too late for the last kitten. She had crawled into the watery den and carried the last baby out. When the mother returned, Spirit of the Mountain had carefully given the wiggling bundle of fur to her. The cougar was never tame enough for Spirit of the Mountain to touch her, but the cat was always there when she went into the forest, protecting her, keeping her company.

At that time, Spirit of the Mountain had had hope, but this morning brought her little. Her white skin had spared her, but what kind of life would she have as a slave? Spirit of the Mountain had no doubt she was being taken to the trading post on the New River, where her father had traded for many years. There, the Shawnee would trade her for guns and ammunition, which were scarce among Indians and of great value to them. Spirit of the Mountain struggled to keep going, to push back her sense of hopelessness.

The day was long. She could no longer feel her feet because the numbness was crawling up her legs. Each step became more difficult, and she feared each step would be her last. Spirit of the Mountain's foot came down on a branch, and before she could stop herself, she stumbled to her knees. She tried to stand, but failed because her legs were once again unable to support her.

The warrior behind her kicked out; his well-placed foot to her side encouraged her to move on. But she

16

could not. Her captor jerked on her tether, causing Spirit of the Mountain intense pain. She crawled onto her hands and knees. Another kick to her ribs sent her tumbling back onto the ground.

Spirit of the Mountain rolled over and looked up. Tears blurred everything, but she made out shadowy forms as they gathered about her. One warrior knelt beside her, but she couldn't be sure who he was. He jerked her to her feet. Her Shawnee captor shook her hard and yelled. She didn't understand the words, but his warning was clear: She must not fall again.

Four nights had passed since Spirit of the Mountain's capture, and another was coming upon the small party. They moved through the shadows of the forest with stealth and quickness, Spirit of the Mountain keeping pace. She had learned to keep up, her sore ribs a constant reminder of what would happen if she didn't. Bruises still colored her neck, but the poultices had kept the wound from becoming infected and helped it to start healing.

Sounds of the day gave over to those of the night; the darkness was a comfort to Spirit of the Mountain. It was the time she had always preferred, and even now she looked forward to the simple pleasures it brought. An owl's hoot echoed around them, his cry alerting a gray fox that hunted nearby, drawing the fox's gaze from the tufted titmouse he chased. His wary golden eyes watched the travelers pass by as his tail fluffed against the cool night. Bats fluttered into flight. A red wolf howled in the distance.

The Shawnee and their captive trudged on. A mist drifted about them, bringing sweet smells of night.

Spirit of the Mountain stopped. The tether about her neck jerked painfully, but she did not move. Her captor turned back and gave her a frightful look, then pulled her on. She dug in her heels and motioned for him to let go. Somehow, she got her point across. Finally, he released her, watching her curiously.

She sniffed the air and quietly moved past the Indians. They watched her closely, but she wasn't concerned with them. She stared into the dark shadows. Spirit of the Mountain sensed it was there. No, she smelled it was there.

The bear rose onto her hind legs only a few feet from Spirit of the Mountain, its massive paws slicing through the air menacingly. The animal growled a warning. Slowly, carefully, Spirit of the Mountain backed away. The Indians raised their weapons, but she cried out, stopping them, and the bear ran off. When her captor tried to follow the animal, she stepped in front of him.

"No," she shouted with as much authority as she could muster. "Let the bear be. She's protecting her cubs."

The fierce-visaged warrior stared down at her. At first, anger showed in his dark eyes; then his look softened. She tried to explain her actions with sign language, but became frustrated when he showed no response. Spirit of the Mountain turned away from him, but he forced her to turn back.

He pointed to his nose, then sniffed the air. When curious eyes looked into hers, she nodded. She had smelled the bear long before they could have known that they were walking right toward her and her cubs. Admiration glimmered in his eyes. He picked up her tether, and they continued on.

A full week passed before the party arrived at the trading post. Spirit of the Mountain's dread was fully warranted by the dismal place, more so by the dismal people there. The Shawnee camped with her for another night outside the post on the banks of the river. The usual sounds of night were broken by the noises that drifted to them from the cabin. Raucous laughter shattered the soft croaking of the frogs; shouts overwhelmed the gentle lull of the river as it rolled by.

Spirit of the Mountain curled into a tight ball to keep the night's chill from her. She wished she could keep the noise from penetrating her mind as easily. Each sound, piercing and strong, stole away the sleep she desperately needed, as it bluntly reminded her what the morning would bring.

The next day, they returned to the trading post. Her Indian captor spoke to the trappers, and for the first time, Spirit of the Mountain realized he spoke French. It had been many years since her French mother had tutored her in the language, but she understood enough. The Indians were from a northern tribe of the Shawnee, and she would be sold to the highest bidder.

Several trappers eyed her, their interest apparent. She cringed as she watched the dirty men drinking heavily. She could not understand exactly the words they spoke, but their intent seemed as filthy as their bodies. Her Shawnee captors were more acceptable than these men. Panic twisted in her mind.

The bidding took on a frenzied pace. The men shouted against each other, their glassy-eyed stares telling her of their determination to own her, and worse. Finally, she tugged at her captor's arm, drawing his gaze to her.

She spoke in French. "You cannot let these filthy pigs buy me. Even you could not be so cruel."

For a moment only, Spirit of the Mountain thought she saw pity, but his sympathy was short-lived. He turned back to the group of trappers.

Tears sprang to her eyes, blurring the ugliness in front of her. She ground her teeth in vexation and wiped at her eyes angrily. Then she pulled her shoulders back and raised her chin in defiance.

Only one trapper did not participate, and she studied him, trying to ignore the loathsome men who fought to buy her. He remained in the corner, shadows obscuring his face. His long legs remained propped on a table, revealing a casual, uncaring attitude. An empty plate, a drink, and the stub of a cigar littered the table, making her think he might be taking a nap after his meal, if anyone could possibly sleep with so much noise.

The clamor ended, drawing her gaze back to the other trappers. The auction was over. A short, square-looking man had outbid the rest. His smile revealed a mouthful of decaying teeth, several already missing. A dirty beard framed his face, unknown matter clinging to its shaggy growth; his hair hung in greasy clumps about his neck and shoulders. He stepped closer to Spirit of the Mountain, his foul breath stinging her sensitive nose. She turned away in disgust.

"What's the matter, little girl?" He jerked her face back to his. His fingers dug into her cheeks, hurting her. "You'd best be nice to Pierre, or I'll not be so nice to you."

He laughed. The sound chilled Spirit of the Mountain, its meaning clear enough to horrify her. Slowly, he pulled her closer and kissed her wetly. She thought she would be ill.

Raucous laughter filled the smoky, dim building. The overpowering smells of hides, ale, and unclean bodies closed in about her. She couldn't breathe. Desperate for air, she pulled free and whirled about. Distorted faces—leering, laughing—flashed by. She pushed past them toward the door.

"Don't let her get away," Pierre shouted.

Hands grabbed for her. She gouged, bit, and fought her way clear of the men, toppling anything she could put between them and her. This defiance only seemed to incite them further, and they moved in on her. Spirit of the Mountain clawed at the door and finally jerked the latch free. Fresh air urged her on, giving her the strength she needed.

She sprinted for the trees, but one trapper remained right on her heels. He dragged her down and turned her over, his body heavy atop hers. Her hands were still tied, but she scratched at his face, leaving four long, bloody marks on his cheeks. He hollered in anger and raised his fist to strike her.

Pierre stopped him, a leer still twisting his lips. "No, I don't want her face all marked up—not yet anyway."

Spirit of the Mountain was jerked to her feet, and

the leather tether about her neck painfully guided the maiden behind her new owner.

Nathan Walker watched the dirty Frenchman disappear into the trees, dragging his new possession along behind him. It had taken every bit of willpower he had not to interfere earlier during the bidding for the young woman. But the odds against him had been too great. He could have done her no good fighting the Indians and all the trappers simultaneously.

Even now, he knew it would be best if he walked away from the whole affair. The woman was no business of his. Yet he couldn't desert her. She was a white woman, first a captive of Shawnee warriors, now of a French trapper. Nathan could not abide Pierre's crudeness. Nathan knew of the man: His cruelty had earned him fierce and deserved notoriety.

Nathan gritted his teeth. He would do something he would probably regret. If he got the woman away from Pierre, then what? He was a fool to let those sad blue eyes get the best of him. A great fool!

Nathan packed his canoe and departed from the trading post, leaving behind any common sense he might have had when he had arrived earlier that day with furs to trade. He followed the river as he knew Pierre would.

Chapter Two

Spirit of the Mountain knelt to start the fire, carefully nurturing the small sparks into flames. Pierre jerked on her tether. When she winced from the pain, he laughed. He delighted in reminding her of his presence, his dominance. She glanced only briefly at his lounging form, then went about preparing their meal. The man grunted, as if satisfied she was aware of him, and returned his attention to the bottle of whiskey he cradled in his arm.

From the corner of her eye, she continued to watch Pierre guzzling the potent drink. His actions slowed and his speech slurred as the liquid took hold of him. The drunker he got, the more liquor drizzled down his bearded chin. Spirit of the Mountain almost wondered if any had made its way down his throat at all, but the glassy look he gave her was answer enough.

The short, squat man tried to stand, but failed when his legs proved too rubbery to hold him. He slumped against a tree, panting from the slight exertion. Slowly, he wound the length of leather about his hand, drawing Spirit of the Mountain to him. Although his lascivious grin made her sick, she had no choice but to move closer. She did not try to fight him as he reached for her. Instead, she smiled.

Pierre's grin widened. "Come here, little girl. Come and make Pierre a happy man."

She pointed to the whiskey, then to herself.

"You want a drink?" He handed it to her.

Again she smiled, then tipped the jug up to her lips. She took a small sip, the liquid burning all the way down her throat. She gasped, and Pierre cackled. He grabbed the whiskey back and took another long drink.

"Have another, *ma chere*. It will make you feel good." He handed the jug back to Spirit of the Mountain.

She accepted, but when she tried to take another sip, he grabbed her about the neck and pulled her tight against him. Spirit of the Mountain struggled, but he forced the liquid down her, nearly drowning her in whiskey. Finally, he let her go.

Spirit of the Mountain scrambled away, coughing and choking on the foul brew. Pierre nearly fell over with laughter. She had never seen anyone turn so red in the face. When he could breathe again, he drained the last of the bottle.

"Get me another," he hollered, throwing the jug at her.

She caught it, then moved to the pack. Spirit of

the Mountain pulled out another jug. Impatient, he tugged on her tether. "Don't dawdle. I've a thirst."

He reached for the bottle, but paused and looked up at her. "And I've a desire only you can quench, girl."

Pierre reached for her, but she stepped back in repulsion, the bottle still firmly in hand.

"Don't play shy. I'll not stand for it!"

"And I will not stand for you pawing me, you filthy dog."

His eyes widened in surprise when he heard her speak English. Calmly, Spirit of the Mountain raised the heavy ceramic jug and brought it down on his head. Whiskey ran over his shocked face. Panic rose in her when he did not move. His eyes stared at her blankly. Finally, he fell forward, his face hitting the ground with an odd thud.

Wasting no time, she pulled the offending tether from her neck and threw it onto his still body. "Dog," she spat.

"Now, I don't think that's very friendly. Do you, John?"

Spirit of the Mountain looked up to find two of the trappers from the trading post casually watching her. She pushed back her panic and faced her new foes, their posture no longer casual as they shortened the distance between them.

"But then," the one called John added with a wide grin, "she did take care of ol' Pierre for us."

"Did a right good job of it, too," the tall, lanky one agreed, giving the unconscious form a nudge with his foot. Only a groan came in answer. "He won't be up for a while. Looks like we'll need to take care of the woman for the ol' boy."

"Good idea," John drawled.

Spirit of the Mountain eyed the men warily. The one called John made the first move; the taller one followed his lead. They closed in, but Spirit of the Mountain dodged John and twisted about just in time to catch the other on the chin with her fist. It was more surprise than the punch that stopped him, but his hesitation gave her the precious seconds she needed to escape. Spirit of the Mountain fled into the thick growth of birch and oak that surrounded the small campsite.

Darkness blinded her, but instinct guided her footsteps as she ran. The two trappers were right behind her, the noise of their clumsy tracking keeping her aware of their position. Sharp as bird talons, branches of shrub maple tore at her arms and clawed at her face, yet she pushed on. Her lungs burned for lack of air, and her legs trembled from weakness. The long, horrible nightmare had taken its toll on her body: Little sleep and even less food had robbed her of the strength she needed to escape them.

Even as Spirit of the Mountain fell to her knees, she could hear her pursuers not far behind. She tried to stand, but her legs refused. Tears blurred the dark shadows as she desperately searched for a place to hide.

Nathan heard the woman's soft sob and felt a strange sensation twist his heart. He saw her try to stand, only to fall again. His footsteps fell like feathers on the matted ground, silent and swift. He was upon her before she became aware of his presence, and he covered her mouth with one hand to keep her from crying out.

The young woman fought him, but her efforts cost her dearly, and she collapsed from exhaustion. Nathan lifted her into his arms and carried her away, his steps quickening when he heard the commotion behind them. The trappers closed in, forcing Nathan to seek cover. A large, hollow log lay across the path, and he gently placed his charge inside, covering her with leaves and debris. He followed inside just as a trapper made his way across their trail.

When the young woman stirred, Nathan's hand muffled her soft moan before the man standing only feet away could hear it. Nathan watched the feet moving about in a circle. For a long moment, the man just stood and listened. Nathan felt the woman tense. He tightened his grip. She struggled, but he held tightly and leaned closer to her. "Stop it, or we'll be found out," he whispered in her ear and she stilled.

Another set of boots appeared. "Where the hell did she go?"

"She couldn't just disappear. She's got to be here somewhere."

"You search that way, and I'll go this way."

Nathan watched the trappers split up and leave. "If I take my hand away will you promise to keep quiet? I don't particularly want to have to fight both those trappers to save your hide. It would be easier if you'd cooperate in this rescue attempt."

When the woman did not move, he asked, "Do you understand me?"

Still she did not speak, and he sighed, thinking

that rescuing her wasn't going to be easy. Slowly, he took his hand away. She did nothing. Nathan put his finger to his lips, motioning for her to be silent. This time she nodded. He slid from the log, then helped her crawl out. He took her hand and led her through the trees toward the river.

The soft sounds of water filtered to Spirit of the Mountain as they drew near the riverbank. She gathered her thoughts and tried to decide what she should do. First, she would see what this man had planned. It was strange, but she felt comforted by the way his hand held hers.

They stopped. The man dropped her hand, and a sense of loss crossed her weary mind. He moved along the muddy bank, searching until he found his canoe, covered with brush. Wasting no time, he pulled the tree limbs away, then turned back to her. He waved for her to come.

Uncertainty coursed through Spirit of the Mountain as she considered her options. His hand had been warm, and she had felt a kind of safety or comfort with him. Still, confusion plagued her, keeping her feet from moving. He again motioned for her to come, urgently this time.

Noises drifted to Spirit of the Mountain, and fear moved her toward the canoe and the stranger helping her. She crawled into the canoe and moved to the front. He pushed off, the canoe sliding silently into the water.

Spirit of the Mountain picked up an oar, and they coordinated the slight splashes of their strokes, sending them downriver with ease. The moon was full, its circle of white light beaming down on the river to guide them. Within minutes, the river became rough, the strong current pulling them along its course. The man began to paddle toward the bank. Spirit of the Mountain poked him with her oar and waved him on. When he continued to move to the shore, she persisted.

"You want to go on?" he shouted, the river loud and violent around them. When she pointed down the river, he said, "You're crazy. Can't you hear? There are falls down river."

Spirit of the Mountain motioned again for him to go on. When he hesitated, she pointed to her ear.

"You are crazy."

The canoe bobbed over the churning water, bouncing off the rocks and boulders as it zigzagged toward the falls. The sound of the rushing water heightened to a deafening roar, the river cascading in a turbulent drop into the abyss below.

Spirit of the Mountain grabbed the side of the canoe before they dived over the edge and rode the wet beast down. She could do nothing but hold on as the river carried them along, plunging them over a second, even longer, drop, the rapids now a cauldron of water and foam, their canoe slight in the great expanse of motion.

As they approached a bigger fall, Spirit of the Mountain motioned for them to paddle to the riverbank. The man obliged. When they finally struggled close enough, he jumped from the canoe to pull it from the current that threatened to drag them on. They stumbled onto the mossy bank just as the fierce river ripped the canoe from his grip and swallowed it.

They lay for a long moment, neither moving nor speaking. Finally, he broke the silence. "You seemed game enough to go over the first two falls, exactly what stopped you this time?"

Spirit of the Mountain kept her silence. The man had a kind face, and she liked the sound of his voice. It was deep, with a soft tone, but weary confusion still reigned. Her instincts told her she could trust him, but common sense demanded she be cautious. He stood and walked over to where she sat. He was taller than any man she had known.

"Do you understand anything I say?"

He leaned down, the sharpest, greenest eyes she'd ever seen studying her, the darkness of his hair and beard intensifying their color. She felt as if his eyes penetrated her very soul.

"My name is Nathan Walker."

"I am"—Spirit of the Mountain turned away from his intense gaze, a feeling she had not experienced in a very long time tickling her belly—"Spirit of the Mountain."

Nathan smiled, the crinkles at the corners of his eyes deepening, the vivid green of his eyes paling with the twinkle that suddenly lit them. "You do speak English."

"Of course." Spirit of the Mountain tried to stand, but she lacked the strength. He lifted her into his arms and carried her to the shelter of the giant oaks and tulip trees that edged the river. He lay down beside her. A haze of sleep drifted over her, the warmth of his body seeping into hers, relieving the numbness that had long ago overcome her. No longer able to fight her exhaustion, she gave in, drifting into the comfort of sleep, secure in this stranger's embrace.

Nathan stared at her heart-shaped face, which somehow seemed particularly appropriate for a woman so courageous. Long dark lashes fanned her pale cheeks, but he remembered the beautiful blue pools that lay beneath her closed lids. Gently, he wiped at the smudges of dirt and blood that marred her beauty. He settled down, comfortable against her. Within minutes, he felt his own lids grow heavy with weariness.

Spirit of the Mountain heard the man's heart, her ear warm against his chest. The steady pounding was comforting, its steady rhythm matching her own heartbeat as it began to throb inside her head. Slowly, she opened her eyes; his heavy breathing told her he still slept. She pulled away from his embrace, then regretted doing so.

It was still dark in the trees, but morning light dusted the mountaintops with a spray of gold. The river beckoned to her. Its cool, clear water wakened and refreshed her when she waded in. Careful to keep from the strong current, Spirit of the Mountain bathed away the dirt and grime of the last grueling week. If only she could be cleansed of the memories branded in her mind.

Grief and fear twisted together in the pit of her empty stomach. As she looked about, a rush of emotion intruded upon her weariness. She did not know where she was. Was this man, this Nathan Walker, to be trusted? Her instincts told her yes, but recent experiences cast doubt on her feelings.

Thoughts of her family brought forward the grief

she had put aside. Her emotions overwhelmed all else. A tremendous pain ripped through her, tearing apart her fragile composure. Tears choked her, and Spirit of the Mountain struggled to the shore, where she sank to her knees, sobbing. Visions assaulted her, haunting her with their horror. The memories were too fresh, too tender. She gave in to her heart's pain and wailed.

A short distance away, Nathan watched the young woman the Indians called Spirit of the Mountain. He wanted to comfort her, but didn't. Her sobbing slowly subsided, and in its place came the Cherokee death song, the notes gaining strength as she sang the song of mourning. He had heard this song before, but never had it touched him as it did now. Her sadness became his; her grief swelled inside him.

He tried to move away, but couldn't. His feet were moored to the spot as if with leaden weights. He imagined what she must have endured. Perhaps she had witnessed the deaths of those she now mourned. These conjured visions consumed Nathan, plunging him into a flurry of emotions he rarely experienced. Entranced, he struggled to free himself from the unwanted feelings. He didn't like being out of control. His frustration became anger, its potency finally ridding him of the spell.

Nathan turned away. Despite the coolness of the early morning, sweat had accumulated on his brow. He impatiently wiped it away. Again, he wondered what he was getting himself into.

When her tears were spent, Spirit of the Mountain returned to where Nathan waited. He noted the pain that remained etched on her face. He also noticed how beautiful she was, with her wet doeskin dress clinging to her.

The silence seemed awkward, and Nathan cleared his throat. "You never did tell me why you wouldn't take the final falls."

Spirit of the Mountain waited a long moment before speaking, as if she were tired and found answering difficult. "I do not understand."

Nathan walked to the water's edge. "You urged me to take the first two falls when I would have come to shore. Then before we reached the last, you stopped me. Why?"

"The last fall was too large. We would not have made it in one piece."

Nathan was confused. "You've been here before?"

"No."

"Then how do you know this?" She was right, they could not have made the last fall, but he would not have thought they could have made the first two. "And how could you have known the first two were safe enough to cross in my canoe?"

When Spirit of the Mountain turned away from him, her look cautious, nervous, he reached out and pulled her chin back. He looked into eyes that seemed to tell all. "It wasn't just your own life you were risking." Then he added, his own eyes widening, "You didn't know."

She sighed heavily, as if giving in. "I could hear the difference between the falls. The third was too large."

Nathan could feel the heat rising to his face. "How could you hear the difference? It was all just a loud roar!"

33

"It's hard to explain," she whispered, twisting free of his hand.

"I lost my canoe, all my traps and supplies," he said evenly, but he knew the muscle in his jaw twitched, giving him away. "I lost everything except the pack on my back and my rifle, so you'd best explain."

Spirit of the Mountain stepped back in confusion. "I sensed the first two were safe, but the last one—"

He didn't let her finish. "What do you mean by sense?"

Nathan waited for Spirit of the Mountain to answer. It was as if all about them had fallen silent: The trees, the animals, even the soft breeze were still, waiting for her answer.

"I trust my instincts. They never fail me."

Nathan just stood and stared. When he finally spoke, anger sparked each word. "Your instincts— you trust your instincts."

"Yes, I do." Spirit of the Mountain walked away. "I will go now."

This action stopped Nathan's thoughts cold, like a splash of water on a flame. His anger sputtered out, its fire gone as suddenly as it had come. "You aren't going anywhere, Spirit of the Mountain."

She walked farther into the cover of the forest. "I am going home."

Nathan made up the short distance she had put between them in a few long-legged strides. Gently, he grabbed her arm and stopped her. "Hold on."

She said nothing, but her look told him she was not happy with his persistence. "How did you end up with the Shawnee? That was a Cherokee song you were singing."

"The Shawnee attacked my people's village and took me captive."

"Your people? The Cherokee? They are who you want to go home to?"

She nodded.

"You can't go home. There is nothing to go home to." This was just a guess, but Nathan was almost certain of it. It would have been unlike the Shawnee to leave anyone or anything behind.

"I will." She jerked free of his hold. "Go home. You cannot stop me."

It was true. Nathan couldn't stop her. But he felt he should for her own good. Flashes of old memories and old pains tramped across his mind, devastating any doubts he might have had. Although he was certain he was in the right, he threw up his hands. "No, I can't stop you. Unless—"

"Unless what?" she asked, eyeing him warily.

"Unless I tie you up and carry you with me."

Her mouth rounded as did her blue eyes; the fear he saw in them made him regret his threat. "I don't want to hurt you, Spirit of the Mountain. But I can't let you wander off alone in this wilderness. You admitted yourself you've never been here. How can you find your home? How long has it been since the Indians took you?"

"Eight nights," she whispered.

"You will come with me."

"No," she declared and started off again, her chin tilted stubbornly, the stomp of her feet showing her steadfast purpose.

"I won't let you commit suicide," he hollered, following her.

When she continued on without answering or looking back, Nathan gritted his teeth in vexation. Her pace hastened, and so did his. Soon, he was running after her as she darted deeper into the dense wall of trees and undergrowth. He could no longer see her, but he followed her noisy retreat easily.

His irritation grew with each slap of the thick brush across his face. Catching sight of her just ahead, he quickened his step. As he fought to be clear of the scrub, he decided she had gone this way on purpose. Each scratch, each sharp branch that reached out to hinder him seemed somehow personal. Finally, he caught up with her and grasped her arm firmly.

"Leave me be, Nathan Walker," she cried, her voice stressed with pain. "I must go home to my people!"

"They are not your people," he shouted back. "You are free to go home to your own kind. Don't you see? You are no longer a captive. You are free!"

"You do not understand," she said. "I was not a captive. They were my family!"

Nathan tried to keep her flailing fists from connecting, and at last, he pulled her to the ground, his arms locked about her. She struggled to break loose, but she was too weak to escape his stronger hold. She stilled, deep sobs shaking her.

Spirit of the Mountain wept again, and this time, Nathan understood her pain. She cried for herself, for her family, for her people. He held her tight, comforted her. His whispered words were gentle and caring as he cradled her in his arms.

"It will be all right," Nathan said. "I'll take care of you."

She looked up into his eyes, and the trust he saw shining in hers stirred him greatly.

"Why?" she asked. "You don't know me. Why do you care what happens to me?"

Nathan considered her question before he answered. "I don't know, but I do know I can't walk away. I couldn't last night, and I sure as hell can't leave you here alone today."

"Take me back to my village."

Her request seemed simple, but it was impossible. "Is your Indian family still alive?" he asked. The pain that flickered across her face told him the answer. "I can't take you back, Spirit of the Mountain."

"I will find another tribe to live with."

He brushed a stray tear from her pink cheeks. It was good to see some color in her face. "You're a white woman: You might not be accepted as family. You could end up a slave or worse."

Nathan looked away from her troubled blue eyes and studied the scarred bark of a birch tree. A piece of withered velvet still clung to the rough white surface where a buck had rubbed his antlers, trying to be free of the tender, bleeding skin.

Memories of his years as a captive, a slave, crept forward, strong and unyielding. Just thinking what the Indians might do to her made his flesh crawl. The chill of a sunless forest cooled his flesh, but it could not touch the heat that scorched his mind. No, he would never take her back with the small hope she would be adopted as she apparently had been before.

"Where will we go?"

Nathan got hung up on the fact she had said we, and a moment passed before he focused on what she asked. Where could he take her? Perhaps a white settlement would take her in. Quickly, he discarded that notion. Too often, a white woman had as much difficulty returning to her own kind as she would have staying with the Indians. He couldn't do that to her.

"Surely you have someone. Perhaps a distant relative of some kind?"

The name of Samuel Jacoby drifted across Spirit of the Mountain's mind. She allowed only a moment's hesitation. "No."

He raised his brows. "You do have someone. I see it in your eyes."

Spirit of the Mountain became uncomfortable that a stranger could read her thoughts so easily. She stood and walked away. And although a forgotten moment drifted across her mind from long ago, suddenly real and unyielding, she stuck to her answer. "No, there is no one."

Her response made Nathan smile, then laugh. The sound was soft and gentle. The humor didn't mock her attempt at lying, and the twinkle that lit his eyes made her feel good. She laughed with him, but she was determined, just the same, to remain firm in her answer.

"You don't lie well, Spirit of the Mountain."

"I have had little practice."

Nathan could see her stubbornness in the set of her jaw, the squareness of her shoulders. He understood she would not give in easily. He could play that game, too. He shrugged his shoulders and turned away from her. "I have no choice but to take you to the nearest settlement. Perhaps the church there will take you in."

"I do not wish to be taken in by strangers."

Her voice shook slightly, and he knew he was on the right track. "Since there is no relation to take you to, I'll have to do the best by you I can. You do understand I have no choice, don't you?"

She nodded, but fresh tears came to her eyes. Nathan felt his own resolve weaken. "Come on then. We've a good spell of walking ahead of us."

Nathan headed off, but Spirit of the Mountain did not move. He looked back, waiting. A beam of sunshine filtered down through the ceiling of branches and leaves, casting her in its soft light, bringing a golden blaze to her loose hair. It struck Nathan how one moment she was stubborn and strong, but the next fragile and frightened.

"I have a grandfather."

"Where is your grandfather?" He moved back to stand by her.

"Boston."

Nathan's smile returned. "Then I will take you to Boston."

"He might be dead. Or"—she paused, uncertainty strong in her voice—"he may not want me."

"Why not?" Nathan was appalled to think anyone would not accept their own flesh and blood.

"Samuel Jacoby did not approve when my father married my mother. She was French. Because of this my father and mother left Boston. They left Samuel Jacoby to begin a life of their own, free from his disapproval. He will not welcome me any more than he did my mother. I cannot go to him."

"How do you know he would not want you? Maybe he's changed."

"Maybe he has not."

Nathan smoothed his beard and gave what she said some thought. "Have you ever heard the saying two wrongs don't make a right?"

Spirit of the Mountain nodded her head. "My mother believed it was so."

"Would your mother have wanted you to give your grandfather the benefit of the doubt?"

Spirit of the Mountain tried to put the vision from her mind, to put aside the memory of her mother's dying words:

Please, Neil, I beg you. Take Samantha back to Boston and settle this anger between you and your father once and for all. Our daughter deserves better than this. You deserve better. You gave up everything for me, for us. I beg you to go home. Do not stay in this godforsaken land once I am gone. Promise me you will do this so I will not die with this unrest in my heart.

Her father had failed to make good his promise.

Tears fell onto Spirit of the Mountain's cheeks. "Yes, she would."

Chapter Three

"Nathan Walker."

Nathan stopped and turned to Spirit of the Mountain. "Yes?"

She, too, had stopped, her face pinched and pale. Nathan quickly moved to stand beside her. Since he could see she was trembling, he put his arm about her shoulders for support.

"Do you think we might rest a moment?"

The weakness reflected in her voice made Nathan regret having pushed so hard to put distance between the trappers and themselves. His concern that the men would follow them became secondary. "Of course. I didn't think."

He put his hand to her forehead. It was hot. "You've got a fever. When was the last time you had something to eat?"

Spirit of the Mountain turned away. "I only need a moment to rest; then I can go on. Please do not concern yourself."

Nathan felt even worse. He lifted Spirit of the Mountain into his arms. "There are some caves not too far from here. We'll stop there for the night."

Spirit of the Mountain felt the burning in her eyes and knew he was right: She needed food and rest. She was embarrassed by her weakness, yet she felt comforted by the strong arms that carried her so effortlessly. The muscles beneath Nathan's buckskin shirt were hard and defined. Giving in to her feelings, she allowed him to carry her, her head cradled on his shoulder, her arms tight about his neck. The earthy scent of the animal hide and his own musky male odor became one, filling her senses. Despite her near exhaustion, Spirit of the Mountain felt the stirring of desire so long dead inside her.

Had it been nearly two years since her husband had held her in his arms? This stranger was the first man who had broken through her grief and loss. Spirit of the Mountain wondered how she could be attracted to a man she did not know, how she could trust her life, her future, to him.

"You can let go now," Nathan said, interrupting her thoughts.

Spirit of the Mountain opened her eyes, meeting his gaze. Then she realized they had stopped and he had spoken to her. "What?"

"You can let go now, Spirit of the Mountain."

Regretfully, she unwound her arms from his neck, and he gently set her upon the ground. They were standing at the mouth of a huge cave. "Do you think the Frenchman will follow us?"

A deep sigh reached her ears, and she turned to Nathan. "Pierre can be very dogged. He won't take this lightly."

"You know this man called Pierre?"

"I know of him. He's a dangerous man."

This answer confused Spirit of the Mountain. "I do not understand why you have put yourself in danger, Nathan Walker. Why would you do this for someone you do not know? It does not make sense."

"No," he conceded, "I guess it doesn't at that."

Spirit of the Mountain stepped closer and put her hand to his face. His beard was soft yet prickly against her palm. "You must not take such risks. You must go on without me."

Like a cloud covering the sun, a dark shadow passed over Nathan's face, stealing all the lightness from it, leaving only a hardness Spirit of the Mountain was frightened of.

"We've already gone over this. I'll not speak of it again."

His words were definite. Although Spirit of the Mountain sensed she should take heed, she chose to argue the point. "You are a stubborn man, but it is foolish to stay. I can take care of myself. I do not need your sympathy or protection."

Nathan couldn't believe what he was hearing. She thought he was stubborn! He'd had mules less contrary than this woman. "I suppose you didn't need my protection last night when those two trappers were hot on your trail? Do you have any idea what they would have done to you if they had caught you?"

He was angry—angry with those men for their in-

43

tent, angry with Spirit of the Mountain for discounting the danger facing her. He grabbed her shoulders and shook her hard, ignoring the fear that had crept into her soft eyes. "Do you?"

Tears were his answer, making the blue of her eyes stand out against the paleness of her skin. Her lower lip trembled, but she bit it to keep it still. She blinked back her tears and pulled away from him.

Spirit of the Mountain said nothing. What could she say? He was right, and she could do nothing to make him go away. Perhaps in time she would understand his reasons for staying better.

"I'm"—Nathan paused when she turned to him— "going to see if I can snare a rabbit."

For a long time after he disappeared, Spirit of the Mountain merely stood, staring. Finally, she closed and opened her eyes to relieve the burning and moved farther into the cave. She gave herself a moment for her eyes to adjust to the darkness and found a small lagoon of water inside the stone room. Water spilled down the rock wall, which was worn smooth where the water followed its twisting path to the pool. The sound soothed her. She knelt down and rinsed the dust from her face. Weariness tugged at her eyelids, but she shook free of its demands. She must gather wood for a fire.

Spirit of the Mountain tried to stand, but weakness kept her down. She tried again, then decided she would rest a moment.

Nathan shook Spirit of the Mountain gently. Slowly her eyes opened. Like a cat, she uncurled, stretching her legs and arms as she did. She yawned widely.

"You'd better eat something." He handed her a rabbit leg, the skin charred and brown from the fire where it had cooked on a spit. Her eyes widened, and she looked about in dismay.

"You must think me lazy, Nathan Walker. I should have built a fire while you were gone. Instead I fell asleep."

He smiled at the shy blush that colored her cheeks. "I would never think you lazy."

His mood, the soft tone of his voice, and the look in his eyes moved the warmth in her cheeks through the rest of her body. Spirit of the Mountain concentrated on the rabbit leg she held. Never had anything smelled so wonderful or tasted so heavenly. She devoured the meat.

Nathan offered her another morsel, and she accepted with a wide smile. "I can remember my mother saying a lady should never eat as if she was truly hungry." She took another big bite, swallowed, then licked the grease that smeared her lips. "I was never very good at being a lady."

"I prefer you as you are—honest and strong."

Spirit of the Mountain's smile disappeared. "As you can see, Nathan Walker, I am not so strong. You have had to care for me as if I were a child."

"I think you are stronger than any woman I have ever known. Many would not have survived what you have been through."

Remembrance assaulted Spirit of the Mountain, robbing her of the good feelings inside her. She shivered and whispered hoarsely, "Death had me in his grip." She touched the cut on her neck. "Why am I not with my family? Why did the Spirit of Death not take me?"

Nathan heard the agony in her voice and saw the pain written on her delicate face. He wanted to answer her questions, to ease the grief in her heart, but he couldn't. He didn't know why she'd been spared. He was helpless to find answers to his own questions, let alone to hers.

"I don't know, Spirit of the Mountain." He sighed. "Perhaps it's best we don't know why things happen the way they do."

"Yes," she said, putting aside the meat she still held. "That is best."

When Spirit of the Mountain yawned again, Nathan pulled his blanket from his pack and put it around her shoulders. "You'd best sleep some more."

She was asleep almost before he had finished the words. Nathan smiled and tucked the blanket around her. A strange sensation touched him, and he thought of how good it felt to take care of someone. He had been alone many years. He would have thought being responsible for another's safety and comfort would be an irritant rather than the pleasure it was. She had stumbled into his life, catching him totally unaware. Within 24 hours, she had settled into a place in his heart he thought had died with Sarah long ago.

He shook his head in wonder. Why, indeed. Nathan settled back against a broad, flat rock and watched the woman sleep. Curled up in a ball near the fire, Spirit of the Mountain looked childlike. Yet he knew she was anything but. Too many times when she looked at him with her round blue eyes, he had been all too aware she was a woman.

Nathan closed his eyes and tried to gather his composure. It could be a long walk to Boston, and he'd better get control of his feelings—and keep control. Yet even with his eyes shut, his mind's eye conjured visions of her berry-red lips and honey-colored skin. With a groan, Nathan stood and walked away from the fire; the heat inside him was enough to keep him warm in the coolness of oncoming night.

He stood at the mouth of the cave, watching the sky change color, the soft blue becoming purple, then black. Stars popped out against the inky backdrop, winking and blinking as he studied their age-old patterns. The night was clear, but his mind remained cluttered, cloudy.

Still, when Spirit of the Mountain cried out, the sound cut through his troubled thoughts to his very soul, pulling him back into the cave and to her side. She was sitting up, her mouth still open from her outcry, tears wetting her cheeks. Nathan knelt down and reached out to her, but she seemed not to see him. Visions of her nightmare seemed to control her.

"It's just a dream," he said softly, pulling her into his arms. "It's just a bad dream." He pushed back the tendrils of hair that clung to her face. She was still warm from fever, and her eyes shone too brightly against the paleness of her face. He rocked her back and forth, stroking her head to sooth her as best he could.

Slowly, Spirit of the Mountain found her way back to reality. Like a beacon of light, Nathan's hushed voice pulled her clear of her troubled dreams. The nightmare brought back the horror of remembrance, its hold on her strong and unyielding. Yet the steady beat of his heart drowned out the cries of her people; his earthy smell overcame the taint of death. Her hands held on to a body that was warm and giving, and her mind released the dead spirits that haunted her.

Spirit of the Mountain found Nathan's intense green eyes, the look in them chasing the last of her dream away. "Nathan Walker," she whispered, her gaze never leaving his.

"Just call me Nathan."

"Nathan."

"Yes," he said, his breath warm against her cheek.

She blinked and tried to gather her composure. "I am sorry to be so much trouble to you." Spirit of the Mountain knew she should pull free from his arms because his closeness confused her. But she didn't.

Yes, Nathan thought, she was trouble all right— only a different sort from what she was thinking.

Unable to stop himself, he bent his head and kissed the lips that troubled him so much. They were soft, parted slightly; he could taste the sweetness of her mouth. His tongue touched hers. Her hands slid to his neck, her fingers cradling the base of his head. He pulled her more tightly into his arms. Her body molded to his as his hands explored her delicate curves.

The explosion inside Nathan was so intense that it took his breath away, then shook him so thoroughly he pulled away. He sucked in a great gulp of air to clear his thoughts, to cool the heat that scorched his body. He held her at arm's length. When he dared to look into her eyes, he saw confusion and pain, and he dropped his hands from her shoulders.

"I'm sorry. I didn't mean—" He didn't finish. He had meant to kiss her, and more. That was what frightened him. Nathan turned away from Spirit of the Mountain and went back outside. He should be standing watch, not seducing a woman who trusted him.

Back in the cave, Spirit of the Mountain started to call after him, but stopped. The sudden awakening of desire and long-forgotten needs had overwhelmed all else. Even her grief had become secondary to this startling passion. Guilt washed over her, and shame heated her face. Yet even before she could fully comprehend the array of emotions rushing through her, Spirit of the Mountain felt a pang of hurt because he had pulled away from her.

Unable to rid herself of this feeling, she sat back down and curled up in the blanket he had given her to keep warm. It smelled of smoke, earth, and Nathan. He didn't need to be present for her to see him. His image remained in her mind, clear and distinct. He was taller than most men; his broad shoulders were appropriate for his great height. Long dark hair framed a bearded face, but it didn't camouflage the strong, proud lines of his heritage.

Spirit of the Mountain thought he had a fine, handsome face, but it was his eyes that dominated all else. They were the color of a lush green forest. Sometimes when he laughed, they were the bright green of new growth; but mostly they were the shadowed green that appeared just before darkness.

She rested her chin upon her knees and waited for

49

Nathan to return. Should she say something or pretend that nothing had happened?

A dull ache in her head kept Spirit of the Mountain from thinking straight. She felt weary. Nathan's look told her their kiss had been a mistake. She should consider it a mistake, too. This thought prompted a sigh. Spirit of the Mountain didn't think their kiss so. She touched her mouth, imagining his lips on hers. She liked his kiss and wanted to feel it again.

Her eyelids drooped, then closed. This time, her dreams were of Nathan, of a man loving her again, as a woman should be loved.

Nathan berated himself for kissing Spirit of the Mountain. He had barely had the thought to keep a close reign on his desire before he was doing just the opposite. Again he wondered at the sudden turn his life had taken. He had passed many years in the wilderness, alone, content with his solitude. So what the hell had possessed him to put his nose where it hadn't belonged? He should have walked away and never given the young woman another thought. But he hadn't.

He had allowed a moment of weakness to control him; his own haunting memories made him interfere. Nathan closed his eyes, the vivid recurrence of old emotions striking hard, pushing forward memories for his mind to repeat. Seven years of indentured service and three years as a Huron slave had left scars—deep, unhealed marks upon his soul. He had thought the unwanted mental baggage long gone. Yet after one quick look into Spirit of the

Mountain's fearful blue eyes, he was lost to his tortured past all over again.

Nathan pushed the pent-up air from his lungs. His jaw set, he pushed the memories from his mind as well, focusing on something more immediate. How was he going to get himself out of this mess?

He would do as he promised. He would take Spirit of the Mountain to her grandfather in Boston. Then all would be right. And along the way, he would keep his hands to himself.

"You are a man of your word," Nathan mumbled aloud, as if hearing the words would make them true. "You'll not act like a schoolboy again."

Pierre bit off a chunk of dried venison. It was the second night he had spent without a fire. "Damned woman," he growled.

It had been easy to pick up the trail of the two trappers, and he had followed them as they followed the girl. Pierre gathered from the short arguments between the two that the girl had gotten away from them with the help of a third man in a canoe. The man and girl hadn't gone over the last falls. Instead, they'd started off on foot. They couldn't be far away.

A smile twitched one side of Pierre's mouth as he thought of the girl. She was sure to please him. He would let those fool trappers lead him right to her. Maybe they'd even kill the son of a bitch she was with. Then all he would have to do was kill them and pick up his property.

Chapter Four

Nathan shifted uncomfortably. The night had seemed long and unending, but the day would dawn in another hour. He found himself looking forward to heading out again. Perhaps then he would keep his mind on the travel, not on Spirit of the Mountain as it had been most of the night.

A quiet noise roused him, causing him to stiffen against the broad tree. It was so subtle a sound it might have gone unnoticed by most men. But to Nathan, it signaled the presence of another human being. He didn't know whether the intruder was Indian or white. It didn't matter. He slowly lowered the barrel of his long rifle, still casually propped in his bent elbow, but ready should he need it.

A twig snapped, and the usual forest noises hushed. Nathan did not move. He stilled even his breathing so he could listen. The slightest movement in the thick wall of trees told him where the man was.

The man lunged forward, and Nathan fired. When the smoke cleared, Nathan saw the man had disappeared back into the lush growth. Nathan took out after him.

Spirit of the Mountain heard the gunshot and froze, the piece of wood she held in her hand poised above the fire she fed. As a shadow crept into the cave, she stood and raised the chunk of wood.

The trapper rushed her, and she brought her makeshift club down on his head. The man cried out in pain, but he seized her wrist before she could strike him again, forcing her to drop the wood. He wrestled her to the ground, his much greater weight giving him the advantage. Then Spirit of the Mountain bit his hand and twisted free. She crawled away from him, kicking at his grabbing hands.

Steellike fingers caught her, wrapping about her ankle. Spirit of the Mountain clawed at the ground, but she couldn't keep the trapper from dragging her back to him. A sinister chuckle filtered into her mind. Hands slid up her bare thighs. She screamed, yet her rage seemed only to excite the man further, and his laughter mocked her anger.

She turned around and hit the man hard on the chin with her fist, but the blow did not seem to bother him. His head nearly even with hers, Spirit of the Mountain stilled. The light of victory burned in his eyes. She closed her eyes, unable to look at his vile face. For one slight moment, she felt him relax as he pulled up her dress.

Quickly, Spirit of the Mountain brought her head up, butting the man's nose with her forehead. He sat back, hands to his broken and bleeding nose. She struggled free and scrambled to her feet. But her escape was blocked because the Frenchman stood in the entrance to the cave.

Spirit of the Mountain looked back. The trapper, also apparently afraid of Pierre, stood, one hand still holding his nose, the other held up as if to stop whatever Pierre might do.

Pierre held a knife—a large, long, ugly knife. Slowly, he stepped closer, his head moving back and forth.

"You shouldn't have tried to take my woman, John." Pierre shook his head. "It was not a good thing to do to Pierre."

"We . . . just wanted—Ah, hell, Pierre, it ain't often we get a chance at a white girl. You really can't blame us none."

"It's true," Pierre said. Now his head moved up and down. "White women are hard to come by out here. But—"

Spirit of the Mountain dared a glance at the trapper named John, whose face went white when Pierre didn't finish his thought. She could see his hand shaking as it reached for his own knife, still in its sheath at his waist. The cave was damp and cool, yet beads of perspiration dotted John's face. He had the look of a man about to die. Spirit of the Mountain swallowed hard and looked back at Pierre.

He seemed unaffected by the man's fear. A cold, hard look shone in his eyes—the look of a killer. Killing was a part of the wilderness, a matter of survival for man and animal alike. Killing was something Spirit of the Mountain understood. But she saw something different in the depths of this man's pale gray eyes, and it chilled her. He liked to kill. Her stomach twisted and she felt ill. This man was more than dangerous: He was evil.

Making the first move, the trapper dived at Pierre. They came together like two angry bears, grunting and twisting together. Spirit of the Mountain tried to get past them, but couldn't. Nathan appeared at the mouth of the cave just as Pierre's blade disappeared into John's middle. The two men stopped their struggle and Pierre shoved the dead man from him.

When Spirit of the Mountain moved toward Nathan, Pierre said, "I could understand the other two interfering and taking the girl—"

Pierre's words stopped Spirit of the Mountain less than a foot from Nathan. Then she turned around.

Pierre's stance was casual; he was seemingly unconcerned as Nathan lowered his rifle directly at him. "But I am a bit surprised at you, Walker."

"Well"—Nathan shrugged his shoulders—"I don't really understand it myself."

Pierre laughed and wiped the blood from his knife on John's dead body, then put it away. "She is pleasing to look at."

A shudder traveled down Spirit of the Mountain's spine.

"Judging from the tracks I followed, I thought maybe an Indian had helped her get away. I never understood why you dressed so much like the savages, Walker. But then, you've always kept to your-self. That's why I don't understand you interfering in another man's business."

"Maybe I want her for myself."

Pierre laughed again. "For the likes of him"—he pointed at the dead man—"I'd believe that. Even the likes of me! But you, Walker? No, you've always struck me as a man of principle. A man who'd want better than a whore who's been used by filthy ani-mals since she was old enough to be mounted like a dog."

The ugliness of his words struck Spirit of the Mountain so hard she saw red. She would have charged the horrible Frenchman if Nathan hadn't grabbed her around the waist and stopped her. She screamed her anger, the sound echoing off the cave walls. His efforts cost Nathan the advantage he had on Pierre.

"She's certainly a handful." Pierre straightened his arm and pointed his pistol directly at her. "I like that."

The jerk of Pierre's pistol told them to move away from the cave's entrance. Nathan all but carried Spirit of the Mountain back into the cavern.

"Give me the girl, Walker. I've no fight with you."

Spirit of the Mountain looked up at Nathan. His eyes were shuttered; no emotions showed as he stared at the gun. Only the slight twitch of a jaw mus-cle showed his anger. His arm tightened about Spirit of the Mountain's waist. He wasn't about to give her to Pierre. A part of her was relieved, yet a part of her became more fearful. He should not risk so much for her sake.

"I'll not give her up to the likes of you, Pierre. I wouldn't let you screw a mongrel dog, let alone a real woman."

The pistol quivered as red slowly crept up the Frenchman's neck, over his face. "I don't think you have much choice in the matter, *n'est-ce pas?*" He sprayed spittle with each shouted word. "I have the pistol, you son of a bitch." Pierre waved the pistol about in the air to punctuate his point. "I'll not ask again."

At that moment, the second trapper stumbled in, bedraggled and angry. He fired his rifle. The ball struck the rock wall, missing the Frenchman, who fired his pistol in turn. The trapper fell dead to the ground.

Nathan and Spirit of the Mountain took advantage of the distraction and moved back into the darkness of the cave. They made their way into the musty caverns, following the underground passage into the mountain.

"You're a dead man, Walker." Pierre's threat reflected off the damp walls, the distorted echo a reminder of his pursuit. "She's a whore! You're going to die for a whore!"

When Spirit of the Mountain stopped dead in her tracks, Nathan took her hand and pulled her behind him. "Don't listen to him, Spirit of the Mountain."

"But he speaks lies, Nathan."

He turned and looked into her eyes. "I know he speaks lies."

Pierre was close, and they moved on, the darkness drawing the walls tight about them. They climbed higher into limestone caverns, tall columns and fringes of stone standing watch over their flight. Nathan lifted Spirit of the Mountain up a steep bank of rock. Water weeped from the walls, covering the floor. They sloshed through it.

Spirit of the Mountain fell to her knees. Nathan knelt down to help her up. Above him the walls moved, and the blackness came alive. They stood, sending the bats into flight. Screeches filled the air, deafening Nathan as he tried to avoid the creatures' fluttering wings.

Nathan pulled Spirit of the Mountain into his arms to protect her from the bats. She was warm, but all around them was chilled wet stone and darkness. When the bats finally disappeared, silence descended upon them. Time seemed to stand still, leaving them alone in the world.

But Nathan knew they weren't alone or safe. "We must go on."

Sad eyes gazed into his. "You risked all for me, Nathan Walker. I will not forget this."

"I can't bear the thought of him touching you."

This reply prompted a shy smile. "At least there is one thing we agree on."

They trudged on, slipping and sliding over and up the damp rock. Suddenly a small light appeared in the distance, higher up in the cave. They followed it. Together they scaled the pathway, finally arriving at the end.

A watery veil cascaded down in front of them. Their only way out was a sheer drop into great falls that roared down from overhead from its secret source within the mountain. Nathan looked out into the churning white water plunging into a blue hole, an abyss of darkness and light.

"There's no other way out, Walker," Pierre shouted from behind them.

Nathan looked back to Spirit of the Mountain, his eyes questioning her. She took his hand into hers and smiled. The courage he saw took his breath away. Then they turned and jumped.

Pierre watched Walker and the girl disappear into the curtain of the falls, but it took a moment for his mind to register what they had done.

"Damn fools," he whispered. He crossed to stand at the edge of the cliff, water spraying on his face. Surely no one could survive such a fall. Then again, it would be just like Walker to do the impossible.

Pierre headed back the way they had all come, angry it would take half the day to backtrack and get around the mountain to see what he could find. If they survived, he'd track them to hell and back. He'd bought the girl fair and square, and no one, not even that son of a bitch Walker, would take her from him.

He'd been surprised at how well she'd cleaned up. She was even prettier than he'd imagined once the dirt and grime had been washed away. Once he got her out of the squaw dress and into something proper, she'd be stunning. The vision his mind created made him smile. Something red, something low cut and tight.

There were times when it didn't matter to a man what a woman looked like, only that she was a warm body to relieve the ache in his loins. But now, as Pierre thought about the girl, he wanted her even more. Lust combined with fury consumed him. If she'd survived the fall, he'd teach her not to run from him. As for Walker, he'd make certain his death was painful. But before he killed Walker, Pierre would make the bastard watch as he made the woman his own.

He felt the sudden hardness between his legs. *"Mon Dieu,"* he whispered, awed by the effect that mere visions of her in his mind had on him. The promise of her delights made Pierre laugh aloud.

"You will be mine and no other's." He was pleased by the sound of his voice as it echoed again and again.

Spirit of the Mountain felt Nathan's hand pulling her from the violent water. It felt as if the river was trying to pull her back, fighting to claim her. But Nathan's strength prevailed, and he dragged her to the river's edge. They crawled over moss- and lichen-covered boulders, slipping and sliding to the grassy bank.

Exhausted, Spirit of the Mountain collapsed into Nathan's arms. When the burning in her lungs eased, she began to laugh, softly at first, then out loud. She rolled onto her back to look up at Nathan. He smiled, the joy of being alive evident in his eyes and face.

Out of breath again, though delightfully so now, she stilled, her gaze fixed on his green eyes. Spirit of the Mountain took a deep, cleansing breath, both to relieve the ache in her lungs and to calm the sudden beating of her heart. Unable to bear the intensity of his look any longer, Spirit of the Mountain turned away.

Nathan reached out and gently pulled her face back to his. "I've never known a woman with as much courage as you have. You are remarkable."

The turmoil his softly spoken words caused her was enough to leave her speechless. But the expression on his face and the unspoken words in his gaze were too much for Spirit of the Mountain, and she pulled away. She was shivering from cold, yet she was on fire inside.

"You're turning blue. We'd best dry you off," Nathan said.

Panic brought her from her daze. "Do we dare take the time? Will the Frenchman follow us?"

Nathan nodded. "I'm sure he won't give up on you—even if he just wants to make sure you're dead. But it will take him some time to get down here. We'll warm you up and get something to eat. We wouldn't get far if you came down with a bad chill."

"I will gather some wood."

"Damn," Nathan said, checking his powder. "It's wet. It will take some time to make a snare."

Spirit of the Mountain studied the river a moment, then smiled. "You tend to the fire. I will get us some fish. It will not take as long."

His dark eyebrows rose in question. "You don't have anything to catch it with."

Her grin widened. "I can manage."

Curious, Nathan followed her as she climbed back over the boulders, searching for a place where the river was calm. She stepped into the shallow pool and stilled, letting the muddy bottom settle back into place. Quietly, she waited.

Chuckling to himself, Nathan turned away, certain she would come up short of the promised fish. He would see what he could find.

"Nathan," Spirit of the Mountain called out to him.

He glanced back, and she held a plump, wriggling fish in her hands. She tossed it to him. He bent over to pick it up, then shook his head in amazement. When he looked back, she was intent on catching another, as promised.

Spirit of the Mountain ran her finger over the engraved handle of the tomahawk. "What tribe's markings are these?"

Nathan swallowed the bite of fish he had taken before answering. "Huron."

It was a single word, yet something made Spirit of the Mountain take closer notice. "Did you live with the Huron?"

Pierre's words came back to her, and she studied Nathan's clothing. He wore a deerskin shirt and a beaded belt with his knife and sheath. Leather breechcloth, leggings, and moccasin boots completed his native dress. Even his hair was long and worn loose about his shoulders. Only his beard played false to the image. "Is that why you dress as an Indian?"

He didn't look up, seemingly intent on finishing his meal. "I lived with the Huron for some time."

She wanted to ask more, to discover everything about this man so he would not be a stranger to her. But she understood the subtle change in his voice and did not wish to intrude. If he wanted her to know, he would tell her.

Her soft sigh seeped in past the wall Nathan had put up. He took her hand into his and gave her a reassuring squeeze. "They're three years I've tried

62

hard to forget, Spirit of the Mountain. I didn't mean to put you off."

This honest reply prompted a small smile that told him it was okay. "I am sorry it was so hard for you with the Huron."

"You were happy with the Cherokee?"

It took a moment for Spirit of the Mountain to reply, a faraway look seeming to steal her thoughts. "Yes, I was the adopted daughter of Chaser of Dreams, shaman of the Cherokee tribe of *Shaconage*."

"*Shaconage*?"

"It means place of blue smoke. It was my home."

Sadness touched her words, and a slight quiver in her voice reminded Nathan he was taking her away from a place she loved as her home. "How did you come to be with the Cherokee?"

"I was hunting and had gone farther down the mountain than I realized. It was spring, and a sudden storm hit. I came across Running Deer, Chaser of Dreams's son. He was pinned beneath a fallen tree, and I helped him."

Nathan was astounded. "Why were you out hunting alone?"

Spirit of the Mountain's look was curious, as if she didn't really understand his question. "I needed to eat. There was no one to hunt with."

"What of your parents? Where were they?"

"My mother died when I was ten, my father a year later."

His amazement turned to concern. "How long were you alone?"

A small wrinkle furrowed her delicate brow, as if

she was confused. "I stayed at my home for over a year. After I helped Running Deer, I began to stay at the village for long spells and eventually was adopted into his family. That is when I became Spirit of the Mountain, blood brother to Running Deer."

"But you are a woman. How can that be?"

"To Running Deer, it made no difference. We became inseparable as children. Even my husband could not claim a part of my heart that belonged to Running Deer."

Her next words seemed to catch in her throat, and she said no more. Nathan stood, turning his face away from her gaze, certain it was his reaction that had stopped her as she related her story. He cleared his throat, suddenly nervous and strangely angry. "You didn't tell me you had a husband."

"I do not."

This answer prompted his anger to dominate him. "You aren't making any sense. You just mentioned a husband. Then you tell me you don't have a husband. Which is it?"

"I was married at sixteen," Spirit of the Mountain whispered, her eyes filling with tears. "Two years later I buried my husband and child together."

As if someone had punched Nathan in the stomach, the air rushed from his lungs. Finally, he recovered, but his breathing didn't relieve the ache in his heart created by his own foolishness. "I'm so sorry, Spirit of the Mountain. I didn't mean—"

"He was killed in a hunting accident," Spirit of the Mountain said. "I was pregnant with our first child, and when they told me, I went into labor. The baby was born too early. He did not survive more than a few minutes."

She brushed her tears away and pulled her head back. "My only comfort was that his father was there to guide him into the spirit world."

When a sad silence descended on them, Spirit of the Mountain stood and put the fire out. "I think we should be going."

"Yes," Nathan said.

Chapter Five

The day that had started with sunshine became stormy and gray. Dark clouds crawled over the sun, blocking its light and warmth. A slow mist inched along the ground as Nathan and Spirit of the Mountain trudged on. A storm was hard upon them. The weather suited Nathan's mood. Neither of them had talked much since their conversation that morning.

It began to rain hard. As much as Nathan hated to stop, he knew Spirit of the Mountain was struggling to keep up. He turned and called, "There's an abandoned cabin not too far from here. We can spend the night there."

He took her hand and moved into the trees, creating a path through the thick growth. "I hope it's still standing," he hollered over the noise of the rain, its heavy drops soaking them quickly and thoroughly. After fighting through the thick growth for some time, they broke through to a clearing, the tiny cabin at its center a haven in the storm.

Nathan pushed open the door and went inside. It took a moment for his eyes to adjust to the dimness. A dank, stale odor was heavy in the air, but it was light compared to the memories that broke free in his mind. Memories he had purposely hidden in a dark place in his heart. A place where he could not feel the pain that had come close to destroying him.

"At least it's dry," he said, trying to focus on the moment at hand. Nathan turned to Spirit of the Mountain, who had followed him inside.

She nodded, pushing back a length of hair that clung to her face. Nathan stepped over to stand in front of her and ran his finger over her wet cheek.

"It seems we spend most of our time wet and hungry." He laughed softly, his gaze moving from hers to the dreary room. Guilt from the past mingled with new remorse. "I've not done much of a job taking care of you."

"I have no complaints, Nathan."

Spirit of the Mountain sighed. Her eyes were sad. "It is my troubles you have taken on. You could not know that crazed man would pursue us so determinedly."

Nathan grinned. "I've no complaints."

Thunder cracked, rattling the timbers with its fierceness, foretelling the stormy night to come. Nathan walked back to the door. It hung precariously on one leather strap; another strap had torn free.

"Dinner might be a bit scarce in this storm. I'll see if I can't scrounge something to eat."

"I will see to the fire." Spirit of the Mountain knelt in front of the stone fireplace. Then she placed on the hearth some kindling and shavings left in a holder by the cabin's long-gone resident.

Nathan handed her a flint. "There used to be a shed at the side of the house. You might see if there is some dry wood out there."

The cry of a cougar filled the air, the sound pulling Spirit of the Mountain's attention from Nathan.

"Sounds like we've got company." He laid his hand on her shoulder. "It shouldn't bother us any."

Spirit of the Mountain's soft laughter stirred Nathan with its sensuality. "Of course not. She has been following us since we turned off the trail. She is cautious and curious, but not dangerous."

Again, the strangeness of what she was saying and the manner in which she was speaking set off questions in Nathan's mind. "How do you know she has been following us? It is hard to spot catamounts in the wild, even to know when they are about."

"As I said, she is very cautious."

"How do you know it is a she-cat?"

"I just know." Spirit of the Mountain didn't really know how to explain, and if she did, she didn't think Nathan would understand. Although her answer wasn't satisfactory, Nathan didn't question her further.

"The rain's let up for the moment. I'd better go before it starts again."

Spirit of the Mountain watched him leave, then stood at the door until he disappeared into the dark shadows of the forest. She propped the door against its opening to keep the wind from chilling the room.

The cat called to her again, and this time, she went outside to wait.

Spirit of the Mountain felt the cat's presence before she could see her, her golden-brown coat blending with nature's pallet. Spirit of the Mountain crouched down and patiently waited for the animal to come to her.

Still wary, the cougar moved slowly, her golden gaze never leaving Spirit of the Mountain. When the cat was only a few feet away, she snarled and pawed the air.

"Do not fear, my friend," Spirit of the Mountain said quietly. The animal inched closer, then casually stretched out on the ground. Only the occasional flick of her long tail showed she was even aware of Spirit of the Mountain's presence.

Spirit of the Mountain continued to talk to her, enjoying the unexpected visit of a sister in nature. Another bolt of lightning tore through the dark clouds, the bark of its thunder close behind.

Nathan stood at the forest's edge, watching the scene at the cabin door. It wasn't dark yet, and he could see the cougar clearly. But that didn't keep him from doubting what he saw.

He remained in the shadows, uncertain what to do. The wild animal had relaxed in Spirit of the Mountain's presence, even to the point of lounging on its side. Nathan could tell Spirit of the Mountain was talking, but he was unable to hear her words. Somehow, he understood the words didn't really matter. It was the tone of her voice and the way she communicated with the cougar that made the difference.

Spirit of the Mountain was different from any woman or man he'd ever known. She seemed confident and assured in everything she did. She had said she trusted her instincts. But it was more than a second sense. He knew that now. It was something unconventional, something Nathan wasn't certain he wanted to know about. Even as he witnessed it, he wanted to explain it away, to make some sort of excuse for her odd behavior.

The strange feeling Nathan had experienced before returned, only now it was strong and undeniable. He wanted to turn away and dismiss it all. Still, he found himself mesmerized. As he continued to study the woman and the cougar, he began to imagine subtle similarities in them. It was as if Spirit of the Mountain became the cat. This thought made him turn away.

Nathan started to move back into the dark shadows of the trees, but stopped. He wanted to go on, to find something for their dinner as promised. But as much as he wanted to walk away, memories pulled him from his purpose and took him to the spot where he knew it would be.

It took him a few moments to find it, the weeds and forest having grown over the small grave long ago, the earth taking back its own. Carefully, he uncovered the handmade cross, revealing the letters he had so lovingly carved into the wood. Nathan ran his fingers over Sarah Walker's name.

"Hello, Sarah," he whispered. "It's been a long time."

Spirit of the Mountain

*   *   *

The cougar tensed and sniffed the air. The wind had changed, alerting the animal to Nathan's presence. Spirit of the Mountain studied the woods and saw a slight movement. The cat stood and screamed a warning.

Spirit of the Mountain smiled. "You had best go now, my friend."

The cat was gone in an instant, and Spirit of the Mountain went back inside to tend the fire. Once the fire was going, she had enough light to look around the cramped single-room cabin. A few pots and pans, blackened from use, lay neglected, rusted.

The fireplace commanded the wall at the far end. Only one small window broke each flanking wall; shutters locked over them to keep the weather out. A rough-hewn trestle table with benches filled the center of the room. A log bed with a ripped cornhusk mattress and a single chair completed the meager furnishings.

Dried herbs still hung from the ceiling rafters, and Spirit of the Mountain used the chair to reach them. She also found husks of dried corn and gathered an armful. Tonight they would have corn cakes, and in the morning, mush.

In a short time, Spirit of the Mountain had the cakes baking, and she started straightening the cabin, cleaning and sweeping it as best she could. She shooed the mice away with the broom. Their squeaks and squeals told her they weren't happy about her intrusion.

She laughed at their objections. "Tonight, this place is mine. Tomorrow it shall be yours again."

Fela Dawson Scott

"Do you always talk to animals big and small?"

Nathan stood in the doorway, watching her. His voice held humor, but his eyes were serious. Spirit of the Mountain understood his curiosity stemmed from her earlier company.

"Yes, I suppose I have."

Carefully, Nathan put the door back in place and stepped into the room. The fire had driven the chill off, and Spirit of the Mountain was bathed in a soft golden glow of light. She was beautiful. Dark honey-blond hair cascaded down her back to swirl about her hips with each movement; the doeskin dress she wore accented every womanly curve God had given her.

Nathan put his mind on other things. "Have you always tamed wild animals with such ease?"

Spirit of the Mountain placed the broom back beside the fireplace and sat at the table. Nathan took a seat across from her. The darkest of blue eyes looked back at him, unsettling him further.

"I am Spirit of the Mountain. It is what the Indians call the cat of one color. The cougar is my sister in nature, and I am blessed to have a special relationship with these animals. She was merely acknowledging my presence in her home."

At first, Nathan did not say anything. Her explanation was the most curious thing he had ever heard. Finally, he chuckled. "You're joking, aren't you?"

When her seriousness told him she was not, he looked away, suddenly nervous, the strange feeling accosting him again. "You aren't joking."

"No," she said, her voice telling him of her disappointment. "Before I came to be with the Cherokee, even before my parents had died, I befriended a mother cougar. She remained my friend for many years. The Indians gave me the name Spirit of the Mountain because they thought me much like my cougar friend, living in the dark shadows of the mountain, wild and free."

Nathan brightened. "And this is that same cat?"

"No, I have not seen my friend since I went to live in the village."

"I'm afraid I don't understand, Spirit of the Mountain."

Spirit of the Mountain took a deep breath and plunged on. "It was difficult leaving the only home I had ever known, but my adopted family gave me a new life, a new heritage. It was as if God was giving me the chance to know two worlds and bring them together as my own. But it wasn't until my cougar friend came to me in a dream that I truly believed."

"Believed what?" Nathan took her hand into one of his and covered it with his other. "What was this dream vision?"

"The cat came to me, and our spirits united so she would never be apart from me again. The Great Spirit granted me a Spirit Sister so she could remain inside me forever. My sister in nature has blessed me with her strength and wisdom, things I need in my life's journey down the red path."

Nathan was silent for a long moment. "You believe you have a cougar's spirit inside you?"

She nodded. "My friend's courage and cunning guide me; her wild instincts are my own. She is forever a part of me."

A million thoughts blazed their way across Nathan's mind, destroying his composure and patience. But one rose above them all. "You believe all this nonsense?"

Spirit of the Mountain stood, the bench scraping the dirt floor, nearly toppling at her sudden movement. "I shall finish dinner."

She reached out and picked up the ruffed grouse Nathan had brought in. Her gaze did not meet his as she moved back to the fire. Spirit of the Mountain began to pluck the feathers from the bird, each pull showing her anger. Nathan tried to calm his own surge of emotions, wanting to find the right words to say.

But he failed. It was a good thing he was taking her to her family in Boston. He only hoped he wasn't too late. "You will understand better when you've gotten back to your own kind, Spirit of the Mountain."

This remark made her look up. "What is it I will understand better? That I am white and not a true Cherokee? That what I believe to be true will somehow become a lie when I again live among Christians? That the God of the Indian people is not the same God as of the white people? You have a narrow mind, Nathan Walker. I would have thought better of you."

He moved to her side. "What of your mother and father? Didn't they teach you Christian values? Have you forsaken all for the red man?"

The color drained from her face. "What do you know of the red man?"

"I know how cruel and inhuman he can be. I spent three years"—Nathan drew in a long, shaky breath, visions of his past torturing his mind, haunting him as if they had taken place only yesterday—"as a Huron captive. No, a slave. I know of the torture and humiliation I suffered at their hands. How can you be faithful to an adopted Cherokee family? Faithful to a people like the Huron and the Shawnee who massacred your family and sold you for guns and ammunition?"

"You are angry with the Huron for what they have done to you?"

The answer seemed so obvious Nathan couldn't fathom her question. "They took three years of my life. Don't I have a right to be angry?"

"No."

"No," Nathan said in amazement.

"The Huron treated you as a captive because that is how you thought of yourself. You rejected their life and their beliefs, giving no thought to any other than your own. You never saw them as brothers, only as your captors, so they saw you only as their slave."

Nathan leaned against the stone of the fireplace and stared into the fire. He said nothing; he didn't trust himself to.

Spirit of the Mountain went on. "During the years you were with the Huron, did you not learn from them? Did you not learn what it takes to survive in the wilderness? Has not this knowledge been what has kept you alive these past years?"

Her questions brought his gaze back to hers. "How would you know?"

She pointed to his clothing. "Look at you. You chose what teachings you wished to benefit from. You want to believe the Hurons took three years of your life, but the truth is they gave you much more. They gave you a future, a future you would not have had if not for those years with them. It was your own anger that kept you a captive, Nathan Walker, not the Huron."

Nathan felt the anger in him renewed. "You are the damnedest woman I've ever met."

"And you"—Spirit of the Mountain met his anger eye to eye, nose to nose—"are the damnedest man I have ever known."

He wanted to strangle her. "Don't you betray your parents' memory every time you speak of such things as a Spirit Sister? How can you turn away from your true God-given heritage?"

"My mother was French, my father English. To which heritage should I be faithful? Is there a written rule that says I should not honor them both and that of my adopted people as well? Why is it I cannot take the good of each and create my own complete heritage? I am my own person, my own soul, and I shall honor all my family in my own way."

He wanted to erase the turmoil from her face, to tell her it was all right. But he couldn't. The long-nurtured anger inside him was unwilling to let go. "Are these the values your Cherokee family has given you?"

"No," Spirit of the Mountain answered, sadness causing her voice to tremble. "It was my mother. She also taught me anger and pride are a long-suffering combination, bringing only sorrow to one's heart. Nothing I say will change the way you feel, Nathan Walker. Only you can do that."

She turned her attention back to preparing their

dinner. Nathan couldn't believe how stubbornly Spirit of the Mountain clung to her Indian family and their way of life. But he could see he was getting nowhere arguing with her.

"I'll get some more firewood."

It was dark, the night air cool and damp as the rain continued to pelt the earth. The chill relieved Nathan of the heat that had built up inside him. He stood for a long time allowing his mind to clear as well.

He decided the problem would solve itself when they reached Boston. Nathan couldn't believe Spirit of the Mountain would remain faithful to Indian ways once she had a life with her own people, her own kind.

Nathan had learned this lesson the hard way. An old pain snuck into his mind—memories of his youth, of his broken dreams. He had not understood the differences in the classes, thinking himself the same as the wealthy family he had grown up with in England. He hadn't realized the limitations of his own heritage.

Nathan pushed back his hair with both hands and lifted his face to let the rain fall on it. His eyes closed, he let his mind take him back.

"Why do we have to leave, father?"

"Your mother is very ill, and we can't stay here any longer."

Nathan couldn't believe the Rothwell family would ask them to leave. "But where will we go?"

The Rothwell estate had been the only home he'd ever known until the day his family had been forced to leave. Nathan's father had been the family's tutor, and his mother worked in the household. They had lived in a small cottage behind the main house, comfortable and secure in their life. James Rothwell, the oldest son, was the same age as Nathan. Nathan and he had grown up together like brothers. Nathan had the same schooling, the same riding lessons, the same fencing instructor. They shared everything. Yet, in the end, their relationship meant nothing.

Nathan's family moved into a one-room apartment on the poorer side of town. His father could find work only in a foundry. He became ill also, not of the consumption Nathan's mother suffered, but from a broken spirit. William Walker was a sensitive, educated man. Losing his position with the Rothwells seemed to break his heart. Nathan was unable to care for both his parents, and they were taken to a filthy hospital for the destitute. They died there.

The next two years were hell for Nathan, who had to work and scrounge to get by. In desperation, he indentured himself for seven years for the chance to go to America.

Once he had gained his freedom, Nathan found life to be much the same as it had been in England. Determined to be his own man and make his own way without being subject to another's whims, Nathan journeyed into the wilderness. A greenhorn who knew little of surviving in the wilds of America, Nathan was captured by the Huron.

This brought his thoughts back full circle to what Spirit of the Mountain had said: *It was your own anger that kept you a captive, Nathan Walker, not the Huron.*

"Damn woman," he grumbled and headed to the side of the cabin to look for some dry wood. It unnerved him how much she understood. True, he had survived the last seven years because of what he had learned during his captivity with the Huron. The cruelty and humiliation he'd endured had hardened him, giving him the steely reserve needed to live in the wilderness, as he thought all men should. In the wilderness, money held little to no value, and a man was judged by who he was, not what he had.

In the lean-to, Nathan gathered a load of wood. He stopped in front of the cabin door before entering, trying to compose himself against those sad blue eyes. He kicked the door open with his booted foot and went inside.

Spirit of the Mountain straightened up from her work, having turned the bed's mattress to its cleaner side. Without saying anything, she returned to the fireplace and removed the meat from the spit, where it had been cooking. She placed the meat and some bread on the table, then sat.

Nathan dumped the load of wood and fed the dying fire. He brushed the wood chips from his hands, then went to the table.

"I set a bucket out to collect rainwater. Would you mind getting it?" she asked.

"Certainly," he said, just as politely.

He retrieved the bucket, and they ate in silence. Then they cleaned up in silence.

"You look tired, Spirit of the Mountain. You'd best get some rest."

Spirit of the Mountain nodded and moved to stand by the bed. It had been a long time since she had slept in a real bed, and she approached it timidly. She sat, then reclined. The husks were stiff, crinkling from dryness as she laid her weight on them. The fabric was old and worn. She curled up on her side, putting her back to Nathan, who remained at the table.

The storm still raged outside, but the weather seemed less volatile than the mood inside the cabin. Spirit of the Mountain closed her eyes, clearing her mind of their argument. It was time to sleep. Reliving what had been said would do no good.

Nathan waited until he heard Spirit of the Mountain's even breathing in sleep; then he moved to the bed. He lay down beside her, politely turning away. Nathan found it difficult to keep his mind from the gentle curve of her back. His awareness of her and the feelings it stirred pushed him headlong into guilt. This place, this cabin, and the bed in which they slept were haunted by Sarah's ghost. His wife had died long ago, but now it seemed like yesterday.

He had learned too late the wilderness was no place for a woman, with its isolation, hardship, and constant danger. Sarah's delicate nature, both mental and physical, had been unable to cope with the life they had made for themselves here. Nathan had failed his wife. He would not fail Spirit of the Mountain.

Chapter Six

Nathan looked down into Spirit of the Mountain's blue eyes, their brightness flecked with gold. Dark lashes. Perfectly arched brows. Exotic. Soft pink stained the creamy white of her cheeks, and roses colored her full lips.

Spirit of the Mountain lay curled at his side, her head resting on his shoulder. He felt the silky smoothness of her arm, his hand sliding upward to her gently rounded shoulder.

The dream was so real, so arousing, Nathan awoke with desire strong in his blood. He felt the intense beating of his heart at his temples and the strangled breath dormant in his lungs. Even the feel of her in his arms remained. Nathan opened his eyes, struggling to bring his raging emotions under control.

Slowly, he became aware that Spirit of the Mountain was sleeping in his arms.

Just as in his dream, she lay against him, cuddled close, her leg intimately draped over his, her arm across his belly, his hand caressing her. Only her eyes remained closed; the passion he witnessed in their depths was imaginary. Nathan labored to reconcile his disappointment and subdue his desire for her.

Spirit of the Mountain stirred, a sense of security warming her in her half sleep. It felt good to be held by a man. It had been too long since—

She stiffened, unable to move, unable to breathe. Shyly, she turned her head up, catching the twinkle in Nathan's green eyes as he watched her. The mild warmth that permeated her intensified, bringing her longings to the surface. Then she started to pull away.

He held strong. "You needn't move." He smiled, slow and easy. "I was enjoying the feel of you next to me."

The heat moved up her neck to her face. She felt unable to respond to his softly spoken words. But her body rushed ahead of her mind, the feel of his leg between her thighs stirring a need deep within her. It took every bit of control for her not to move against him. What little control she had shattered when he did. Involuntarily, her hips moved to meet the gentle pressure of his leg, a low moan escaping her lips.

Nathan's hand moved to her neck, cradling her head in his palm. Spirit of the Mountain closed her eyes when he kissed her forehead. His lips moved down to the crease in her eyelids, to the contour of her cheekbone. His tongue traced a line to her lips, but he did not take them with his.

Spirit of the Mountain opened her eyes. "It has been too long since I have been held by a man." Her voice sounded strange to her own ears, a deep sensuality resounding in each word.

The passion in Nathan's eyes became confused, pained. He drew in a long, shaky breath, then pushed her gently yet firmly from him. Throwing his long legs over the side of the bed, he sat up. "I'd best start a fire."

Tears stung her eyes, but Spirit of the Mountain determinedly blinked them back. She didn't understand his reaction, yet pride kept her from asking. "Yes," she mumbled. "It is cold."

Nathan built the fire, pretending to be preoccupied with it instead of the turmoil in his mind, but the silence was uncomfortable. "Did you love him?"

His question brought Spirit of the Mountain's troubled gaze to him, and he regretted asking. "Did I love who?"

"Your husband," he said, suddenly insecure. His unsureness was a rare experience, and he didn't like it.

"Of course. Why else would I marry him?"

She sounded so definite, so confident in her feelings. He wanted to know more, yet at the same time, he didn't. Curiosity won out. "Have there been no other men? You are a beautiful woman, Spirit of the Mountain. Why didn't you remarry?"

"No," she whispered, her voice taking on a faraway tone. "There have been no other men." She looked down, seeming to study her hands clasped tightly in her lap as she sat on the side of the bed. "There could have been other men, but my adopted father understood there was no room in my heart for them. He did not declare my mourning over, and I was not expected to remarry until he did."

"And now?" Nathan moved to stand in front of her. She looked up at him. "Is there room in your heart for another? Has your mourning ended?"

Spirit of the Mountain wanted to say yes, to let him continue with the delights he had teased her with only moments before. But she remained silent, unable to say yes or no. Her body seemed ready, wanting, yet her mind clung to her grief, to a first love that could never be again.

Nathan turned away. "You must have loved him very much."

"Yes, very much." Memories flooded Spirit of the Mountain's mind, good feelings surging with them. "I was young. He was brave and handsome."

She wanted to see Nathan's face, to understand what he was thinking, what he was feeling. But he stood with his back to her. "He was Running Deer's best friend. At first, Red Hawk seemed angry with me when I took my place by Running Deer's side, not only as his sister, but as his blood brother. Then, as time passed, he thought of me as an irritating little sister, always in the way."

Easily she recalled the very day the tension between them changed. "It was as if Red Hawk woke up one morning and saw me as a woman, not the child he had seen before."

Nathan's back remained to her as she said, "Not long after that, Red Hawk came to my father and brother and asked permission to take me as his wife. He brought many horses, more than I had ever dreamed of for my family. My father was very proud."

Her words brought his gaze back to hers. "Is that what it takes? Many horses?"

The anger in his eyes was clear, echoed in each harsh word he spoke. Spirit of the Mountain was confused by his sudden mood. "What do you mean?"

In two long strides, he was in front of her, reaching out to pull her up. "Pierre paid highly for you, an entire year's trappings to make you his. Was this not enough? Is that why you ran from him? If he had paid more, would you have willingly gone to his bed?"

His words hurt her. It was more than she could stand. "It is the way of my people. A hundred horses would not have been enough had I not loved him."

Nathan knew that. He just couldn't contend with the hurt her words of love for another created in him. He wanted only to hurt her back. His anger was preposterous. This total stranger, a woman he'd known only a few days, was driving him mad. He was being irrational, and he hated being irrational. He'd experienced so many ups and downs since she came into his life he was dizzy.

He tried to clear his thoughts. "That was unkind. I'm sorry." What had possessed him to say such things? One moment he wanted to throttle her; the next, he—

His lips came down on hers, unyielding and relentless. Nathan forced his tongue into her mouth and felt her tense. Anger still controlled him, and it was reflected in his kiss. Disgusted with himself, he twisted away.

"No," he yelled, more to himself than Spirit of the Mountain. He had buried one wife in the wilderness; he could not bear to bury another. "There can be nothing between us. Nothing."

"What is it you are afraid of, Nathan? Me? Or does loving a woman frighten you so terribly?"

His gaze came to rest on her. He felt certain his eyes, his face, his very being reflected the torture that plagued him. "You can't understand."

"Understand what?"

"I made my choice long ago. This is my home." His hands swept around him in a grand gesture. "The wilderness is my life. I belong here."

"You are right," she said. "I do not understand."

"There is no place for a woman in my life." His heart constricted as the vision of his wife, young and innocent as she lay cold in her grave, burst forward in his mind's eye. "This is no place for a wife and family."

"The wilderness, the mountains—they are my life, my soul," Spirit of the Mountain said. "I was born here. I want to die here. In what way do I not belong?"

Agitated, Nathan began to pace. "Are you blind? You lost both your parents to the wilderness: Your husband and child have been taken by this land's cruelness. Your Indian family was massacred by the harshness of this land's people. It is no place for a woman. You will be better off in Boston with your real family."

"If this land is so brutal and heartless, what has

beguiled you into staying, Nathan Walker?"

Nathan remained quiet for a long moment. "This land gives me something that far outweighs its disadvantages. It is a place where I can be a man, free of society's misguided concepts and constrictions. I am judged by who I am, not what I have or will never have. I've lived by others' rules, others' whims. I'll never do so again, not as long as there is breath in my body and strength in my soul. I shall remain here till I die."

"Is it so hard to believe that this place, this wilderness, might be in my blood as well?"

"You choose this place because you've never known anything else. How can you be so certain Boston is not where you want to live out your life?" Nathan stood directly in front of Spirit of the Mountain and took her hand into his. "Don't you see? I must take you home. What you do with the rest of your life will be up to you and your grandfather. At least, then, you will have been given a choice."

"It is not a matter of choice, Nathan. My spirit belongs to the mountains, to *Shaconage*. It is my destiny. I do not need to travel to Boston to know this."

He let her hand drop. "I know what's best for you. Trust me, Spirit of the Mountain."

"Trust you? You do not understand who I am or what is important to me. You do not know what I believe in, how that is inseparable from me, part of me. How is it that you are to decide my fate? Is that not for me to do?"

"No," he replied simply, his look warning her not to argue further. "I must take you home."

Spirit of the Mountain considered what to do. "I

will make some corn mush. Then we will go."

She moved past Nathan and began breakfast. An uneasy truce settled over them. Spirit of the Mountain dumped the last of the ground corn into the boiling water, stirring the mixture until it thickened. She lifted the pot and took it to the table.

Nathan sat. Spirit of the Mountain started to sit, but stopped. She looked about, an alarm in her head sounding.

"What is it?" Nathan asked.

Spirit of the Mountain walked to the door. She didn't need her eyes to see the danger; her instincts gave her sight. This time, the cougar's cry was a warning, telling her of the danger she already sensed.

"He is here," she said calmly. Nathan stood and crossed to her, his rifle in hand, his look deadly.

"Walker," Pierre yelled. "Walker, I know you are in there."

Nathan pulled Spirit of the Mountain away from the door. Looking about the cabin, his gaze settled on the rafters in the ceiling. Nathan pointed above him. "I'll lift you up there. I want you to hide. Under no circumstances are you to come out. Promise me."

Spirit of the Mountain started to say no, but something in his eyes made her stop. He ran his finger over her cheek; then he smiled and said, "I'll be fine."

"Walker," the Frenchman called out again, his voice taunting, his laughter like an echo in the early dawn air. "Walker, don't make me come and get you."

Nathan hoisted Spirit of the Mountain up into the

rafters, waiting only long enough to see that she was hidden. He jerked open the door, leaving it hanging on its single shaky hinge. He walked out into the soft morning light, as if all was right in the world.

Pierre's lips moved into a lopsided grin, the smirk evident in the tone of his words as well. "You have been a lot of trouble, Walker. What am I to do with you?"

"Pierre, you've been as obstinate as a male dog after a bitch in heat."

This insult made the Frenchman's smile disappear; the ruddy red of his skin brightened with anger. His eyes narrowed, and his nose flared. "Tell the girl to get out here."

"The girl"—Nathan stressed Pierre's usage—" is gone. She ran away last night while I slept."

"You lie," Pierre screamed. "Why would she run away."

Nathan shrugged. "Woman are fickle. Who can explain why they do what they do?"

Pierre snarled and pushed past Nathan into the cabin. Spirit of the Mountain could see him from her perch as he walked about the single room, pushing and kicking everything he came in contact with. His grumblings were offensive, but less so than the man himself. He stepped directly below her, and she held her breath in fear.

Pierre reached out and picked up the pot, scooping up the thick mixture with his fingers. Pierre shoved them into his mouth, the pasty corn mush clinging to his mustache as he licked his fingers clean. He belched, then threw the kettle aside. It clattered across the table to the floor, its contents marking its path of flight.

The bed caught his attention, and he stepped to stand beside it. He stood and studied it; then his hand reached out to touch the indentation where their bodies had been. A low rumbling from his throat erupted into a horrible cry. Pierre stomped to the fireplace and picked up a burning log. He threw it on the mattress, the old covering blazing instantly, dry husks feeding the flames.

Pierre remained for a while, watching the fire spread. The orange flames ran along the dry wood, taking hold and devouring it. In just a few minutes, the room was filled with smoke. Spirit of the Mountain covered her mouth to keep from coughing. Pierre was finally forced from the burning room.

The fire moved up the walls, flames licking at Spirit of the Mountain's feet as she huddled on the beam. She turned around and braced herself, her back against the rafter, her feet flat on the mud and grass roof. Spirit of the Mountain kicked out, cracking the roof. She pushed with all her might and finally broke through.

Spirit of the Mountain crawled onto the roof with smoke concealing her. She carefully moved to the edge and peeked over. The roof of the lean-to was just below her. She lowered herself down to it.

Nathan ran back to the cabin, his heart in his throat. The fire had already consumed much of the old wood, the walls aflame, the door blocked. Pierre stood only a few feet away, laughing.

"What is the matter, Walker?"

Nathan tried to go inside, but the heat drove him back.

Pierre was directly behind him. "I do hope she was worth dying for."

The Frenchman laughed again, drawing Nathan's gaze back to him. The repulsive man pushed his face close, his eyes filled with hatred.

"Tell me, Walker, did she squirm beneath you with delight as you filled her with your seed? Or is she one of those cold bitches who lie like a corpse until you are finished with her?"

Anger erupted in Nathan as if from a dormant volcano, spewing forth in violence. He lunged for the Frenchman, grabbed him about the throat, and pulled him to the ground. It felt good to tighten his grip, to see the ugly man's eyes bulge as air no longer reached his brain. Nathan was intent on killing him, but a sudden pain ripped open his head, and darkness relieved him of his fury.

Spirit of the Mountain slid over the wall, smoke blinding her, her lungs burning from lack of clean air. Her feet dangled unsupported, not quite reaching the ground. She let go, but strong arms grabbed her before she landed.

She struck out, her elbow landing squarely on a rib. She twisted free of grasping hands and sprinted away. Clear of the blinding smoke, she ran for the trees. Just as she reached cover, her Shawnee captor stepped out in front of her. She slammed into him. It was like hitting a wall, and the breath was knocked from her. She would have collapsed had he not caught her. His grip on her was unbreakable.

The Shawnee lifted her and carried her back to

where Pierre watched the log cabin crash to the ground in flames. The smile Pierre gave Spirit of the Mountain told her that he was not at all surprised to see her.

"It is amazing who you run across way out here in the middle of nowhere." Pierre looked at the Shawnee warriors, the same party he had bought Spirit of the Mountain from. "But then again, we have all been following the same trail north, and I was bound to run into someone. I had hoped it would be you, but I met them instead."

Pierre jerked Spirit of the Mountain from the Shawnee's arms and pulled her next to him. He pointed at Nathan's unconscious body. "While you two were rolling about in bed, I passed you and came onto the Shawnee camp in the night."

Spirit of the Mountain struggled to get free. Finally Pierre allowed her to go to Nathan. "He's not dead, *ma chere*. At least, not yet."

She glared at him, all the emotions she was feeling surging forth in a storm of hatred. "You are lower than a dog. You are not even worthy of the vermin that crawls the earth!"

This insult lifted his brows, amusement never leaving his twisted lips. "Is that the best you can do?" He stood above her as she knelt by Nathan's still body. "I expected more of you."

Spirit of the Mountain leaned over to look at Nathan's wound, blood marking the spot where he had been hit. Her fingers wrapped about the handle of his knife. In one sudden, fluent motion, she rose, arching the blade at the Frenchman, the tip slicing across his middle, cutting through his shirt and flesh.

He stared in surprise, then glanced at his wound. It only made him laugh, the Shawnee joining in as they closed about her. Pierre raised his arm to stop them. "Do not hurt her," he called out in French. "I want some fight left in the girl."

"You"—Spirit of the Mountain spoke in French as well—" are not man enough to take the fight from me, you French dog."

The Shawnee whooped and hollered. Pierre did not find her words so humorous.

"Ma chere." He smiled, but the smile did not reach his eyes. "What makes you say such things? I have yet to show you what it is like to be bedded by a real man, a Frenchman. You have yet to know the true delights of the French."

"I think you know only how to delight Frenchmen, *n'est-ce pas?*" She saw how her words hit him. It made her feel good, powerful. *"Mon Dieu!"* she said, laughter tinging her voice. "Perhaps you prefer little boys? Little boys for the little man."

Spirit of the Mountain thought Pierre's head might split apart from anger. He hurled himself in her direction, his entire body lifting from the ground. She easily sidestepped his bulk, bringing her blade down to cut into his arm as he stumbled by. The Shawnee made no move to help him. Their postures were relaxed as they enjoyed the exchange between Pierre and her.

A loud harumph sounded as Pierre hit the ground, rolling away from Spirit of the Mountain's direct attack to his back. He scrambled to his feet. Her knife sliced the air again and again, forcing him to back away from her persistent charge.

Finally, the fierce-visaged Shawnee warrior came forward and caught her arm, wrenching the knife from it. Spirit of the Mountain was nearly insane with anger. She fought against his superior strength. Unable to keep her still, he struck her hard across the jaw.

The pain halted her only momentarily. She doubled her fist and hit him back, her efforts doing more damage to her knuckles than his chin. She did not flinch at his hard look, but waited for the reprisal.

None came. His fingers rubbed where she had struck him. He grunted, as if pleased with her; then he put his hand out to her. She did not move. Slowly, he reached out and took her hand to examine the bleeding skin.

"You are headstrong," he said in French, his voice gentle, almost sympathetic. "You should not be so foolish next time."

Spirit of the Mountain nodded, wincing from the pain she had inflicted upon herself. "Your chin is definitely harder than my fist. I will think better of it in the future."

Pierre started to pull her away, but the warrior stopped him. His look warned the Frenchman.

"Don't you forget, Long Knife. The girl is mine."

Long Knife nodded, unintimidated by Pierre's manner. "The girl is yours. We go now."

She looked at Long Knife. "Where are we going?"

It was Pierre who answered her, his sneering words making her fearful again. "There's a Shawnee camp not far from here. We are going there so we can all take pleasure in Walker's death. It will be quite a celebration, *ma chere*."

The blood drained from her head, and she thought

she might fall. She balanced herself on the Shawnee's arm. "What does he mean? The Frenchman has me back. Why must Walker die?"

Pierre guided her away, his touch unusually gentle as Long Knife continued to hover nearby. He spoke English so the Indians could not understand, his breath hot on her neck. "These bloodthirsty savages need no reason to torture their enemy. Have you never witnessed a man being burned alive? Surely, your Cherokee brothers did this many times while you were living with them? Perhaps it is something you enjoy yourself?"

Bile rose in Spirit of the Mountain's throat, and she feared she would be sick. "You cannot mean to let them kill Nathan?"

Her words came out weakly, and Pierre seemed delighted by them. "Of course I do. I, too, shall find great pleasure in seeing him die so cruel a death. No one interferes in my business, *ma chere*. No one."

"Please." Tears blurred the vision of his unyielding face. "I beg you, Pierre. Do not kill him."

This made him laugh. "You beg me. *Mon Dieu!* You have nothing to bargain with. Nothing at all!"

She pulled her head up, her chin tilted in defiance. "I've everything you want, you vile pig. Let him live, and I'll not fight you any longer."

"Perhaps I like a woman with a little fight in her."

"Perhaps" she said, teasing him with her voice, "you have no idea how good it can be when a woman gives it willingly?"

Pierre's eyes squinted as he thought on her offer. "You make me hard just thinking about it, *ma chere*.

But"—he paused for effect—"I think I want him dead more than I want you soft and willing."

His laughter mocked her, and this time, she could not keep the tears back.

Chapter Seven

Had it been only 11 nights since she had slept in the security of her lodge with her Cherokee family? So much had happened in so short a time. Spirit of the Mountain felt dread swell inside her; it rested like a weight about her heart. Even when she had been taken captive she had not known such dismay. At that time, she had had no control of her fate; nothing she might have done could change what happened. Then Nathan Walker's path had crossed hers. This was what she found unbearable.

"I should not have gotten into the canoe," she moaned in agony.

Nathan pulled himself up from where he lay. "Why do you say that?"

"If I had not allowed you to rescue me, we," she

said, then corrected herself, "you would not be in this predicament."

She knew that darkness obscured her face, but the tone of her voice made her feelings clear. And though Nathan's hands were tied, he still managed to take hers into his.

"If we had it to do all over again, I'd not change a thing."

"Then you are a fool, Nathan Walker." Tears choked Spirit of the Mountain, her voice breaking as she fought to suppress them.

Nathan pulled her to him, encircling her with his arms, his tied hands behind her. Her head rested in the valley of his neck, her breath warm on his skin. "Well, maybe there is one thing I'd do differently," he whispered into her ear.

When Spirit of the Mountain looked up, he didn't need the light of day to see the question in her eyes. He didn't need to see the sparkling blue depths he seemed always to drown in. She was forever branded on his mind, each and every detail.

"I think I would have made love to you." Nathan drew in a long, shattered breath, then closed his eyes to relieve the sudden ache in them. "God, how I want you."

Spirit of the Mountain knew that physically one's heart could not break. Still, she suffered no less than if her heart had actually done so. If Nathan was to die, a part of her would die as well. She buried her head against his shoulder, tears surging forth in a sob.

"Remember, it was of my own choosing to help you. You have done your damnedest to be rid of me."

"No." She placed her hand upon his cheek. "In my heart, I wanted nothing more than to be with you. But nothing is worth your dying."

"There are a few things in life worth dying for." Nathan's voice became hoarse, and he paused to clear it. "And you, my sweet, are one of them. Do not think otherwise."

She touched her lips to his. "There has been no room in my heart since Red Hawk's death, but you, Nathan Walker, have found a place. A place no other will ever know."

Unable to bear his touch any longer, Spirit of the Mountain left the warmth of his embrace. He was virtually a stranger, yet he'd quickly become a part of her—a part she would carry with her for her entire life.

The long night stretched on, seemingly endlessly, yet dawn eventually prevailed, and with it came the promise of grief and horror. The small party traveled on, each second, each minute, each hour haunting Spirit of the Mountain with the promise of impending death.

Finally, they came out of the darkness of the forest and overlooked a long valley. Fog lay low, hugging the glacier-dug canyon surrounded by ancient ridges, markings of long ago. A faint trail led down to the Shawnee village huddled on the valley's edge.

Thoughts of her family filled Spirit of the Mountain's mind. She asked Long Knife if any of her people had been brought here. He shook his head no, then pointed north. Disappointment distracted her for a moment, and she prayed the women and children would find some sort of peace and happiness there.

As they drew near the village, a cry went up, bringing the Shawnee from their lodges and their work. Children swarmed about, their cries of joy interrupted by the sharp barks of dogs that ran at their feet. Old women shuffled along with the help of wood canes, sticks they expertly wielded to prod Nathan when he passed. The younger women huddled together shyly. Their dark eyes dared to peek at the warriors, then turned quickly away. Other warriors hollered welcome to their brothers and fierce war cries for the prisoners.

Work was left undone. Skilled hands stopped, leaving weapons unfinished; skins being scraped and plied into softness were ignored. Racks of deer meat, fish, and wild fruits were left to dry in the sun, unprepared foods forgotten. Nimble fingers stopped weaving intricate designs in baskets. All was secondary to the returning warriors. Babes unable to walk were carried at their mothers' breasts, while the elderly were helped along by strong hands. They all came; they all anticipated the time of celebration.

This kaleidoscope of smell, sound, and sight brought forth a homesickness in Spirit of the Mountain. Heartache filled her, remembrance of her own village, the similarities strong as she looked about her. Yet the Shawnee were more of a warring tribe, their attack on her own peaceful village evidence of that.

Part of her understood their dependence on making war with other tribes. For many, there would be no life without the prospect of war, no useful purpose to be upon mother earth. It was nature's way, and in their eyes an honorable occupation. Their enemies' greatness was a direct reflection upon them: the stronger their spirit, the greater the conquerors' own might. It was considered an honor to torture a man of tremendous courage; the longer it took for him to die, the better for those inheriting his prowess.

This thought made Spirit of the Mountain despair. Nathan would not die quickly; his ordeal promised the warriors the glory of vanquishing a noble enemy. Her stomach twisted into a painful knot. All the strength drained from her legs, and they threatened to buckle beneath her. She willed herself to remain standing. She could not show signs of weakness. She would not.

The warriors herded Spirit of the Mountain and Nathan to the center of the village. Everyone gathered about them, excitement in every high-pitched cry and squeal. Young men anxious to prove their courage ran forward to face Nathan, eye to eye, their looks ferocious. Some merely stared; some pulled weapons in threat, brandishing them menacingly. Nathan's features remained hard, showing his courage in return.

The tribe's leader shuffled through the crowd, and the noise quieted. The man's back was bent from age, his hair gray, his skin dried and wrinkled. But as he moved to stand in front of Spirit of the Mountain, she saw the wisdom his great age had given him reflected in his faded brown eyes.

Pierre spoke to the elder, Long Knife interpreting for him. A great cry of joy deafened her as the Shaw-

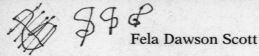

nee shouted their appreciation over the event to come. They dragged Nathan away and tied him to a post. The women gathered wood and piled it at his feet. Their chatter drifted on the breeze to Spirit of the Mountain like that of a flock of birds settling into a tree for the night.

Desperation drove all other emotion away, and Spirit of the Mountain stepped forward. She raised her voice to be heard above the commotion, the anger in her tone stilling all those about her. "I am Spirit of the Mountain, blood brother to Running Deer, adopted daughter of the shaman of the *Sha-conage* Cherokee."

She spoke in French, Long Knife relating what she said to his chief. A change moved the old man's stone features, and his lackluster eyes glowed in anger.

She did not back down. "I have been blessed with the Spirit Sister of the cat of one color. How can you dishonor this sacred spirit by giving me to this dog of a Frenchman?"

Spirit of the Mountain spit into the dirt at their feet. "You treat this man as if he were a brother. I am more brother to you than he."

When Long Knife's interpretation was given, her statement made the Shawnee chief's face scrunch into a wrinkled knot of anger. "You are but a woman. How can you be blood brother to a Cherokee warrior? It cannot be."

"I speak the truth." Spirit of the Mountain stuck her hand out palm up to show the scar of the blood ceremony. "I bear the mark of our solemn oath."

She took a step forward to show she would not back down to his fierce countenance. "I am Spirit of the Mountain in all ways. My sister in nature runs strong in my blood."

The old man seemed to consider her words, but his doubt did not lessen. "Why would the Great Spirit bless you, a white woman, with a Spirit Sister?" He pointed a bony finger at her. "You lie. I should kill you for twisting the truth with your white woman's tongue."

"Then you will dishonor the Great Spirit and his wisdom with your insolence." Spirit of the Mountain faced his accusations. No fear showed in her voice or her demeanor as she waited for Long Knife's Indian translation.

The chief's lips puckered together, a thin line marking his stubbornness. "You will die in the fire with the Frenchman's captive."

Pierre objected, but immediately shut his mouth at the look the tribal leader gave him.

The chief's fierce glare did not keep Spirit of the Mountain quiet. "The cat of one color has been my sister for many years, and the blessings of its spirit are mine."

She drew in a long breath before continuing, but there was nothing else to lose by plunging on. "It is my right to prove the truth of my words. I will prove the strength and cunning of the Spirit Sister who guides me. My very soul belongs to this animal's spirit. Are you so frightened by me, a white woman, you will not grant me this right?"

A great stir moved the crowd when her words were repeated in Shawnee. Their gasps of surprise at her audacity were loud, but silence immediately followed as they awaited their elder's words.

Suddenly, his grim lips smiled. "You have great courage for a white woman. The Frenchman can have you. It would be a shame to kill such a spirited female."

He started to turn away, as if the matter were settled. But it was not settled for Spirit of the Mountain. "Are the Shawnee cowards? I dare you to put me to the test of truth. I will prove the Great Spirit has blessed me. Do the Shawnee fear the truth?"

The tribal leader turned back, his movements slowed by age. His look was indignant, his manner proud. The years that had passed since his birth did not influence this part of the man. "Spirit of the Mountain, I have listened to you, and your words stir a great anger inside me. But I will put aside this anger and allow you what no woman has ever been allowed before—the chance to prove the truth of your words."

Silence still claimed the people, but the Frenchman stepped forward. "I bought this woman in good faith from your warriors. She is mine. You cannot determine the fate of one who does not belong to you."

Pierre waited for Long Knife's interpretation and the old man's response. The leader's words, directed to Spirit of the Mountain, ignored the trapper. "When the sun again touches the faraway mountains, you will begin this trial of truth."

The old man then looked to the Frenchman. "You and this woman will be taken to the place of prayer, many miles from here. A torch and a knife will be placed here in front of the ceremonial fire where the captive is tied. The one to reach it first will determine his fate. But take heed. My warriors will be waiting in the forest, and you must get past them as you make your way to the village."

The Frenchman looked as if he wanted to dispute this decision, but he didn't.

"If you reach the captive first, you will have proved your worthiness of the honor of a Spirit Sister," the tribal leader said to Spirit of the Mountain. "You and the captive will be allowed to go free."

He then turned back to the trapper. "If you arrive to set the torch to the wood, the captive will die as promised, and the woman is yours."

"But she is already mine," Pierre ground out.

"It seems you have been unable to keep her yours." A slow smile forced the chieftain's lips into a crooked slit across his face. "Is any woman worth what you must endure, Frenchman?"

A wry smile curled Pierre's lips in turn. "I believe this woman is." He laughed out loud, taking away the tension that had hung in the air like a stale odor. The crowd, too, laughed, then proceeded with the preparations for the new and exciting event added to the ceremony of fire.

Spirit of the Mountain felt Long Knife tugging on her arm, pulling her away. "You must prepare for the ordeal."

She turned to see Nathan, but he was being taken to another part of the camp. Long Knife insisted, and she had no choice but to go with him.

Spirit of the Mountain rose from the pallet where she lay. Sleep would not release her from the torment of her mind or relieve the sadness that haunted her heart. Earlier, she had cleansed her body and mind in the sweat lodge. She prayed to the Great Spirit to guide her Spirit Sister and give her strength. She felt prepared for the trial that would begin at dawn. Yet she longed to see Nathan, to spend with him the last minutes before she must leave.

The Shawnee had spent the entire night in song and dance, their festivities a prelude to her ordeal and Nathan's. Joyous laughter mocked her apprehension and fear; it tormented each waking moment.

Unable to bear her growing anxiety any longer, Spirit of the Mountain ducked through the doorway and stepped outside. Long Knife had remained close. She pulled a fur blanket tight about her and faced him squarely. "I wish to go to him."

Long Knife understood. He turned away from her. "It is forbidden."

Spirit of the Mountain reached out and placed a hand on his muscular forearm. Her touch brought his gaze back to her.

There had been no words of distrust, but Spirit of the Mountain tried to ease any doubts he would have that she might try to escape. "My honor has been questioned." She spoke quietly, sincerely. "I will prevail, and the truth will be known."

Long Knife's dark eyes studied her closely; then he nodded and walked away. She followed him through the maze of lodges, stopping only when he did. He turned to her, his expression giving away little of what might have gone on in his mind.

"I will not be far, Spirit of the Mountain." He disappeared into the darkness.

Before she went inside, Spirit of the Mountain studied the night sky, seeing that morning was not far from dawning. She ducked inside.

A fire burned in the center of the lodge, the meager light it cast showing Spirit of the Mountain where Nathan was. He sat on a pile of furs, his back resting against a pole, his wrists tied behind him and secured to it. Nathan had been stripped naked, but a fur lay across his lap.

He looked up, surprise registering on his face. "What are you doing here?" he whispered, thinking she might disappear if he spoke too loudly.

She walked to his side, then knelt. He saw a myriad of emotions in her eyes. Spirit of the Mountain touched his face, her hand soft against his cheek. She rubbed the clean-shaven skin, then smiled.

"You have a handsome face, Nathan Walker. You should not cover it with hair again."

Nathan's eyes closed, her words sending shivers down his spine. "I'll have to remember that." He opened his eyes to study hers and tried to smile. "I feel like a turkey that's been cleaned and dressed for the fire."

This remark made her look away, and he regretted his words. "Did you bring a knife with you?"

Spirit of the Mountain looked confused. "A knife?"

"Yes"—he leaned forward and wriggled his hands—"to cut me free."

She shook her head. "I cannot free you."

"What?" It was his turn for confusion.

"I promised Long Knife—"

There was no need to finish. He understood what

107

she had promised. Still, he could not hide his disappointment.

"He would not have let me see you if I had not."

"Tomorrow. When they take you to the place of prayers, you must try to get away. Run as fast and as far as you can away from the Shawnee and the Frenchman. Promise me."

"I will not leave you."

"You must." Nathan tried to be firm. "You will."

Her sigh was soft, sad. "I will not leave you, and I cannot run away, Nathan Walker."

"I cannot save you this time, Spirit of the Mountain. You must do as I say." Even as he spoke he knew his argument fell on deaf ears.

"You said there were some things in life worth dying for. I believe honor is one of them. Without it, there is nothing. I cannot do as you ask."

Nathan wanted to deny her claim, to say it was not so. But he couldn't, not even to save Spirit of the Mountain or himself. Disheartened, he looked away from the honest emotions he saw so clearly on her beautiful face.

"Please, Nathan." She took his face in her hands. "We have so little time." Her breath was warm and sweet, her smile provocative.

"Have you come to grant a condemned man his last wish?"

Tears filled her eyes, but she blinked them back. "Why must you say such things?"

"I don't know." Nathan swallowed hard to relieve the dryness of his mouth. "It's the only way I know how to face hardship. It's inconsiderate."

Spirit of the Mountain

Spirit of the Mountain put her finger to his lips. "I know a better way."

Slowly, deliberately, she leaned closer, her lips pressed softly against his. He pulled away, looked into her eyes. What he saw took his breath away. "Has your grieving passed?"

"My time for grief is over." Spirit of the Mountain backed away from Nathan and let the fur drop to the ground, baring her body to his heated gaze. She liked what she saw in his eyes. "It is now time to love again."

"I have one favor," he mumbled hoarsely. "What is your name? The name your mother and father gave you?"

She inched forward and smiled. "Samantha. Samantha Louise Jacoby."

"Samantha," Nathan whispered into her ear.

Bumps rose on her flesh. She liked the way Nathan said her name. She liked the feel of his lips on her neck. Spirit of the Mountain slid her hands over his bare chest and moved them up to pull his lips to hers. A warmth stirred her blood, slowly bringing forth the needs of a woman—needs she had buried beneath her grief, needs she could no longer deny.

As if a new life had been born within her, Spirit of the Mountain allowed long-forgotten desires to control her. She explored Nathan's hard-muscled body with her fingertips, reveling in the maleness of him. His scent filled her senses; her tongue tasted the saltiness of his flesh.

Nathan wished his hands were free to touch and feel Samantha. But in another manner, his restriction added a maddening sensuality to his building passion. Her lips were hot and wet as they marked a trail over his chest, then back up to his throat. He ached to feel her soft lips against his, to slide his tongue into the sweetness of her mouth.

There was no shyness in her look, no timidness as she pulled away the fur that covered his manhood. She was a woman, neither virgin nor whore. Spirit of the Mountain, Samantha. Nathan saw her willingness, her honesty. She was unlike any other woman he had ever known, would ever know.

With animallike grace, she straddled him. He captured one round breast, the nipple taut and hard beneath his tongue. He traced a wet path to the other, accepting its fullness into his mouth. A soft moan told him of her pleasure.

Spirit of the Mountain bent her head to smell the dampness of his hair. Then she nipped at the lobe of his ear. Her hands wound into the long length of his hair as his tongue continued to lick and tease her. The drumbeat of the Shawnee celebration filled the air, crawling into her head, matching the strong, powerful pumping of her heart.

She felt the spirit inside her move to its rhythm, the magic of their lovemaking pulling her farther into its world. Spirit of the Mountain understood only the pulsating need deep inside her, carrying her from thought. Only pleasure and longing remained. Slowly, she slid down, her hunger meeting Nathan's.

He sucked air into his lungs, a surge of pleasure washing over him as she accepted his fullness into her. Spirit of the Mountain was warm and wet, the feel of her as she began to move on him firing his blood. He wondered if he'd already died and gone to heaven. Surely it was not meant for man to experience such delight on earth.

Yet when his release came at the same moment as hers, Nathan knew he had not. He felt Spirit of the Mountain trembling from the intensity of their lovemaking and understood why she had come to him. Whatever happened with the coming of dawn's light, they would have had this one time.

Spirit of the Mountain continued to hold Nathan tightly. Even when the heat of their lovemaking dissipated and her heart slowed its race within her chest, she held strong.

Finally, she pulled away. She picked up the fur and wrapped it snuggly about her. She wanted to say something, but words remained unformed in her mouth. Spirit of the Mountain looked down and found Nathan's darkened green eyes filled with sorrow. She touched his cheek and smiled.

Nathan seemed to struggle with his own words. "If—" He did not finish, but turned his head to kiss her palm. "If I should—"

"My Spirit Sister will not fail me."

Nathan looked doubtful, wanting to believe her, yet unable to.

"Do not worry, Nathan Walker. I have enough faith for us both." Spirit of the Mountain turned and left, unable to look back again.

Chapter Eight

Spirit of the Mountain's eyes remained closed, but subtle changes in smells and sounds told her sunrise had blushed the night sky with red. Birds began their daily chatter. The trees rustled with squirrels and chipmunks rising as the night creatures sought places to rest.

A light mist sprayed Spirit of the Mountain's face. The dampness clung to the air, mixing with the pungent smell of earth and forest in this sacred place away from the camp. The cry of a hawk opened her eyes, and she lifted them to watch the animal circle above her. With great ease, it glided on the wind's current, magnificent and powerful.

The gurgle of a stream soothed Spirit of the Mountain. Her mind now belonged to the forest that surrounded her. A raccoon stopped in its morning trek to the water, the animal's black eyes watching her as she watched it. Unconcerned, it moved on. A white-tailed buck moved through the brush, nibbling on tender new leaves, but it darted off when Long Knife appeared.

It was time for Spirit of the Mountain to go with him. Just before they left the cover of the trees, Long Knife turned to her.

"Standing Bear will be among the warriors in the forest." His dark eyes showed an unusual quality of caution, his words reflecting the warning they gave. "He has not forgotten I stopped him from killing you. He will try again."

"Why does he wish to kill me, Long Knife? I have done nothing to him."

Long Knife looked as if he might not answer her, but then he spoke. "He believes your scalp would bring him luck. When the sun's light shines on your hair, it reflects the color of the sun. With such a scalp, he could bring the power of the sun to him."

Part of her regretted asking the question, part of her was glad to know she had such an enemy. "I will take care."

Spirit of the Mountain walked past Long Knife and into the clearing, where the trial of truth would start. Long Knife called to her, and she turned back to him.

He offered her his war club, its handle intricately carved with stories of his bravery. "Take this." Long Knife pushed it into her hand when she did not take it. "You have shown much courage, Spirit of the Mountain. I am honored to have taken such a captive."

"Thank you, Long Knife." Spirit of the Mountain

shoved the club into her belt. She was ready.

The Frenchman, too, looked prepared. His hard features told her he was not happy to be put through this ordeal. If she failed, he would be sure to make her pay. Resolutely, she pushed all thoughts of failing from her mind.

She concentrated on the strong, steady beat of her heart. The rhythm grew louder as her mind gave way to its powerful magic, coursing into the veins of her body with each pulse of her heart. Her blood heated, speeding through her as the spirit inside her came forward. The smell of the Frenchman, stronger now, curled her nose in distaste. Every fiber of her being was alert and ready.

Long Knife dropped his raised arm, the signal to start. The Frenchman took off, disappearing into the cover of trees within seconds. Spirit of the Mountain noted the direction he took, then started off in another. If she could avoid him, she would. There would be enough trouble ahead with Shawnee warriors lying in wait.

With the thick wall of trees blocking the meager dawn light, she felt as if she'd crossed into a dark tunnel. Darkness still prevailed over many parts of the hilly terrain, waiting for the sun's warmth to spread as it gained height in the sky.

Darkness was like a friend, and her eyes quickly adjusted to it. Like her sister cat, Spirit of the Mountain had sight that was sharper in the shadows. All her senses were keener in the forest, the place she called home. Her feet barely touched the softly mulched earth. She was guided by senses that took her away from the more familiar trails worn smooth by the Shawnee. The warriors would expect her to take the trails to the village. She would not.

Within minutes, she came upon the fresh markings of a warrior. The Shawnee seemed unconcerned with hiding their own trails, confident in her inability to get past them. Spirit of the Mountain did not slow her pace, even when she spotted the Shawnee as he moved to stand in her path. He let out a war cry, but it trailed off in surprise when she ran straight toward him.

Spirit of the Mountain neither veered nor hesitated in her attack. Just as the warrior struck out, she rolled past him and leapt to her feet before he could react. Spirit of the Mountain brought Long Knife's club down onto his head, not hard enough to kill, but hard enough to knock the Shawnee unconscious.

A twig snapped, and Spirit of the Mountain whirled about. Her arm rose to deflect the blow of another warrior, and their clubs cracked together loudly. She twisted to the side and brought the club down across the Shawnee's shins, sweeping his feet out from beneath him. As he hit the ground, Spirit of the Mountain struck him, rendering him unconscious as well.

She ran on. The terrain steepened, but Spirit of the Mountain kept her grueling pace. She scaled the rocky face of the mountain that lay between her and the village. Ignoring the pain of her scraped and bruised skin, she thought of only one person. As climbing became harder because the mountain was rockier, the beat inside her head became stronger.

115

She moved, as if in a dream, ignoring hardships and overcoming obstacles.

The hair on the back of her neck bristled, and she looked behind her. The Frenchman had spotted her. He was following her up the rocks. She continued on, but his longer legs carried him to within feet of her. Spirit of the Mountain turned and kicked out just as he grabbed for her ankle. He lost his footing and slid back down several yards before he could gain a firm hand hold to stop himself.

Spirit of the Mountain crested the hill before the Frenchman could catch her again. Again on level ground, she ducked into the thick bramble of undergrowth. Twigs and branches tore at her, slowing her flight as she fought her way through them. When her lungs burned, she stopped to catch her breath and listen for the Frenchman.

He did nothing to hide his pursuit, his large frame sounding much like a bear charging through the forest. This time, she waited for him.

When the Frenchman burst upon her, he nearly ran her over, unaware she had stopped. Spirit of the Mountain reacted with quickness and agility, bringing her knee up into his unprotected groin. The big man fell to his knees in agony, and she stepped away from his bungling attempt to grab her.

Suddenly, Standing Bear was just behind the Frenchman, who was grasping himself in agony. Spirit of the Mountain's gaze locked with Standing Bear's, and she knew the warning Long Knife had given her was true. Standing Bear wanted her dead. He would not be content with just impeding her progress to the village.

Spirit of the Mountain fled. Daring to glance back, she saw Standing Bear wasted no time on the Frenchman. He merely pushed the injured man aside, then went after her. She ran as fast as she could, but knew he would easily gain on her. The trees thinned, and she broke into a small clearing.

Standing Bear's heavy breathing seemed loud in her ears, and she realized there were only seconds before he would catch her. She could not see the drop-off, but she sensed it was there. A warning sounded in her head, but Spirit of the Mountain plunged on. She leapt with every bit of strength she had, the earth beneath her feet disappearing. She flew across the chasm to the other side, dropping several feet before she hit solid ground.

She rolled to break her fall, but slid off the cliff, her feet dangling precariously over the edge. Spirit of the Mountain struggled to pull herself up to safety and hugged the earth thankfully when she had. Finally, she pushed herself up onto shaky legs and looked across the gully she had jumped. Standing Bear was there watching, his stance angry, his cry chilling as it drifted to her.

Suddenly, he whirled about and backtracked. Spirit of the Mountain breathed a sigh of relief, then turned to find her way down from her lofty perch. A flash of color caught her eye, and she looked back. Standing Bear took flight and floated on air as he followed to her side.

As he landed, Spirit of the Mountain climbed down, carefully moving over the rocky decline. He remained close behind, giving her no respite. Once she found more secure footing, she broke into a full run.

Spirit of the Mountain was light and fast on her feet, but Standing Bear had a longer, more powerful stride. He closed the distance between them. Reaching out, he grabbed a handful of her hair, forcing her to slow down, then stop.

Standing Bear jerked her into his arms; her struggles against him were useless. He chuckled, his delight showing clearly in the dark brown of his eyes. With deliberateness, he pulled his knife from its sheath, his hand forcing her head back at a dangerous angle.

Suddenly, the soft, wet earth beneath them gave way, and they both slid down a muddy embankment. They landed in a heap of arms and legs, mud making it difficult for either to stand. Spirit of the Mountain crawled on her hands and knees to get out of his reach, but his hand clamped onto her ankle. He dragged her back to him, but she twisted and kicked out, landing a blow directly to his chest. As the air whooshed from him, she tugged free of his grip and scrambled away.

Once again on solid ground, Spirit of the Mountain darted off down a trail with Standing Bear close behind. She sensed someone just ahead. A flash of color told her it was the Frenchman. Her nose confirmed it. He crouched, waiting, ready to strike.

Spirit of the Mountain slowed down enough for Standing Bear to close in on her. The Frenchman did as she expected and jumped into her path. She swerved just before she ran into him and ducked beneath his outstretched arms. The Frenchman could not react before Standing Bear appeared at a dead run and slammed into him full force.

While the two men grappled with each other, Spirit of the Mountain rushed ahead. She came to a river, started to cross it, then stopped. Another Shawnee warrior stood on the opposite bank. He searched the outline of trees, apparently hearing the now subdued noises of the Frenchman and Standing Bear.

Spirit of the Mountain sank down into the water and dove when the Shawnee entered the broad stream. He stopped so close she could see his legs. He did not move on. Her lungs began to burn for lack of air. Looking about, Spirit of the Mountain spotted a beaver's dam and swam underwater to it.

Rising inside the animal's den, she sucked in large gulps of air. When she felt safe, she swam back out to see if the warrior was still there. He had gone onto the bank and walked toward the sounds he'd heard. She crossed to the other side and crawled from the water.

A surge of renewed energy pumped through her. She was ahead of the Frenchman. The village could not be far off. Spirit of the Mountain sprinted on.

Spirit of the Mountain studied the village before entering it, eyeing the center where Nathan was tied. One last warrior stood in her way, his face fierce as they approached each other. Standing Bear's angry cry stopped him.

The other warrior stepped aside, and Standing Bear came toward her from behind where the other had stood. Standing Bear pulled his hatchet and knife from his belt. From the side, Long Knife emerged and stepped between her and Standing Bear.

Since Long Knife spoke in Shawnee, she did not understand him, yet his tone displayed immense anger. The warriors came together like two great stags, grunting and pushing, testing each other's strength. But Long Knife had earned his place as a great warrior because of his skill, and he quickly turned the tables on Standing Bear. Within seconds, Long Knife had the other warrior on the ground. Long Knife's blade quickly, deftly cut Standing Bear's throat.

The Frenchman appeared at the edge of the village, and Spirit of the Mountain gave no more thought or time to Standing Bear. She ran for the knife that had been placed on the ground in front of Nathan. Then her hand wrapped about the handle and pulled it from the soil.

"Watch out!"

Nathan's warning followed her own senses, and she turned on the Frenchman. He jumped clear as she slashed the air. Then he plowed into her, throwing her aside as if she were but a sack of flour. The Frenchman grabbed the torch, using it to keep her at bay as she struck out with the knife. Again and again, she sliced the air with the blade, and the Frenchman's counterstroke barely missed her with the flame.

Despite her many attempts, Spirit of the Mountain couldn't get close to him. His slow laughter erupted. He casually touched the torch to the dry, brittle wood. It began to burn, flames devouring the great pile that lay at Nathan's feet. Smoke rose and choked

Nathan, the fire spreading rapidly.

Desperately, Spirit of the Mountain tossed dirt in the Frenchman's face and ran past him. She still couldn't get close enough to cut Nathan free because the wall of flames stopped her.

Barely able to see, Spirit of the Mountain took the only chance she had to save Nathan. She took a deep breath and threw the knife, recalling the many hours she and her brother had practiced as children. Her aim accurate, the blade imbedded in the post where the leather ties bound Nathan's wrists. Quickly, he cut himself free and jumped clear of the fire.

The Frenchman tackled Nathan, and they rolled about, smoke and dust making it difficult to see who was who. With each twist and turn, the two men moved closer to the flames. Spirit of the Mountain started toward them, but Long Knife pulled her back, his strong arms keeping her from interfering.

"You have proven your worthiness, Spirit of the Mountain. You have prevailed in the trial of truth. It is now time for these men to settle their dispute."

She did not agree, but Long Knife's grip on her made certain Spirit of the Mountain could do nothing but watch.

The Frenchman knocked Nathan from him and pulled a burning stump of wood from the fire. He attacked, the flame missing Nathan's head by precious little. Nathan rolled onto his back and brought his legs up into his chest as the Frenchman landed atop him. Nathan kicked out, sending the Frenchman backward. He teetered, then fell onto the blazing pile of wood.

The Frenchman's shirt caught on fire, engulfing

him in flames within seconds. He screamed and scrambled to his feet, then ran for the river, batting at the fire with his bare hands.

Long Knife let go of Spirit of the Mountain, and she ran to Nathan. He pulled her into his arms.

"Thank God, you're safe," he muttered, his eyes filled with tears. "This has been the longest day of my life."

Nathan pulled back and looked at Spirit of the Mountain, making certain she was all right. He hugged her again.

The Shawnee leader shuffled over to them. They stood apart to face him.

"Spirit of the Mountain, the Great Spirit has most certainly blessed you. Your Spirit Sister is strong and cunning. You have earned your freedom. Go."

Spirit of the Mountain looked up at Nathan and smiled.

Nathan grabbed his rifle and knife from the warrior who held them out to him. Then he took Spirit of the Mountain's hand. "Let's go. We've a long way to travel."

She nodded, but paused. Taking the war club Long Knife had given her, Spirit of the Mountain handed it back to him. Neither said anything. There was no need.

"Let's go, Nathan. We've a long way to travel.

Pierre lay in the mud along the riverbank, allowing the ooze to ease the pain of his burns. When he was able, he stood and stumbled into the cover of the trees. He gathered goldenrod and coneflower to make a poultice that would soothe his blistered skin.

A deep, seething anger rose through his agony, the desire for revenge giving him an unrelenting drive to survive. If it was the last thing he did, he would see that bitch suffer. Terribly.

Chapter Nine

"Nathan," Spirit of the Mountain called out to him, his long legs having carried him several yards ahead of her. He stopped and turned back to wait for her to catch up.

"You do not have to go so fast." Spirit of the Mountain smiled, believing she understood his reasons for doing so. "They will not change their minds, Nathan."

Nathan took her hand and started off again. "I don't want to take any chance they might. I'll carry you if I must."

She jerked free of his hand and laughed. "If you must."

This response stopped him again, but when he turned back, his eyes showed her teasing was effective. He swooped her into his arms, his deep laughter mixing with hers. It produced a pleasant sound, one Spirit of the Mountain liked, one she wouldn't mind hearing often. She placed her hand on his face, a sudden warmth spreading through her like fire.

"I could not bear it if you were to die on my account, Nathan Walker. Promise me you will not frighten me so again."

"Me," Nathan cried, his eyes rounding with amazement. "You nearly frightened me to death with your stubbornness. I've never known such hell as I went through this morning."

Spirit of the Mountain knew he would not understand her faith in her Spirit Sister. She couldn't help but be a little disappointed. "We are free. That is all that matters."

"What happened, Sam?" His eyes were serious.

"Sam," Spirit of the Mountain whispered. "My father used to call me Sam."

Gently, he put her feet to the ground, but his arms still held her. "You aren't going to tell me, are you?"

"No," she replied, hoping that would be the end of it.

"Was it so terrible?"

"It was as they said, no more."

He didn't seem satisfied with her answer. "How—"

"I cannot explain what you will not believe. It is done. Let it be."

It was obvious he didn't want to let it be, but he did. He walked on, this time a little more slowly so she could keep up with his long-legged stride.

* * *

125

The sun had long since disappeared behind the mountains, but golden patches of light still capped a hillside here and there. Slowly, all faded into darkness as the dark shadow of night crept over Spirit of the Mountain and Nathan. They stopped.

"We can spend the night here." Nathan pointed to a secluded spot, then to the stream nearby. "There's plenty of water."

Spirit of the Mountain nodded and began gathering wood for a fire. Nathan went off in search of food. Once the fire was going, she walked down to the water. Tall white oaks shaded the bank in an umbrella of glossy new leaves, casting dark shadows in the gray light of evening.

Unable to keep from the beckoning crystal water, Spirit of the Mountain pulled her moccasin boots off and set them aside. She untied the beaded belt from her waist, then dropped it and her dress. A cool night breeze lifted her hair from her shoulders, touching her skin with its chill.

Ignoring the cold, she waded into the water, which revived her. Since the stream was shallow, she splashed water up onto her arms and face. Quickly, she cleansed the dust from her body, the weariness from her mind. Spirit of the Mountain felt Nathan's presence, but kept her back to him.

"You certainly make a pretty picture."

She still didn't look around. "Do I?"

"Yes," Nathan said, but a note of concern filtered into his voice. "You should wait to bathe until I'm here, Sam. Anyone could walk up on you."

His concern made her turn to his dark silhouette. "I knew it was you, Nathan."

"You couldn't have known it was me. I was too quiet."

Spirit of the Mountain sloshed through the water to stand a few feet in front of him. Her eyes closed, and she lifted her head to sniff the air. "I could smell you." Her eyes opened, and she looked at Nathan again, though it was too dark to see his face. "You smell good, Nathan."

Nathan knew she was naked. The outline of each curve fired the passion building inside him. The night cloaked her like a sensuous veil, revealing little, promising everything.

He had never been told he smelled good, and he didn't know what to say in turn. Spirit of the Mountain—Samantha—intrigued Nathan. She was a mystery to him. There was a part of him that liked that, another part that wanted to know everything. But even more strongly, he feared the truth.

The hardness in his loins increased; the heat inside him intensified. Nathan lay his rifle aside and shucked off his clothes. He splashed into the stream, spraying Spirit of the Mountain as he moved toward her. Soft, delightful laughter greeted him, the sound intoxicating, pulling him more deeply into her spell of seduction.

"You are so beautiful," he muttered, pulling her into his arms. He buried his head in the mass of her wet hair, the chill soothing his heated face.

Small, delicate hands explored his back, and he wondered how someone so petite could be so capable. A shudder moved through him as his thoughts scattered, then focused on a vision of what she must have endured that morning. Nathan sucked in fresh air to relieve the sudden ache in his chest.

Spirit of the Mountain felt Nathan tense, then pull back. "What is it, Nathan?"

"Nothing," he mumbled, drawing her back into his arms. "I just want to hold you and never let you go."

Nathan's words were comforting, yet they held a promise she did not believe he meant. Spirit of the Mountain was not so gullible as to believe that, once she was safely deposited with her grandfather in Boston, Nathan would stay as well. He would leave.

She kissed his shoulder tenderly. Love him she would, no matter what the future held. Spirit of the Mountain cupped water into her hands and began to wash the broad expanse of his chest, then his shoulders and arms. Slowly, deliberately, she rinsed his flesh; each movement, each moment was a pleasure as she bathed Nathan from head to toe.

Nathan's lips sought hers, hot and wet, his tongue uniting with hers. His hands slid down to the roundness of her buttocks, gently squeezing, then lifting her to him. The hard maleness of Nathan made her hips move closer, but it still was not enough. Spirit of the Mountain wound her legs about his waist, lifting herself. Then she slid down over him with relief.

The fire inside Spirit of the Mountain kept the cold night away, and she moved to the silent rhythm of love. Slowly at first, then faster, harder, the need within building, driving. She felt the slow ache burst, sending its tingle clear to her toes, curling them as they remained locked behind Nathan. She clung to Nathan, his own release shaking him as he thrust one final time, then fell quiet.

His heavy breathing tickled her ear. When it

calmed down, Spirit of the Mountain slid her feet back into the water. Without words, she once again washed him, cleaning the sweet scent of their love-making away, leaving the feel of their bodies a memory to savor.

Then, lovingly, Nathan did the same, the water rinsing the last of their bodies' heat from her. He lifted her and carried her to the mossy bank, where they dressed.

Nathan lay awake for a long time. Curled in front of him, Spirit of the Mountain's soft, even breathing comforted him in an odd way—just like the way she fit perfectly against him, her body warm and pleasant to hold close. He found the sensation difficult to put into words.

Thoughts drifted through his mind, taking Nathan back to a time when he was a child. The security he had had then was a comfort he had not known for a very long time. How strange that this particular woman would give him this. They had so little in common.

This brought on other sensations that impinged upon the good ones. How could she so easily work her way into his heart? She didn't belong there with him—he knew that for certain. Long ago, Nathan had become a part of the wilderness. Long ago, he had realized he was to live out his life alone. It was the only way, the only place he had ever been able to be his own man, complete and uninhibited by others' notions of what he should be.

He wouldn't give that freedom up for anyone or anything. Even this nagging sense he somehow belonged with Spirit of the Mountain. He could not allow this tiny feeling to beguile him, to cause him to deny the truth of who he was and where he belonged.

Spirit of the Mountain should be with her family. Their home was the best and most proper place for her. He had no second thoughts on the matter. What kind of life could he give a woman? His was a life for a man alone. There could be no wife, no children, no home. He had learned that the hard way.

His mind settled on this one thought, which left no room for argument. He would think on it no more.

Nathan yawned, stretching wide as he worked out the cramps from sleep. He looked about and saw the fire was going, but he did not see Spirit of the Mountain anywhere. He stood and began to search for her, not out of a sense of urgency, but from a sense of loneliness.

"Sam," he called out. No answer. He wandered farther from where they camped near the bank of the stream. "Sam."

"Good morning." Her voice was soft, drifting to him from a direction he could not determine.

"Sam, where are you?"

"Up here."

Looking up, Nathan spotted her perched on a wide branch above him. "What are you doing up there?"

Spirit of the Mountain held up a honeycomb and smiled triumphantly. "Getting breakfast."

Now he saw the hive she had raided, its inhabitants buzzing about her head by the hundreds. Fear rushed over Nathan as Spirit of the Mountain's safety became his most immediate concern. "Sam. Be still."

She licked the honey from her lips, then used the back of her hand to wipe at the sticky liquid that ran down her chin. "Would you like some, Nathan?"

"No," he said evenly. "Just come down now. Before you get stung."

Spirit of the Mountain tossed the honeycomb down to him. "They will not harm me. I have been stealing honey since I was a child. They do not seem to mind."

Nathan gathered his tightly strung emotions in and breathed a sigh of relief. He should have known.

Spirit of the Mountain pulled her arm from the hole in the tree, a large chunk of honeycomb grasped firmly in hand. She stilled and sniffed the air. "Nathan," she shouted.

Darkened with concern, green eyes looked up to Spirit of the Mountain. "What is it?"

The 500-pound bear rose onto his hind legs, extending the animal to his full six feet height. He stood eye to eye, nose to nose with Nathan. Neither moved for a second. Then the bear let out a growl, and Nathan shouted, "Christ Almighty!"

The creature lunged forward, a massive paw tearing through Nathan's deer-hide shirt and into his flesh. Spirit of the Mountain jumped from the tree, landing next to them as the bear took Nathan down, rolling him about. Nathan was helpless against the animal's tremendous strength as powerful and deadly claws ripped and tore at him.

Spirit of the Mountain yelled, drawing the bear's

attention from Nathan. She moved close enough to touch the animal. Nathan managed to stand, then fell to one knee again.

"Run, Sam," he cried out weakly, but neither she nor the bear moved.

Nathan's face was only inches from the animal's paw. Spirit of the Mountain called out, "Move away, Nathan. He will not harm you further."

Nathan struggled to his feet, swayed precariously. Then Spirit of the Mountain slowly moved toward Nathan and slid her arm about him for support.

"Go now," she said directly to the bear. The animal dropped down onto all fours, a deep grunt accentuating his shift in weight. Black eyes watched her, yet she gave no sign of fear.

She extended her right hand, still full of the drippy, sweet honeycomb. "Here," she offered, her voice soft, holding no threat or anger. "It is your favorite."

The same paws that had shredded Nathan's flesh so easily reached out and pulled her hand to its mouth. His tongue, rough and raspy, licked the honey she offered. Spirit of the Mountain put the honeycomb into the bear's mouth, then pulled free of his sharp teeth without a scratch.

Quietly, while the bear finished his treat, Spirit of the Mountain helped Nathan back to their camp. She guided Nathan to the stream, then told him to sit down. She pulled his bloodied shirt from him.

He moaned at the movement, but when he turned to her, his eyes were twinkling. "It could scare a man to death running into a giant like that." Nathan chuckled, but stopped at the discomfort his laughter caused him.

"I am sorry, Nathan," Spirit of the Mountain whispered, gently washing the blood away.

"Whatever for?" Nathan asked hoarsely, pain underlining each word.

Spirit of the Mountain looked at him, sad and worried. "I did not warn you quickly enough to get out of his way."

He stopped her ministrations and took her hand into his. "How could you know the bear was there?"

Confusion plagued her. "He must have been downwind of us. Then, the wind shifted—"

"You smelled him the way you smelled me last night?"

She nodded.

"My God." Nathan dropped her hand, his mood changing in that instant. He didn't want to believe what she was saying, but how could he deny what he had witnessed firsthand? Obviously, she wasn't in danger from the wild animals.

"You can go right up to wild animals. You have a sixth sense no one else seems to have. You can steal honey from a beehive. You can smell and hear better than anyone I've ever known. What are you? Are you a woman? Or are you an animal?"

"I am a woman, yet an animal's spirit lives inside me. It gives me abilities I would not have without its presence."

Nathan was willing to accept the notion that she had some sort of special relationship with animals, but he couldn't give credit to the idea of an animal's spirit being inside her. "This Spirit Sister nonsense you told me about?"

"It is not nonsense, Nathan Walker. It has saved your hide many times already." Her voice took on an angry tone. "If I were you, I would not make light of it."

"Well," Nathan said with a drawl, "you aren't me."

She stood, stiffness in every movement and word. "No, I am not, and I am glad. I would not want to be so stubborn and ignorant."

Anger pushed all else away. "Ignorant."

"Yes, ignorant."

Nathan reached out to grab her, but the pain stopped him short. "I ought to—"

"You ought to clean yourself, Nathan Walker."

Spirit of the Mountain started to walk away, but could not resist one last comment. "You ought to put something on those wounds when you are done."

Something akin to a growl followed her back to the fire. She stubbornly kept her back to him, refusing to watch as he tended to the lacerations the bear had crisscrossed over his chest and arms. Even when she heard him approach, she did not look at him.

"Are you ready to go?"

Shock brought Spirit of the Mountain from her self-imposed silence. "Perhaps you should rest before we go on."

"I'll rest when I need to rest." His voice still sounded angry. "Let's go."

"You are angry." It was a statement and needed no response. He gave none. "It will only bring you grief. I will tend to your wounds."

When she reached out, he pulled away. "You needn't bother. I'm fine."

Worry defeated her own anger. But she did not argue further with him. It would do no good. After the fire was put out, she followed him, saying no more.

By late afternoon, Nathan's eyes were dulled from pain, his stride slow and sluggish. Spirit of the Mountain's concern finally exceeded her perception of his stubbornness.

"Nathan, you cannot go on."

He turned back to stare at her, his gaze unseeing, anguished.

She took his hand. "Please. You will become ill if we do not tend to your wounds."

"Does this disturb you?"

His voice sounded strange, distant, his question just as unusual. "Of course it would disturb me."

"Why?"

Spirit of the Mountain didn't know what answer he wanted. She said the only thing she knew to say: "Because I love you, Nathan Walker."

Something flickered in the dark green eyes that stared down at her. Something she couldn't interpret or put meaning to. Then it was gone, leaving a vacant stare. Nathan dropped to the ground, unconscious.

Kneeling beside him, Spirit of the Mountain tugged his shirt from his back. He had lost a lot of blood. His face was pale and drawn. He roused, and she managed to get him up, helping him to a secluded spot off the trail they were following.

Nathan continued to drift in and out of wakefulness as Spirit of the Mountain gathered pine needles to make a poultice. When she was done, Nathan opened his eyes once again.

"Sam," he whispered. "There is a homestead not far from here, a half day or so northwest. You must go on. It's the Taylor farm. They are friends."

A surge of irritation ran through Spirit of the Mountain's mind. "You are always telling me to leave you, Nathan. I will not. You need not ask again."

"I can't make it, Sam. You must go get help."

Spirit of the Mountain set her jaw, clamping her teeth together in vexation. "I will not go without you."

"But—"

"I will make a litter. We will go together."

Nathan's face scrunched up in pain. "Damn you, woman. You never listen."

"Why should I?" she asked, already gathering long, sturdy branches to lash together. "What you say makes no sense."

"Why, you ungrateful—"

Spirit of the Mountain knelt down and put her finger to his lips. "Ssshhh, you need to rest quietly."

She pulled his knife from the sheath on his belt and set about digging for roots to lash the litter together. It was dark before Spirit of the Mountain completed her work.

They would start in the morning. Tonight she would rest.

"Ma! Ma!"

The young boy ran ahead of Spirit of the Mountain, calling out. His mother came to the cabin door, wiping her hands on the long print apron that covered her dress. She raised her hand to block the sun from her eyes. Seeing Spirit of the Mountain dragging the litter behind her, the woman ran out to meet her.

"Jack," she called out to the small barn that housed animals. "Jack, come quick."

When she reached the litter, recognition came to her face. "Nathan Walker," she whispered in surprise.

Jack Taylor came running, his boy on his heels. "Here." Jack pulled the litter from Spirit of the Mountain's hands. "I'll take it on up to the house. Libby, you'd best see to the girl. She's near exhausted."

Exhausted didn't seem adequate to how Spirit of the Mountain truly felt. She had reached that point long ago. Now she felt like the walking dead. Libby's strong arms helped her the last few steps, and she was grateful for it.

"Now don't you worry none. We'll see to Nathan." Libby Taylor's voice was sweet, almost childlike. Spirit of the Mountain liked it. At one time, Libby's expressive face may have reflected youthfulness, but years of hard life had stolen it away prematurely. Without words, the deep lines etched into her sun-darkened skin told a story that saddened Spirit of the Mountain.

"Thank you for your kindness," Spirit of the Mountain said.

"What's your name?" the woman asked as they entered their home.

Spirit of the Mountain looked about the small frontier cabin. Although sparse, it gave over an instant homey feel. Something cooked on a spit in the stone fireplace. Mending lay on the trestle table, and benches sat on each side, a homemade chair at each end.

"I am Spirit of the Mountain."

Jack carried Nathan in and laid him in the bed. A patchwork quilt hung from the ceiling to provide a measure of privacy for the husband and wife. Another covered the bed. Libby pushed the meat aside and hung a cast-iron pot on the hook, filling it with water.

"I am Libby, and this is my husband, Jack Taylor." Jack nodded in Spirit of the Mountain's direction. "This is our son, Tibias."

Tibias had stood back out of the way, but he came forward when introduced. "How do you do, miss. What happened to Nathan?"

It was as if she had to think back, because her mind was dull and slow. "He ran into a bear."

Libby stood at the bed, examining Nathan's wounds. "You did good with your poultice. He just needs some good food in him and some rest."

Dark brown eyes rose, and Libby's gaze came to rest on Spirit of the Mountain. "He'll mend right enough."

Spirit of the Mountain smiled, despite the energy it seemed to take. "Yes, he will mend right enough."

"Tibias," Libby said, motioning to him. "Get the miss some cool water."

Libby bustled back over to Spirit of the Mountain. "You can rest here." Libby pushed her down onto a small cot in the corner. "I'll have something to eat in no time. No time at all."

Spirit of the Mountain

Tibias offered Spirit of the Mountain a cup of water; its wetness soothed her parched throat. Before she could even mutter a word of thanks, sleep closed her eyes.

Chapter Ten

"He's sleeping."

Spirit of the Mountain turned to Libby, who stood in the open doorway, a bucket of water in one hand. "He has a fever."

"Yes." Libby nodded and placed the bucket on the table. "It's to be expected after tussling with a bear like that. He just needs to work it out of his system."

"How can you be so certain?" Spirit of the Mountain didn't feel Libby's confidence.

Libby took the kettle of water that heated over the fire and poured it into a large pan. She came up beside Spirit of the Mountain and placed the pan on the small table by the bed. "I've nursed many a man through worse than this. Don't you worry none."

She patted Spirit of the Mountain's hand, then sat down on the chair next to Nathan.

"What can I do?"

"You just rest." Libby wrung out a cloth and continued ministering to her patient.

Spirit of the Mountain stood there, uncertain what to do. She had rested plenty, and she felt she should be doing something, anything. She also felt a stranger in a place with people she did not know. She did not wish to impose any further than she had already. She walked outside.

Sunlight pushed through a few clouds. Spirit of the Mountain watched the white billows skid across the blue canopy overhead like puppies chasing each others' tails.

"Miss."

She looked down at Tibias, his round, freckled face anxious. He looked like his father, with an unruly crop of reddish-brown hair and hazel eyes. "Yes?"

"I was just wondering if Nathan was going to be all right?"

Smiling, she rumpled his already tousled hair. "It would take more than a big bear to hurt Nathan Walker."

His brown eyes grew large. "How big was it, miss?"

"As big as any I have ever seen. This tall," she said, reaching up as high as she could. "Over five hundred pounds, maybe six."

Tibias's mouth became round in surprise. "Did Nathan kill him?"

Spirit of the Mountain put her hand on his shoulder and walked with him to the small barn. "No, Tibias. There was no need. That bear was as startled as Nathan."

"Wow," he muttered under his breath. He picked up his fishing pole. "Would you like to go fishing, miss?"

"Fishing?"

"Yes, miss. Pa's been busy in the fields, so I've been catching fish for our meals. With you and Nathan visiting, I'd better catch extra."

A notion struck Spirit of the Mountain "It must be a lot of hard work for your mother and father here?"

"Yeah." The boy scuffed the dirt floor with his worn boot. "It's plenty hard. When I get older, I'll be able to put meat on the table, not just fish."

Spirit of the Mountain smiled. "I know you will. You will be a fine hunter, Tibias."

"Maybe next year."

"Next year," she agreed and watched him run off toward the river, fishing pole in hand. Her idea seemed right.

"Tibias," Spirit of the Mountain called out to the boy. He looked up from the bank, where he sat waiting for the fish to bite.

"Yes, miss."

"We are going hunting."

He rose and pulled his line from the water. "But Pa said I'm not old enough to shoot the rifle yet. It's taller than I am."

"It is not taller than I." She laughed, eyeing the long rifle. "At least not much taller."

Tibias ran up to her and smiled shyly. "You, miss. You are going to go hunting?"

"No. We are going hunting." Spirit of the Mountain pulled the boy along with her. "I am in the mood for some meat. How about you?"

His eyes lit up. "Some wild turkey would taste mighty good."

"Then turkey it is."

"Ma," Tibias ran into the cabin, his eyes bright, his breathing heavy. "Look what we shot!"

Libby put her finger to her lip, shushing her son. Curious, she walked past him to the door where he pointed. Spirit of the Mountain stood in the doorway, a large, plump turkey in hand.

"What on earth?" Libby exclaimed, her mouth dropping open at the sight of the tom.

"I thought you might like this for dinner, Libby. Tibias said Jack has not had much time for hunting while working in the fields."

Libby took the bird in hand. "My, oh, my," she mumbled, her eyes filling with tears. Suddenly, her look became concerned. "Tibias, your father has said you can't go hunting yet. You didn't disobey him, did you?"

"No, Ma. Miss here did the shooting. I just went along."

Warm brown eyes turned to Spirit of the Mountain. "You shot the bird?"

Spirit of the Mountain nodded. "Your son is perfectly safe with me. I have been hunting for many years."

Libby's lips puckered strangely, and she looked down at the floor, her hands wiping at her apron. "Why it isn't a proper thing for a woman to do, Spirit . . . uh, Spirit of—"

"If it is easier, you can call me Samantha or Sam."

Spirit of the Mountain could see Libby's dismay and uneasiness.

"Samantha, why that's a beautiful name. Is that the name your parents gave you?"

"I was born Samantha Jacoby."

"Do you remember your parents?" Libby plopped the turkey on the table and began to pluck it.

Spirit of the Mountain understood the other woman's curiosity. "Yes, I did not go to live with the Cherokee until I was twelve."

Shock distorted Libby's normally kind face. She quickly controlled herself. "You went to live with the Cherokee willingly? You weren't a captive?"

Confused, Spirit of the Mountain answered the only way she knew how. Honestly. "Of course not. I loved my Indian family, just as I loved my real parents."

"Oh, my." Libby sat, her hands no longer pulling feathers.

"What is it? Have I said something to upset you?" Spirit of the Mountain sat on the bench across from Libby. "Have I done something wrong?"

Sympathy replaced the shock on Libby's face, once again kind and caring in appearance. "I'm sorry, Samantha. I just assumed you were with the Indians against your will. It's just not a common thing. I've never known anyone who—"

"Who lived with Indians as a daughter and not a slave."

"Yes." Libby pulled a weak and unconvincing smile, then started plucking again. "Well, it's a blessing you weren't taken as a captive. Too many whites have suffered at the hands of those savages. You were a lucky one, all right, Samantha."

The woman's words hit chords within Spirit of the Mountain she had not known existed. Yet, Libby seemed to think nothing of her then. She acted as if they were talking about the weather. A strange tightness constricted Spirit of the Mountain's heart, and a lump formed in her throat. She could not speak. She could not move.

"Are you sure you didn't overdo it today? You look as white as a ghost."

Libby's voice reflected her concern, bringing Spirit of the Mountain's thoughts away from her pain. "I am tired. I think I will rest." She stood and walked to the door.

"Where are you going, Samantha? You can lie down on the cot if you'd like."

"It is a beautiful day. I will find a sunny spot to rest." She needed to get outside, to get away from this place. "Send Tibias for me if you need any help."

"You go on. Don't you fret over what needs to be done. I'm doing fine." Libby waved her on. "Tibias, fetch me some potatoes from the cellar. We're going to have a feast."

Spirit of the Mountain's pace quickened. She nearly ran to the cover of the trees just beyond the clearing of the Taylor farm. Once the shadows had swallowed her, she fell to her knees, tears choking her. She didn't understand Libby's words. They haunted her, feeding the pain within her chest.

It was a blessing . . . she was lucky . . . whites have suffered . . . savages.

As a child, Spirit of the Mountain had lived alone with her family in the mountains, and as a young woman, she'd been safe in the love of her adopted family, an Indian family. She had not known there would be a difference to others. She knew only how she felt.

A dark fear climbed forward, a fear she had given no thought to before today. Would it be the same in Boston? Would her own grandfather feel she was lucky? Would he believe that the Indians were savages, that her adopted family was responsible for the suffering of the white man?

"It is a lie," Spirit of the Mountain cried out to the trees, birds fluttering away in surprise at her outburst. She raised her head up, looking to the sky, looking to the Great Spirit. "How can I live with a people that believes in lies?"

"How do you feel, Nathan?" Spirit of the Mountain touched his forehead. It was cool, the fever broken.

"I've felt better. But then, I've felt worse, too."

She smiled. "You've looked better, too."

This response made Nathan smile in turn, then chuckle. "I suppose I have at that." He rubbed the bristle on his cheek. "I guess you'll be wanting me to shave this stubble off?"

"It was nice to see your face."

His grin widened. "Then I will shave."

The past came to her mind, a strong vision touching her with its pleasure. "I used to watch my father shave when I was little. I begged him to let me try; then it became our daily ritual."

"Then"—Nathan's eyes twinkled mischievously—"you can shave me. Yes, I think I'd like that."

The look in his eyes told her more than his simple

assent implied. "I shall see what I can do."

Libby returned to the cabin and immediately walked to the bed where they talked. "I see you're finally awake."

"How long have I been here, Libby?"

"Just a couple of days." She busied herself with cleaning up, her mood light and cheery. "Didn't think there was a bear alive that could put you in a bed for two days, Nathan. I'd almost think you're getting old."

"I am getting old," Nathan complained good-naturedly.

"I'll have you something to eat in no time."

Nathan pushed himself up, wincing slightly as he sat on the side of the bed. "I'm starving."

Spirit of the Mountain gently touched one deep scratch. "You should be careful, Nathan. You might start bleeding again."

He pulled her hand away and kissed it softly, but dropped it before anyone else might see. "How did you get me here? I don't remember."

"I made a litter, as I said I would."

"You are amazing, Sam." Nathan wanted more than anything to take Spirit of the Mountain into his arms, but he resisted. Libby wouldn't understand. She was a pious woman and would not approve of their relationship. This made him wonder about it himself. He had put Spirit of the Mountain in a very difficult position, compromising her before she even had a chance at a life with her family.

"I've not been a very valiant savior, my sweet. I have done wrong by you."

"I do not understand. You have done all that is

right by me, Nathan. You make no sense."

Nathan turned away from her honest, caring eyes. "How about helping me down to the river. I'd like to wash up a bit."

He stood and with Spirit of the Mountain's help walked a few steps. Libby stood in front of them, blocking their way.

"What on earth are you doing out of bed, Nathan?" Her face showed disapproval.

"I need some fresh air, Libby. Don't worry, Sam will be with me."

She didn't change her look. "I don't know—"

"I do," Nathan said confidently. "She got me here, didn't she?"

Libby stepped aside, but she obviously still didn't approve.

Spirit of the Mountain put her arm about Nathan's waist, his arm casually draped over her shoulder. She could feel his chest rumbling as laughter shook him.

"Libby's a kind soul, but she can be too smothering at times." He walked slowly, but his arm pulled her closer. "I've got to confess, I'm not nearly as weak as I put on."

Looking up, she saw the twinkle reappear in Nathan's eyes. "What do you mean?"

"I just wanted to put my arm around you without Libby's dour disapproval."

"Why does she disapprove? What is between us is of no concern to her."

Nathan was silent for a long moment. "It's a different world away from your Indian family, Sam. I should have prepared you better. I just didn't think far enough ahead."

Spirit of the Mountain smiled shyly, a warmth coming to her cheeks. "We have been busy with other things, Nathan." Then she turned serious. "I do have some questions about Libby, about what is proper."

When they reached the river and sat, Nathan asked, "What do you mean proper?"

"Libby said it was not proper for a woman to hunt. I think I understand this. Women did not hunt among the Indians, and they thought it strange that I did. My mother, too, objected, but my father insisted it was important I learn how to survive. My mother taught me the things a daughter should know, and my father trained me as he would have a son. It saved my life when I ended up alone on the mountain."

"Then what is it that's bothering you, Sam?"

The great pain returned to her chest, bringing tears to her eyes. Spirit of the Mountain blinked them back and steeled herself against the hurt. "I am afraid, Nathan. Afraid of what is beyond my mountains. Libby said that I was lucky to be adopted by the Cherokee, that it was a blessing. She said—" Spirit of the Mountain stopped to still the tremble of her voice. "She said too many whites have suffered at the hands of savages."

"Libby is a kindhearted Christian woman, Sam. She has known a life of hardship and adversity. Many like her and Jack come to the edge of the wilderness to live, to find a life that isn't under the yoke of another."

He paused. Spirit of the Mountain waited, wanting to know what made people come here, what made people like Libby think the way they did.

"They face a hard life filled with toil, disease, wild animals, and Indians."

"Then why do they come out here?" She wanted to understand, to rid herself of the pain inside her.

"The Taylors," Nathan said, then paused. "We all came for one reason. The wilderness means freedom. Your own parents came to the mountains to be free of a disapproving family. Jack Taylor and I indentured ourselves for seven years to come to America. America meant freedom."

He drew a deep breath, as if the memories disturbed him. "Seven long, hard years working for another, never having anything to call my own. It's hard to feel like a man when the world endeavors to keep you down, denying you even the most basic of needs—pride and honor. Without heritage and wealth, you're condemned to a life of poverty and forever tied to your station in life."

Spirit of the Mountain felt his pain, the hurt of his struggling to be his own man on his own terms.

"So," Nathan continued, "for men like Jack and me, the only place left to start a life of freedom is the wilderness. Wives like Libby go where their men go. It seems we want this land as badly as the Indians want to keep it for themselves. All are willing to fight for it, willing to die for it."

Nathan took Spirit of the Mountain's chin and turned her face up to his. "And for many people the Indians are savages." His voice was soft, sympathetic. "Their ways are different, violent. The very things that bring pride and honor to the Indians are abhorred and feared by the white man. Few have lived with and loved both white and Indian families. You are special, Sam."

A single tear slipped from her eye and trailed down her cheek, then into the corner of her mouth. "Then why do I feel so"—she groped for the right word—"dirty. I feel dirty, as if I have done some horrible thing I should be ashamed of."

"It's not you, Sam. It's others who do not understand."

Nathan closed his eyes. Spirit of the Mountain waited for him to explain it all so it wouldn't hurt anymore.

"You must never feel ashamed of who you are or where you have been. You are one of the most honest and loving women I have ever had the pleasure of knowing. The ignorance of others is not your fault."

"If a kindhearted woman like Libby feels this way, what will others think? What must I face in Boston?"

It was an honest question, one he wished he didn't have to answer. "It could be worse for you. I'll not lie and say it will be all right."

"The Frenchman assumed I was a whore of the Cherokee." Spirit of the Mountain's mouth went dry; the words were distasteful to say. "Is this what other whites will think?"

"Many will assume it."

"If they learn of my husband and child, will that make me worse than a whore in their eyes? Will no one understand?"

Nathan's eyes told her his answer.

"Nathan," she whispered, "how can I go to a family that will think this?"

"You don't know what your grandfather will think. Blood is thicker than anything."

Spirit of the Mountain became frightened. "But you do not know this for sure. I am part French. He disapproved of my mother because of her heritage. How can he get past all of these things to take me in as his family now?"

"I think it might be best if we do not tell anyone other than your grandfather about your Indian past."

"How can you say this?" Spirit of the Mountain was shocked. "You tell me to not feel ashamed; then you tell me to keep my past a secret." She turned to run away.

Nathan grabbed Spirit of the Mountain's wrist before she could leave. "Listen to me."

She didn't want to listen. She wanted to run away from everything and everyone. "Let me go."

"No." He pulled her back to him. "Don't you see? It's for your own good."

"It is not for my own good. Perhaps, it is for your good, Nathan Walker."

He let go. "For my good? Just what the hell does that mean?"

"I think you want me to hide my past because you are ashamed." She hugged herself with her arms, tears now flowing freely. "You make love to me, but do not want anyone to know it."

"Only because it would make things worse if it were common knowledge. It's considered a sin for two people to make love to each other without being married!"

Never had Spirit of the Mountain been so confused, so torn. "They will think me a whore, so I will act like a whore."

In a flash, Nathan stood before her, his face a mask of anger. He took her roughly by the shoulders and shook her. "Don't you ever say anything like that again. Do you hear me?"

He pulled her into his arms. "Don't ever say that again, Sam."

Pain was reflected in each word, and she knew he was sincere.

Chapter Eleven

Libby sat by the fire sewing while Nathan and Jack enjoyed a pipe of tobacco after their supper. Libby paused and looked about, a worried look crossing her face.

"Nathan, where's Samantha? It's getting dark. She shouldn't be out so late by herself."

"She went down to the river." Nathan puffed on the pipe again. "Sam doesn't seem to mind the dark."

This answer made Libby stand. "What on earth is she doing down at the river this time of night? It's dangerous, Nathan."

Nathan grinned. "She's bathing, and if I've learned anything about Samantha, it is that she can take care of herself."

"She'll catch her death bathing in the cold." Libby's face did not give up the tension lining it. "I've never known anyone who bathed every night like that. It's not natural."

"She seems to think it is." Nathan could see he was fighting a losing battle. Libby stood with her hands on her hips, a grim set to her jaw. "All right, I'll go find her."

Tibias stood. "I'll go, Nathan. No need to interrupt your smoke with Pa."

He rushed out the door, his mother on his heels. "Now, Tibias, you ask if she's decent before you get too close, and hide your eyes like a proper boy."

Nathan's chuckle brought her scolding look back around to him. "And you, Nathan Walker, could learn some manners, if you ask me. It's right shameful how you look at that woman."

"Now, Libby," Jack said. "Seems that isn't any of our business. You'd best mind your place."

Her brows shot up, and her eyes grew round. "Jack Taylor, you be minding your own place. It isn't proper, and I don't want to see Samantha hurt by others' scorn when she and Nathan reach town."

"You're right, Libby. I've not considered what everyone will think. I never meant—" What he'd meant to do no longer mattered.

Jack drew a long puff and blew the smoke into the air, the sweet scent of tobacco drifting with it. "Seems to me folk will not take kindly to her having lived with the Indians. They can be real unforgiving to women who try to return to their own kind."

"That's why I'm taking her to Boston. Samantha has a grandfather there. At least we hope she does."

Libby's look brightened. "Good. Family can be more understanding than others. But I do think she should attempt to dress like a white woman, Nathan. It will draw less attention in your travels than that Indian garb she wears."

Nathan sighed, knowing it would not be easy—for Spirit of the Mountain or for him—to convince Libby what was best. "I'll see what I can do. Do you have anything she could wear, Libby?"

The woman smiled an all-knowing smile that told him she was way ahead of him. "That's what I'm working on now, Nathan. But there's still a problem."

"What's that?" Nathan asked.

"It will raise many an eyebrow for a man and woman who aren't married to travel together."

Nathan stiffened. "Now, Libby, you aren't suggesting—"

"No." She held up a hand to stop his blustering. "I'm not saying you should marry the girl. I know how you feel about that. I do think you should say Sam is your wife, though. It would be simpler."

"Yes." Nathan hadn't thought of that.

"But—"

Nathan knew there would be a lecture now.

"I'm surprised at you, Nathan. You seem to have no guilt over compromising the young woman, knowing full well you won't be doing the honorable thing by her. I am deeply disappointed."

He felt uncomfortable beneath her righteous glare, but he stood his ground. "And you, Libby Taylor, do not know what is between us. You only guess at the nature of our relationship. You do not know what has gone on, and you will not know. Do not tell me what honor demands of me."

"He's right, Libby," Jack said. "As I said, you'd best mind your own affairs, not Nathan's. But I am a bit curious, Nathan. If the girl has been with the Cherokee, how is it she is with you? I've never known you to go so far south before."

"I didn't. The Shawnee attacked her village and killed her adopted family. She was taken captive."

"Oh, my," Libby whispered, drawing their gazes back to her. Her eyes were round with fear. "You stole her from the Shawnee?"

Nathan understood her instant fear of the Shawnee, their uneasy neighbors. "No, I didn't steal her from the Shawnee, Libby. They took her to trade for guns and ammunition. I was there when they sold her."

Her eyes grew even rounder. "You bought Samantha?"

"Good Lord, woman. Let the man tell his story without your constant interruptions." Jack's words made his point, though they held a kindness that made Libby smile at her own impoliteness.

"No, I did not bid for her." Nathan's mind recalled vividly the humiliation Spirit of the Mountain had suffered, his own difficulty in not becoming involved in the auction. "A Frenchman ended up buying her. She cost him his whole year's trappings."

Libby could not be quiet. "Not that Pierre? What a crude animal he is."

Nathan laughed. "Well, at least we do agree on one thing, Libby—except my description might be a little more colorful than yours. He is worse than an animal. I helped Sam escape from the Frenchman."

A low whistle came from Jack's lips. "Lordy, Nathan, he's not a man you'd want as your enemy."

"I've since learned that," Nathan drawled.

"He's been after you?"

"Like a dog hot on our trail."

"I'm sorry, Nathan." Libby's voice was soft, her eyes tearing. "You've risked your life for her. I should not have judged you so hastily."

Nathan took her hand and kissed it kindly. "Perhaps your judgments are not so off, Libby."

"The girl was lucky you were there," Jack said.

"Sam is a woman, not a girl." Nathan's voice took on a tender and loving sound distant even to his own ears. "And I am not a saint, but a man."

"It is right you are taking her home to family, away from this slow death." Libby's voice softened. Embittered and hard as her life was, she knew well the dangers of life on the frontier. "Take her home, Nathan."

They had all known their own share of difficulty. Libby was a plaguing reminder of what wilderness life did to the women who loved their men enough to follow. But their troubles all seemed to pale when compared to the pain in Spirit of the Mountain's short life.

"She's so young, and she has known so much death," Nathan said. "Her parents died within a year of each other, leaving her alone in the mountains to survive by her wits. Then she found the love of an adopted family, even that of a husband. She buried her husband and child together more than two years ago."

Nathan paused and gathered together his rampant emotions. "If that wasn't enough, the Shawnee massacred her adopted Cherokee people and took her captive. She has endured far more than her share. I have promised to take her home to her family so she can have a life without so much killing and loss. I want to give her this more than anything."

"We"—Libby looked at her husband, love shining in the depths of her dark brown eyes, the moments of bitterness forgotten—"shall do what we can to help Samantha."

"Thank you," Nathan mumbled, his mind distracted by the hardship that taking Spirit of the Mountain home would cause him. Less than two weeks had gone by since she had come into his life. Yet as each day passed, he became more and more aware of how difficult it would be to be without her. He had not thought much about love since the death of his wife. Was he falling in love with this woman? Even so, he knew he would take her home and leave her behind. It was the only thing he could do.

"Miss," Tibias hollered. "Are you decent, miss?"

Spirit of the Mountain turned to the trees where Tibias was hidden. He backed out toward her, his hand covering his eyes. She smiled at his manners, knowing Libby probably prompted him to be careful.

"Yes, Tibias, I am decent."

He dropped his hand and turned. "Ma was worried about you being out after dark. I came to fetch you."

"Come sit with me a moment." She motioned for him to sit and continued to work the tangles from her wet hair.

He sat, but he didn't seem too comfortable. "Ma

won't like it if we don't come home right away."

Spirit of the Mountain stopped her combing and smiled. "Okay, we will go back." She stood, then stretched, long and slow. It was beautiful here, and she regretted having to leave this spot.

Tibias was already a few feet ahead of her. "Ma says you'll catch your death bathing in the river like you do. She says it's not natural."

"Oh, but it is natural, Tibias. Animals bathe constantly."

He waited for her to catch up. "I guess I never thought of it that way."

Spirit of the Mountain put her arm about his shoulder. "You can learn a lot by watching the animals, Tibias."

A scuffling in the underbrush drew Spirit of the Mountain's attention. Slight growls drifted to her ears. The gentle breeze blew away from them, so she could not tell what was there, but her senses told her of danger.

"We must hurry, Tibias." She pulled him along.

Another deep, menacing growl stopped her. This time she saw shadowy forms sliding in and out of the brush.

"Wild dogs, miss," Tibias's voice wavered in fear. "They roam in packs scavenging for food."

"Dogs?" Spirit of the Mountain had never seen wild dogs.

"Yes. Other settlers brought them. Some of the settlers left, some were killed by Indians, some died from sickness. The animals were left behind to fend for themselves, and they turned wild." He tugged on her arm. "We'd best run, miss."

"No, here." She pulled him toward a tree. "Get up there and stay. No matter what, stay in that tree."

Tibias pulled away. "You, too, miss."

"Do as I say, Tibias. I will be fine."

She practically lifted him into the branches of the tree, and he scampered up out of reach. Another growl, closer this time, made her turn back.

The dog was huge, the hackles on the back of his neck standing on end. He bared his teeth and drooled in long strands that reached to the ground. Spirit of the Mountain had never seen an animal act this way. Golden eyes stared at her.

"Miss," Tibias called down to her. "Miss, he's gone mad."

"Mad?" She still didn't understand.

"He's got rabies, miss. A sickness."

The animal inched forward, and she felt fear quicken her heart, send it racing.

"Run to the water, miss," Tibias cried out. "Run."

Spirit of the Mountain took off, the animal following right behind. She splashed into the water just as the dog closed in. He stopped short, veering away from the river.

He snapped and howled in irritation. Suddenly, a short yip interrupted his sounds, then silence. Spirit of the Mountain studied the edge of the trees, then spotted the dark silhouette of a man that walked from them. She moved from the water, then sensed the newcomer was not Nathan or Jack.

She breathed a great sigh of relief when she finally made out Long Knife's form. His stony features were a comfort at that moment.

"Long Knife," she called out in French as she approached him. "What are you doing here?"

He rested his arm on his long bow, his arrow having killed the rabid animal. "We were hunting when we came upon your camp. We found bear tracks and blood, so we followed. You are not hurt?"

"No, I am fine. Nathan had a run-in with the bear, but he is better now." Spirit of the Mountain was surprised by the Shawnee's concern.

"He should be more careful."

Spirit of the Mountain laughed. "I am afraid I was distracting him at the time."

Tibias's cry of outrage cut through her, and she ran back to where she had left him. A warrior had hauled Tibias from the tree, but he was having a difficult time holding the boy, who kicked and yelled his loudest.

"Let me go!"

"It is all right, Tibias. He will not hurt you." She turned to Long Knife, who had followed her. "You will not hurt these people?"

The slightest twitch of his brow told her of his surprise she ask such a question. "These people are friends of yours, Spirit of the Mountain?"

"They are Nathan's friends, and they helped Nathan when he was hurt. So now they are mine as well." Tibias ran to Spirit of the Mountain, and she put her arm about him.

"We have left these people to live in peace for many years. I see no reason to do differently now."

Spirit of the Mountain felt foolish. "Thank you for helping me." She pointed in the direction of the river. "I do not know what I would have done if you had not come along, Long Knife."

"My warriors will burn the dog. The madness must not spread to the other creatures."

"What's going on here?"

Nathan walked toward them, his rifle propped in the crook of his arm. Jack followed close behind.

"A mad dog came upon us. Long Knife killed him."

Moving to Spirit of the Mountain's side, Nathan protectively took her elbow. "We're grateful, Long Knife. But what are you doing here?"

Spirit of the Mountain explained the situation to Nathan and Jack.

Jack didn't look very comfortable, but he did what he apparently thought best. "You helped Samantha and my son. Me and the missus don't have much, but you're welcome to share our food."

Spirit of the Mountain translated Jack's words, then Long Knife's response. "He does not wish to cause any hardship for you and Libby. They will camp on the river tonight and leave in the morning."

Libby's face drew into a mask of terror. "They are camping here?"

"Yes." Jack took her by the hand and led her back to the chair she had been sitting in by the fire. "They will be gone in the morning, Libby. There's no need to be so frightened."

Tibias went to his mother's side. "Ma, they saved me and Sam from that mad dog. You should have seen them." His eyes grew large with awe. "They were fierce looking."

This remark did nothing for Libby's composure. She held on to the arms of the chair with a white-knuckled grip. "Jack, I don't think—"

"They helped my son. I'll not tell them to leave, Libby. They're staying, and you might as well accept it."

When she did not seem to, Jack's voice took on a softer tone. "Libby, it's only for one night."

Her lips remained set in a grim, straight line. "They could murder us in our sleep, Jack."

Spirit of the Mountain could be quiet no more. "They will not harm you or your family. Long Knife said so."

"And you believe him?" Libby rose from her chair, her stance, her eyes, her tone accusing Spirit of the Mountain of being gullable.

"He is an honorable man," Spirit of the Mountain replied softly in Long Knife's defense, an odd sense of pride touching her.

A wild look filled Libby's eyes, a look that confused Spirit of the Mountain. "He's a murderer," she yelled. "He killed your Indian family. How can you stand up for the likes of him?"

A slow, hot anger rose inside Spirit of the Mountain, but she tried to remain calm. "It is the only way they know how to survive. I do not believe in the manner in which they do this. But I do understand, just as I am trying to understand why you come onto their land and claim it as your own, then call them savages when they fight to keep what is theirs."

"You were born a Christian, Samantha. How can you condone war made upon innocent men, women, and children? They are savage and brutal."

"War is their way of life. They know nothing else. They know no other way. When has there ever been war that was not waged against the innocent? You

164

come from a country whose history flows red from wars, wars fought in the name of religion and state. The inquisition terrorized the people of the fourteenth century—in the name of God. It is all savage and brutal."

Libby's frantic eyes turned hard and angry. She reached out and slapped Spirit of the Mountain on the cheek. "You will burn in hell for speaking of such things, Samantha."

Spirit of the Mountain said nothing. It would do no good. She walked outside and away from the cabin. The cool breeze relieved the heat inside her. She walked to the river and watched the fire that burned at the Shawnee camp. Long Knife came to stand in front of her.

"You have confused me, Long Knife, and I do not know what to believe any longer. You came into my life a part of a hellish nightmare."

She looked up at the star-filled night to keep her tears from falling. "You killed my family and people I loved with all my heart. Then you killed Standing Bear in my defense. For reasons I do not understand, you came all this way and saved me from a mad dog."

Confusion tore at her mind. How had her world gotten so mixed up? "I should hate you."

Long Knife reached out and wiped away a tear, an uncharacteristic look of tenderness in his dark eyes. "Do you hate me, Spirit of the Mountain?"

"No," she confessed. "I do not hate you."

"I am sorry for the pain I have caused you."

Somehow Spirit of the Mountain knew he was not a man who apologized easily, especially to a woman.

She didn't know what to say.

"You are a special woman, and I am glad to have known you. I think we could have been friends if not for what has passed between us."

"I think," Spirit of the Mountain said softly, "we are friends, Long Knife."

He gave her a rare smile. "Friends."

She returned his smile. "Good night, my friend."

Spirit of the Mountain turned to leave, but paused and looked back. "Good bye, Long Knife."

Long Knife raised his hand, acknowledging the fact that they might never see one another again. She didn't need him to tell her that he, too, found their parting sad. It was something she understood.

Spirit of the Mountain saw Libby sitting outside the cabin as she approached. The other woman's hands were clasped tightly in her lap, her head bowed. "Libby," she said, drawing the woman's gaze.

Libby stood. "I've been waiting for you."

"You did not need to wait up for me."

Libby sat again and patted the seat beside her. Spirit of the Mountain took it. "I wanted to speak to you. To say how sorry I am I struck you. No matter our differences, I should not have acted so hateful toward you. It was unkind of me."

"It is forgotten, Libby."

Libby gave her a stiff nod. The grim set of Libby's mouth made it clear to Spirit of the Mountain that she was still ill at ease with her and the Indian camp just beyond on the riverbank. Having nothing more to say, Spirit of the Mountain stood to go inside.

"I have something for you." Libby handed a bundle

to Spirit of the Mountain. "I thought it would be best if you had a proper dress to wear while you and Nathan travel to Boston."

Spirit of the Mountain heard the slight emphasis on the word proper, but she dismissed it. She shook the dress out and held it up to her. "It is beautiful, Libby. I have not had a dress this fine for many years."

"Perhaps you can try it on tomorrow? I can make any adjustments, if needed, then."

"Thank you, Libby."

Chapter Twelve

The cabin was dark and quiet. Spirit of the Mountain moved across to the table and found a razor upon it.

"You said you'd shave me."

She turned to find Nathan standing in the doorway, a wide grin on his face. As he came closer, the fire's light revealed the twinkle in his eyes.

"Where is everyone?"

"They're all working in the field." Nathan pulled her closer, wrapping his arms about her, his lips tickling her neck. "We're alone."

Spirit of the Mountain wriggled free and laughed. "If you are feeling so spry, perhaps we should be helping them?"

"I am feeling quite well, but Libby insisted I give my wounds one more day of healing."

"But I can help them." Spirit of the Mountain started back out the door.

Nathan stopped her. "I think they were trying to give us some time alone."

This explanation surprised Spirit of the Mountain. "That does not sound like Libby."

"I think she feels we need to talk."

An uneasy feeling came over her. "About what?"

He picked up the razor and rubbed his chin. "First things first."

Since there was already water heated, Spirit of the Mountain poured some into a pan, then pointed to the chair by the bed. "Bring that closer to the fire, Nathan. I would not want to cut you."

"Yes, dear. Is the blade sharp? I've a few days' growth to scrap off."

Nathan sat down and lifted his chin. He was looking forward to this much too much.

Spirit of the Mountain wrung out a towel in the hot water and wrapped it about his face. "It will be fine."

Her voice was soft, enchanting. Just the closeness of Spirit of the Mountain was enough to stir the fires inside Nathan. She leaned close, and he smelled the sweet scent of her. "You always smell wonderful."

She pulled back, her eyes showing her pleasure. "My mother always smelled good. I liked that." She seemed to be recalling times gone by. "I rub wildflowers on my skin when I bathe. It makes me think of her."

"Was she beautiful?"

A smile came to her full, sensuous lips. "Yes, very."

Nathan ran his finger over her bottom lip. "You must look like her."

Spirit of the Mountain reached up and pulled on a cord tied about her neck and took off the medicine pouch. From inside, she removed a tiny object. She opened the locket and showed Nathan small portraits of her parents.

"Do I?" she asked as Nathan put the towel aside to examine the portraits.

"Yes," Nathan said quietly. He looked up and saw the happiness glowing on her face. "But you are even more beautiful."

She took the locket back and carefully placed it back inside the pouch and around her neck. "I think you are prejudiced on that point."

"Am I?" Nathan's mood remained playful, but she slapped his roaming hands away. He laughed out loud.

"Do you want me to shave you or not?"

Folding his hands in his lap, he pretended to get serious. "I want you to shave me."

"Very well," she said, lathering his cheeks and chin liberally with the soap. When he tried to speak, she ran the soapy brush across his mouth, forcing him to be quiet or get his mouth full of lather.

Slowly, carefully, Spirit of the Mountain began to scrap the remnants of his beard away, revealing soft, slick skin. Nathan remained still, but found doing so more and more difficult as she pulled him this way and that way. His head rested against her breasts as she moved up his neck, her face only inches away as she made each stroke with the razor. Her breath was as honeyed as her skin, making the discomfort in his loins worsen.

"Maybe this wasn't such a good idea," he groaned in the seconds she paused between strokes.

She pulled away. "Why? I have not even nicked you."

Nathan swallowed hard, then wrapped his fingers about the wrist of the hand that held the razor. He drew her closer to him. "I suddenly have other things in mind. To hell with the shave."

"What of your wounds? Libby would be—"

"To hell with my cuts. To hell with Libby." He kissed her deeply.

Spirit of the Mountain wanted him desperately. But she twisted away. "No," she cried out, stepping away from his arms as he tried to pull her back.

"What's wrong, Sam?"

Nathan's question was filled with anguish. More than anything, she wanted to take that pain away, to know only the pleasure he gave to her and she to him.

"I do not know." Her voice trembled. She tried to think, to clear the confusion in her mind. "It seems to be wrong in their home, with their disapproval."

Passion clouded his mind, but slowly clarity came to him. She was right. He knew that; still he had cast aside his principles for desire and allowed his lust to control him. Shame doused the heat inside him, and he brought himself under control.

"You are right, Sam." He sighed deeply. "One moment alone with you, and I lose all my good sense."

Spirit of the Mountain handed him the towel, and he rubbed the remaining soap from his face. Tenderly, he reached out and wiped the suds that clung to her face after their kiss.

"I am so confused, Nathan. I no longer know what to do, who to be. In my heart, I am Spirit of the Mountain. I do not think I can be this person you want me to become. I fear I can never be Samantha Jacoby again."

"Once we get to Boston, it won't be so difficult. I promise. What you learned with the Cherokees will fade with time. It'll be all right."

Spirit of the Mountain wanted to believe Nathan, but she couldn't. "I did not learn how to be a Cherokee, Nathan. I became a Cherokee. I cannot take it from me, any more than I can remove my heart and live."

She picked up the dress Libby had made for her. "Putting on this dress or pretending to be a proper white woman will not make me one."

"You must." Nathan took her shoulders, aggravation clear in his eyes. "You will. You have no choice."

"I have a choice. I can stay." Her voice reflected her longings. "Alone, or with you, and never again know this torture that is ripping me apart."

Nathan pushed her away angrily. "You know that isn't possible."

"Or I can go to Boston and die, for you will be taking me away from the very thing that gives me life: my mountains."

"Do not be so dramatic, Sam. You aren't going to die if I take you to Boston. It's physically impossible."

She turned away to keep her disappointment and hurt from him. "Are you willing to risk my life on this assumption?"

"Yes. You belong with your family in Boston. In time, you will not even remember this argument."

Spirit of the Mountain said nothing. There was no more to be said. Nathan would not, could not, understand.

He came up behind her and turned her around. His eyes were no longer angry. They were gentled, as was his touch. "I wouldn't do anything to hurt you, Sam. You know that, don't you?"

She did believe he meant what he said. She nodded.

"If I didn't take you home, I could never live with myself. Believe me, I know what's best for you."

Spirit of the Mountain was not convinced. "You could not possibly know this."

Nathan turned away in frustration. "I know the wilderness is no place for a woman."

"Do you cling to this belief because of Sarah's death?"

His back stiffened, and Spirit of the Mountain knew she had touched on a forbidden subject. But she could not go back. "I am not Sarah, Nathan. You must learn this."

"Who told you about Sarah?"

"Libby. She thought it would help me understand you better."

"Do you?"

"I understand what it is you fear, Nathan. I know how difficult it is to lose someone you loved, how much it hurts."

"No, you do not understand. Our losses were not the same."

The guilt in his voice tore at her heart. "You were

not responsible for Sarah's death, Nathan."

"I brought her here. I saw how difficult it was for her, but I couldn't go back. Even when she grew weaker and her mind started to slip away from reality, I stayed. I killed her with my stubbornness."

Spirit of the Mountain moved in front of Nathan and took his hand into hers. "I am strong, Nathan, and I have already lived some twenty years in the wilderness. I do not fear it as you do, as Sarah did. It gives me life, not death."

"Yes, you are a strong woman, stronger than any I've ever known. But it is not enough. You've spent your entire life surrounded by family. First, your mother and father, then your adopted family. They cared for you, watched over you."

"You could be my family, Nathan."

Nathan pulled his hand away, then stepped away. "I—"

Spirit of the Mountain could see all too clearly the guilt and pain that tormented him in the expressions that twisted his face. She understood that these emotions would not allow Nathan to give in to her even before he said the words.

"I can't be your family, Sam. I can't."

Anger overwhelmed the hurt of his rejection. "Damn you, Nathan Walker. I am not Sarah."

"My decision isn't based solely on Sarah's death, Sam. Libby's strong, but look at what the wilderness has done to her. She's an embittered woman, old beyond her years." Nathan turned back to Spirit of the Mountain, his look sad but sincere. "You belong with your family. Don't you want to be with your family?

Isn't that what your mother would have wanted for you?"

For the second time since Spirit of the Mountain had met Nathan, visions took her back to her mother's death, to the promise her father had failed to fulfill because of his own unexpected death. For her to go to Boston, to her grandfather, was exactly what her mother would want. Spirit of the Mountain understood the danger this would mean for her, but family, love, and honor seemed more important.

"How is it you know what my mother would want of me?"

"By the way you speak of her, by what she taught you. I think you are very much like her, Sam."

"I hope so," she whispered, doubt still troubling her.

"Promise me you will try it my way."

Spirit of the Mountain did not reply.

"Please, Sam."

Tears came to Spirit of the Mountain's eyes, but she blinked them back. "I promise, Nathan."

She understood fully how much she loved Nathan Walker. She would trust her life to him. Deep down, Spirit of the Mountain knew her Spirit Sister could not live away from the mountains. Still, she would abide by Nathan's judgment, willingly and lovingly, in the only way she knew how. She would honor her family's memory, fulfilling her father's promise to her mother.

The evening sky was dusted with orange, the edges tinged purple and gray. Slowly, the small colony tucked against the thick wall of trees was cast in darkness. The river lay like a dark ribbon, meandering around its edge. Lights appeared in the windows, and smoke rose from the chimneys.

Spirit of the Mountain had never left the protection of the mountains before. She held back, remaining in the cool shadows, uncertain about the town she watched. Once, she had gone with her father to a town. As a child, it had proven exciting. Now, it felt sad—like saying farewell to an old friend.

Spirit of the Mountain mourned her loss. It was more a melancholy wondering than a heart-wrenching pain. Would she ever return to this land she loved? What did her future hold?

"We'd better go, Sam. It'll be dark soon."

She turned to Nathan, fear gripping her. "Couldn't we just stay here tonight?"

He shook his head. "You've got to get used to towns. It's best to start small and work up to Boston."

Nathan took her hand, and they traveled the rest of the way side by side.

"Remember, you are Samantha Walker. At least, while we're traveling."

"I remember."

He stopped. "Do you understand why?" Concern edged his voice.

"I understand." He seemed to be waiting for her to go on.

"We will draw less attention traveling as man and wife."

"I do understand, Nathan. More than you think. You do not want my reputation tarnished. Besides, it may be the closest I ever come to being Mrs. Walker."

The look on his face made her immediately regret what she had said.

"Are you ready, Sam?"

"I think so." They walked on.

A myriad of smells drifted to her sensitive nose, as many sounds came at her simultaneously. People still milled about, heading to their homes for the night. Nathan and she approached the center of town. Chatter was sharp compared to the dull roll of wagon wheels. The high-pitched barks of dogs and the whinnying of horses was interrupted by the low grunts of pigs. Smoke hung heavy in the air, mixing with the pungent smell of trash, manure, and dust.

The town was fascinating, frightening.

A small inn and tavern stood in front of them, the night breeze swinging its sign back and forth, the hinge squeaking. They walked into the dingy interior and found a crowd of people.

Nathan asked for the proprietor and got a room. It was on the second floor, facing the street they had just come from. Nathan closed the door behind them and lit a candle.

The room was small, but it had all that was necessary: a bed with a colorful quilt covering it and a single night table beside it. An old dressing table with a cracked mirror stood across from the bed, a chair to the left. A privacy screen was positioned in one corner, the necessity tucked behind and a washstand, bowl, and pitcher to one side.

"It's not fancy," Nathan said.

Spirit of the Mountain moved to the bed, pushed on the mattress, then sat. "It is fine, Nathan. Very comfortable."

He crossed to stand in front of her. "It's comfortable?"

"Yes." She nodded. "It seems to be."

He grinned widely. "Maybe we should try it out?"

She widened her eyes in mock surprise. "But what about my reputation? We would not want to tarnish it."

"But we are Mr. and Mrs. Walker here, Sam." Nathan chuckled, moving closer, his hands running up her arms. "It's expected that a man and wife would make love at night."

"I would not wish to shirk my duties as a wife."

Nathan watched the subtle changes in Spirit of the Mountain's eyes and wondered at the passion he saw there. She was the most natural, honest woman he had ever known. She had no pretense or shyness about what she wanted. This thought alone stirred his heart and heated his body.

She was beautiful. She was uninhibited. She was everything a man could want in a woman, in a wife. In a pretend wife, he amended.

Her arms wrapped about his waist, and she lay down, pulling him down atop her. The scent of wildflowers filled him, her skin soft beneath his touch.

"I'm like a man possessed, Sam."

Intense blue eyes darkened with desire and watched him. "In what way, Nathan?"

His finger traced the contour of her lower lip, which was the color of wild strawberries. "I know I should stay away from you—for your sake as well as my own. Yet I have no willpower when it comes to you. One sweet smile and I'm in your arms. One soft word and I'm lost. It is like an addiction. The more

I'm with you, the more I want you."

"Is that so bad?" Spirit of the Mountain asked.

"I think so."

"Then you should not think so much."

Spirit of the Mountain wound her arms about Nathan's neck and brought his lips to hers. She kissed him, long and slow, her tongue touching his.

"Maybe you're right," Nathan said. Only the feel of her lips against his mattered.

"Of course I am." Spirit of the Mountain knew the power she had over Nathan. The thought of it raised her own passion to a higher level. She wanted Nathan to be addicted. She wanted him to need her. She wanted him never to think of being without her.

Pierre huddled closer to the meek fire, feeding it a few branches to take the chill from him. The crude lean-to he had built provided little warmth, and even less comfort. His belly growled, the puny squirrel he had caught for his dinner doing little to stay his hunger.

Anger burned inside him, slow and constant, fed by the hatred he harbored.

His eyes squinted together as he thought about the girl, his one eye closing altogether as the scarred flesh drew tight with healing. He examined his burned face with his gnarled and scarred fingers, the raised welts of flesh testimony of his promise to make them pay.

With a grunt to confirm this oath to himself, Pierre lay down. It was a long time before his eyes closed in sleep.

Chapter Thirteen

Barrel upon barrel lined the walls, filled with everything from flour and sugar to seeds for planting, oats for livestock, and nails for building. The store provided a mixture of dry goods, grocery staples, and hardware supplies for the town. The large room seemed small for the variety of merchandise crammed into its space.

Spices and coffee scented the air, freshly tanned leather and furs muting the pungent odors with their own musky scents. Saws, hammers, and shovels filled shelves or hung from the walls. Tables were laden with bolts of printed cloth. Jugs of whiskey, bottles of wine, and casks of ale stood behind the huge store counter, along with kegs of powder, lead ammunition, rifles, and guns.

Spirit of the Mountain wandered around the

tables, lightly fingering different objects. She had traveled a few times with her father to the trading post, but never had she seen so many items in one place. It was a marvel. The colors, textures, and smells held her interest as Nathan gathered the supplies he needed.

The storekeeper's wife ambled over to Spirit of the Mountain. The woman's rounded stomach and slow, rolling pace told Spirit of the Mountain she was near time for giving birth to the babe she carried.

A delicate hand rested on the woman's lower back, her discomfort obvious. Still, she smiled warmly. "Are you finding what you need?"

Returning the smile, Spirit of the Mountain shook her head. "I am waiting for"—she paused, an awkward feeling overcoming her as she tried to speak the lie—"my husband."

"Sorry for the wait. We always seem to get busy in the spring." The woman patted her stomach. "I'm not much help to my husband these days. Sometimes it feels like I can't take another step with all this weight I'm carrying."

Memories of her own pregnancy came back to Spirit of the Mountain so vividly she almost felt it herself. "You must be close to your time."

"Yes." The woman leaned against a table to take some of the pressure from her swollen feet. "Lord willing, this babe will be born healthy and strong. I lost the last one."

A haunted expression twisted the woman's face, as if the pain she had gone through were only yesterday. Spirit of the Mountain reached out and placed a hand on her shoulder. "I am certain this child will be all right."

The woman straightened and squeezed Spirit of the Mountain's hand. "I'm sure you're right. If you need anything, you just holler."

Spirit of the Mountain watched the woman as she moved through the maze of goods, her feet shuffling. The small place in Spirit of the Mountain's heart that belonged to her own child's memory came alive with grief. Her eyes stung from unshed tears, and her throat tightened. She hoped this woman would know only joy with this new child.

A sudden desire ran strong through Spirit of the Mountain, taking her by surprise. She longed to hold a baby to her breast, to feel its warmth mingling with her own, its flesh pressed against hers. This yearning disturbed her, and she turned away from the picture of motherhood the young woman portrayed. Spirit of the Mountain studied a colorful bolt of fabric, fingering the print with feigned interest.

The small yip of a puppy caught Spirit of the Mountain's attention, pulling her from her melancholy. She walked across to the counter, where a tall, burly man stood waiting his turn.

Shyly, Spirit of the Mountain peered around his elbow to the small bundle of fur that protruded from his pouch. It was a red wolf pup, round eyes peering about in fear and confusion. Pointed ears, much too large for his small puppy face, were alert. He howled, but was silenced with a sharp slap to the head.

"What's this?" the storekeeper asked.

The trapper lifted his bundle of furs to the counter. "I've brought you some furs, Tom."

Tom separated the bundle, examining each pelt with care. Spirit of the Mountain made note of the various animals the other man had trapped, and her stomach twisted into a knot. Several cougar pelts lay on the counter; the last one the storekeeper picked up was that of a red wolf.

The trapper pulled the pup out. "Found this not far from where I caught the wolf. Thought you might want it, Tom. I'll throw it in with the furs."

Tom let out a snortlike laugh. "Whatever for? I've no need of a wolf."

Another man stepped forward and lifted the pup by the nap of the neck to look at him. "I'd buy him, Tom. He could be a good fighting dog."

The sick feeling in Spirit of the Mountain's stomach increased. "How much do you want for the wolf pup?"

All eyes turned to her, as if the men hadn't been aware she was there before. She moved to stand in front of the counter and reached for the animal. The man pulled him away from her grasp.

"I said I'd buy the pup, Tom. I was first to say so."

The storekeeper took the animal from him. "I don't much like what you do, Hank. I've always sold you what you need, but I don't think I'll contribute to the barbaric form of entertainment you provide."

The man's face scrunched up in anger, but his pique seemed to pass as quickly as it came. "You always were a bit too pious for me, Tom." He left the store.

As Tom and the trapper turned back to Spirit of the Mountain, Nathan came up behind her. "What is going on, Samantha?"

She took the wolf pup from the storekeeper and cuddled him close. "Can we buy him, Nathan?"

Nathan took her elbow and pulled her aside. "What do you want him for?"

"That awful man was going to train him for fighting. This pup needs someone to love him, not abuse him."

A softness came to Nathan's eyes. "I would like for you to have the puppy, Samantha, but I don't have enough money. I've got to save it for us to take a coach to Boston."

Disappointment crowded her mind, and fear crept into her heart. "But what will happen to the animal?"

"I don't know."

She turned back to Tom. "I would work for him. Your wife is so near her time. Could I help you here in the store so she can rest a bit?"

Tom looked to his wife, who now stood beside him. The smudges beneath her eyes told him plainly of her need for rest. "No." He shook his head. "We don't need any help, miss."

The trapper disagreed with Tom. "Now, Tom, looks like Rebecca could use a little help around here. I know it ain't none of my business." He held up his hand when Tom looked like he was going to agree. "But I think I've been trading with you folks long enough to speak my mind. I think you should take the little lady's offer. Won't cost you nothing. I'm giving you the pup."

Spirit of the Mountain was surprised by the big man's sensitivity to Rebecca's needs. He was a loner, a man who spent his time trapping and killing animals. Yet he had a deep-hearted kindness for a woman about to give birth.

Rebecca spoke up. "He's right, Tom. I could use some help."

Nathan spoke beneath his breath. "We can't afford to stay longer at the inn, Sam."

"Then we will sleep in the forest." She touched his face tenderly. "It is what I prefer."

"You could stay in the shed out back," Rebecca offered, then looked away, apparently embarrassed she had heard their conversation.

Spirit of the Mountain moved closer to Rebecca, a strange kinship already existing between them. "I can help you when your time comes."

This offer made Rebecca's eyes brighten.

"Ruth will help you deliver the baby, Rebecca. Just as she has the others," Tom said.

"Ruth is a hundred years old." Rebecca's voice became stronger, more determined. "I would prefer this woman."

"My name is Samantha."

"This woman is a perfect stranger. You know nothing about her." Tom looked unswayed.

"You're right. I know nothing about her, except that she has a kind heart. She is willing to work to make that wolf pup her own. Not many would bother over the animal."

Nathan took Samantha's hand. He could see the love she already had for the orphaned wolf. She would not be swayed on this point, any more than Rebecca would be swayed the matter of letting her stay and work. "I think, Tom, we have lost. We'd best retreat while we still can."

A crooked smile overtook Tom, only one side of

his mouth lifting as he grinned. "All right, Rebecca. Samantha can work out the cost of the pup, and they can stay in the shed."

The trapper slapped Tom on the back and laughed, as if he, too, had won the battle. "I'll be seeing you folks at the end of summer."

He turned and looked at Spirit of the Mountain. "Take care of Rebecca, little lady. I want to see a healthy baby when I come back."

"I will, sir." She gave him a grateful smile.

As the trapper ducked under the doorway, he paused and looked back. "What are you going to name the little critter?"

Spirit of the Mountain looked down into the pup's sweet face. He yawned wide, comfortable and safe in her arms. "How about Red?"

"Red," the trapper repeated, then nodded. "I like it."

As if in agreement, Red howled, his high-pitched tone echoing about the room. Everyone laughed, and Spirit of the Mountain hugged him to her.

Spirit of the Mountain peeked in the door, the loud cries of children telling her where to find Rebecca. "Tom said it would be all right to come up."

Rebecca looked up from the booty she was knitting. "Come on in." She started to stand.

"No need to get up."

The young woman sighed deeply, then smiled. "I'm not sure I can anyway."

"It must be very uncomfortable for you." Spirit of the Mountain sat across from Rebecca, her two children resuming their loud play. Timothy, the oldest at five, determined what he and his younger brother, William, three, would do. With all the importance a child could muster, he took responsibility for each and every action they made. The younger boy willingly followed his lead.

"Tom said you've done more than enough to pay for Red."

Rebecca's comment drew Spirit of the Mountain's attention back to her. "Yes, he told me today."

"You've worked hard, and with Nathan hunting every day and bringing us the meat—" She paused, her eyes showing her gratefulness. "Well, it's been wonderful having you here."

"You have been most generous." Spirit of the Mountain felt relaxed and comfortable with Rebecca, who was petite, with a kind, round face, sparkling, pale blue eyes, and dark hair.

Rebecca turned away, but Spirit of the Mountain caught the sadness that came over her face. "I will miss you. It's been nice having another woman's company."

"I will miss you, too, Rebecca." Spirit of the Mountain was reminded of the quiet moments with her adopted Cherokee mother. Sometimes they would work without talk, the silence they shared warm and companionable. Then there were times they could chat and laugh, enjoying the special feeling that existed only between mother and daughter.

Timothy began to wheeze from playing too hard, gasping for each short breath of air he could pull into his lungs. Rebecca tried to calm him.

"Poor Timmy." Rebecca smoothed his rumpled hair and kissed his head. "He's had asthma since he was just a baby. Nothing seems to help him."

"I think I can help him, if you do not mind." Spirit of the Mountain stood and crossed to the fireplace. She put the kettle on to boil, then pulled a pouch from her skirt.

"I noticed Timmy had trouble breathing yesterday, so I went out this morning and gathered some jimson weed. I will brew a broth. If you give Timmy some when he suffers an attack, it will relieve his troubled breathing."

A few moments later, Spirit of the Mountain had the hot tea ready for the child. He sipped it and breathed more easily.

Rebecca's face lit up with joy. "How can I ever thank you?"

"There is no need."

"I had hoped you would be here when the baby was born." Her hand rubbed her belly tenderly.

Spirit of the Mountain put her hand to Rebecca's stomach. "It will not be long."

Rebecca's voice softened to almost a whisper. "I'm afraid, Samantha. Not only did I lose my baby the last time, but I nearly bled to death as well. I don't think I could bear losing another."

"It is difficult. You spend all those months dreaming of giving life, and when death comes instead, it is hard to accept. Babies are so tiny, so innocent, and you cannot understand why they have been taken from you." Spirit of the Mountain, her old pain strong, closed her eyes to keep from crying.

"You've lost a child?" Rebecca asked in amazement, her eyes rounding in surprise.

Spirit of the Mountain drew in a deep breath. "Yes, a few years past."

A blush stained Rebecca's cheeks with embarrassment. "Somehow, I thought you and Nathan were newlyweds. The way you act is like a couple first in love."

Guilt assaulted Spirit of the Mountain, and she had to turn away from Rebecca's honest face. Suddenly, all her lies were unbearable. She was ashamed she had misled this woman, whom she had come to think of as a friend.

"I cannot lie any longer, Rebecca. Nathan and I are not married. I was married before. I lost my husband and child within a few days of each other."

Rebecca took Spirit of the Mountain's hand and squeezed it reassuringly. "It doesn't matter, Samantha. I can see you love each other. That is all that matters."

"It is not the worst of it," Spirit of the Mountain said, unable to stop the flow of truth. "My husband was a Cherokee warrior. I lived with the Cherokee for many years."

It took a moment before Rebecca could answer, her voice low, almost unhearable. "Whatever your past, it is no concern of mine."

Tom pushed open the door and stepped into the room. "But it is mine."

His face was hard, twisted by hatred. Rebecca stood awkwardly, faced her husband. "Do not judge her, Tom. We do not know the reasons for her being with the Indians. I don't want to know."

"She's guilty of fornication, Becky. That alone is reason enough to send her on her way. But to have lived with those heathen murderers is an abomination I cannot abide."

Rebecca turned to Spirit of the Mountain. "Tom was married before. His wife and children were attacked while he was out hunting one day."

"What they did to my wife was unspeakable, but the children—I never found the children. I can only pray that they are dead, that they were not taken by those savages. It's unbearable to think they might still live."

"Samantha is not responsible for your loss, Tom. Do not take your anger out on her."

Tom turned to Rebecca. "Do not dare tell me what to do, Becky. It is my grief, not yours." He turned back to Spirit of the Mountain. "You can stay the night, but I expect you to be gone in the morning."

Spirit of the Mountain wanted to say something that would ease the pain she saw in his eyes, something to make him believe not all Indians were hostile and savage. She found no words that would achieve those things. She realized there were no words that could still the years of strife between the white man and the red man. She turned to leave.

Rebecca grabbed her hand as she passed. "Samantha—"

It was obvious she didn't know what to say either.

"Rebecca, you are kind and generous. I will miss you."

Chapter Fourteen

"What's going on, Sam?"

Nathan's figure filled the doorway to the small shack; his face was blocked out by the light from behind him. Outside, the sun was setting in a blaze of color. The interior where they had slept these past few nights was dim and windowless. Spirit of the Mountain had neglected to light the oil lamp, wishing to remain in quiet darkness, which seemed to ease the torment inside her, like cool water to a hot brow. Nathan stepped into the room and pushed the crooked door shut. He moved to the table, where the lamp sat, and struck a flint to it.

The wavering light showed him more clearly where she sat, and he moved to stand in front of her. "What's wrong?"

She raised her eyes to meet his gaze, but quickly

looked away. "Nothing. I just wanted to sit awhile in the dark."

His hand pulled her chin around so she had to meet his look. "I told you that you don't lie well, Sam. What's wrong?"

"What is wrong is that I do not lie well."

Nathan pulled a stool up and sat beside her, taking her hand in his. "Go on."

"It is over, and it no longer matters, Nathan. We will leave in the morning."

He wasn't satisfied. She could tell by the stubborn twitch of the muscle in his jaw. But he let the matter go at that, saying no more.

"Okay," he said. "We leave in the morning."

Spirit of the Mountain picked up Red, who had been sleeping at her feet, his whimpers drawing her attention. She hugged him to her, knowing he would love her unconditionally. Tears came to her eyes. Why couldn't people love unconditionally?

"God, I hate it when you do this."

Nathan's anguish was obvious, and it brought her from her private thoughts, making her consider how he felt. "I am sorry. I do not wish to hurt you, Nathan."

"Don't you see? When you block me out, you do."

She turned away. Too much swarmed in her mind, leaving her distraught. She felt anger and hurt, but mostly, she was confused. "I do not know what to do. I cannot lie. You have said yourself I do not do this well. Yet when I tell the truth, people are angry and hateful."

Nathan's sigh reached her ears, and she turned back to him.

"You told them didn't you? That's why Tom was so cold when I took some grouse to him for their supper."

"I told Rebecca. Tom overheard. Rebecca said it did not matter, but Tom—" Spirit of the Mountain recalled the ugly look that had twisted his face, the even uglier words that had come from his mouth. "It mattered to Tom that I had lived with the Cherokee. He has much hatred for the red man and no forgiveness in his heart for what he believes me to be. He asked us to be gone in the morning."

Nathan took Spirit of the Mountain into his arms and hugged her tightly. She could feel the movement in his chest as his heart beat softly, steady and strong. It calmed her, yet it tortured her. She pushed away. "You tell me to lie, but I cannot."

"It is for your own good. I've explained that. Surely, now more than ever, you can see that."

She stood and walked away from Nathan, holding Red close to her. It was as if Red were the one and only thing in this world she could hold on to. Even Nathan had promised nothing, except to take her home, which he believed he must do. When that was done, he would leave. "I see only that I cannot change what people will think. I am willing to accept this."

"Even if it is their hatred you must endure?"

"Yes," she whispered, rubbing the top of Red's head against her cheek. He was soft and warm. "It matters little what others might think. My hurt feelings are of little consequence. What is of consequence is how I feel about myself, whether I do honor to what I am, who I am. I cannot lie again about these things without dishonoring what is of great importance to me."

"I don't know if I can stand them hurting you."

The hardness in Nathan's voice drew her gaze back to him. She could see her pain was his. This touched her beyond words. "There is nothing you can do to protect me, Nathan."

She turned her back to him, and he moved to stand behind her. He placed his hands on her arms to keep her from walking away. "There must be something we can do. Perhaps a compromise."

"I do not know."

Her words were a whisper he barely heard. He felt more than heard the slight tremble in her voice, the pain that scored its notes. Slowly, firmly, he turned her to look at him.

"I know you don't understand all this, Sam. I've asked you to trust me on this. Is that so hard?"

Samantha licked her dry lips and considered his question. "I cannot lie, Nathan. It is not within me to do so."

"Then what if you merely do not speak of your past. That would not be lying."

"It would be most fortunate, indeed, if that was all that it took. What if people ask me direct questions? How can I ignore them?"

"Then I shall come to your rescue." Nathan smiled. "I shall rescue the beautiful damsel in distress. That's what I'm here for. Together," he said pulling her close, "we will find a way so your conscience doesn't bother you."

"And what of us?" She stepped away from him, his closeness nearly shattering her new purpose. "I do not wish to continue to Boston under the pretense that we are man and wife. That, too, is a lie."

Nathan knew he should put an end to their relationship, but he had put off doing so. "You are right. We can no longer pretend to be man and wife or play at being lovers, Sam. In a few days, we can catch a coach to take us to Boston. Then you will be under the care of your grandfather, and—"

"You will leave me."

"Yes." He already felt the pain of their imminent separation. "You know it can be no other way."

"I understand it can be no other way."

"Good."

A part of Nathan was glad she understood, but another part wanted her to cry and wail, to plead for him to stay with her. He felt cold, his heart shutting off the feelings within. Nathan knew what was best, and so did Spirit of the Mountain.

"Good night, Nathan."

"Good night, Sam." He turned and left her the bed they had made together, choosing the cold, hard floor on the opposite side of the small room. It would be a long night.

The loud knock awakened Spirit of the Mountain, but Nathan was already to the door before she had even turned over.

He opened it and found Tom standing there, lantern in hand, a grim look written upon his face. "Rebecca's asking for Samantha."

Spirit of the Mountain rose and crossed to Nathan's side. "What is wrong, Tom?"

The lines on his face hardened, and he did not look

her directly in the eye. "It's the baby. She's been laboring since early last night. It's the same as last time. She's afraid and asking for you."

"I will be right up," she said without hesitation.

Tom started to turn away, but stopped and faced her. This time his eyes met hers. There was no sympathy or kindness in them. "I'm not asking for myself, mind you. It's Rebecca who insisted I come for you. It changes nothing between you and me. I'll feel the same whether you help my wife or not."

She met his glare. "I am not doing this for you. I am helping Rebecca. I expect nothing from you in return."

His nod was firm, telling her the matter was settled. Spirit of the Mountain preferred it this way. She followed him out into the darkness.

Rebecca turned wide, fearful eyes to Spirit of the Mountain when she walked into the bedroom. Spirit of the Mountain didn't need to see the blood on the bed to know Rebecca had started bleeding. Spirit of the Mountain could smell it, like death in the air. She forced herself to smile and take the woman's outstretched hand into her own. Rebecca was cold.

"Samantha," she cried, then clenched her teeth as another spasm shook her. "Please help me. I'm going to lose my baby. Please help me."

Spirit of the Mountain pushed back strands of sweat-soaked hair from the other woman's pale face. "You must not talk so, Rebecca. You and the baby will be fine. You will see."

"It's just like the last time," she whispered, weakness stealing her strength.

"Tom," Spirit of the Mountain called out, knowing he was standing at the doorway. "You will do no good standing there and staring. Get out of here."

He hesitated, and Spirit of the Mountain wondered for a moment if he would refuse. It was obvious he didn't trust her, but he finally disappeared, closing the door behind him.

"He didn't want to get you. He's a proud man."

"I was surprised he did come for me." Spirit of the Mountain managed a small smile. "How did you manage that?"

This question made Rebecca laugh, though faintly. "I told him if he didn't fetch you, I'd never let him touch me again."

"Rebecca," Spirit of the Mountain said, trying to keep their conversation light, to distract Rebecca from her pain and fear, "I did not know you had such a devious streak in you."

Nathan watched Tom pace back and forth, his steps agitated and nervous. They had spoken little in the last hour, and Nathan couldn't take the silence any longer.

"Perhaps, you should have a drink, Tom. It would calm you a bit." Nathan moved to the back of the counter, where the rum was stored. He poured a generous portion in a mug for Tom, then got himself one as well.

Tom took the mug and drained it in one quick swallow. "Can that woman of yours really help my Rebecca?"

Nathan poured them another drink and wondered

himself. "I don't know Samantha well enough to tell you."

After that drink was gone, Tom wiped his hand across his mouth and held the mug out for another. "I guess I can't blame you none for taking her to your bed. I've not been innocent of partaking of the flesh in my own past. But even a whore you have to pay for is better than a woman who's been with them stinking Indians."

A slow, intense heat rose in Nathan until he could no longer control it. He swung at Tom's face, which was twisted with hatred and anger. His fist landed squarely on the man's jaw, sending him flying backward to the floor.

Tom moaned, rubbing his sore chin. "What on earth did you do that for?"

Nathan pointed a finger at Tom, and each word he spoke was filled with fury. "That woman has more goodness and kindness in her than a dozen people like you and me. She loves unconditionally, which is something we could all learn if you ask me."

"She was married to a savage, you fool." Tom stood, but he kept his distance from Nathan. "She has no morals at all, fornicating with you, admitting it openly, with no shame. They've turned a good white woman into trash. No, even worse, an Indian-loving whore."

Taking a step forward, Nathan swore beneath his breath, "Damn you, I ought to—"

"To what?" Tom sneered. "I don't see you marrying the girl. Bedding her, yes, but taking her as wife, no. You're no different from me, Walker."

A sick feeling struck Nathan. "I'm not marrying

her for reasons you couldn't understand. Her past has nothing to do with it. Nothing at all."

"If you say so." Tom shrugged, clearly not believing a word of what Nathan said. "I still say she's an Indian-loving whore. But maybe that's the type of woman you like. Does she do things no God-fearing white woman would do?"

A low growl came from Nathan, warning Tom as he closed in.

"Leave him be, Nathan." Spirit of the Mountain stood just inside the room. Nathan wondered how long she had been there.

Tom quickly moved to her side. "How's Rebecca?" Then his eyes riveted to the small bundle Spirit of the Mountain carried.

"You have a baby girl, Tom." Spirit of the Mountain held the squirming child out to her father. "Rebecca is sleeping. She will be fine, given time to rest and regain her strength."

Tom's shaking hands took the child. "A girl?"

"Yes, a girl."

Spirit of the Mountain watched as Tom carried his new daughter back up the stairs to be with his wife. Spirit of the Mountain was saddened. Born totally innocent of hatred and prejudice, the child would soon be taught by her loving father to feel and do as he did. Perhaps one day they would meet, and the very child Spirit of the Mountain had helped into the world would turn away from her in disgust.

"You have much too much goodness in you, Sam. How can you be so tolerant of a man like that?"

Nathan's question seemed absurd to Spirit of the Mountain. "It is for Rebecca, not Tom, and I fear if

I returned his hatred, I would be the same as he is."

"Come on." Nathan took her hand. "We can still get a few hours' sleep before morning."

This time, loud shouts woke Spirit of the Mountain from her sleep. She rolled over just as the door to the tiny shack was kicked open. Light poured in, blinding her to the body that stood in it.

"You were told to be gone by morning."

Spirit of the Mountain looked about for Nathan. She stood and moved to the doorway, hearing his voice outside, his pushing through the crowd of people gathered there.

"Get your things," Nathan said, his tone calm, yet an underlying urgency relating the seriousness of the situation. She did as he said, quickly gathering the few things she possessed. Carefully she put Red into a bag he could ride in comfortably and pulled the strap around her neck.

When she stepped out into the early morning light, she saw that many of the townspeople had assembled. A tenseness hung in the air. Their manner and looks told her Tom had wasted no time in spreading the facts about her past.

Tom came out and joined them. He had said nothing would change between them, and he was right.

"Tell Rebecca I said good-bye," Spirit of the Mountain said, but Tom did not answer.

"Indian whore!" someone in the crowd shouted.

The words struck her like a slap across the face, but she ignored them. Nathan did not look so inclined. She took his hand and started to walk away. He pulled free.

"You people should be ashamed of yourselves," Nathan said, but his words fell on deaf ears.

"She is the one who should feel shame. Look at her," one woman yelled. "She has no shame for what she's done."

Spirit of the Mountain stopped. "Exactly what is it I have done that you people consider to be so shameful?"

"Living with the Indians was bad enough," Tom said, "though we might have understood if you had been taken against your will. But you married one of them savages and bore him a child. It was a sin against God, and he took your baby as punishment. A moral woman would have killed herself before she would be wife to a heathen."

Tom's words cut deep, hitting the small part of Spirit of the Mountain that belonged to her dead baby. Grief and pain mixed with her anger.

"I do not believe God is so cruel he would take out his wrath on an innocent child. I loved my husband. There is no shame in that."

A clod of dirt pelted her on the arm. Another followed. Nathan pushed himself between Spirit of the Mountain and the crowd, protecting her from the onslaught.

"Leave her be, you fools."

They did not stop. Nathan huddled over Spirit of the Mountain, guiding her through the people. One man reached out and grabbed Nathan, pulling him from her side.

"You have fornicated with this she-devil and should be punished for your sins as well."

A clenched fist struck him in the face, bloodying

his nose, before striking him again in the stomach. Three others struck out, pounding him to the ground, numerous feet kicking him when he was down.

"No," Spirit of the Mountain cried out, fighting her way to Nathan's side. When she reached him, she felt for his knife and pulled it. She swung out in an arch, the knife's blade insuring safe space.

"Get back," she hissed.

Tom approached her. "Do not compound your sins, Samantha."

"You make me sick." Spirit of the Mountain heard the venom in her own voice, something she had had little experience with. "How is it that a woman as sweet and kind as Rebecca has found herself married to a man like you?"

The rage that hit Tom made the hatred in his eyes intensify. He stepped forward, his hand raised in threat.

"Do not test my patience." Spirit of the Mountain punctuated her words with the knife she held, aimed directly at his heart. "You people have not endeared yourselves to me. I would stand aside if I were you."

"How dare you threaten me," Tom sneered, his hate-filled eyes scrunching into tiny slits.

Spirit of the Mountain supported Nathan with her arm. "I not only lived with those red savages. I became one."

Slowly, Tom stepped aside. The others followed, clearing a path for them.

Spirit of the Mountain struggled forward, supporting Nathan on her shoulder. They cleared the crowd and moved into the protection of the forest. Once they were out of sight, she helped Nathan to sit. "Are you all right?"

Nathan looked up at her, one eye already coloring and swelling. "I'm fine. My pride might be a bit bruised, as well as my body, but I'm all right. How about you?"

She looked away. She wasn't fine. She was livid. Never had she been so angry. It frightened her— what she might have done? "We should go if you can walk."

"I'll walk." Nathan smiled, but winced from his split lip. "But I'll not run."

"Agreed. We will walk, not run."

Nathan rinsed the dirt and blood from his face, wishing he could clean the ugliness from his mind as well. The shouts of the townspeople haunted him, chased him each step of the way as they had walked from the village.

Samantha said nothing as he washed in the stream. She had said nothing about what had happened, and he felt unable to speak of it. Anger still churned inside him. When the townsfolk had insulted Spirit of the Mountain, he had felt murderous. Their vile words and beliefs had caused more damage than the physical blows he had suffered.

The smallest of doubts sneaked forward to claim control of his muddled mind. Was he doing the right thing by her? Would it be any different for her in Boston? A sick feeling twisted his stomach at the possibility of her grandfather rejecting her. No, he

Fela Dawson Scott

could not think this way. He would not.

"Are you ready, Sam?"

When she nodded and handed his rifle to him, Nathan understood there was no turning back.

Chapter Fifteen

The sway of the coach lulled Spirit of the Mountain and the other passengers, who were jerked back to reality as a wheel fell into a hole. The rutty road assured everyone there would be no real rest.

Spirit of the Mountain had never known a day to be so long as the one she had spent in the crowded conveyance. Dust rolled in past the canvas that covered the window, choking the already stale air. Too many bodies were crammed inside; knees knocked against each other as the passengers were thrown about in the coach making its way down the narrow road to Boston.

Directly across from Spirit of the Mountain sat a large woman, her dour-looking daughter, and an even more sullen-looking child. A thin, pale man completed the wall of people, dust irritating his already persistent cough. Nathan sat to Spirit of the Mountain's left, and a young man sat to her right; an older gentleman had squeezed himself into the last seat.

The child moaned from sickness, and his grandmother fanned herself incessantly as she droned on and on about her ailments. The daughter sat quietly, meek in the shadow of her overbearing mother. The man hacked constantly, almost in rhythm with the woman's whining.

"I think that filthy beast should be put up top."

Spirit of the Mountain raised her gaze to meet the woman's glare of indignant annoyance. Spirit of the Mountain found it amusing, despite the many attempts already made to get a reaction from her.

Surprisingly, the young man next to Spirit of the Mountain spoke up. "The puppy hasn't bothered anyone, Mrs. Webber."

A brow was raised, its meaning as haughty as the woman's words. "It is bothering me, Mr. Kincaid." Her menacing look turned back to Spirit of the Mountain. "What kind of puppy is it anyway?"

"It is a small puppy," Spirit of the Mountain replied evenly. "Too small to put up on top, Mrs. Webber. I am sorry he is bothering you."

"No more than the child's crying," said the older man, a traveling merchant named Henry Howell, coming to Spirit of the Mountain's defense.

Stroking Red's head, Spirit of the Mountain smiled at the child. "It must be very uncomfortable for you, Albert. How old are you?"

Shyly, the little boy smiled back, the first glimmer of a smile since they had embarked on their unbearable journey. It was his mother who answered. "He's five. The movement of the coach seems to have upset his stomach."

"It is quite tight in here." Spirit of the Mountain looked about at the rest of the tired, drawn faces. "I think we all feel a bit uneasy."

Since morning, they had already had a broken wheel and several near turnovers as the driver hurled the four-wheeled vehicle toward their destination with as much speed and carelessness as imaginable. Spirit of the Mountain would have preferred to walk the rest of the way to Boston, but Nathan said it was quicker by coach. She was beginning to wonder if they would make it at all.

"What takes you and your husband to Boston?"

Spirit of the Mountain returned her attention to the gentleman with the persistent cough. She tried to remember his name. "Mr. Walker is not my husband, Mr. Lindfield. He is merely escorting me to my grandfather's. He lives in Boston."

"I'm so sorry, miss. I just assumed—" He didn't finish, an uncomfortable look appearing on his face.

"There is no need to apologize," Spirit of the Mountain offered, trying to ease his embarrassment. "Mr. Walker has been very kind, and he has gone to a lot of trouble to see I get to my family safely."

Mrs. Webber's fanning increased. "Why, it's not proper for a young woman to be alone with a man. You should have a chaperon, young lady."

Nathan could no longer hold his tongue. The woman was beginning to wear on his nerves. "It seemed that it was more important to find her family than to consider etiquette. I'm sure you would have done the same."

"Where are your parents?" Mrs. Webber asked hotly, ignoring Nathan and his statement.

"They were killed. If not for Nathan, I would have been, too."

This answer seemed to quiet Mrs. Webber questions, but her disapproval did not abate. She made that quite apparent by her stern countenance. Nathan was impressed with Spirit of the Mountain's patience.

The passengers once again fell silent, but the droning of the rolling wheels, the curses of the driver, and the thunderous plodding of the horses' hooves were loud in their ears.

It had been almost a week since Tom and the others had driven Spirit of the Mountain and Nathan from the settlement. Nathan had not spoken of the incident since. Nor had they been together as lovers.

Clouds rolled in, covering the sky with premature darkness. The sun remained hidden in the blackness; the light of day was gone behind the storm. Rain pelted the coach, and the road quickly turned into a muddy bog. The wheels turned more slowly, sucked down into the quagmire. Soon they came to a complete halt.

"Everybody out!"

Everyone got out and waited for the coach to be pulled free, the men all wading through the thick mire to push or pull, depending at which end they struggled. The horses became skittish, uncontrollable. The thunder blasted about them, each clap making them tremble with fright. The driver became

A Special Offer For
Leisure Romance Readers Only!
Get
FOUR
FREE
Romance
Novels
A $21.96 Value!
Travel to exotic worlds filled with passion
and adventure —without leaving your home!
Plus, you'll save $5.00 every time you buy!

Thrill to the most sensual, adventure-filled Historical Romances on the market today...

FROM 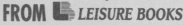 LEISURE BOOKS

As a home subscriber to Leisure Romance Book Club, you'll enjoy the best in today's BRAND-NEW Historical Romance fiction. For over twenty-five years, Leisure Books has brought you the award-winning, high-quality authors you know and love to read. Each Leisure Historical Romance will sweep you away to a world of high adventure...and intimate romance. Discover for yourself all the passion and excitement millions of readers thrill to each and every month.

Save $5.⁰⁰ Each Time You Buy!

Each month, the Leisure Romance Book Club brings you four brand-new titles from Leisure Books, America's foremost publisher of Historical Romances. EACH PACKAGE WILL SAVE YOU $5.00 FROM THE BOOKSTORE PRICE! And you'll never miss a new title with our convenient home delivery service.

Here's how we do it. Each package will carry a FREE 10-DAY EXAMINATION privilege. At the end of that time, if you decide to keep your books, simply pay the low invoice price of $16.96, no shipping or handling charges added. HOME DELIVERY IS ALWAYS FREE. With today's top Historical Romance novels selling for $5.99 and higher, our price SAVES YOU $5.00 with each shipment.

AND YOUR FIRST FOUR-BOOK SHIPMENT IS TOTALLY FREE!
IT'S A BARGAIN YOU CAN'T BEAT! A Super $21.96 Value!

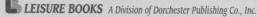

LEISURE BOOKS *A Division of Dorchester Publishing Co., Inc.*

GET YOUR 4 FREE BOOKS NOW — A $21.96 Value!

Mail the Free Book Certificate Today!

Get Four Books Totally FREE — A $21.96 Value!

▼ Tear Here and Mail Your FREE Book Card Today! ▼

PLEASE RUSH
MY FOUR FREE
BOOKS TO ME
RIGHT AWAY!

Leisure Romance Book Club
65 Commerce Road
Stamford CT 06902-4563

AFFIX
STAMP
HERE

irritated and began to whip them, making them even more unruly.

"Let me try," Spirit of the Mountain yelled to the man, his hand raised to strike again. He stopped and turned to her, his look astounded, then skeptical.

"You're joking, miss?"

"I don't think she is," Nathan said from behind her. It did not surprise Spirit of the Mountain he was near. He was never far from her.

The man stared at Nathan, his mouth opening for a moment before he finally snapped it shut. "She might get hurt. I'll not be responsible."

"Sir, you seem to have had little regard for our safety as you pushed these poor horses and this rickety contraption you call a coach to the limit to remain, as you so often have said, on schedule."

This rebuke did not set well with the driver's already impatient, if not surly, attitude. He pointed a dirty finger at her. "I'll not be talked to in such a way by a woman." His angry gaze moved back to Nathan. "If she were my wife, I'd be shutting her up before she causes trouble."

The slightest twitch of one eye told Spirit of the Mountain that Nathan was losing his temper, but he held on to it and said simply, "If she were my wife, and if she were out of line, I might consider it."

Spirit of the Mountain stepped closer to the driver, whose appearance was as unkempt as his manners. "I can get these horses to pull the wagon free. Do you want to waste more time struggling with them? Or do you want to keep to your schedule?"

"What makes you so damn sure you can do what I can't?"

This question merely made her smile. It was Nathan who answered him. "Believe me. She can do what you can't."

The driver's look remained doubtful, but a glimmer of something else touched his dark eyes, echoed in the challenge he threw at her. "I'll eat my hat, miss, if you can pull us free."

Saying nothing more, Spirit of the Mountain took the whip from his hand and tossed it into the mud. She thought he might explode from anger. "You two help the others at the back of the coach."

Nathan did as she asked. The driver followed, but with obvious reluctance. Spirit of the Mountain walked to the horses and began talking to them. Her voice soothed their fear, and their shrill shrieks calmed to normal whinnies. The animals' quivering eased as did their struggles to free themselves. They listened and responded to her.

She prompted the horses to pull, and they strained forward to free the coach from the muck. Slowly, they moved, each muscle of the great animals straining until they were clear.

The driver came up to her, his mouth gaping again, this time in amazement. Spirit of the Mountain smiled. "There is really is no need to eat your hat, sir. I am glad to help."

All the passengers crawled back in and spent the rest of the afternoon in silent, damp discomfort. They arrived at the overnight station late. Dinner was cold and unpalatable. The passengers picked at the fare provided. Exhaustion kept everyone silent.

"Are you doing all right?"

Nathan's voice was soft, almost apologetic. Spirit

of the Mountain looked up into his brilliant green eyes. Her heart tightened painfully. "I am fine."

"I know it's uncomfortable and the people are a little surly, but I thought it would get us to Boston more quickly."

"I am sure you are right, Nathan. Do not worry over me."

His eyes told her he did. "You've handled yourself well—with Mrs. Webber, I mean. She'd scare the hell out of most people with that sour look of hers. But you hold your own."

Spirit of the Mountain couldn't help but smile. "Mrs. Webber is not so bad. She is merely an unhappy woman."

"Only you would think that." Nathan brushed a smudge from her cheek. The look in his eyes changed, the green darkening with passion. He turned and walked away.

Spirit of the Mountain made no attempt to stop him. She knew they could no longer be together. Yet each night that passed left Spirit of the Mountain feeling more alone than ever. Each mile that brought her closer to Boston brought her closer to heartbreak. It was inevitable—she understood that now. But that didn't make it easier.

Spirit of the Mountain tried to play the game as Nathan expected. They had achieved an uneasy existence. She did not lie about her past, but merely failed to offer all the details. She had learned how people could be, and she was learning how to deal with them as well.

Nathan crossed the room, anxious to put some distance between Spirit of the Mountain and himself.

He couldn't even touch her without his passion rousing. She controlled him, and he was helpless to stop her.

Too many times in his life he had been unable to control what others did to him. That was his whole reason for living alone in the wilderness. He didn't like losing his will to another—not even a woman like Spirit of the Mountain.

"She seems quite a remarkable woman."

Henry Howell's statement brought Nathan from his tormented thoughts. "Yes, she is."

"She mentioned today you are taking her to a grandfather in Boston."

Nathan nodded. "Yes, if he still lives."

"She does not know if he is alive?"

"No." Nathan tried to hide his annoyance with Mr. Howell's questions. It wasn't really the man's curiosity, but Nathan's own troubled emotions that made him wish to be left alone. "I don't think her grandfather even knows Samantha exists. I hope he is alive, for Samantha's sake."

Mr. Howell sighed heavily, his round stomach straining against the buttons of his vest. "For your sake as well?"

Not liking Mr. Howell's question or his tone, Nathan leaned closer. "What do you mean by that, sir?"

Mr. Howell held up his hand as if to stop Nathan's cross words. "Now, now, Mr. Walker. I do not intend to be impertinent. I simply cannot help what I see."

"What is it you see?"

Henry Howell clasped his fingers together and rested them across his ample belly, thinking a while before he spoke. "The truth, as I see it, is that you are in love with the woman and she in love with you."

Nathan raised an eyebrow, suddenly amused rather than irritated. "Is that how you see it?"

"Yes, sir." Howell's lips pursed out in thought. "I think it is a shame you two cannot do something about this."

For the briefest of seconds, Nathan wondered about this, too, then stopped himself. "There is nothing to be done, Mr. Howell. I must return Samantha to her family. It is the right thing to do."

"Perhaps you are right. Forgive me my sentimentality, young man. I hope no offense was taken by my rambling on."

"Not at all."

Henry Howell started to walk away, but turned back. "If you don't mind one more question—"

"And what would that be?" Nathan asked, unable to deny the man's wide smile and amiable face.

"I travel a great deal and have many clients in Boston. I thought I might be of help in locating the girl's grandfather. What is the man's name?"

"Samuel Jacoby."

The expression that crossed over Henry Howell's features prompted an alarm to go off in Nathan's head. This response increased as he heard the man suck in air. "Do you know the man?"

"I'm not sure. I know of a Samuel Jacoby." He came closer before continuing the conversation. "Do you know what Samantha's grandfather does for a living?"

"No, we haven't talked about him much. I only know his name."

He took a step in Samantha's direction. "Perhaps we could ask."

Nathan followed, curiosity mingling with uneasy foreboding. "Why not?"

"Samantha," Henry Howell said, approaching Spirit of the Mountain.

"Yes, Mr. Howell," Spirit of the Mountain purposely did not look at Nathan, but kept her eyes on the gentleman who spoke to her.

"I was just telling Mr. Walker I might know your grandfather. Samuel Jacoby, isn't it?"

"Yes."

Howell settled down on the bench beside her. "Do you know what it is your grandfather does in Boston?"

"I believe he was, or is, a shipbuilder."

"Oh, my," Henry Howell muttered.

"What is it?" Spirit of the Mountain felt anxious at his look. "Is there something wrong, Mr. Howell?"

"Oh, my, no." He took her hand into his and patted it. "I'm sorry if I caused alarm, dear. It's just that it is such a surprise."

"What?" Nathan's voice was colored with exasperation.

Spirit of the Mountain wanted Mr. Howell to be more precise. "Mr. Howell, please. What is it that has surprised you?"

"Why, that you are the granddaughter of one of the richest men in Boston. Samuel Jacoby isn't just a shipbuilder. He owns one of the largest shipyards in America."

"My grandfather is wealthy?"

"Very." Henry Howell seemed to consider

something. "You can prove you are Samuel Jacoby's granddaughter?"

"Why would I claim to be his granddaughter if I was not? That would be dishonest."

"There are a lot of people who would do such a thing, Sam," Nathan said in a hushed voice.

The expression on his face caused Spirit of the Mountain concern, but she was distracted by Mr. Howell's next statement. "Your grandfather might wish to have verification, since he doesn't know of you."

It was beyond her comprehension, but she tried to understand what they were telling her. "I believe I can establish who I am to my grandfather."

This response made Mr. Howell smile widely. "Excellent. I am so pleased to be a part of such a wonderful reunion." He wandered off, exclaiming, "To bring a family together—what a joyous occasion."

Nathan felt empty, the realization that Samantha was part of one of the richest families of Boston leaving him numb. It was as if a final, impenetrable barrier had risen between them.

Old memories came forward, destroying the value he had put on what he had known to be right. Her grandfather's wealth was a barrier he couldn't get beyond. He wasn't as joyous about Spirit of the Mountain's good fortune as Henry Howell seemed to be.

"What is wrong, Nathan?"

He turned to find Spirit of the Mountain's blue eyes staring at him, questions mirrored in their depths. "Nothing is wrong, Sam."

She stepped closer and placed her hand on his

arm. "You do not lie well yourself."

Just her light touch was enough to send his already confused state of mind into turmoil. He drew in a deep breath to still the sudden fast beat of his heart. "You must be very happy to find out your grandfather is so well off."

"I do not know that it makes any difference," she whispered softly.

Nathan stiffened. He knew it would make a difference. "Things will be very different for you."

A furrow creased her beautiful brow. "In what way?"

He didn't know how to explain it. Maybe he was wrong. Maybe for her there would be no difference. She was family. Samantha Jacoby would not be tossed out into the streets with no afterthought. Jacoby blood ran in her veins. He had no right to compare his own past disillusionment with what might happen to her.

Reaching out, he caressed her cheek. "It will be fine," he said, hoping if he lied he was doing so convincingly. He hoped she would find happiness with her new family.

Spirit of the Mountain doubted what he said, but she said nothing more. She could tell he was uncomfortable with this new turn of events. What it could be that made him uneasy, she didn't know. She had no idea what to expect or what to think about her grandfather or the fact he was supposed to be wealthy.

Her parents had done their best to give her a complete education, but her learning did not include the interpretation of the differences between classes.

Spirit of the Mountain had read many books that made clear that the wealthy and those less fortunate did not live, work, or play together. It was as if there were different worlds for different people. What the books did not explain was why.

"I am afraid, Nathan."

"Now what have you to be afraid of? We left the Shawnee, the Frenchman. We've left everything behind there is to be afraid of, Sam."

She sighed heavily. "I understood the reasons that the Shawnee attacked my village and took me captive. Even the Frenchman was a man I could understand. But I do not know what to expect from my grandfather. Will he love me? Will he hate me? That is what I am afraid of."

"How could he not love you, Sam?"

Although Spirit of the Mountain wanted to believe Nathan's kind words, she said, "For the same reasons we were run out of the settlement. For the same reasons I must keep my past from everyone. I loved my adopted family, but I must not say it aloud. I can only remember how I felt in my heart in silence."

"In time you will understand all this better. Be patient."

Nathan's words were meant to comfort her, she knew. But they didn't. "I feel that Samuel Jacoby's wealth makes a difference to you, Nathan. Should it make a difference to me?"

"No, it shouldn't make a difference to you."

But she knew it mattered to Nathan. As hard as he tried to say it didn't, it did. Spirit of the Mountain felt lost in a strange world, her only comfort a man she had known less than a month. Now, she was no

Fela Dawson Scott

longer secure in the fact Nathan would be there when she faced her greatest fear: rejection by her grandfather, possibly severing forever the last remaining tie to any of her family, leaving her totally alone in the world.

Chapter Sixteen

Spirit of the Mountain awakened and rolled over onto her side, her mouth covered with her hand to still the sob that shook her. Her dream had been so vivid. Nathan's lovemaking had aroused her desire easily, but reality left it to ache inside her without release. Tears stung her eyes as she tried to gain control over the havoc her dream had created.

The room became stifling. The air was stale from the sleeping bodies that claimed the floor randomly on makeshift beds of meager straw mats. Quietly, she rose. Even Red was undisturbed. Placing each step carefully, Spirit of the Mountain made her way to the door. Lifting the latch, she inched open the door and slipped silently out into the dark night.

The crisp, damp air revived her, clearing her muddled mind of the dream and its devastation. It had stopped raining, yet wetness clung to everything, casting the night in a shimmering glow. She walked away from the station to the forest's edge. It was like soothing medicine, calming her soul, easing the pain in her heart.

Sounds of the night played like music in her ears. Spirit of the Mountain drifted away to another place, another time. She closed her eyes and visions accompanied the songs of nature, visions that brought back the happiness of a simpler existence.

She played as a child with her adopted brother, Running Deer, his laughter mingling with her own. Love for her adopted family filled her: the gentleness of her mother, the pride that lit her father's eyes when Red Hawk had courted her. Spirit of the Mountain relived the youthful, tender love she experienced when Red Hawk made her his wife and a woman.

"You shouldn't wander off alone like this. It's dangerous."

Spirit of the Mountain opened her eyes, startled. She had been so immersed in her daydreams that she had not heard anyone approach. "Mr. Kincaid," she muttered, still not totally released from the other world.

"Are you all right, Miss Jacoby?"

Concern edged his voice, and Spirit of the Mountain pulled herself together, pushing away the memories to which she wanted to cling. "I am fine. I just needed some air."

He stepped closer. "As I said, it isn't safe for you out here alone. These woods are filled with wild animals, and there might even be Indians about. You should be more careful."

"She wasn't alone, Mr. Kincaid."

Nathan's voice came from the shadows. Spirit of the Mountain was not overly surprised he was there.

"Oh." Mr. Kincaid seemed to be caught off guard by Nathan's presence. "My apologies. I—"

He didn't finish, but walked off.

Nathan moved to stand beside Spirit of the Mountain. "He's right, you really shouldn't wander off in the night."

"I did not go far. There is no danger, Nathan."

His shadowed face looked down on her, the night obscuring his features. "Perhaps none from wild animals and Indians."

She said nothing in reply.

"I think we embarrassed young Mr. Kincaid."

"In what way?" she asked, not understanding his meaning.

"I think," Nathan whispered, his voice soft and captivating, "he believes we came out here together. Clandestine lovers seeking a moment alone."

Spirit of the Mountain found it difficult to think. "I came out here to be alone. Why are you here, Nathan Walker?"

"To keep you safe, Samantha Jacoby."

She stepped away from Nathan. His body was too close, too arousing. "I think I prefer the danger of wild animals and Indians to your protection."

"Yes," Nathan said, his voice cracking from suppressed emotion. "We do have a tendency to lose control when alone."

"I suggest we go back. Before we do something we

will regret." Spirit of the Mountain fought hard to maintain control of her feelings. She wanted to fall into his arms and let him kiss away her sadness. Instead, she turned from him and walked toward the station, her heart once again heavy with pain.

Nathan didn't follow immediately. He needed a moment to gather his thoughts, to clear his mind and senses of the woman who tempted him more strongly than he had known was possible. He wondered what she had been thinking earlier, standing alone in the darkness, wrapping the wilderness about her as another woman might a shawl.

He had sensed her departure into another world, another place that seemed to bring her happiness. But it had all disappeared as soon as he and Mr. Kincaid appeared. Many events had brought her here, yet Nathan felt responsible for the sadness he saw in her eyes of late. But what more could he do? Indeed, he should have done less.

Nathan returned to the cabin. Inside, he waited a moment for his eyes to adjust to the dimness, not wanting to step on the people who slept. Finally, he could see the shapes lying about, and he saw that Spirit of the Mountain had returned to her place, her back to him as she curled up beside Red. A strange pang of longing struck him, and he turned away from the sight of her.

The next day brought sunshine, which mixed with the dampness to make it muggy and uncomfortable for the travelers. The rain had washed down the narrow, winding road they followed, leaving deep trenches for the wheels to fall into hazardously. Finally, one hole wrenched the spindles too far and broke a wheel, jolting the coach so far to one side it crashed onto its side.

The passengers were tossed from their seats to land in a pile of arms and legs. Mrs. Webber lay atop the overly thin Mr. Lindfield, her stout form thrashing about. Spirit of the Mountain couldn't help but be reminded of a fish out of water as Mrs. Webber tried to hold on to air in her attempts to get up.

Suppressing a laugh, Spirit of the Mountain reached out to help the old woman. It finally took three of them to pull the wailing Mrs. Webber from her compromising position atop poor Mr. Lindfield, whose face was pale and drawn when the rescue was accomplished.

"Are you all right, Mr. Lindfield?"

Spirit of the Mountain's question was answered by a fit of hacking, the air he was finally able to breathe disrupted by his ailment. She put her arm about his frail form and all but lifted him from the coach. Nathan and Ryan Kincaid helped the women crawl out, and both lent a hand as Henry Howell struggled to the ground. Young Albert was frightened and clung to his mother, tears coursing down his red cheeks.

Mrs. Webber continued to wail, causing Albert to cry harder. Spirit of the Mountain put her hand on Melissa's arm. "I will look after Albert. You had best see to your mother. She seems quite upset."

Melissa hesitated only a second, but her mother's high-pitched tone moved her to action. She handed Albert to Spirit of the Mountain and smiled gratefully.

"Thank you. He's just frightened. I'll see if I can calm mother."

"Come on, Albert. We had better see if Red is all right."

Large, tear-filled eyes stared up at Spirit of the Mountain but sobered at the mention of the puppy. Spirit of the Mountain carried the boy Albert over to a quiet spot off the road, where a large tree offered shade. Kneeling on the grass, Spirit of the Mountain put Albert down, then twisted the pouch she carried Red in about so she could peek inside. The pup usually rode with his head poking out, but he had slipped down inside to hide during the commotion.

"He is fine, Albert." She smiled and lifted Red from his comfortable home. The puppy was always content as long as he was close to Spirit of the Mountain. Albert reached out and petted his soft head, a smile now replacing his frown of fear.

The wolf pup yipped and pranced about playfully, anxious for attention. In minutes Albert was laughing, his frightening experience forgotten. Spirit of the Mountain, too, forgot the discomfort of the day and simply enjoyed the child's company and Red's playfulness.

"I think that's the first I've seen the boy laugh."

Nathan stood looking down at them. Spirit of the Mountain shaded her eyes to see him better, but the sun was bright behind him, casting his face in shadow. "Is everyone doing all right?"

"Yes. A few bumps and bruises, but nothing serious." His slow, soft chuckle rumbled forth, the sound soothing to her. "I think Mrs. Webber might never be the same."

This remark brought a smile to her face, the vision of Mrs. Webber on top of Mr. Lindfield forever branded in her mind. "Poor Mr. Lindfield. I thought he might suffocate before Mrs. Webber got off him. He seems so frail and slight in comparison to her."

Nathan's chuckle breaking into full laughter, he smiled brilliantly as he casually slung himself down onto the grass beside Spirit of the Mountain. It was the first time in over a week they had been at ease with one another.

Albert's energy spent, it was only minutes before sleep overtook him. He lay curled up with Red tucked into his small arms. Both the boy and the pup were content to take a nap.

"You are good with children, Sam."

"I had hoped to have many children." She looked away, and the good feelings disappeared in the same instant.

Nathan saw the slightest blush come to her cheeks, telling him her reaction to his statement. "You are young, Sam. You can still have a whole brood of babies."

Her face remained turned away so he could not see her face, but her shoulders slumped ever so slightly. "I suppose you are right."

Nathan knew she had tried to keep her feelings from him. He suddenly understood that his casual comment went much deeper than intended. "I'm sorry, Sam. I didn't mean for any of this to happen. I never meant to hurt you."

Pride brought anger to Spirit of the Mountain, and she was dismayed that he could read her so easily. She turned carefully guarded eyes back to him. "You have not hurt me, Nathan Walker. When my husband and child died, I felt the pain of their loss. At that time, I was hurt. You merely reminded me that I am still a woman, that I had not died with them as I feared I had. For that, I am grateful." She lied, but this time she was determined for him not to see her words as such.

Nathan felt as if someone had hit him in the gut. "Grateful?" He was appalled. No, he was hurt. The very emotion he thought he had caused in Spirit of the Mountain was now ripping him apart. It was ironic that she could turn the tables on him.

He found himself wanting something from her she was not giving him. Perhaps he wanted to believe that she was lying to him, that he had meant more than that to her. "Is that how you really feel? Grateful?"

"Exactly how is it you want me to feel, Nathan? You tell me we can never marry. You plan to leave as soon as you deposit me on my family's doorstep. What—" Spirit of the Mountain paused and took a moment before she continued. "What is it you want from me when you offer so little in return?"

"I want the truth. At least I have always been truthful with you, Sam. I've never lied to you."

"I think you are lying to me now. I think you have been lying to yourself even more."

Nathan began to deny her accusations. "Perhaps you're right. You mean more to me than I care to admit, to myself or to you. I have lived my life so much the same these past years, one day pretty much like another, each year going by with little difference to mark its passing."

He wasn't even certain what he was trying to say, but he rambled on, hoping to make some sense. "Then you stumbled into my world like a great breath of fresh air, stirring me back to life from the meager existence I maintained all those years."

Leaning closer, his lips near her ear, Nathan whispered, "You've made me doubt myself. All I've believed in for thirty-two years is suddenly unclear in my mind. You confuse the hell out of me, Samantha Jacoby, and I'm at a loss to know what to do about it."

"What does your heart tell you?" Spirit of the Mountain had turned her head to him, her lips almost touching his, her breath sweet and warm.

"When I am close to you, my heart tells me to take you into my arms and make love to you."

Determinedly, he leaned back, breaking the spell between them. "But I cannot."

"Someday, you will learn to listen to your heart, Nathan. It speaks the truth when your body or mind may betray you or speak falsely. When you understand this, you will know what is best."

Nathan pulled himself up from the ground and stood. "What would have been best would have been to leave you to the Frenchman. I put my nose in another's business, and I've been paying for it ever since."

"Yes, it would have been best if you had."

"Damn you." Nathan knelt down, anger pushing through all else. "Don't be so noble when I'm being a selfish cad. You know damn well I couldn't have left you to him."

He stood again, unable to bear her closeness. It

was uncanny how easily she could rattle him. "I might be confused about everything I feel, but I do know one thing for certain: I'll not give up my life and everything I believe in on a whim."

"Is that what you believe love is? A whim?"

"Isn't that what it is? We've known each other less than a month. How can it be anything but a whim—a mad, passionate whim."

Disappointment ran through Spirit of the Mountain, but it was nothing compared to the undermining realization that Nathan believed their love to be nothing more than a whim, a fancy, a lark that would pass, much like a bad meal that lay uneasily on the stomach. At that moment, all hope vanished.

"They are ready to continue on." Ryan Kincaid's voice broke the silence that had descended between Spirit of the Mountain and Nathan.

She looked up and nodded. "Thank you, Mr. Kincaid."

She started to lift the sleeping boy, but Nathan gently pushed her aside and gathered Albert into his arms. Spirit of the Mountain placed Red back inside his pouch and followed Nathan back to the coach.

"Mr. Lindfield."

The man Spirit of the Mountain spoke to looked up, his handkerchief covering his mouth as he coughed. The accident seemed to have irritated his ailment, each minute of the long afternoon ticked off by his hacking.

"Yes, miss?"

"I thought this might help." She handed him the cup she held.

"What is it?" he asked cautiously, watery eyes of gray looking at the cup, his long nose sniffing the hot brew.

"It is an Indian tea." She pushed the cup closer. "It will help ease your coughing. I promise."

He hesitated only a second more, then accepted the cup. "Thank you, Miss Jacoby. How is it you know of such things?"

Waiting until he had drunk the cup down, Spirit of the Mountain took the cup back and smiled. "My mother taught me."

When she turned around to put the cup back on the table, she noticed Nathan watching her, a look of relief on his face. She understood he had been nervous about how she would answer Mr. Lindfield's question.

Spirit of the Mountain moved away from Nathan's watchful eye and stood in front of the fireplace. For a moment, she saw nothing on the mantel, her mind still occupied with Nathan. Then, slowly, she became aware of the objects that lined it. Many Indian artifacts lay upon the rough-hewn wood—a hatchet, a round balled club, a pipe, a flute.

The station owner came up next to her. "It's interesting how artfully Indians carve. Even their weapons are made beautifully."

He picked up the hatchet, a bundle of eagle feathers dangling from the handle. "It's from a Huron warrior," he said proudly, holding the object up to examine it again, perhaps for the hundredth time.

Spirit of the Mountain feared to ask how he had come by the items and instead focused on the flute. As she touched it, memories floated across her mind.

"Do you play, Mr. Crandell?"

"Naw." He placed the hatchet back and picked up the flute. "I'm tone deaf. Can't seem to make it sound the way the Indian did that traded it."

She knew she shouldn't ask, but she couldn't help herself. "May I try?"

"Of course." He handed the flute to her.

Moving back to the bench that braced the long table, Spirit of the Mountain sat. At first she just fingered each hole in the flute; then she tested the holes for their individual sounds. Each note was low and soft. The maker had produced an instrument of haunting quality.

Taken back to her past, Spirit of the Mountain recalled her father's patient teachings and the hours he had spent playing the flute he had carried from Boston, the same flute he had played as a child. It had been easy to pick up the melodies of the Cherokee, and she had spent many nights playing for her adopted people long after her father was gone from her life. His talent and teachings remained a part of her, and she longed to play once again.

Before she began, Spirit of the Mountain looked up at Mr. Crandell. "It was made for the tone and rhythm of the Indian songs, so I will play it as it was meant to be played."

The music stopped the idle chatter that filled the room. The notes were strong and clear. Henry Howell moved closer, pleasure clear upon his round face. Ryan Kincaid and Nathan came to sit beside Spirit of the Mountain. Even Albert quieted his play to listen. Mr. Lindfield's coughing had ceased for the first time in days, giving him the opportunity to enjoy her playing as well.

Mrs. Webber was left with no one to complain to, so she gave her full attention to Spirit of the Mountain. Mrs. Crandell left her work and joined her husband to stand before the fire.

The song started muted, the tempo slow and easy, gathering momentum as Spirit of the Mountain played on. The notes became stronger, the rhythm faster, whirling everyone into its world of mysterious tones.

Spirit of the Mountain felt the yearnings of her past stir her, tears blurring the images of those who watched. She was no longer in a station with strangers, on her way to Boston and a family she had never known. She moved back in time, back to the people who had taken her in, giving their love and sharing their life, their heritage, their culture.

The melody entranced Spirit of the Mountain, and she could no longer keep the tears back. They flowed down her cheeks as the music flowed into the air, unguarded and passionate. When the song ended, it was as if everyone had been enchanted. No one seeming to notice she was crying.

Spirit of the Mountain brushed the tears from her face and handed the instrument back to Mr. Crandell. "It is beautiful. Thank you for letting me play it."

The station owner handed it back. "I want you to have it, Miss Jacoby. Surely, it was made for you."

"I will treasure it forever."

Chapter Seventeen

The small settlements Nathan and Spirit of the Mountain had stopped at before could not possibly have prepared her for the large city of Boston. The way stations and inns were primitive compared to the clusters of buildings that sprang up before them, towering like wooden and brick mountains, tightly knit together to accommodate thousands of people.

Spirit of the Mountain, Nathan, and Mr. Howell had taken a hired cab after debarking from the coach. Their arrival had been claimed by all the passengers to be a miracle. Spirit of the Mountain could not take in all about her; her senses were overloaded with all there was to see, hear, and smell. Everything sped by in a fast blur, leaving her numb and a little frightened by it all. Even Red felt the change about them and hid safely in his pouch.

Dust stirred by hundreds of feet became mixed with the smoke of fires built for warmth, cooking, and industry. Pigs rooted through the garbage in the streets, and horses worked hard, providing transportation of every sort and means. As Spirit of the Mountain, Nathan, and Mr. Howell drew near the wharf, a salty breeze stirred the air, and they heard a dozen different languages for every dozen people they passed.

Merchants of all sizes and shapes hawked their wares with singsong choruses, tempting customers to them and away from their competitors. Giant warehouses commanded long blocks; workers, sailors, merchants, and immigrants lined the walkways that covered the docks.

Dogs, horses, cows, goats, chickens, ducks, and pigs could be heard, their calls combining with men's curses, women's laughter, children's shrieks, and babies' cries. It was a kaleidoscope of sound, color, shape, and smell.

Spirit of the Mountain felt dizzy. Her neck strained from craning to see everything. "Is it always like this, Mr. Howell?"

Henry Howell laughed at her obvious awe of the city. "Yes, my dear. Is this your first time in a big city?"

Spirit of the Mountain nodded. "I have read about places like this, but I never truly imagined it as it is."

"Your grandfather shall have a marvelous time showing you all that Boston has to offer a new resident. It will be a delight for you, Miss Jacoby, I'm sure."

At the mention of her grandfather, Spirit of the

Mountain felt dread pool inside her. Almost five weeks after Nathan had rescued her from the Frenchman and determined they would go to Boston to find her grandfather, the time had arrived. She found herself unprepared.

Just the mention of her grandfather made her heart lurch and her breath strangle in her throat. She wanted to turn and go back to the wilderness she loved, back to the life she had known. Instead, she remained quiet in the carriage seat, her hands clutching the pouch where Red hid. She no longer saw the sights of the city. Its sounds no longer filled her head.

She forgot why she had agreed to come here. Why had she given her promise to Nathan to try it his way? What had he hoped to accomplish by this? She couldn't remember. It all jumbled somewhere in the recesses of her mind; nothing made sense in the chaos of memories and reality.

"Here we are," Henry Howell announced jovially.

How could the man be so happy when Spirit of the Mountain was so miserable? Couldn't he see she didn't want to do this?

Nathan jumped from the carriage and held out his hand to help her down. His dark green gaze touched her, and she could see the sympathy in his eyes.

"Promise me one thing, Nathan."

"What's that, Sam?"

Her heart jumped, then raced on. "Promise you will not leave me if I am not wanted. I could not bear it if you did."

He tucked her hand into the crook of his arm; his other hand lay comfortingly on top of hers. "You

234

know I wouldn't do that to you. But don't fear. Your grandfather will want you. I can feel it in my bones."

This reassurance made her smile. "It is all so strange, so frightening." She looked up into Nathan's expressive eyes and felt better knowing he would be there with her.

"You're trembling."

"The Shawnee did not frighten me so terribly as the thought of meeting my grandfather for the first time. I know that seems silly—"

"It's not silly, Sam."

"I suddenly do not feel the courageous woman you have claimed I am."

It was true. Nathan had seen her face the Shawnee, the Frenchman, even death without hesitation. Yet now she trembled like a scared child, her eyes round with fear, her face pale and worried. He wished he could take her into his arms and hold her until her apprehension went away. But he couldn't.

"Right in here." Mr. Howell led the way into the main office of Jacoby Shipping Lines, his chest puffed with importance as he took charge.

Inside, he went up to the young man sitting amid a pile of ledgers and paperwork at a desk near one end of the room. "We would like to see Mr. Jacoby, please."

"Do you have an appointment?"

"No, sir. We have only just arrived in the city. The young woman would like a moment of Mr. Jacoby's time. Please tell him it is of grave importance to him and to the young lady."

The man's face showed no emotion. "Who shall I say is here to see him?"

"Miss Samantha Jacoby, his granddaughter."

This statement caused the slightest lifting of the brows, but no more. "Please take a seat, and I shall see if Mr. Jacoby is in."

Henry Howell returned to stand by Nathan and Samantha. Samantha leaned close to Howell. "Surely he knows if Samuel Jacoby is in or not."

"It's merely a polite way of saying he will check to see if Mr. Jacoby wants to take time to see us or not."

Her eyes grew even rounder. "He may not even take the time to see me?"

Nathan tried to calm her. "He may not, Sam. He may not believe you are his granddaughter. If he doesn't, we may have to try another way."

"That does not seem very polite," she mumbled, her fingers twisting together nervously.

"It would not be very polite, indeed," a man said from the doorway of his office. He was tall, almost as tall as Nathan. His hair was gray, but his stature spoke of a man once vital and strong. Samantha had not moved. Nathan could see she was afraid to turn around and face the man.

"You may go inside," the bookkeeper announced.

Henry Howell smiled widely and offered his hand to Nathan. "I will leave you now."

Nathan shook the other man's hand warmly. "We are grateful for your help, Henry."

"I am glad to be a small part of reuniting Samantha with her grandfather." His gaze moved to Spirit of the Mountain. "My warmest wishes, young lady."

"Thank you, Mr. Howell. I shall always remember your kindness."

They watched Henry Howell leave. Then, as gently

as Nathan could, he turned Spirit of the Mountain about and guided her into the office Samuel Jacoby had disappeared into. The older man stood beside his desk, his back to her. Nathan took her to a chair that sat a few feet from him.

Spirit of the Mountain did not sit, but waited for Samuel Jacoby to acknowledge her. Slowly, he turned around.

Spirit of the Mountain didn't know what she had expected, but what she had never thought of was how much her grandfather would look like her father; the same eyes, the same square jaw and lips. The only difference was the gray hair. Her father had died young, when his hair had still been brown. Her heart raced even faster inside her chest, and she gripped Red's pouch even harder.

As she studied her grandfather, he appraised her. She could feel his intense blue eyes examining each and every detail of her.

"My God," Samuel Jacoby mumbled beneath his breath.

A long moment of silence followed. Spirit of the Mountain finally sat, her legs trembling from emotion and fear.

It was Samuel Jacoby who finally spoke. "I would have thought it was your mother sitting there. You look just like her. How old are you?"

"Twenty."

"Yes," he muttered, walking closer. "Just about the same age she was when I saw her last. Over twenty-one years ago."

He reached out and lifted her face so he could see

her better. "Except for your eyes. You have your father's eyes."

She looked into dark blue eyes that mirrored her own and wondered what thoughts lay behind them.

Samuel Jacoby let go and moved behind his desk. "Where's your father. Why hasn't he come with you?"

"They are both dead, Mr. Jacoby."

Sadness gripped him. There was no doubt in her mind.

"When?"

"My mother died when I was ten, Papa a year later."

Jacoby was silent a moment. "Why did you not come to me sooner?"

Nathan stepped forward. "I am the one who insisted she come to Boston to find her family."

"Who are you?"

"I am Nathan Walker."

Samuel Jacoby seemed to be waiting for more. "And?"

Spirit of the Mountain thought it best to be the one to tell him of her past. "About a year after the death of my father, I went to live with a Cherokee tribe. I was adopted into the family of the shaman, Chaser of Dreams. I lived with them the past eight years. I was married, but I lost my husband and our child two years ago."

She paused to take a breath and to gather herself for the possible rejection and hurt that might follow. "Six weeks ago my tribe was attacked by the Shawnee, and I was taken captive. Then I was sold to a trapper for guns and ammunition. Nathan helped me to escape from the trapper, and he said it was best if I tried to find you. There was no one else to whom I could go."

Samuel Jacoby listened to the girl's story, her telling of it dry and emotionless, as if she were guarded and prepared. Many things ran through his mind. He felt sadness at the death of his son, though truthfully he had lost him long before that. He also had sudden joy that he might indeed have a granddaughter. But as her story unfolded, he'd felt horror at what she revealed, then dismay.

What did she expect him to do? Take her in without any reservations, without any doubts as to the truth of her claim? "How do I know you are truly my granddaughter? You could just look like my daughter-in-law."

"What is it you want, Mr. Jacoby?"

"Some proof," he stated with no hesitation.

"Yes," she said and stood. "I was told you might wish something to substantiate my claim."

"You have something that will do this?"

Spirit of the Mountain nodded and pulled the medicine pouch she kept tied about her neck out from its hiding place beneath her dress. Carefully, she removed the locket that contained the pictures of her parents and handed it to him.

Jacoby didn't need to open the locket to know what was inside, but he did. His fingers trembled as he touched the image of his son. "This was your grandmother's locket. She gave it to Neil just before she died."

"My father treasured it. It is all I have left to remember them by."

"Why—" Samuel Jacoby had to stop and clear his

throat. "Why didn't Neil come home? Why did he stay away?"

Spirit of the Mountain's pretty brow wrinkled in dismay and confusion. "You disowned my father and did not approve of my mother. Why would you think he would come home?"

"I had hoped he would forgive my stupidity and pride. I had hoped—" He could not finish.

"My mother and father loved each other very much. They made a new life in the wilderness where it did not matter he was a Jacoby and she French. It did not matter I was a child of that unblessed union."

Spirit of the Mountain feared to feel for the man. She was afraid to understand his pain. Nevertheless, she did. Inside her rose the smallest hint of love—a love she never knew might exist for a grandfather she had given no thought to all these years.

Still, the pain she had inherited from her father and mother remained. She was not ashamed of who she was, and she should not allow this man, this stranger, to break into her heart. She struggled with the turmoil inside her.

"Until this moment, I never dreamed I had a grandchild, a granddaughter as beautiful as her mother was. No, even more so, I daresay." Tears swam in Jacoby's eyes; grief lined his face.

"Why did you send them away?" Spirit of the Mountain asked, pain tinting her voice before she could mask it.

"Because I was a fool, my child. I have regretted my actions all these years. Can you forgive an old man his arrogant pride? Is it possible to begin anew?"

Spirit of the Mountain feared to believe him. "My father carried the grief you caused him to his grave, as did my mother your rejection." She took a deep, calming breath. "I do not know if I can forgive you that."

Samuel Jacoby moved to her side and took her hand into his. "I shouldn't expect anything else, but in my heart, I long for it to be."

"What of my past, my life with the Cherokee? Can you accept where I have lived? The family I have loved? The man who was my husband, the child I buried beside him?"

"You are a part of my son, and I will love you, Samantha. Whatever your past will remain in your past. It no longer matters. What matters is that you take your rightful place in the Jacoby family as my granddaughter and heir. Would you grant an old man this one bit of hope and happiness in his last days?"

Spirit of the Mountain wanted to say no; she wanted to deny his request. She opened her mouth, but nothing came out at first. At last, she said, "I do not know you, Mr. Jacoby."

"We will get to know each other. I promise."

"I—" She tried again, but failed again.

Samuel Jacoby looked hopeful. "I beg you. Please don't deny my happiness."

The small flicker of love in her heart stirred to life. It kept her from saying no. This man was her only family. Without him, she was alone in the world. Deep inside, she longed for the very thing he offered. This need grew inside her, pushing aside her doubt and fear. How could her mother have known it would be so?

"I do not think it could hurt to get to know each other better."

The look on his face spoke his joy. The hug he gave her confirmed it. Disturbed by her grandfather, Red finally stuck his head out from the pouch and looked about curiously.

"What's this?" Samuel Jacoby laughed; then he scratched Red's head affectionately.

"This is Red, Grandfather. I hope you do not mind?"

The look that crossed Jacoby's face told her it had not gone unnoticed that she had called him grandfather. He sniffed loudly, then smiled. "Not at all, my dear Samantha."

He stepped away, sobered. "Samantha," he repeated and the smile returned. "My son named you after me."

Spirit of the Mountain returned the smile, this time with warmth, even love. "It was my mother who insisted on Samantha. Despite all that had happened, she was the one who told me about you. My father rarely spoke of you."

"Perhaps he was too much like me. Such traits can carry more harm than good."

Nathan cleared his throat. "I think I should leave you two alone to get better acquainted." He turned to leave, but Samuel Jacoby stopped him.

"Not so fast, young man."

Nathan waited for Jacoby to go on, but he addressed Spirit of the Mountain instead. "I think we should all go home." Then his gaze moved back to Nathan. "I owe you everything, Mr. Walker. I would be pleased if you would be my guest for as long as you like."

An uncomfortable feeling descended on Nathan. "No, I best be going."

Spirit of the Mountain's look became fearful once again, and Nathan felt the agony of leaving her. She moved to stand in front of him, her face telling him all.

"Please, Nathan. I could not bear it if you went so soon. You are the only friend I have."

This time, Samuel Jacoby cleared his throat nervously. "Yes. It would be helpful for Samantha to have a familiar face about while she adjusts to her new life."

When Nathan did not answer, Spirit of the Mountain's look became desperate, an emotion Nathan had never seen on her face.

"You have risked your life many times over for my benefit, Nathan Walker, and I have no right to ask this of you. Yet I find I need your help in facing a world I know little about. I beg you."

The feelings Nathan fought so hard to suppress rushed to the surface. He struggled to control them. He had to get back to his own life. "You know I'd do just about anything for you, Sam. But I cannot stay."

"Just a little while. Then you can return to your life in the wilderness. I promise," she whispered.

Tears filled her eyes, and Nathan was lost. "All right, I'll stay. But remember, just a while longer."

A single tear spilled over her dark lashes, but she brushed it away and smiled. "I will remember."

"Good." Samuel slapped Nathan on the back. "Let's go home, Samantha."

Fela Dawson Scott

*   *   *

"I wanted to take a moment to speak with you in private, Nathan."

Nathan walked over to the leather wing-backed chair Samuel Jacoby pointed to and sat. The library was large. Shelves of books lined the great expanse of walls; a spiraling staircase led to the second-floor galley. Even Jacoby's desk was grand, its cherry wood glistening. The top inset with tooled leather matched the chair he now sat in.

Jacoby had left Samantha in her rooms to rest, but Nathan knew better. There was too much to take in for her to sleep. He could almost see her discovering each and every item in her rooms—seeing, touching, smelling the many objects that must be in them.

Nathan took the brandy Jacoby offered, knowing from the look of the man he wanted to talk about something serious. Nathan had a good idea what.

"To say I am grateful for what you've done says little, Nathan. Words are insignificant when it comes to what I feel about having my granddaughter here with me."

"I had hoped for Sam's sake it would be so. I am happy and relieved that you are willing to accept and love her. It's important for her to be with family."

"Family is everything. Do you have family, young man?"

Nathan looked up from the glass he drank from. "No, there is no one."

Samuel Jacoby nodded in understanding. "My granddaughter seems very fond of you."

It was difficult to keep the emotion from his voice. "Yes, we have been through much together. We've come to trust and depend on one another."

"I would say Samantha is in love with you."

What could Nathan say to that, except the truth? "I believe she is."

Jacoby stepped around the desk to sit directly across from Nathan. "Do you love her?"

"Whether I do or not doesn't matter, Mr. Jacoby. I've made it clear to Sam from the beginning that she belongs here with you, not with me in the wilderness."

A look of great relief flooded Jacoby's face. "Call me Samuel, Nathan."

It wasn't what Nathan had expected to hear, though he expected the man's obvious delight in knowing Nathan did not intend to stay. Old bitterness rose and kept his back rigid, his face devoid of what he truly felt.

"I think you have a great understanding of what is right, my boy. You've done the right thing by bringing her to me."

"She doesn't see it that way," Nathan said, his voice carefully controlled. "But I believe, in time, she will come to understand the decisions that have been made for her."

"You are so right. I am pleased you think this way."

Nathan lifted his snifter in salute. "Here's to your beautiful granddaughter, Samantha."

"Here, here."

Chapter Eighteen

"Are you awake, Samantha?"

Samuel Jacoby stuck his head inside her room after knocking. Spirit of the Mountain looked up from the book she read and smiled. "Yes, grandfather."

He stepped inside. "Why aren't you resting, dear?"

"It seems a strange thing to do, rest in the light of day."

His laughter warmed the pleasant room. "Not many women I know would agree with you."

Spirit of the Mountain put the book aside, then lifted Red from her lap, where he slept. She stood, then put the pup back down. He opened his sleepy eyes, then shut them again, content to remain in the sunshine that spilled over the window seat. "This is a very beautiful room. I never imagined anything so grand in all my life."

"It was one of your grandmother's favorite rooms. She would want it to be yours."

Tears sprang to Spirit of the Mountain's eyes, and a sudden sadness filled her. "I am sorry I never had the chance to know her. Father talked about her often."

Samuel cleared his throat as an old tightness came to it. "She would be pleased we have been given the chance to be together after all this time. It means a lot to me, child. Perhaps God has seen fit to allow me the chance to make amends for all the unhappiness I've caused in the past."

Shyly, she took his hand. "I am pleased, too."

"Come, sit." Samuel pulled her across to the chairs in front of the fireplace. She sat and he took the one opposite hers.

A troublesome thought lingered inside Samuel, left over from his talk with Nathan Walker. "I've spoken with Nathan, and he seems to agree you belong here with me."

"Yes." Spirit of the Mountain looked away to hide her feelings from her grandfather.

He was not fooled. "I can't help but wonder at what has happened between the two of you. Do you love him?"

Again she said yes, but nothing more.

He could feel her pain, and a protective surge warmed him. "This isn't the place for a man like Nathan. You do understand that?"

"I understand, Grandfather."

Suddenly, Samuel felt uncomfortable. He had only just discovered he even had a granddaughter, yet he found himself immediately acting as a parent or guardian would. He did not know if she would want him to assume these responsibilities so soon. "I must pose a very delicate question, Samantha. One I hope you will be truthful about."

Spirit of the Mountain could guess at his query, but waited for him to ask nonetheless.

"I see you two have come to an understanding of your relationship, but as your guardian"—Samuel paused a moment, as if he might not continue—"I must ask if you have been intimate with Nathan."

Spirit of the Mountain had not known what she would say, yet she somehow found the words inside her. "It has been difficult for me to understand the hatred and anger I have witnessed against the red man since leaving the wilderness. Already it has been made painfully clear my past is looked upon with condemnation and ignorance. People have not taken into consideration that I loved my adopted family and my Cherokee husband. They have not thought the loss of my child should have caused me grief."

Spirit of the Mountain stopped because her feelings were difficult to put to words. She took a moment to will the tears away and put the grief of her past into its proper place. "Nathan tried to warn me, to convince me I must not speak openly of my life. I had to learn this lesson, but it does not change what is in my heart."

"The young man is right. Many will not understand. For your own sake, Samantha, you must do as he advised."

Spirit of the Mountain stood and paced in front of her grandfather, too many emotions twisting inside her, creating a fierce energy. "I do not wish to bring shame to you or to the family. I will not speak of my past."

"It is for the best."

"I will not speak of my past, Grandfather." She stopped again and faced him, knowing the seriousness of her tone held his attention. "I consider what was between Nathan and me a part of that past. The truth of our relationship will remain unspoken."

Samuel did not look happy. "I am your grandfather, and you will do as I say."

His words were filled with pride and the same arrogance she was certain had caused the rift between her father and him. "I shall abide by your decisions from this day forward, but you cannot change what has been. You cannot influence what is in my heart."

"Samantha, you do not understand what the consequences of your actions might mean."

"I am not a child."

"Yes." Samuel sighed deeply. "I know you are not a child."

Spirit of the Mountain sat back down. "What is it you are afraid of, Grandfather?"

"I am afraid you and Nathan were lovers."

"And why do you fear this possibility?"

This question seemed to surprise him. "Why? Because it is a shameful thing, Samantha. Shameful indeed."

"There is no shame in loving. I feel no shame in loving my Cherokee people, no shame in loving Nathan." She placed her hand upon Samuel's cheek, from which age had taken the softness. "Honor means everything to me, Grandfather. I would die before bringing dishonor to those I love."

This declaration brought a smile back to his face, and he leaned across to kiss her cheek. "I cannot ask more than that."

Samuel Jacoby stood and moved back to the door. "I've sent someone to find clothes for you and Nathan to change into. Is there anything else you need, Samantha?"

"Yes," she said, following him. "I would like to bathe."

"I'll send someone to help you."

"Please do not bother anyone. I can manage. I just need to know where to find the things I need."

His laughter filled the room again. "That's what the servants are paid to do. They will see you have what you need, and I'll send Lillian to act as your lady's maid."

"A lady's maid?"

"Yes, dear. She will help you dress, do your hair—whatever it is ladies need assistance with."

Spirit of the Mountain felt a blush crawl up her face. "I am not certain I know what it is that ladies need assistance with, Grandfather."

He patted her cheek. "Well, never you mind. Lillian will know what to do. Just follow her guidance."

"Thank you. I will try."

Samuel pulled the door open. "Don't you worry, Samantha. It will all come in time."

She watched the door close behind him and wondered if it really would all come in time. It was all new and confusing. Spirit of the Mountain looked about the sitting room of her two-room suite.

One wall was devoted to a large bay window that had a window seat filled with burgundy floral pillows that invited her to curl up on them and enjoy the sunshine. Velvet drapes the color of the dark green leaves in the pillows framed the window, a sheer veil of burgundy floating behind them.

A huge fireplace took up an entire wall, delicate ceramic tile and brass drawing Spirit of the Mountain's eye. Two comfortable chairs and a cherry table sat in front of it; an ornate lamp was on the polished wood between them. A beautiful desk completed the furnishings.

Spirit of the Mountain walked into the bedroom; this room was bigger than the entire cabin she had grown up in. She would never have thought a single bed could be so big or braced by posts as large as trees. The canopy of delicate lace and silk spread out above it. A satin cover stretched across the great expanse of mattress. Nightstands out of the same rich cherry wood stood beside the bed, ornate lamps exactly like the one in the sitting room sitting upon them. Thick wool rugs warmed the polished mahogany floors.

A giant armoire and a trunk stood open, ready for clothing, though Spirit of the Mountain couldn't imagine needing so much room. Another bay window and chairs, a privacy screen, and a washstand offered all the comforts anyone could ever need in such an elegant room.

Her grandfather had said the rooms were hers now, but they didn't feel like hers. She had known only two homes in her life. The cabin where her mother and father had raised her—two small rooms and a loft—was comfortable, simple. In the Cherokee camp, she had lived with three maternal generations in one lodge. After her marriage, as tradition demanded, her husband had come to live with them.

Now, she was to stay alone in these huge rooms. She studied the bed, and her mind turned to Nathan. She longed to search him out, to—

She stopped herself. She had consented to live in her grandfather's home, and she must show him respect. She must not dishonor him.

Spirit of the Mountain considered her grandfather similar to the way she imagined her father would have been in his older age. She had feared her grandfather's rejection, but he had welcomed her with open arms. Part of her felt joy, another part, apprehension.

As lovely as his home was, it wasn't hers. She longed for the simplicity she had known. Her suite was lavish and large, yet it felt stark, bare of nature's beauty. No birds sang. No trees stirred, tickled by the breeze. Sweet dogwood didn't scent the air, and the soft sounds of the Cherokee camp were only memories in her mind. Homesickness struck her hard, a deep longing. The past weeks she had concentrated on surviving, on getting to Boston. Now, she was there.

Red's howl drifted from the other room, and Spirit of the Mountain returned to the sitting room. He sat in the window seat, looking as lost as she felt. She picked him up and cuddled him close. "Yes, I know," she cooed, quieting his anxiety. "It will be all right, Red."

She continued to comfort him, knowing her words were as much for herself as for the wolf pup. A knock sounded, and a young woman entered. About the same age as Spirit of the Mountain, she was dressed in a black skirt and crisp white blouse. She curtsied and smiled. "I am Lillian."

Spirit of the Mountain didn't know what to do. So she curtsied back, which made Lillian giggle. "I am Samantha."

"May we set up your bath now, Miss Samantha?"

"Yes, thank you," she replied, finding it strange to have someone else waiting on her.

Other servants entered, and it was but a few minutes before a tub was sitting before the fire, filled with steaming water.

"Shall I stay and help you undress?" Lillian asked.

"What?" Spirit of the Mountain wasn't certain she had understood the maid.

Lillian moved closer. "Shall I stay, miss? To help you?"

"I can manage. Thank you."

The young woman nodded politely. "Then I shall see if your dress is pressed. I will return in time for you to dress for dinner. If you need anything, just ring the bell."

Spirit of the Mountain looked about and did not see a bell. "What bell?"

Walking over to a long tapestry pull, Lillian pointed to it. "It will ring in the servants' quarters, Miss Samantha, and I will come right away."

"I would not wish to disturb you, Lillian. I will be fine."

Again, Lillian giggled, but she ended with a shy smile. "You could never disturb me, miss. It is my job."

"But I cannot imagine I would need help for any-

253

thing. I have been taking care of myself for many years."

Lillian looked dismayed. "If you would prefer another maid, I shall talk to Mr. Jacoby."

Spirit of the Mountain had not meant to cause the other woman worry. "No, you most certainly are the best choice, Lillian. It seems I am not very good at being taken care of. I will try harder."

"Good." Lillian's smile returned. "Your grandfather has asked me to take good care of you, and I would not wish to disappoint him."

"No, we would not wish to disappoint him."

"Charles," Samuel called out to his nephew as he walked past the library door. "I'm glad you're home. Could I have a moment of your time?"

Samuel looked at Charles's fiancee, Prycilla, standing now beside Charles. "We won't be but a minute, Prycilla. Charles will join you in the dining room shortly."

"Certainly," she replied smoothly, though Samuel caught the flash of impatience in her eyes.

Prycilla Ryan was not a woman to Samuel's liking. But he knew Charles loved her, and he would not interfere. Charles Haddock was Samuel's sister's only child, and Samuel had taken him into his home upon the death of his sister, the boy's father having died years before in near poverty.

It had been 12 years since his sister's death, and he had begun to think of Charles as his son. Since Samuel's own son, Neil, was gone, there had been no heir to the fortune Samuel had amassed. Charles had eventually taken that position in the Jacoby family—until now.

Samuel had no intention of disinheriting Charles. Samuel loved him, and Charles would be well taken care of for the rest of his life. But Samantha was Samuel's rightful heir, and he must see to his only grandchild. When Samuel was gone, Charles would run the shipyard. The boy was an integral part of the business. Samuel hoped Charles would understand his obligation to the child of his only son.

"I don't know quite where to begin," Samuel said.

Charles sat across the desk from Samuel. "What is it, Samuel? Is there something wrong?"

"No." Samuel smiled. "Actually, everything seems to be right, Charles."

Leaning forward, Charles waited for his uncle to continue. Whatever the news was, it had made Samuel happy. That was apparent by the look on his face, not a common one for his uncle.

"As you know, my son left some twenty years ago. We had a foul disagreement about the woman he wished to marry. I refused to give my blessing, believing her unworthy of the match."

"I remember this." Suddenly, a hopeful notion struck Charles. "Have you had word of your son, Samuel?"

"Yes, I have word of Neil."

It took Charles's breath away. "Is he alive, uncle?"

Samuel looked away and whispered hoarsely. "No, my son died about ten years ago."

"I am sorry."

"The truth is, I lost him long ago. I've no one to blame but myself for this grief. But another blessing has come my way, Charles. I am a fortunate man."

Charles tried to remain patient, but his uncle had a way of prolonging his presentation of even the simplest of notions. "In what way?"

Samuel cleared his throat. "It seems my son and his wife had a child, a girl they named Samantha. I have a granddaughter, my boy."

Shock claimed Charles. "You know this for certain?"

Samuel's firm nod told Charles it was so.

"Where is she?" Charles asked.

"She is here." Samuel's eye lifted to indicate upstairs. "I've put her in the rooms across from you, Charles."

Everything was changing around Charles. He held his breath. It was a long moment before he relaxed a bit and drew in air.

"I know this must be a shock to you, Charles. It was to me as well. But she is my son's daughter. Too many things make it undeniable."

Pulling himself together, Charles stood and offered his hand to Samuel. "I'm very happy for you, Uncle. I know how much it must mean to you to find out Neil had a daughter."

Samuel shook his hand. "This changes little, my boy. Of course, Samantha will be my heir, but she will need you to continue running the business."

"Of course. I would have it no other way, Uncle. You've been more than generous in taking me into your home and business. I am forever grateful."

"I must ask a favor of you, Charles."

"Anything. You have only to ask."

"Samantha has lived her life in the wilderness. She

knows little of Boston or of the kind of life we lead. She could use a friend to help her through what I know must be a difficult, even fearful, time for her."

Charles smiled. "She is my blood as well, Uncle. I would love her without your asking."

"Good!" Samuel put his arm about Charles's shoulder affectionately. "Shall we go to dinner?"

"Yes," Charles drawled. "Prycilla is probably getting impatient with us by now."

"Yes, I'm sure she is."

Chapter Nineteen

Nathan stood outside Samantha's door, waiting for her to answer his knock. He pulled at the collar of the shirt he wore, the high button choking him. Samuel had seen to it he had new clothes to wear, apparel more fitting a gentleman than a man of the wilderness. Nathan knew Samuel would be waiting downstairs for dinner, so he impatiently knocked again.

A servant answered it. "Just one more moment, sir. Miss Jacoby is almost ready."

The servant closed the door, and Nathan stared at the wide expanse. It was but a few seconds before the door opened again, allowing him to enter. He walked into a large sitting room, and the young woman motioned for him to sit.

Before he had even descended upon the cushion, the servant was gone, disappearing into the bedroom. It was obvious from the whispers and giggles Samantha was dressing in there. Red ran up to Nathan and wiggled all over, showing his happiness to see the man. Nathan picked the pup up.

"Feeling a little outnumbered by females, are you?"

Smiling, Nathan looked about the room, which was pleasant and soothing in color and feel. His own room was impeccably decorated, though it had a more masculine tone. So far, everything about the Jacoby home showed wealth and status; every niche was filled with elegant artwork and furniture.

"I am sorry to keep you waiting, Nathan."

Nathan stood and turned to Spirit of the Mountain's voice, the sweet tone sending shivers through him. But the sight before him took his breath away. The midnight-blue velvet of the gown was the same dark shade of her eyes, the color of a clear night sky, almost black in nature. The intricate gold embroidery sparkled against the rich fabric, much like the lamplight reflecting off the honeyed gold in her hair, so carefully arranged to tumble down the lovely curve of her neck.

"I seem to be quite ignorant about most of the clothes I am expected to wear. Lillian proved very helpful."

"Isn't she beautiful, sir?" Lillian asked.

Nathan's gaze remained fixed on Spirit of the Mountain. "She is more than beautiful."

The peachy blush that came to Spirit of the Mountain cheeks was natural and shy. Nathan put Red down and stepped closer, extending his arm to escort her.

"You look quite handsome yourself, Nathan. But I do not think I prefer you in these clothes over your buckskins."

He fidgeted with his collar once more, trying to loosen it without actually undoing the button. "I think I prefer my buckskins, too. But you are perfection in that gown."

Her flush deepened to a rosy hue, her dark blue eyes sparkling vividly. "I feel like I will explode from all the ties, buttons, and petticoats layered beneath this gown. How do women breathe in all this?"

"Miss Jacoby," Lillian whispered in shock. "A lady does not speak of such things with a gentleman."

Nathan laughed out loud. "I might agree, if I were a gentleman."

"And I am far from being a lady, Lillian." Spirit of the Mountain touched Nathan's cheek affectionately. "You need not worry about us. We have been through much and need not feign propriety when together."

"I wish," Nathan whispered for Sam's ears only, "we could toss aside propriety altogether. I would gladly loosen your ties and buttons so you might breathe easier."

Spirit of the Mountain turned away from his heated look. The promise of his words was enough to send her heart thundering. "Lillian, I wonder if I might ask a favor?"

"Anything, miss."

"It took us so long to dress this evening, I have not taken Red for his walk. Would it be a great bother to take him?"

Lillian nodded, a wide and toothy smile splitting

her face. "Not at all. He's the sweetest little thing."

"Thank you. I will allow more time from now on."

"Don't worry over Red. I'll take good care of him while you enjoy your evening with your grandfather. I believe they are waiting for you in the dining room."

"Yes," Nathan said. "We'd best go."

"Is dinner always so formal?"

"Yes." Lillian adjusted a final curl. "Mr. Jacoby has always preferred dressing for dinner. It is tradition in this house."

Nathan pulled Spirit of the Mountain from the room, his look telling her they were late. The same nervous energy she had experienced earlier that day returned.

"There's no need to be nervous, Sam."

Just having Nathan by her side helped calm her, and his look of confidence soothed her fear. "I fear I will never get used to all this formality, Nathan. I already long for the simplicity I left behind."

"I can understand that."

"But you seem so self-assured. You look as if you were born to this sort of life."

His gaze drifted off, a sudden sadness taking the light from his eyes. Spirit of the Mountain stopped before they started down the stairway and made him turn back to her. "What is it, Nathan?"

"It is nothing."

"We should not lie to each other. We know it does not work well."

"I grew up on an estate much like this one. The memories it brings are not welcome."

Spirit of the Mountain became acutely aware of

how little she knew about this man. His youth was a total mystery to her. "Where was this—in America?"

"No, in England."

"There is so much about yourself you have not told me. We have been lovers, as close as any two people can be. But you are still a stranger, Nathan."

Since leaving England, Nathan had never spoken to anyone about his life there. It was something he didn't like to think of, let alone talk about. "My father was a tutor for a wealthy family. I enjoyed all the benefits of wealth without being born into it. It didn't last."

"What happened?"

Nathan's throat tightened, and he had to clear it to continue. "My mother got sick, and the family asked us to leave. I'd lived always on the Rothwell Estate. I didn't know any other life. My mother died, then my father. I was forced to work at thirteen. I barely survived the sweatshops, and in hopes of a better life, I indentured myself to come to America."

Tears came to Spirit of the Mountain's eyes, and Nathan brushed her cheek with a finger. "I found that life here was no better than in England."

"That is why you traveled to the wilderness—to build a life for yourself."

"Something like that," he said. "We'd best get downstairs before they send someone after us."

"Yes." Spirit of the Mountain put her hand back into the crook of his arm. "We had better go downstairs."

Charles took another drink of the sherry he held, needing the extra guard against Prycilla's sharp wit.

262

She seemed in rare form, but that wasn't what he dreaded. The moment he dreaded was yet to come.

He knew his cousin would be down soon. What Charles was not looking forward to was the moment Prycilla learned that Samuel Jacoby had a grand-daughter, an heir who would inherit his fortune.

Taking another drink, he watched his fiancee as she talked with his uncle. An outrageous flirt, she was self-absorbed, but extremely beautiful. Charles suspected she was marrying him merely for his money. What if she broke the engagement because of Samantha Jacoby?

Charles frowned. He knew that Prycilla was no good. But he was hopelessly, helplessly, in love with her. He could not bear the thought of her leaving him.

"Charles." Prycilla's high lilting voice broke into his thoughts.

"Yes, Prycilla?"

"You are frowning, darling. Are you feeling all right?"

"I'm fine."

"Well," she complained, "we all might die from hunger if dinner isn't served soon."

"We apologize if we have inconvenienced you," Nathan said.

Charles looked toward the man's voice, but he did not get past the beauty who stood by the stranger's side. He hadn't really thought about what he expected his cousin to look like, but it wasn't this. He stood and followed Samuel Jacoby to the doorway.

"Not at all," Samuel bellowed. "You look lovely, Samantha."

"Thank you, Grandfather. Lillian works miracles."

"Grandfather?" Prycilla remained in the spot she had been in when Samantha and Nathan entered the room, surprise apparent in the expression on her face.

Samuel took Samantha's hand. "Charles, Prycilla, I'd like to introduce you to Samantha Jacoby, my granddaughter."

Charles stepped forward and bowed graciously. "Welcome home, dear cousin."

"You are my cousin?" Spirit of the Mountain asked.

"Yes, Charles Haddock." His smile prompted another from his cousin. He felt rewarded by the brilliance and warmth of it. "May I present Prycilla Ryan, my fiancee."

Spirit of the Mountain nodded in the direction of the woman her cousin introduced. Immediately she sensed the woman's character. Prycilla was not to be trusted.

"My pleasure," Spirit of the Mountain replied politely. The woman merely nodded, her eyes telling Spirit of the Mountain she felt no pleasure at all.

"This is Nathan Walker," Spirit of the Mountain said, and Nathan and Charles shook hands.

Spirit of the Mountain felt the tension that assaulted everyone, and she wished she could go back to her room. Suddenly, she felt tired, the strain of the day catching up with her. She was not one to run away from a problem, but tonight she was not up to dealing with Prycilla Ryan. Her head began to ache.

"May I escort you into the dining room, cousin?" Charles asked.

"Of course." Spirit of the Mountain tried to smile convincingly.

Nathan watched Spirit of the Mountain and knew something was wrong. When Prycilla swayed up to him and offered her hand for him to take, he knew what was wrong. The look in the woman's eyes told him.

"Nathan, isn't it?"

"Yes."

"What a surprise," she cooed, "to find out Samuel has a granddaughter after all these years."

"Yes."

The hand delicately touching his arm tensed. He stopped and pulled out a dining chair.

"Thank you, Nathan."

"You're welcome."

Coyly, she lifted her gaze to meet his. "You don't talk much, do you, Nathan?"

"I do when I have something to say."

"Tell me. What do you have to do with all this?"

"All what?"

Nathan knew he was irritating Prycilla, but he couldn't stop himself. She maintained a cool exterior. Only the snap in her eyes told him how she truly felt.

"What have you to do with the sudden appearance of Samantha Jacoby? I can't help but think this is quite strange, for her to suddenly appear out of nowhere."

"Yes, I suppose it could be thought of as strange."

Brown eyes darkened with anger and turned away. Then Nathan took the seat Samuel pointed at across from Spirit of the Mountain. His gaze met hers. He

Fela Dawson Scott

felt her anxiety and wished he could ease it.

"Samuel," Prycilla said.

"Yes, my dear."

"I don't mean to be the one to question this heartwarming reunion, but how do you know this woman is who she says she is? It has been over twenty years since your son went away."

"I have no doubt Samantha is my granddaughter. That should be sufficient for you and Charles."

Samuel Jacoby had more patience than Nathan would have thought.

"If you say so, Samuel."

"I say so."

Prycilla bit her lower lip, as if calculating her next move. Nathan watched her closely, certain she, not Charles, would be the one to cause trouble for Spirit of the Mountain. For a brief second, his gaze moved to Charles. No, it would be the woman to cause trouble.

"Tell me, Nathan," Samuel said, drawing Nathan's attention from Prycilla. "What did you do in the wilderness? Trap?"

"Yes."

"Nathan lost his canoe and all his traps on my account," Spirit of the Mountain said. "He also used all the money he made this spring to get us here."

"It doesn't matter," Nathan said firmly. Then he added more gently, "It was worth it, Sam."

"I shall see your losses are made up to you, my boy. You will never know how much it means to me to have my granddaughter home with me."

"I can imagine, sir. As I said, it doesn't matter."

"No sense in—"

"It was my choice. I expect nothing for what I have done."

Spirit of the Mountain heard the finality of Nathan's words. She regretted having mentioned his valiant efforts on her behalf. But she wanted him to have the things he had lost risking his life to save hers. Pain pounded at her temples.

"Is that where you have been all these years, Samantha? In the wilderness?" Prycilla asked sharply.

Turning to the woman, Spirit of the Mountain concentrated on her words, the pain in her head making doing so difficult. "Yes, I was born in the Smoky Mountain wilderness."

"I thought only Indians lived in the wilderness," Charles said.

His question made Spirit of the Mountain turn her head to him. Her movement was uncomfortable and stiff. "My father and mother had a small cabin in the mountains. The Indians left us alone."

"How frightening!" Prycilla moved her hand to her throat to touch the lace that spilled forth. "I can't imagine such a life."

"It was a good life," Spirit of the Mountain said with pride. Prycilla had made it sound like a curse.

"Of course." Prycilla smiled, but no warmth touched her eyes, which remained unbelieving.

The layers of clothing covering Spirit of the Mountain became stifling, the bodice too tight, pushing the air from her lungs. She struggled to bring her breathing and thinking under control.

"I have a wonderful idea, Samuel," Prycilla said.

"What is that, Prycilla?"

"Samantha might need a woman's guidance while

she becomes familiar with her new home and Boston. Since Charles and I will be wed this next winter, I could go ahead and move in. That way I can be here for Samantha."

The dread Spirit of the Mountain had experienced earlier intensified. "It would be too much to ask of you."

"Not at all, darling. I would love molding you into a fine lady—a lady deserving of the Jacoby name."

"Samantha's just fine the way she is," Samuel said. "But it might not be a bad idea. I'm sure Samantha could use some guidance, as you said."

"I could start moving my things tomorrow." Prycilla's eyes took on a determined gleam. "I thought I might take the beautiful rooms at the end of the hall, Samuel."

"I put Samantha in those rooms, Prycilla. You'll have to choose others."

"Oh."

"It would be no trouble to change, Grandfather." Spirit of the Mountain didn't know exactly why she was making such an offer.

"Nonsense. You don't mind, do you, dear?"

Prycilla's eyes widened, but her smile was perfect, as was her voice. "Of course not. I just remembered how beautiful they were. You stay, Samantha. I wouldn't dream of moving you."

"Then it's settled," Samuel declared happily.

Charles wondered at his fiancee. He had never known her to be generous of her time, especially for another woman. He found himself suspicious of her motives. He loved and desired her, but he didn't trust her—not for a moment.

268

*   *   *

"Are you all right, Sam?"

Spirit of the Mountain and Nathan had stopped in the hall, only a step from her bedroom door. She took a deep breath to ease the pulsating beat in her head. "I seem to have a headache."

Nathan laughed, making the wonderful warm sound that Spirit of the Mountain liked so much. She looked up into his green eyes and found the twinkle that always accompanied his laughter.

"I can understand why. Prycilla seems to be a woman we will have to contend with."

"Yes," she agreed, then realized what he had said. "We?"

"I couldn't abandon you to her—not until you are better equipped."

This promise made her smile. "In what way do I need to be better equipped, Nathan?"

His face turned serious. "You are too trusting, Sam. You need to learn about these people and how to deal with them."

"These people?"

Nathan looked ahead, his gaze no longer on her. "The rich lead a different life. They think differently, act differently. Everything about them is related to money, heritage, and family in ways very unlike anything you have ever known."

"What if I do not wish to be a part of this kind of life, Nathan?"

"Give it time, Sam. Your grandfather can give you everything you could ever wish out of life."

She thought on this statement. "Would you accept this life, if it were given to you?"

Nathan sighed. "At one time, it was all I thought I wanted."

"But given the chance now, what would you do?"

"I wouldn't stay. I would go back where I belong."

"You tell me I belong here, with my family, my blood. But in my heart, I belong to the mountains."

A great sadness filled his eyes. "How can you be so certain you belong to the mountains?"

She smiled and placed her hand on his. "I just know. My spirit belongs to an animal that is wild and free. How can I live here, away from the wilderness, the very thing that gives my spirit life?"

Nathan reached out to open her door. "Will you be all right?"

Spirit of the Mountain understood his question. "It will take some getting used to, but I will be fine."

She looked away, suddenly shy. "The bed is so large. It will seem empty."

"I'd best say good night," Nathan whispered, his voice strained, "or I'll not be going at all."

"Good night, Nathan." Spirit of the Mountain quickly brushed a kiss across his lips, then slipped inside. The room was dark, except for a small lamp that burned by the door. She picked it up and made her way to the bedroom.

Seeking out the basket where Red slept, she put the lamp aside and picked him up. He opened sleepy eyes and yawned wide. She hugged him to her. "At least I have you to keep me warm, my friend."

Chapter Twenty

"Good morning, Nathan."

Nathan looked up and smiled. As always, the green depths of his eyes twinkled with pleasure. Spirit of the Mountain felt the same delight in seeing him. The night in her new room was long and endless, the bed strange and empty.

"You are up early," he said softly.

She pulled a chair out and started to sit across from him. The cook stopped her work and gasped. "Miss Jacoby," she stuttered in surprise. "I didn't know you'd be up so early. You should have rung, dear. I would have sent a tray up to you."

Spirit of the Mountain could see the servant's dismay in the blush that crept up her neck finally reaching her plump cheeks and face. "I would not wish to bother you. With so much to tend to, you need not worry over me."

Another gasp came from the portly woman. "It is no trouble, no trouble at all."

Uncertain what to do, Spirit of the Mountain looked to Nathan for guidance. She did not wish to do anything to offend the cook, but she certainly did not need a breakfast tray brought up to her room. His smile widened, and she knew he would be of little help to her.

"Mrs.—" Spirit of the Mountain realized she did not know her name. She had been introduced to so many members of the household staff that their names had not stuck in her mind.

"Mrs. Winters," the cook offered with a blink, a nod, and a smile.

"Mrs. Winters, would it be all right if I had something to eat here?"

This request made her eyes widen further. "Here? In the kitchen, miss?"

"Yes." Spirit of the Mountain hesitated, seeing the look of horror on the woman's face. "I would like to join Mr. Walker."

Mrs. Winters's round eyes traveled to Nathan, then back to Spirit of the Mountain. "If it is what you wish, Miss Jacoby, I will set you a place on the kitchen table. Would you prefer coffee or tea with your breakfast?"

"I will have whatever Mr. Walker is having."

"Yes, miss."

When the cook turned back to her work, Spirit of the Mountain sat. She leaned over and spoke in a whisper so the cook wouldn't hear. "What is so terribly wrong with having breakfast with you, Nathan?"

"I don't know that it's having breakfast with me. It's more where you are having it. Most ladies of the house would not eat in the kitchen."

"Why not?" The notion seemed absurd to Spirit of the Mountain.

"The kitchen table is for servants and staff. Many ladies would consider it beneath them."

"But you are here, in the kitchen."

He sighed, as if weary of their talk. "It's different for me."

"Why is that? You are my grandfather's guest and should not be expected to take your meals with the servants."

Nathan looked away, and Spirit of the Mountain wasn't able to see what came to his eyes. "I am his guest, but I am not his equal. The kitchen is where I belong."

Spirit of the Mountain placed her hand over his. "But you and I are the same. After all we have been through, nothing can change what we are."

Nathan turned back, and a hardness claimed his eyes, a look Spirit of the Mountain had not seen before. He pulled his hand away. "You and I are no longer the same, Samantha. What we had, what we have been through, is all in the past. Everything has changed."

"Only you think this. I do not."

Nathan found himself frustrated by her stubbornness. How could he convince her of the barrier that lay between them. "You and I come from two different worlds, Sam. We cannot change that."

"But we are not from different worlds. You are the one who fails to see this. Neither the blood that runs in our veins nor the color of our skin matter. What does matter is what lies in our hearts, where our spirits long to be."

"You are wrong. You belong here with your grandfather, your family."

"No," Samantha whispered sadly, her eyes filled with the dismay that vibrated in her voice. "I came here because it is what you believed was right, because my mother would have wanted me to. I will stay because it is what my grandfather longs for. But do not let what I do for the sake of others deceive you. I know what lies in my heart. I belong in the mountains. I belong with you, Nathan Walker."

Nathan stood. He could not bear to listen any longer. A small part of him was beginning to think what Spirit of the Mountain had said was true, but he knew his heart was merely teasing him with what could never be. He understood that as plainly as the fact that day came after night.

"You cannot be with me, Sam. It's best you understand this and go on with your life."

Prycilla did as she said and moved in. It amazed Spirit of the Mountain that any one person could have so many things. The string of people carrying Prycilla's personal property to her new rooms was endless. Her voice broke the quiet. Her commands to the servants were sharp, brooking no argument. "Don't wrinkle that dress, you fool."

"Yes, miss."

Spirit of the Mountain paused before she entered

her own room. Lillian scurryed out of the suite down the hall, tears swimming in her eyes. Spirit of the Mountain motioned for the servant to come to her room, and they entered her sitting room.

"Yes, miss. Is there something you need?"

"No." Spirit of the Mountain smiled. She took the girl's hand and led her to the window seat. She pointed to the pillows, and they sat. "You must not let Prycilla's harsh words upset you, Lillian."

"No, miss."

"I think Prycilla is best taken in small doses."

"Oh, Miss Jacoby." Lillian's eyes widened in surprise, but a tremble of a smile threatened to appear. "You shouldn't say such things."

"It is true. I am afraid I do not know any other way but to speak the truth."

A giggle finally escaped, and Lillian brushed the tears from her eyes. "Thank you, Miss Jacoby. You seem to understand people very well."

"I have known Miss Ryan only a single day, but already I think it best we face her together. Perhaps if we team up, we can keep from doing her harm."

This offer made Lillian burst out laughing. Spirit of the Mountain couldn't help but join her.

"Miss Jacoby, you are so funny."

"But, Lillian, I am quite serious. Prycilla is a person who could try the patience of a saint."

"Yes, I believe she is." Lillian suppressed another giggle.

"Then we agree. We shall support each other when Prycilla is around."

Lillian nodded. "Agreed."

A sharp, rapid knock sounded. It was obvious that

the very woman they spoke of was behind the door. Spirit of the Mountain patted Lillian's hand and stood. "You stay here. There is no need to get up."

Spirit of the Mountain went to the door, but before she could reach it, another impatient knock came. She purposely hesitated a moment before answering it.

"Yes, Prycilla."

"I'm looking for that silly girl. What's her name? Lilly?"

"Lillian?" Spirit of the Mountain asked innocently.

"Yes," Prycilla drawled, her eyes scrunching up with anger. "She's a clumsy idiot, but it seems she's the best I can do in this house. Have you seen her?"

"I have been out walking Red. I just now returned to my room."

"And *what* is Red?"

Spirit of the Mountain had always thought herself a patient person. There had been few people she could think of in her life she disliked. But now she found herself having to control her emotions, to hide the fact she wanted nothing more than to slam the door in this woman's face. What was more amazing was it was for little reason other than that she felt distrust and dislike when she was near Prycilla.

"Red is my pet."

"Your pet? What kind of pet, Samantha?"

Each word, each second that passed between them only intensified Spirit of the Mountain's instincts. This woman was not to be trusted. "He is a puppy."

"What kind of puppy?"

"He is a wolf. A red wolf." Whatever possessed

276

Spirit of the Mountain to be so blunt was beyond her at that moment.

Prycilla sucked in air, the sound reminding Spirit of the Mountain of a snake. The woman recoiled, just like the reptile Spirit of the Mountain had imagined. It was almost too much for her to keep the smile that twitched at her lips down. Her irritation was relieved for the moment.

"You have a wild animal in this house?"

"Yes, I guess I do."

Prycilla puffed up with importance. "We shall see just how long you keep the dirty little creature."

Maintaining her composure, Spirit of the Mountain merely smiled. "I will keep Red as long as he lives, Prycilla."

Narrow eyes became tiny slits, the hate in them unleashed. "That can be arranged."

Spirit of the Mountain grabbed the woman's wrist as she backed away and pulled her closer. "Since we are being honest with each other, Prycilla"—she increased the pressure on Prycilla's wrist, and pain showed clearly in the woman's eyes—"I want you to know I would not like it if Red were harmed in any way. Do I make myself clear?"

"Let go of me, Samantha."

"Do I make myself clear?"

"Yes," Prycilla mumbled weakly, then stepped back when Spirit of the Mountain let her go. Prycilla pulled her chin up haughtily, but a little fear remained in her eyes. "I was just joking, Samantha. You really must learn when someone is jesting."

"You may jest about many things, Prycilla." Spirit

of the Mountain's voice remained hard. "But not about Red."

"I will remember that."

Spirit of the Mountain watched Prycilla scramble back across to her rooms.

"Is it true?" Lillian asked.

She turned to Lillian. "Is what true?"

"That the puppy is a wolf."

"Yes. Does that make a difference?"

"No, miss. He's just about the cutest little puppy I've ever seen. I'll make sure Miss Ryan doesn't hurt him."

The devotion on the girl's face was touching. "Thank you, Lillian. I do not trust Miss Ryan."

"Are you feeling a little more settled this evening, Samantha?" Samuel asked.

Spirit of the Mountain looked up from the plate of food she studied. She had decided most of the dishes—the chowder, the fish, the variety of vegetables, and the brown bread were quite good. But the oysters were not to her liking.

"Yes, everything is fine, Grandfather."

Samuel seemed to think on something; then he addressed Charles. "Charles, perhaps you should take Samantha and Nathan for a ride tomorrow."

"What a lovely idea," Prycilla piped up; then her brow wrinkled in dismay. "You do know how to ride?"

"Yes, I do."

"Wonderful." Prycilla smiled politely, but her eyes challenged Spirit of the Mountain.

"I've decided to have a ball to present Samantha to Boston," Samuel said.

This announcement brought Spirit of the Mountain's surprised gaze back to her grandfather. "A ball?"

"Yes, I want all of Boston to know you have come home."

She didn't know what to say.

"Are you pleased, Samantha?" Her grandfather looked anxious.

"Yes," she mumbled, uncertainty too obvious in the single-word reply. Spirit of the Mountain tried to repair the damage. "I am very pleased."

"Samuel," Prycilla said, breaking into the conversation. "Perhaps it is all a little much for Samantha. After all, she knows nothing of society and what is expected of her."

"Nonsense." Samuel waved his hand through the air. "Samantha has nothing to worry about."

This assurance made Spirit of the Mountain wonder just what there was to worry about. The thought of meeting Boston society did not put her at ease. In fact, it created a pain in her stomach. But the last person in the world she wanted to know this was sitting across from her, a caring look carefully posed on her face.

"I will be fine, Grandfather. When will this ball be?"

"Saturday night. I've already arranged for you to be fitted for a new wardrobe." He glanced at his nephew's fiancee. "You will help her with all this, Prycilla?"

"Of course." She smiled, as if victorious in some

unknown way. "That is what I am here for: to help Samantha adjust to her new home."

"You're a dear. Nathan, I've also taken the liberty of arranging for a tailor to come to fit you as well. It wouldn't do to have you attend my granddaughter's ball in your buckskins."

Nathan's look never changed. "That was kind of you, Mr. Jacoby."

"Samuel, my boy. Call me Samuel. Is your room comfortable?"

"Very."

"Good. Good. Charles, I think you should spend the next week showing these two Boston."

"It would be my pleasure, Uncle."

Spirit of the Mountain drew in a long breath, filling her lungs with the fresh night air. She raised her eyes to gaze at the star-filled sky. It looked the same as it did in the mountains, only here it felt very different.

Sadness gripped her, strong and unrelenting. Spirit of the Mountain bit her lower lip to keep the tremble still, then blinked back the swarm of tears that filled her eyes. How she longed to leave this place, which was so crowded with people and buildings.

The tree she stood next to rustled softly in the slight breeze, the sound soothing. She closed her eyes and envisioned herself back at home; the trickle of a nearby fountain sounded like the stream in which she had bathed nightly. Spirit of the Mountain sniffed the smoky air. It became no longer the smoke of many fireplaces, but that of the cook fire within her family's lodge.

Mentally, Spirit of the Mountain shed the layers of stifling clothing she wore and returned to the simple dress of the Cherokee. Her feet forgot the uncomfortable aching caused by stiff shoes, and they wiggled in the supple leather of moccasins painstakingly worked into softness by her own hands.

"You look as if you're in another world, Samantha."

Spirit of the Mountain had been aware of Charles's presence, smelling the cologne he wore sparingly, but she had been so happy in her thoughts she'd hoped he would not disturb her.

"I'm sorry if I startled you," he said.

"No, I knew you were there, Charles. I was merely being selfish. I apologize."

"I'm afraid I do not understand."

"I was in another world. I did not wish to return so soon."

"Then I should leave you to your solitude." He bowed low and started to leave.

"No, Charles, please stay."

Charles smiled and stepped closer. "Wherever it was, it made you very happy."

"Yes, it did."

Curiosity got the best of Charles. He wanted to know more about this woman, his cousin. "If I might ask, where did your mind travel to?"

Samantha turned away from Charles to hide the sadness she knew once again overtook her features. "I was back in the mountains."

"Are you not happy here?" The thought that his

cousin might not be happy in her new home, with her grandfather, had not occurred to Charles before.

She waited a moment, as if determining exactly what to say before speaking. "I am happy to have found my grandfather. Family has always meant a great deal to me, and you two are the only family I have now."

Charles didn't speak immediately because she seemed not to have finished her thoughts. Finally, he asked, "And?"

Dark blue eyes watched him, studied him, and he thought how serious they were for one so young.

"I am grateful for my grandfather's acceptance." Spirit of the Mountain looked away shyly. "And yours."

Charles reached out and turned her back to him. "If given the choice, would you go back?"

"It seems the choice is not mine to make."

A sense of the necessity of fairness rose inside Charles. He wanted to know the truth. "Please, Samantha. Tell me what you truly want."

"I would go back."

This answer amazed him. "Go back to the mountains? To the wilderness? But you have everything you could ever want here. You will lack for nothing."

A sigh drifted from Samantha. "My grandfather is here. That is all I am staying for."

"But you are his heir. Someday you will inherit all his wealth. You will be rich beyond your dreams."

Spirit of the Mountain knew Charles could not understand her, not completely. They valued different things in life. "My dreams are not about wealth, Charles. I belong in the mountains, where I was born, where my spirit can survive."

This time, Charles turned away, his hand pushing at his hair in confusion. "You will change your mind when Boston isn't so strange and new to you."

"I have felt at war with the people I trust most in the world. Everyone tells me that I belong here, that this is my destiny. But I know the truth. I know where I belong, if only I could follow my heart's longing."

Charles's eyes moved back to her. "You will stay?"

"I have promised Grandfather the chance to be a family."

"I am glad you did."

His words were sincere. Spirit of the Mountain felt his acceptance. "Thank you, cousin. I must go in now."

Charles watched Samantha leave, then started to return to the house himself.

"What has gotten into you?" Prycilla's sharp voice announced her sour mood; her steps as she approached him told that she had overheard his conversation. It didn't surprise him she had lurked in the shadows eavesdropping.

"I don't know what you mean, dear?"

Liquid brown eyes filled with venom. "You certainly do, Charles. Don't play games with me. You won't win."

It was true. She could outmaneuver and outtalk him any day. "Forgive me, Prycilla. I must have lost my mind for the moment."

"It's that witch of a woman. She's twisting you about her finger already."

Her reaction to Samantha was not unexpected, but

it didn't make it any less difficult for Charles. "I assure you, Prycilla, you are the only woman who has me twisted about her finger."

A slow smile finally turned her frown. "What are we going to do about her, Charles?"

Prycilla's voice had taken on a singsong effect. Charles was aware of her manipulation. He was helpless to her whims. "We can do nothing. The sooner you come to terms with that, the sooner we can go on with our lives as planned."

A delicate, perfect brow told him she did not like his answer. "But, Charles, she's going to get all you have worked so hard for. It's not fair. You've invested years in the business, and she waltzes in here and claims it all."

"She is Uncle's granddaughter. I am his nephew."

Her lower lip pouted out, reminding Charles of a child denied a piece of candy. "You surely cannot mean to let it be without a fight? For once, be a man, Charles."

This comment hurt Charles deeply, but he did not wish for Prycilla to know it. "I intend to be a gentleman about this. I did not come here with my uncle's wealth in mind. He has been more than generous in the past, and he has assured me he will be so in the future. Leave it be, Prycilla. I am still perfectly capable of keeping you in the manner you have grown accustomed to. It will make no difference, I promise."

She said no more, but suspicion reigned in Charles's mind. Prycilla was greedy. What he could give her wasn't enough. But no matter the consequences, he would not turn into the type of man she wanted him to be—even if it meant not having her as his wife.

Perhaps, deep inside, there was a small part of him that wanted her to leave him. But the larger part—a foolish part of him—still loved her deeply, passionately. Charles had fallen for the beautiful, impetuous woman before he had truly known what she was like, and that emotion seemed to dominate him, no matter what common sense told him. He was helpless to end what could be the greatest mistake of his life.

Chapter Twenty-one

"I told Charles and Nathan to go on ahead, that we'd catch up with them." Prycilla turned her head and tossed an innocent look in Spirit of the Mountain's direction. "I hope you don't mind."

"Not at all," Spirit of the Mountain assured her, though a flash of suspicion crossed her mind as they walked to the stables.

The building housed many horses, and each stall was neat and tidy, as was true of the entire Jacoby estate. Spirit of the Mountain had yet to see a speck of dust, a fading bloom, or an out-of-place object.

The Jacoby manor was located in a lavish neighborhood of Boston, its many acres of gardens, stables, and pastures giving it a secluded feeling. Everywhere Spirit of the Mountain looked, busy workers were keeping the place picture perfect.

The stableboy brought their horses out, and Prycilla mounted first. She turned and waited for Spirit of the Mountain to do the same. Spirit of the Mountain didn't have any idea how to sit in the strange-looking saddle the frisky animal sported. A smirk lay just beneath Prycilla's smile, as if she waited for Spirit of the Mountain to make a fool of herself.

Spirit of the Mountain smiled back. "Prycilla, I fear my horseback-riding skills are quite primitive compared to yours. I truly do not know how to mount, let alone sit in this type of saddle."

It seemed Prycilla had not expected a compliment. She opened her mouth to comment, but hesitated before the words came out. "It's really quite simple."

She guided her mare closer. "Just sit sideways. Then wrap your leg about the saddle horn like this."

Spirit of the Mountain did as directed and found herself seated. "It feels odd."

"You will get used to it, I'm sure." Prycilla urged her horse into a gallop. "We really must hurry before the gentlemen get too far ahead."

The stableboy handed the reigns to Spirit of the Mountain, his smile saying much. "Very good, miss," he mumbled.

Spirit of the Mountain understood he wasn't referring to her managing the saddle, but her thwarting Prycilla in her attempt to get the best of her.

"Thank you." She smiled back, then pushed ahead to catch the disappearing mare and its temperamental rider.

Sheer determination and strength kept Spirit of the Mountain on the horse, the saddle's position making her feel she could fall at any time. Slowly, she began to relax, and by the time they caught up to Charles and Nathan, Spirit of the Mountain was actually beginning to enjoy herself.

Nathan rode back to meet her. "I see you managed the sidesaddle. I forgot to warn you."

Spirit of the Mountain pulled to a stop. "I think that is the reason for your being sent ahead, Nathan. It would not have been as much fun if you had been there to rescue me from my moment of ignorance."

Green eyes twinkled mischievously. "I take it it was not as much fun as expected."

Prycilla's moods were quite apparent; even her horse was nervous and skittish as she needled it with her riding crop. Spirit of the Mountain felt sorry for Prycilla. She did not seem a happy person.

Nathan and Spirit of the Mountain followed Charles and Prycilla. They left the Jacoby property and eventually ended up in a park, moving from light into darkness. The trees rose above them in a green umbrella, casting giant shadows, cooling the park despite the sun's warmth.

Spirit of the Mountain smelled the pine-scented air, which was tainted only by the lingering smell of Prycilla's perfume. High in the trees, squirrels scurried from branch to branch, and chipmunks chattered to each other, quickly disappearing from sight as the group rode by.

Bird songs and the rattle of a woodpecker hard at work drifted to Spirit of the Mountain's ears. A shallow stream wound through the trees, and the eyes of raccoons shone in the shadows as the animals washed their food at its edge. The grunt of a wild pig as he rooted for acorns echoed from the thick growth of trees, and the cry of a hawk overhead carried down on the soft breeze. The steady rhythm of the horses' hooves was muffled in the matting of needles and leaves that softened the earth.

It was the closest Spirit of the Mountain had felt to home since leaving the wilderness. "May we stop for a little while?"

Charles slowed and turned back to Spirit of the Mountain. "Of course." He dismounted and helped Prycilla from her horse.

Nathan did the same for Spirit of the Mountain. She felt the brush of his body as his strong arms lifted her to the ground. The sensation his action created was immediate.

He hesitated a second before releasing her. "Have I told you how beautiful you are today?"

The whisper of his words tickled her ear, but the intent in his voice made her shiver. "No, you have not."

"I shouldn't be so neglectful," Nathan said, then stepped away. "You are like a breath of fresh air, Samantha."

The look in his eyes told her he, too, was disturbed by the intense attraction that rose so naturally between them. Unable to bear the heat that sizzled inside her, suddenly too warm in the many layers of clothing she wore, Spirit of the Mountain walked away.

She examined each delicate blossom she came across, enjoying the sweet scents each offered. Lost in her own thoughts, Spirit of the Mountain didn't pay attention to where she wandered; she merely wandered.

Fela Dawson Scott

Charles approached Nathan, a worried frown puckering his forehead. Nathan waited for the question he obviously had on his mind.

"Samantha shouldn't wonder off alone like this."

Nathan merely smiled. "I think she prefers to be alone for the moment."

This answer didn't seem to satisfy Charles. "Someone should be with her, don't you think?"

"No," Nathan answered simply. "She will be fine."

Charles cleared his throat nervously. "I know this isn't the wilderness—"

"No, it isn't."

"But there are wild animals in this park, Nathan."

"Yes, I believe there are."

A redness rose from Charles's neck up into his face. "I don't mean to persist, but I feel I should look after my cousin's welfare."

Nathan grinned. "I know that, Charles. Forgive my bad manners. Your cousin is quite at home in an environment like this. She doesn't need you looking after her, I'm sure."

"Just the same, I'd feel better if one of us was with her." Charles started after her.

Nathan watched him leave, then casually turned his attention to the woman who watched him.

"You two are lovers," Prycilla said.

Her comment wasn't posed as a question, at least not in tone, so Nathan didn't answer. He neither denied nor confirmed the notion in Prycilla's mind.

"It's quite obvious. Neither of you has bothered to hide the fact." When he still said nothing, Prycilla came closer, standing directly in front of him. "I would think you'd be a good lover, Nathan."

Boldly, she reached out and took his hand. She examined it, her fingers lightly running over the callouses. "I would think you'd be a gentle lover, despite such strong, rough hands."

He pulled free. "I would think you'd be an unfaithful lover, despite what you pretend to be."

Her sappy, sweet look turned hard in a flash. The seductiveness in her liquid brown eyes turned to fire. "How dare you speak to me in such a way."

Nathan raised an eyebrow along with his shoulders to show he cared little, dared much. "You brought it up."

Her hand snaked out, but Nathan caught her wrist before she could slap him across the face. His grip was tight enough to tell her she shouldn't attempt such a thing again, light enough not to cause too much pain.

When he let go, Prycilla stepped back, anger darkening her creamy-white complexion. "You arrogant son of a bitch. I should have Charles—"

"Do what?"

"You are no better than a servant to Samuel Jacoby. He's merely tolerating your presence because you brought his granddaughter back to him."

If her words were meant to upset Nathan, they didn't succeed. Stronger, more damaging, hurts from childhood had inured him from such attacks.

"What you or Samuel Jacoby thinks of me matters little to me. Only Samantha's happiness is important. You would do well to remember that, Miss Ryan."

"You are a pathetic excuse for a man."

This insult made him laugh. "And you are a pathetic excuse for a woman."

Prycilla gasped and stomped her delicate foot before she whirled about and walked off in search of Charles. Nathan was glad to be rid of her.

Charles watched Samantha from the cover of the trees, not wanting to disturb the pleasant picture she offered. She sat on the ground in the midst of a bed of wildflowers, a white-tail deer nibbling on some morsel she offered.

It seemed such a natural thing, his cousin feeding and petting a wild animal. He didn't move; he just continued to watch her, wondering what her home must have been like.

"Charles."

Prycilla's angry voice broke the silence and startled the doe. The animal bounded off, and Samantha stood, brushing off grass and twigs that clung to her riding clothes.

"Charles." Prycilla broke through the trees, each step purposeful, determined.

Charles waited for Prycilla to reach him. "What is it, dearest?"

"How could you leave me with that man?"

Confusion clouded his mind. "What man? Nathan?"

"Yes. He is a brute, a cad, a simpleton with no manners."

"What did you say to irritate him, Prycilla?"

"Me," she cried, her eyes widening. "What makes you think I did anything?"

"Just a guess." All this did not bode well.

"Well, you are wrong. Dead wrong. I did nothing.

He is merely a bore, and I'll not spend another second alone with him."

Spirit of the Mountain could hear the whining tone. She did not necessarily need to understand the words to know Prycilla was angry. Regret rose within her. How was she ever to get along with this woman? Although she did not wish to be near the others, she walked over to them.

"I think we'd best start back," Charles said.

"Yes." Prycilla held her hand to her head. "I have an excruciating headache."

"I am sorry you are not feeling well, Prycilla."

The woman turned her back to Spirit of the Mountain. "We must hurry."

Charles lingered with Spirit of the Mountain. "I regret interrupting our outing. You seemed to be enjoying yourself."

"Yes, I was. Perhaps Nathan and I can ride back in a little while. You should take Prycilla home so she can lie down and rest."

"Yes, that seems a good idea." He paused before they rejoined the others. "I hope you don't mind, but I was watching you feeding the doe."

"Yes, I knew you were there."

"I was hidden by the trees. You couldn't possibly have seen me."

"I could not see you, Charles, but I knew you were there."

Spirit of the Mountain left Charles and returned to where Nathan waited. Prycilla was by her horse, her back stiff, her look deadly. Charles appeared and faithfully attended his fiancee.

"I shall see you for dinner then?" Charles asked.

"Yes." Spirit of the Mountain smiled and waved Charles on. "I hope you are feeling better by then, Prycilla."

Prycilla rode off, her riding crop once again thumping the poor animal into a faster pace.

"It seems I am to blame for Miss Ryan's foul mood," Nathan said. He looked serious, but a twinkle remained in his eyes.

"Are you?"

"Yes, I don't think she likes me much."

"Why is that, do you think?"

He stepped closer, the soft scent of him filling Spirit of the Mountain's senses. "I don't seem to have the patience you do, Samantha. How can you maintain such composure with a woman like that?"

"It is not so difficult, Nathan." Spirit of the Mountain stepped away to clear her mind of his presence. He was the one whom she had difficulty maintaining her composure around. "She seems harmless enough."

Nathan reached out and pulled her back around to him. "Prycilla Ryan is more dangerous than you think. You should be careful."

"You need not worry, Nathan. She is only as dangerous as I allow her to be."

"I hope you are right. Did you know we are all alone?" His mood had changed. It was reflected in his tone and the look in his eyes.

"I think," she whispered, her own feelings changing as quickly as his, "you are the one who is dangerous."

Nathan's brows raised in mock surprise. He

stepped closer, and their bodies touched. "Me? Dangerous?"

"Yes." She tried to break the hold his gaze had on her, but found she could not turn away.

His arms slid around her, warm and hard. She closed her eyes. Nathan's lips moved as he spoke, brushing her cheek softly. "I've longed to hold you in my arms, Samantha. I have promised to keep from you, and yet I'd risk condemnation and hell itself to have you."

Soft, wet lips took hers. They were sweet and tender at first, then passionate, desperate. Like water bursting its dam, emotion flooded through Spirit of the Mountain. Even the years she had mourned for her Cherokee husband had not created such longing as the short time Nathan and she had remained apart from each other.

Nathan reeled from the passion that surged through him, the pain in his loins crying out for release. He sensed Spirit of the Mountain's surrender and knew he could take her right there.

It was the hardest thing he had ever done, but Nathan pushed away from her. "God, Sam, what am I to do?"

She said nothing, the confusion in her eyes making him feel like the heel he was.

"We'd best get back home before I change my mind and make love to you right here and now. And damn everyone."

Gently, he guided her back to her mount and lifted her into the saddle.

Spirit of the Mountain said nothing, and Nathan was grateful not to have to speak again.

Chapter Twenty-two

The gown lay across Spirit of the Mountain's bed, its dark burgundy color shimmering almost black with richness in the firelight. Delicate lace spilled out from the neckline and sleeves, a touch peeking out from beneath the hemline gathered in several places with bows.

Spirit of the Mountain studied the dress intently, as if it were a difficult problem she must solve. In a way, it represented just that. In less than a few hours, the Jacoby home would be filled with people—strangers.

Her stomach ached from tenseness, and she wrung her hands. The last week had proved trying; Prycilla's constant attempts to make her life miserable were succeeding. Spirit of the Mountain was able to put off many of Prycilla's wearisome ways, but gradually, the woman had managed to slip past her indifference and touch a nerve she'd protected fiercely.

A strong desire to please her grandfather kept Spirit of the Mountain from giving up. He was happy, content to have her home with him. She could not disappoint him with her inability to cope. She felt at war, pulled in too many directions.

A tiredness seeped into her soul, drawing the vibrancy from her. Spirit of the Mountain knew what was happening, but she did not know what to do about it. She despaired and slumped down in a chair. Spirit of the Mountain wanted to love her new home, to do as everyone said and be Samuel Jacoby's granddaughter. But as each day passed, she longed more for her mountains, for the wilderness. Boston was beautiful and exciting, only not in ways that sustained Spirit of the Mountain.

Simplicity remained a part of her; lush surroundings made her ill at ease. Even the dress, as beautiful as it was, did not bring the delight it should have. The ball her grandfather was giving for her benefit threatened to be a nightmare.

A knock interrupted Spirit of the Mountain's thoughts, and she ran to the door because the soft sound told her it was Nathan. She pulled open the door and all but flew into his arms.

"What is it, Sam?" Nathan quickly shuffled her inside and closed the door as she began to sob uncontrollably.

"Sam." He pulled her arms from about his neck and made her look at him. "What is it?"

She sniffed and wiped at the tears that ran down

her cheeks. "I am sorry, Nathan. I just feel—" What did she feel? Spirit of the Mountain sniffed again. "I am scared. I feel alone."

He lifted her chin to look deep into her eyes. "It will be fine, I promise. You'll be the most beautiful woman there. And," he added with a wide grin, "you're not alone. I'll be there by your side."

"What if I do something to embarrass my grand-father?"

They walked over to the window seat and sat, his arm still around her. "What could you possibly do to embarrass him? He loves you, Sam. You love him. That is all that matters."

"Yes," she mumbled, trying to focus on this certainty rather than the fear that made her insides tremble.

Nathan wiped the wetness from her cheeks. "Now dry your eyes. It wouldn't do to have you swollen and puffy from crying."

Spirit of the Mountain tried to smile, but hiccuped one last sob instead. This made her laugh, and Nathan joined her, the sound soothing.

"Now take a deep breath."

She did.

"Now call Lillian." His look drifted to the gown. "It looks like you will need her help with all that lace and silk."

He turned back to Spirit of the Mountain, a longing look taking the twinkle from his eyes. "I wish I could help you, my sweet. But—"

"But you must dress as well," Samantha said with a push toward the door.

"Yes, I suppose I must."

Nathan opened the door, but glanced back and winked at her. "Don't worry, Sam. It will be fine."

"Thank you, Nathan."

Spirit of the Mountain took another deep, cleansing breath, then moved to the washbowl to splash cold water on her face. Mentally, she felt better. If only Nathan could heal her spirit as well.

"Miss Jacoby."

Spirit of the Mountain saw the woman's mouth moving, but found it hard to concentrate on the words. So many people, so many words—they were all beginning to blur together in one long sound, like the droning of a bee working a flower.

"Yes." She couldn't remember the woman's name. The only thing drifting across her tired mind was the image of the giant powdered wig. Spirit of the Mountain's first thought was of a pack rat's nest, with a little of everything clinging to the encrusted hair. She wished the woman would go away.

"It must have been quite difficult for you, growing up in such savage surroundings."

"I never believed the wilderness to be savage, nor did growing up there seem difficult." Although the woman looked content with Spirit of the Mountain's answer, she did not give any hint of leaving too soon.

Thin, wrinkled lips pulled into a pucker, as if the woman had just eaten something sour. "But the Indians." She gasped, the redness of her mouth stark against her white painted face. "Surely you were in danger every moment."

Despite her numbness, Spirit of the Mountain sensed Nathan coming up behind her. His soft, polite voice confirmed his presence.

"Mrs. Littlebaum, you've managed to occupy this beautiful woman's time so completely I must object." Nathan bowed gracefully and brought the woman's age-spotted hand to his lips. "Surely you cannot object to sharing her with the rest of us."

To Spirit of the Mountain's amazement, a dark blush actually showed through Mrs. Littlebaum's thick coat of makeup, and she batted her thinning eyelashes at Nathan coyly.

"Mr. Walker, I certainly could not object to sharing Miss Jacoby with a gentleman such as yourself."

"Nor must you neglect the others who might wish a moment with the lady."

Spirit of the Mountain saw the gentleman who spoke, a young man she had met earlier. This time, a name came to mind: Joseph Ashton. She also recalled the whispers of the other young ladies. Joseph Ashton was one of Boston's most eligible bachelors. Judging from the giggles and coy looks, Spirit of the Mountain assumed any one of them would have been quite willing and happy to bring an end to that state.

Joseph cleared his throat nervously; then soft hazel eyes met her gaze. "I would be honored if you would grant me this dance, Miss Jacoby."

Mrs. Littlebaum swatted Joseph sharply with her fan. "I believe this gentleman was here first, young man. Mind your manners."

The dismay was plain on Joseph's face, and Spirit of the Mountain felt sorry for him, but it was Nathan who rescued the younger man.

"I surely wouldn't mind staying a few moments

longer in your delightful company, Mrs. Little-baum." He bowed elegantly, granting to Joseph the privilege of the dance.

Spirit of the Mountain smiled thankfully at Nathan, and he winked, letting her know she owed him a favor. Spirit of the Mountain was so relieved to get away from the smothering woman that she didn't think about the young man in whose company she was.

Joseph whirled her about the dance floor, the music carrying them on its soft melody. Expressive eyes watched her closely as he said, "Miss Jacoby."

"Yes, Mr. Ashton."

"You dance very well."

The compliment was so unexpected that Spirit of the Mountain laughed. She felt his muscles tense. "I am sorry," she stuttered, realizing her rudeness. "I have not danced since I was very young, and I did not think I would remember. My mother taught me."

He looked away, but only for a moment. "Is it true that you've lived in the wilderness all these years?"

"Yes."

"I find that fascinating."

She was pleased he did not find her past repulsive. "My life has not been so different from any other."

A flash of admiration lit his eyes. "I think it has been very different. I envy you."

Spirit of the Mountain found herself curious and happy for the distraction this young man provided. "Why would you envy me, Mr. Ashton?"

"Please," he said softly. "Call me Joseph."

"Why would you envy me, Joseph?"

This response made him smile. Whether it was her

question or her calling him by his Christian name wasn't clear to Spirit of the Mountain. He just seemed happy.

"I'm not really sure I know why," he confessed. "I just feel you've lived a life more intense than the one I've known. I've known privilege, wealth, a life of great promise but little challenge."

A sadness struck Spirit of the Mountain. "Do not romanticize the wilderness, Joseph. It is a hard life, a life that has brought me much grief and taken many people I loved. But it holds my heart, my soul. It is my life."

"But your life is here now. You have been plunged into a life of privilege, wealth, and great promise."

"Yes," she said. "It looks as if we both look forward to little challenge."

"Miss Jacoby."

"If I am to call you Joseph, then you must call me Samantha."

"Samantha." Joseph's smile widened. "Would you allow me to call on you? I find myself wanting to know more about you, if you would permit it."

His request came as a shock to Spirit of the Mountain. She wasn't certain what to say. "Perhaps that is something you should ask my grandfather, Joseph."

"Of course. But I would like to know what you think."

Spirit of the Mountain liked Joseph Ashton. He seemed a very nice man. She guessed he must be in his late twenties. "I would like that."

"Then I shall ask your grandfather's permission now," he announced and guided her from the dance floor.

Joseph escorted Spirit of the Mountain to her grandfather. "Mr. Jacoby."

Samuel Jacoby accepted the young man's handshake. "Joseph, I see you are getting to know my granddaughter."

"I was hoping you would allow me to call on Miss Jacoby tomorrow. She has totally enchanted me, sir."

Samuel beamed. "If Samantha wishes it, my boy. But properly chaperoned, of course."

Now Joseph's face mirrored Samuel's; both men were clearly pleased with the whole situation. This made Spirit of the Mountain wonder what they had in mind. It would be just an innocent visit from a young man with whom she had enjoyed a few minutes of conversation.

"Until tomorrow, then?" Joseph said.

Spirit of the Mountain nodded politely, uncertain now about the whole situation. "Until tomorrow."

Joseph bowed, then disappeared into the crowd. Samuel took her arm and guided her toward the large buffet. "Have you eaten anything, child?"

"I am not hungry, Grandfather."

He frowned. "You must keep up your strength."

This statement made her laugh. "I have eaten enough in the last week to keep up my strength for months. I did not know people could eat so often or so well."

Samuel laughed with her. "That's one of the advantages of wealth, my dear. You never have to be hungry again."

Flashes of the long, difficult journey with the Shawnee disturbed her. She remembered hunger

303

Fela Dawson Scott

gnawing at her stomach, stealing her precious strength as she trudged along, desperate to keep up to avoid being beaten for lack of effort.

"Are you all right, Samantha?"

Her grandfather's voice broke through her nightmare, drawing her back to a reality that seemed a dream, as if one day she would wake up and find herself back in her family's lodge in the Cherokee village. It was what she longed for.

"Samantha," Samuel repeated, this time more urgently.

"I am fine. I was just thinking how much has changed in so little time. Not even two months have gone by since the Shawnee attacked my village."

Samuel Jacoby's look changed. "I had not realized it was so recently you lost your adopted family. I am so sorry, my dear. It was quite selfish of me to cast you into the midst of my friends so soon. I should have given you more time to adjust."

Spirit of the Mountain had not meant to upset her grandfather. "No, I am sorry. I did not mean to take the joy from your eyes."

"I only wanted to make you a part of my family as soon as I could. You have made me happy and I desire to share my joy with the world."

"And I only want to make you happy, Grandfather."

"You have, dear child. You have."

"I have been as patient as I can, Sam. I demand this next dance be mine." Nathan's voice was light, drawing her gaze from her grandfather.

"Then I must concede to such demands," she said.

"I was trying to get her to eat a bite, Nathan. She'll

304

wither away if she doesn't start eating more."

"I am fine, Grandfather."

The twinkle remained in Nathan's eyes, but the smile faded. "You do look a little pale, Sam. Perhaps you should heed your grandfather's advice."

Spirit of the Mountain tried to look fierce. "I want to dance with you, Nathan. I demand you do as I wish."

He lifted his shoulders in mock surrender. "What can I do, Samuel? She is quite insistent."

"Then dance with her, my boy."

Nathan pulled her close, gracefully whirled her out into the crowd of people. Spirit of the Mountain felt the ripple of muscles beneath her fingers and wished the fabric of the jacket was not between his flesh and her touch. Determinedly, she put the thought from her mind.

"Are you managing, Sam?" Nathan asked.

"As well as I can."

"You seem to be managing very well. I think Joseph Ashton is quite taken with you."

"Is he?"

"I'd say so. He seems elated Samuel has given permission for him to call on you."

There was the slightest change in his tone, so subtle, so slight. Spirit of the Mountain even wondered if she had heard it at all. "Is this wrong? He seems a nice gentleman."

"Yes, he seems nice enough. It is good you are going to see other men."

Confusion clouded her. "I am merely visiting with the young man, Nathan. You make it sound like he is coming to court me."

"Isn't he?"

She stopped and stared up at him. "We have barely said more than hello, Nathan. What makes you say such a thing?"

Nathan could see Spirit of the Mountain hadn't even suspected men would want to court her. He walked her out into the garden, where they could talk in private.

"You are a beautiful woman, Sam. You must expect young men to come courting," he said, and the hurt that came to her eyes tore his heart in two.

"I do not want young men to come courting, Nathan. I love you. How can I ever love another?"

"You will—in time."

"It is not so simple a thing, Nathan Walker."

"Isn't it?" he asked. The smallest bit of jealousy slipped into his mind. "You loved your husband, and now you claim to love me. Why not another?"

Spirit of the Mountain turned away from him. "I never loved my husband as fiercely as I love you."

Nathan didn't want to hear her confession. He didn't want to feel the pain that came to his heart, the tightness in his throat that kept him from speaking.

"We grew up together, and we were young. It was a first love given me by the Great Spirit because he knew Red Hawk would not be with me long. I believe without that blessing I would not know how to love you so completely."

Unable to bear her words any longer, Nathan walked away, leaving her alone in the garden. He felt shaken to the very depths of his being. The joy her words brought him nearly undid him. He had come close to taking her into his arms and declaring his own unending love. But he couldn't. Understanding this, he walked away from her, away from the temptation that ran strong in his blood.

Spirit of the Mountain didn't try to stop Nathan. She understood the hopelessness of doing so. He was a man of convictions he couldn't let go, even to love her as she loved him. Not wishing to return to the party, she strolled farther into the private garden, the sounds of laughter and music fading away. Lanterns had been placed about, but Spirit of the Mountain intentionally sought out the darkness in the back area, hoping to remain hidden in the shadows of the trees.

She wanted to cry, to ease the pain she felt building inside. But no tears came. Instead, a great weariness claimed her. Spirit of the Mountain thought of her Spirit Sister, the cat who gave her strength and wisdom. Since arriving in Boston she had felt its life waning. Spirit of the Mountain struggled with the grief of losing her, knowing full well that, if her Spirit Sister died, she would die, too.

Life was precious, her instinct to survive great. But honor outweighed all. Without honor, life held no meaning.

"Are you all right, cousin?"

Spirit of the Mountain did not look in the direction of Charles's voice, knowing long before his arrival of his presence.

"I just needed some fresh air."

"Perhaps a break from the people?"

She smiled, appreciating his ability to understand her so well after so short a time. "It is quite numbing.

So many faces, so many names. I am having trouble keeping everyone straight in my mind."

"That's to be expected. Everyone here has known each other for many years, even entire lifetimes. We forget it can be difficult for someone new. Give yourself time."

Time. She didn't have time. "Yes, I suppose you are right, Charles."

He took her arm and guided her to a small bench, secluded beneath a giant oak tree. They sat.

"That didn't sound very positive. Are you still homesick for your mountains?"

A sigh sounded before she could still it. "It is more than homesickness, cousin. But it is nothing to concern yourself with. It, too, will be settled with time."

Charles felt a dread deep inside him. He sensed that, somehow, the solution to his cousin's sadness would not be what he would wish for her.

"Grandfather will probably be wondering where I have gone off to," she said.

Offering his arm, Charles smiled widely. "Then I shall escort you safely back to his side, dearest cousin."

Chapter Twenty-three

Nathan found himself unable to return to the party; the crowd of people had suddenly become unbearable. He sought refuge in Samuel Jacoby's library. He needed to be alone to sort out the confusion that tormented his mind.

Until six short weeks ago, he had been content with the life he had made for himself in the wilderness—content with himself and the person he was.

He knew he should walk away and leave behind the woman who caused his internal suffering. Still, Nathan found himself unable to go. Spirit of the Mountain deserved the chance to be a part of this family, to be with the grandfather who loved her—a chance without the complications Nathan provided by staying.

Logic told him so, but his heart rebelled. The

thought of leaving her was painful, the act unimaginable. He couldn't envision his future without her, alone and unloved. His convictions were becoming less and less important. The very base from which he had proudly guided his life was crumbling before the seduction of love, the notion of a home, a wife, and children.

Nathan recalled Spirit of the Mountain's pale face and tortured eyes. What was taking the life from her? Was it this place? Was it her loving him? A nagging fear surfaced; his instinct told him she was in danger. But from what? A broken heart? No one ever died from a broken heart.

"I thought I might find you in here." Charles closed the door and joined Nathan.

"I needed to be alone," Nathan said, hoping Charles would take the hint, but he didn't.

"You two seem so well suited for each other. I don't understand why you are so determined to leave her here, Nathan. Why don't you take Samantha home with you?"

"It's impossible, Charles. There many things you don't understand, so don't interfere."

A flicker of fire came to Charles's eyes. "I want to understand, Nathan. Why don't you explain the situation to me? Samantha loves you, and I believe you love her. What is so difficult about that?"

Frustration touched a nerve in Nathan, and he could not keep it from his voice. "I can't take her back to the wilderness. Surely you can see that."

"Then marry Samantha and stay in Boston. She wouldn't have to choose between her grandfather and you."

"I never asked her to choose. I want her to be with her family. That is why I brought her here."

"Yes," Charles replied dryly, "that was the noble thing to do. Now she has everything: a family, a home, and a broken heart."

Nathan felt his anger rising. "You do not have a right to condemn or condone what I have done. It is between Sam and me. No one else."

"What if you were wrong to bring her here?"

"I wasn't wrong. Samuel loves her, and she loves him. This"—Nathan pointed to everything surrounding them—"is everything anyone could want in life. She will get over her feelings for me. I am nothing compared to all this."

Charles looked sad. "Somehow, I don't believe Samantha thinks as you do. Look at her, Nathan. She's been here a little over a week, and already the color is gone from her cheeks."

"She has a lot to adjust to."

"Good God, man," Charles yelled, "are you blind? Or are you such a fool?"

Nathan found himself grasping Charles by the collar and raising his fist to strike. Then he stepped back and pointed a finger in warning at Charles. "Leave me be. I've done what I thought best for Sam from the very beginning. I don't know any other way except to leave and let Sam get on with her life."

"She needs you."

Confusion mixed with anger, and Nathan thought he might explode from his inner turmoil. He slammed his fist into the wall, shaking the portraits that hung on it.

The pain diverted his attention momentarily, and

he rubbed his bruised knuckles. "I can't go, and I can't stay."

"It seems we are two of a kind, Nathan."

Charles's statement made no sense to Nathan. "You and I have nothing in common."

An ironic smile touched Charles's features. He sighed heavily. "We are two men bent on our own destruction. You are walking away from the woman you love for her sake. And I"—he paused, then continued on, his look cast to the ground in dejection— "am determined to marry a woman who will bring me only grief, yet I cannot walk away. Strange things we do in the name of love."

"I need a drink." Nathan walked over to the sideboard and poured himself a brandy. Then he gave one to Charles and smiled. "Here's to love—and to fools in love."

Charles lifted his own glass. "Hear, hear."

Spirit of the Mountain folded back the comforter in her bed, but could not bring herself to climb into the empty space. She moved to the window and stared out into the darkness.

"You will catch a chill." Nathan's voice came from behind her.

She knew he had been there for several moments before speaking. Yet she didn't turn around. She feared the sight of him. "What are you doing here, Nathan?"

"I—" He stopped, then started again. "I don't know. I was going to my own rooms and found myself at your door instead."

"Go away," she whispered weakly, already feeling

the trembling deep in her belly. "I cannot bear to see you tonight. Please go away."

The plea in her voice ripped into Nathan's heart; his soul was tortured by her pain. He wanted to ease the hurt, to heal the wounds he had inflicted upon her.

"I only wanted you to be united with your family. I never meant to hurt you the way I have."

Finally, Spirit of the Mountain turned to him, but her face was cast in shadow, and he could not see her eyes—eyes that would have told him more than her words. "I know you did not intend to hurt me, Nathan. You had only honorable intentions from the beginning."

Shame warmed his face and tinted his voice. "Honorable? How honorable is it to seduce you, knowing full well I would only leave you?"

"I desired you, Nathan. It was not a one-sided affair."

"You were vulnerable, and I took advantage of you. I am a cad, and nothing you can say will change that."

Spirit of the Mountain crossed the floor to stand in front of him. "I believe I first made love to you while you were tied and bound to a post. Do not make what was beautiful between us ugly. I do not regret loving you."

Nathan reached out to her, and Spirit of the Mountain stepped into his open arms. His lips took hers, which were soft and warm. Desire burst inside him so quickly and intensely he had no time to claim control. He lifted her and carried her to the bed.

Helpless to stop himself, Nathan pulled the silky

nightgown from Spirit of the Mountain. He trailed kisses down her neck to the gentle curve of her shoulder, then down long, delicate arms. Nathan quickly shed his own clothing, not wanting anything between them. They lay entwined, flesh against flesh, holding each other close.

His passion aroused Spirit of the Mountain instantly. She wrapped her legs about his waist; her hips gently urged him to take her. Her need was so great she felt it as pain only Nathan could ease.

When he entered her, Spirit of the Mountain thought she might faint from the tremor that swept through her. She clung to him in desperation, her love so immense it took her breath away. Tears ran from her closed eyes.

"Don't cry, my love." Nathan kissed her tears away, his tender words sounding like a whispered dream.

"Love me, Nathan." She kissed him deeply, longingly. "Love me tonight as if there were no tomorrow, as if there were no promises to break and no demands upon our honor, no past, no future. Love me tonight."

He touched his lips to hers, sealing their ill-fated desire. "I do love you, Samantha. God help me, I do."

Tears blurred the vision of his face, and Spirit of the Mountain knew happiness. She was content. The spirit inside her could fade away. Nathan loved her tonight and always. She knew it in her heart.

The knock intruded on Spirit of the Mountain's sleep, and she turned away from the sound, pulling the pillow over her head. Another knock sounded more loudly, more insistently.

She moaned and called out, "Go away."

Then the door opened anyway, and Prycilla's sharp voice gave commands, which roused Spirit of the Mountain. She sat up in bed and quickly scanned the room. To her relief, she found Nathan absent.

"What is wrong with you today, Samantha? From what everyone says, you never sleep late." Prycilla bustled into her room and stood at the foot of the bed, hands on her hips. "It's already late afternoon. Even I am up by this time of day."

"What do you want, Prycilla?"

Prycilla carefully patted her hair, brushed the wrinkles from her skirt. "I had a tray brought up for us, dear. I thought you and I could have tea together."

This was an odd occurrence, but Spirit of the Mountain tried to give the other woman the benefit of the doubt. "Tea?"

"Yes, tea. We haven't been spending enough time together, and I feel it's all my fault. I promised your grandfather to do my best to help you adjust to Boston life. We can start today."

"I do not think—"

"Do not deny my chance to keep my promise, Samantha. I'm going to be a member of this family soon, and I'd like to make a good impression with Samuel."

Spirit of the Mountain pushed her tangled hair from her face, trying to make sense of Prycilla's shift in attitude.

"You splash some cold water on your face. I'll be mother and pour the tea."

The woman left the bedroom and started to prepare the tea. Unable to think of a way out, Spirit of the Mountain rose and did as Prycilla had said. Pulling her robe on, she resigned herself to Prycilla's company.

"One sugar or two?" Prycilla waited, poised with the spoon of sugar.

"One."

"Cream?"

"Yes, please." Happily, the woman complied, stirring the tea before presenting it to Spirit of the Mountain. It was the strangest moment, as if Spirit of the Mountain were having a bizarre dream. She sat and took the cup as Prycilla prepared her own cup.

Spirit of the Mountain waited to see what Prycilla would do next. She was curious, if not suspicious. Spirit of the Mountain decided she preferred Prycilla her normal way, mean spirited and selfish. At least, she knew what to expect then.

"Your tea is getting cold, Samantha."

Brown eyes watched Spirit of the Mountain closely, intent on what she was doing. She lifted the cup to her lips, and Prycilla smiled. This alone might have been enough to keep Spirit of the Mountain from drinking, but the subtly bitter smell of the tea made her only pretend to take a sip to satisfy the woman's watchful eyes.

Spirit of the Mountain wasn't in a talkative mood, but that didn't seem to matter. Prycilla carried the conversation easily. Spirit of the Mountain stood and walked about the room, pretending to listen to the other woman's chatter, carefully dumping the tea into a bowl of fresh-cut flowers.

"More tea?" Prycilla asked after a while.

Spirit of the Mountain moved back to the table and held out her cup. "Please."

Prycilla prepared her another cup. "This is so much fun, Samantha. Perhaps we should do this every day."

The other woman's lips had moved, but Spirit of the Mountain had not been listening to the words. "What was that, Prycilla?"

"I think we should do this every day."

"Every day?"

"Yes, dear."

Every part of her objected. Her mind cried out no, but she found herself saying, "Of course. That would be fun."

Lying had never come easily to Spirit of the Mountain, but with Prycilla, it seemed necessary, and it seemed to make the woman happy. This made Spirit of the Mountain suspect her even more.

The aroma of the tea drifted to Spirit of the Mountain's sensitive nose; the rich black tea had smelled good. Suddenly, she realized what it was that was different. The first cup had definitely smelled differently, the slightest bitterness tainting it. Carefully, she took a sip, but she found the tea had been brewed in its usual way.

She placed the cup on the table. "Excuse me a moment, Prycilla. I am a little chilled and my shawl is in the other room."

Spirit of the Mountain allowed sufficient time before she grabbed her shawl and returned.

"I made you a fresh cup, Samantha."

"How thoughtful of you." Spirit of the Mountain

found herself playing Prycilla's game. She didn't sit, but she picked up the cup and strolled about making idle conversation. She moved to the window seat, pretending to study the garden below. This cup had the same bitter odor. Her suspicions were confirmed.

Spirit of the Mountain pretended to take another sip; then she slowly made her way to the flowers. Her mind raced ahead, calculating what she would need to do if they repeated this fiasco on a daily basis.

It seemed as if an hour passed before Prycilla left her alone, having had the tea tray removed before she left. Spirit of the Mountain closed the door and stood with her back against the wood panel. What would she do? What could she do? Nothing.

Was she really surprised the woman would try something like this? It suited Prycilla's personality to try to poison her. Spirit of the Mountain had assumed she was marrying Charles for Samuel's money. Now she was positive. Spirit of the Mountain lay directly in the way of Charles inheriting the money. It was logical for Prycilla to try to remove her.

Spirit of the Mountain immediately ruled out going to Charles. Poor Charles. It would take time for him to realize what kind of woman his fiancee was, and the last thing Spirit of the Mountain wanted was to be the one to tell him. Their own relationship seemed too new, too vulnerable. This wasn't the sort of thing to spring on someone who was hopelessly in love.

She would find out where Prycilla had the poison hidden and simply replace it with something harmless. Prycilla would not know, and she would think her plot was succeeding.

Her decision made, Spirit of the Mountain put the problem from her mind. Prycilla was a fool, but Spirit of the Mountain would play her deadly game until she knew better what to do.

Pierre walked away from the Taylor cabin. Anger made him walk fast; he dragged his burned left leg with an effort.

The Taylors were lying. He knew it.

He could barely see out of his burned eye, his fury causing his face to scowl, drawing the eyelid closed. It didn't matter if they lied to him about Walker and the girl. He'd pick up their trail easily enough.

Chapter Twenty-four

Nathan had been right. Joseph was courting Spirit of the Mountain. It had been nearly two weeks since the night they had met, and he had not missed coming a single day to see Spirit of the Mountain. Tonight, Joseph's parents, Thomas and Beverly Ashton, were giving a small dinner party in her honor.

Joseph's youngest sister, Charlotte, was displaying her talent on the spinet, and Prycilla accompanied her in song. If Spirit of the Mountain had to find one nice thing about Prycilla, it would be her beautiful voice. But the fact Prycilla also thought this did take something away from it.

"Samantha."

"Yes, Joseph."

"Prycilla mentioned that you played the flute. Would you play for us?"

All eyes turned to her. Spirit of the Mountain wasn't certain she was comfortable being the center of attention. She saw the smirk on Prycilla's face and knew the other woman had done this intentionally. Since Spirit of the Mountain's arrival, Prycilla tried hard to embarrass her in any way she could contrive.

"I do not play very well, Joseph. I am certain it would not be as pleasurable as your sister's playing."

"Nonsense," he declared, a glow of pride coming to his face. "I would love to hear you, Samantha."

"I do not have my flute," she said, stating the first and most obvious excuse that came to mind.

Joseph moved to a cabinet near the spinet and opened it. He produced a flute and presented it to her. "There are few instruments this family has not attempted to master."

Prycilla walked over to her, challenge lighting her eyes. "I did notice the flute I saw in your room was quite different. Perhaps Samantha can't play something so sophisticated, Joseph."

"It was handmade, Prycilla—an Indian flute to be exact."

"Oh, really? How quaint."

A flush came to Joseph's face, showing he was ill at ease with Prycilla's rudeness. "Maybe this wasn't such a good idea. It seems I have assumed too much, Samantha."

Nathan stood and crossed to stand by Spirit of the Mountain. His look chilled even Prycilla's impudent one. "I have had the pleasure of hearing Sam play." His gaze moved to her, the coldness in his eyes replaced by a loving warmth. "I would be delighted if you would honor me so again."

321

Spirit of the Mountain had already decided not to let Prycilla get the best of her, but Nathan's subtle message gave her even more confidence she could take the smug look off the other woman's face. She prepared herself, taking a moment to familiarize her fingers and ear to the instrument.

The tune she began playing took Spirit of the Mountain back to a special time she had shared with her father. It was a classical piece that had taken her many hours of tutoring from her loving teacher and many years to master. The music took over, and the people in the room faded away as stronger memories claimed her mind.

She thought of her father and how proud he would be that she remembered the notes. The beautiful melody was as unforgettable as her past. Spirit of the Mountain barely realized tears ran down her cheek, the emotion of the song blending with the stirring of her heart. It was as if her father sat across from her, his face beaming, his eyes approving of her performance.

When the music ended, Spirit of the Mountain's visions did not. She remained entranced, and the mood was broken only when someone touched her on the shoulder.

"I did not know Neil had taught you to play."

Her grandfather's expression told Spirit of the Mountain he had been touched as well, the same ghost haunting them both.

"He took great pleasure in his music. When I play, it is as if my father is beside me and his pleasure becomes mine."

Joseph came to her side. "You never cease to

amaze me, Samantha. That was truly remarkable."

Everyone echoed his sentiment, except Prycilla, who sat by herself, refusing to give merit to Spirit of the Mountain's talent.

Nathan said nothing, but he didn't need to. Spirit of the Mountain could read his thoughts as easily as her own. It was exactly what he had intended, and he seemed pleased. Spirit of the Mountain smiled. This small triumph made her feel better than she had in days.

As the Ashton family chatted on, she saw Joseph slip out of the room with her grandfather. A strange feeling touched her.

"Mr. Jacoby," Joseph cleared his throat nervously. "I wished a moment in private with you to discuss something very important to both of us."

Samuel watched the boy fidget with the snifter of brandy he held and guessed at his motives. "Come out with it, son."

Joseph straightened his shoulders, as if preparing for battle, and faced the older man. "I know Samantha has been home only a short while. I have known her only two weeks."

"Yes." Samuel rather wanted to make this situation easier for the young man, but he found himself enjoying the lad's discomfort too much to do so.

"What I mean to say is I've grown very fond of Samantha. I knew the very first moment I saw her, sir."

"Knew what?" Samuel demanded, intentionally sounding far more gruff than he felt. He willed the smile from his lips.

Fela Dawson Scott

"I knew I loved her," Joseph said.

"You love my granddaughter?"

"Yes, sir. Very much."

"What do you intend to do about this love, sir?" Samuel demanded, nearly causing the boy to drop his drink.

"I intend to marry her, Mr. Jacoby." His words came out a bit loud, a bit demanding. Joseph lowered his voice and added, "If you will give me your blessing, sir."

"You certainly have my blessing, Joseph. But how does my granddaughter feel about you?"

It was as if Joseph had been given something wonderful, then had had it taken away. "That's just it, Mr. Jacoby. I don't know how she feels."

"Haven't you asked her?"

"No," Joseph confessed. "I love her, sir, with all my heart, but I don't think she feels the same way for me."

"Oh." Samuel thought not, too.

"I believe she has feelings for Nathan. She hasn't said this, but it seems to be so. I don't quite know what to do about it."

Samuel put his arm on Joseph's shoulder and gave him a reassuring pat. "Well, now, I wouldn't let that discourage you. Very few marriages begin with love. As a matter of fact, you have a head start with your loving Samantha to begin with. She will come to love you in turn, my boy. But first, you two must get married."

"It's my greatest wish."

"Good." Samuel poured two more drinks. "Then

we will drink to your future together. I couldn't be more pleased."

Nathan closed the door behind him. "You said you wanted to speak with me, Samuel?"

"Yes." Samuel sucked a long draw from the cigar he smoked, then pointed to the chair across from his. "Make yourself comfortable."

Nathan did, but declined the cigar Samuel offered.

"I'll get right down to it, Nathan. Joseph has asked for Samantha's hand in marriage."

Joseph's proposal was not a surprise, but Nathan knew Samuel watched him closely for a reaction. He gave none.

"I have given my blessing."

"I see," Nathan said calmly, despite the sudden rise of temperature inside him.

"The boy says he loves my granddaughter."

"Yes, it seems so."

"You have no objections?"

Nathan found himself very close to saying, yes, that he did object to this marriage. It was almost more than he could bear to think of another man holding Spirit of the Mountain close and making love to her. He remained very still, as if the smallest movement would give his true feelings away. "If I did, would it matter?"

"To me, no. To Samantha, I believe it does."

"You could be right."

Samuel's face grew red. "You're damned right I'm right!"

"All right," Nathan nearly shouted back, his anger breaking free of the tight reign he had put on it. "Exactly what do you want, Samuel?"

"I want to do what's best for my granddaughter, Nathan. I believe her marrying Joseph is best."

A deep-seated pain rushed forward. "Marrying me isn't?"

The older man nodded. "I like you, Nathan. I admire your independence and strength. But the truth is I want more for Samantha."

Nathan stood, walked across the room, and leaned against the fireplace, formulating his response. "I love her. Isn't that enough?"

"I don't believe it is. I don't think you do either."

"I'm not sure I know what I think anymore." Confusion muddled his thoughts. He was no longer clear about what he thought or wanted.

"You believe Samantha belongs here. You risked your life to give my granddaughter all this. Don't take her happiness here away from her now."

"I did believe bringing Sam here was the right thing for her."

Nathan felt a strong sense of wrongness over what he had done, despite the promise he had made to himself and to Sarah. In less than a year, the wilderness had taken the life of Nathan's vibrant, young bride. He had sworn never to marry again, never to let the harsh life he had chosen for himself take another innocent life. Still, the sense of wrongness pushed him on. Spirit of the Mountain's own words haunted him relentlessly: *I am not Sarah. The wilderness gives me life, not death.*

Then, Nathan said, "Since we arrived, Sam has lost so much of herself. She's losing vitality—"

Samuel's snortlike laugh interrupted Nathan.

"Sam isn't losing anything, Nathan. Don't be ridiculous."

"I'm not being ridiculous." Nathan began to pace back and forth, anxiety building inside him. "Samantha told me that she couldn't live here, that her spirit would die. I didn't believe her. I thought it ridiculous."

"What the hell are you talking about?"

Nathan stopped and stared for a long moment at Samuel. "Samantha believes she's going to die."

This reply stopped Samuel. The fear that came to his eyes was real. "Why would my granddaughter think this? She has everything."

"You can't give her the one thing she needs, Samuel: the mountains."

"I don't understand, young man. The mountains?"

Nathan didn't know where to start, how to explain. "Samantha . . . Spirit of the Mountain—"

"Spirit of the Mountain?"

"That's her Cherokee name. She was named for the catamount, her Spirit Sister."

"Spirit Sister?"

Pushing back his hair, Nathan tried to slow his mind down, to clear the clutter so he could explain this better. "I know this is all quite absurd, Samuel. I haven't been very accepting myself. But I honestly don't know what to believe anymore."

"All right, son." Samuel leaned back. "Just try to explain all this to me."

Nathan tried to do just that. When he finished, he waited for Samuel to speak, but the man just stared into space.

"I think the spirit inside her is dying," Nathan said,

"just as she claimed it would."

"Nonsense." Samuel stood. "You can't seriously believe this, Nathan. It's preposterous. If you don't like Samantha marrying Joseph, just say so. But don't concoct an absurd tale of Spirit Sisters to convince me she should return with you to the mountains."

"I didn't believe the wilderness was a place for a wife and family. Now, I'm not certain I wasn't wrong."

"Don't stand in her way, Nathan. Samantha has a home, a family, and wealth. Forgive me, my boy, but you can't give her any of these things. What kind of life can you give her except one of hardship and pain? Don't let your feelings make you selfish. If you truly love her, you will think of what is best for Samantha."

"I am." Nathan sighed, his heart heavy with doubt.

"No, sir, you are not." Samuel's voice became hard. "You are allowing your feelings for Samantha to blur your principles. Your principles made you bring Samantha to me. I beg you to allow your principles to guide you now. You must leave and allow me to arrange a bright and certain future for my granddaughter."

Guilt washed over Nathan, combining with the doubt that lingered in his mind. Together, they overwhelmed his new and vulnerable sense of understanding. "You're right, Samuel. It's best I leave."

Spirit of the Mountain watched Nathan, whose back was to her. She wanted to see his face, to see the green of his eyes, to see if he truly believed what he was doing was for the best. When Nathan had asked her to come into her grandfather's study, she knew something dreadful was wrong. His manner, the way his eyes wouldn't look directly at her, and his blunt statement made Spirit of the Mountain ask what she did of Nathan.

"You cannot ask me to do this," he said.

His voice held the slightest note of pain, but Spirit of the Mountain feared to take heart in it. She moved to stand directly behind him, forcing him to turn and face her.

"I must ask you, Nathan. I must know you can do this. Then I will know you are speaking the truth."

Nathan grasped her arms, his eyes desperate. "It is for the best, Sam. I must leave. You must marry Joseph and get on with your life without my interference."

"Without your love?"

He pushed her away. "You asked for one night. It was all I can give you. Now, it is time for me to go."

"Then prove you don't love me anymore. Give me away on my wedding day. Give me to another man."

"No."

"You cannot."

His desperation turned into anger. "Believe what you want. I will not give you to another man."

Spirit of the Mountain shrugged her shoulders. "Then I will not marry Joseph."

"You must." Nathan pointed his finger at her, as if accusing her of her stubbornness. "And you will."

"You cannot tell me what to do, Nathan Walker."

"I will not marry you, Sam."

She turned away, hiding the hurt she felt. "I did not ask you to."

Nathan knew it would be difficult to convince Spirit of the Mountain marrying Joseph was best. But he hadn't expected her silly request to give her away. "All right, Sam, you win. I'll stay and give you away."

Whether this concession made her happy or sad, Nathan didn't know. She nodded and quickly left the room. He stood, staring at the door she had shut behind her. It felt as if a door in his heart had been closed, forever setting apart the pleasure that lurked on the other side, condemning him to a life of loneliness and heartbreak.

After she ran away from Nathan, Spirit of the Mountain rushed up the stairs, her path blurred by tears that stung her eyes. She collided with Charles as he started down.

"Samantha."

His strong arms kept her from falling. She kept her head bent to keep him from seeing her distress. "I am so sorry, Charles. I did not see you."

"Are you all right?"

She stepped past him. "I am fine, cousin."

Her rooms were only a few doors down. They were her sanctuary against all the trials that lay before her. She wanted only to disappear inside them, to leave behind her pain, to forget the sadness that hounded her like a mad dog at her heels.

Slamming the door behind her, Spirit of the Mountain lay her head back against the dark wood of the door. She closed her eyes, trying to ease the pain in her head. Failing, she went to the large basket where Red lay and picked him up. She buried her nose in the softness of his fur, the feel of it tickling, the smell of it sweet. He wiggled in delight.

"Oh, my dear," she murmured, sliding to the floor in despair.

Chapter Twenty-five

Samuel looked at Spirit of the Mountain, his worry intensified by the paleness of her face. She had dark circles beneath her eyes—eyes that seemed overly large, dull and lifeless as they stared back at him.

"I know you do not understand the reasons you and Joseph should marry, my dear. But you must trust I do know what is best for you."

The smallest of smiles lifted the sadness on her face, only to be beaten down again. "I do understand that you believe this, Grandfather. I will do as you say."

This answer broke his heart more than if she were angry. "Given time you will not even remember you loved another man."

It would never be. Spirit of the Mountain knew this, but to deny her grandfather's assertion would take too much of her strength. "It does not matter." She slowly rose from the chair. The effort it took to keep her growing weakness from her grandfather was a struggle. She crossed the room to stand by his side. "Given time, all will be as it should be."

Spirit of the Mountain stood on her toes and kissed his weathered cheek. She did not want her grandfather to know time was not to be hers. She wanted the short time they still had together to be filled with love, not regret. "I must rest now, Grandfather."

He placed his palm to her cheek. "You do look tired, my child. I will send Nathan for you when it is time to go to the church."

Once she was in her rooms, Spirit of the Mountain did not go into the bedroom. She merely made herself comfortable in a large chair. Red found her lap and curled up contentedly. The warmth and softness of his fur was like an elixir, bringing the relaxation Spirit of the Mountain needed. Willing her mind to be cleared of its clutter, she thought of nothing, her only movement the steady stroking of her pet.

A soft knock came, telling her the time had arrived. Nathan entered. "Are you ready, Sam?"

She nodded and rose, putting Red into his basket to continue with his nap.

Nathan came up behind her. "I am worried, Sam. You do not look well."

Spirit of the Mountain turned around, but she did not look at him. It was too difficult. "Do not worry yourself, Nathan."

He grabbed her chin and lifted her face so she met

his gaze. "But I do worry. Tell me the truth. I must know."

"You already know the truth. What can I say you do not already understand in your heart? You do not want the truth, Nathan. Your mind cries out for me to lie, to ease the worry that strangles you. I cannot."

Nathan let go of her chin and turned away. He stood for the longest time staring out into nowhere. "What are we to do?"

"I am to marry Joseph today. Beyond that, I do not know."

Nathan whirled back around, his eyes filled with anger and grief. "That's not what I meant, and you know it. We must go away right now. We must return to the mountains."

"No." It was all she could say.

"We must"—he softened his voice, but the rest came out strangled from emotion—"or you will die."

"Then I will die."

"No," Nathan cried out in anguish. He grabbed her arms and shook her as if he could shake the stubbornness from her. "I was wrong. I should never have brought you here. I see that now. I beg you, Sam. We must go."

Her heart ached for him. "You were not wrong, Nathan. It was right for you to bring me here."

"How can you say that? You're dying, and I am to blame."

Spirit of the Mountain took his face into her palms, drawing his troubled gaze to her. "You are not to blame. You must believe this. We have merely followed the paths that brought us to this point in our lives. We can do nothing to change what is determined for us."

"We must. I cannot bear to lose you."

Spirit of the Mountain guided Nathan to a chair and pushed him in to it. She sat at his feet, her hands grasping his. "How can I make you understand? You were strong in your resolve when I was weak. Now I see where my duty and honor lie."

"You make no sense. I was wrong in my purpose. We found love together, and I have done everything to keep us apart."

"Yes, we found love, Nathan. We risked death itself to be together. No one can take this away. Nothing can diminish it. But to leave now would be selfish." Spirit of the Mountain thought of her mother and understood her dying wish. Her mother wanted peace between her husband and his father. She put aside her own hurt to heal those she loved. "We would be thinking only of our own needs. By staying, I am giving an even greater gift. My grandfather needs me. He needs to know I will not leave him as my father did."

"He asks too much." Nathan pulled her hands to his lips, kissing them, clinging to her.

"He asks nothing. I am giving of myself, willingly, lovingly, with all my heart and soul."

"Why didn't I listen to you? You said from the very beginning we belonged together. Why am I only now seeing the truth?"

Spirit of the Mountain saw his tears through her own. "But we are together, Nathan. We have lived and loved more in the short time we have shared than most people do in a lifetime. It has taken me this time to see what my purpose was in coming here. We cannot change what is done."

"We will convince your grandfather that if you stay you will die."

She laid her head in his lap. "You were witness to the spirit inside me. You recognized its existence in your heart long ago, yet you denied it. Your mind fought the thought that such a thing might be."

Nathan stroked her head, the feel of his hand soothing the turmoil in her heart.

"But I believe now. Couldn't your grandfather do the same?"

"You have lived in the wilderness and known Indian life, yet you are just now coming to terms with all this. How could my grandfather, who has known nothing other than his life here in Boston, comprehend?"

"We could try." Nathan found himself unable to let go, to give in to losing Spirit of the Mountain. "We must try."

"There is not enough time."

Spirit of the Mountain raised her head and looked deeply into his eyes. She did not have much time. Nathan thought his heart had stopped the moment he read the look in the dark blue depths. He wished for time to stand still—even more, for time to reverse and go back to give him a second chance at having the greatest, most fulfilling love he could ever know in life.

He knew this wouldn't happen. He knew Spirit of the Mountain would not leave her grandfather. She had promised to stay. "Damn your honor, Sam. I do not want to go on without you."

"Without honor," she whispered softly, "life is not worth living."

It had been decided that a small, private ceremony would be best. Spirit of the Mountain knew her failing health had been the reason for her grandfather's insistence it be so. The Ashtons had hoped for a long engagement and large wedding, but they had given in to their son's wish to be married as soon as possible.

As soon as Spirit of the Mountain arrived at the chapel, Prycilla and Lillian helped her dress. Her wedding gown was splendid, with its many layers of lace and satin. None of it mattered to Spirit of the Mountain. She allowed herself to be turned and twisted, primped and prepared for the ceremony ahead.

"I would think you'd be a little more excited than you are, Samantha," Prycilla said. "After all, you are marrying one of the wealthiest bachelors in Boston."

"I would like to speak with Joseph, Prycilla. Would you please go get him?"

Prycilla gasped in horror. "It's not proper."

"I do not care. I wish to see Joseph. Go get him."

Gone was all pretense of good manners. Spirit of the Mountain did not wish to appease the obnoxious woman another second. It was as if Prycilla understood this. For once, she did not argue. She left to find Joseph.

"Lillian, you may go on out to the chapel," Spirit of the Mountain said.

The girl nodded. "You look beautiful, Miss Jacoby. You have my best wishes."

"Thank you, Lillian."

"Thank you, miss. Was my pleasure to help."

The girl disappeared, leaving Spirit of the Mountain alone in the small room. She could not have told anyone what the chapel looked like, or even the room she stood in. Nothing came to mind. Dread occupied her being.

Joseph knocked, then entered. "What is it, Samantha?"

"I wanted to speak with you before we said our vows."

"Surely, it isn't anything that couldn't wait. Everyone is ready for the ceremony to begin."

"It cannot wait, Joseph." Spirit of the Mountain motioned for him to sit in the only chair in the sparse room.

Instead, he took her hand into his. "What is so urgent then?"

"I should have told you this when we first met. It might make a difference in whether you wish to marry me or not."

Joseph cleared his throat anxiously. "If this is about you and Nathan. It doesn't matter. I love you, and I believe you can grow to love me in time."

Spirit of the Mountain turned away from his loving look. "Nathan is only a small part of my past." She squared her shoulders, forced herself to turn and face Joseph directly, honestly. "I have kept the truth of what happened before I came to Boston from you."

Joseph did not make any attempt to stop her, so she continued. "I have lived the past eight years with a Cherokee family. I was not taken captive, Joseph.

338

I went to live with them willingly. I became the adopted daughter of Chaser of Dreams and loved my adopted family as much as they loved me. I am Cherokee, Joseph. My heart and soul belong to my adopted people."

"Is that all?" Joseph laughed, but his laughter was nervous. "That isn't so bad, Samantha. It does not matter."

"Does it matter that I married Red Hawk and became pregnant with his child?"

Joseph did not speak for a moment. "Are they still alive?"

"No, my husband died in a hunting accident. I lost the baby only days after."

"Then—" His voice broke, but he went on. "Then it is time for you to remarry."

She stepped closer, her hand touching his cheek. "You do not have to marry me, Joseph. I would understand if this changes your feelings for me."

"No." He grabbed her hand and touched his lips to her palm. "I love you, Samantha, with all my heart. I don't care what is in your past. It does not matter. The only thing that matters to me is that you spend your future with me. I want this more than anything."

"I do not deserve you, Joseph." It was the truth. He loved her without reservation, and she could not return that love.

"Shall we go?" He offered his arm to her.

She took it. There was no going back.

Prycilla had hurried away from the door and the conversation she had overheard. Now a thousand thoughts ran through her mind, distracting her from the ceremony that took place before her.

She did not see the man who entered the church. She did not see him make his way down the aisle toward the couple repeating their vows—until he stepped forward and grabbed Spirit of the Mountain's arm.

Shock went through Spirit of the Mountain as she locked gazes with the Frenchman. Half his face was burned beyond recognition, his flesh stretched and scarred by the fire. She gasped in horror, not only from the sight before her, but from what his presence in her life meant.

"*Ma chere*," Pierre slurred. "I am hurt you did not invite me to your wedding."

Nathan moved forward, but the Frenchman calmly pulled his pistol and shot him. Spirit of the Mountain saw the lead ball rip open Nathan's shoulder, sending him stumbling backward until he fell. Pierre threw the one pistol aside and jerked another from his coat, the wandering barrel keeping the other guests at bay.

Pierre grabbed for Spirit of the Mountain, but she twisted away and ran to Nathan. She knelt beside him. His eyes were closed. There was blood everywhere. She leaned down to hear if his heart still beat. The sound of her own was so strong in her ears she feared she could not hear his. Nathan moved and his eyes fluttered open. She heard Pierre just above her and felt for the knife she knew Nathan would have somewhere on him.

"You are mine, *n'est-ce pas*?"

Pierre dragged her from Nathan. "You bastard,"

she screamed, drawing on the last of her strength to fight him.

"You will come with me. Be still, or I will kill another." His pistol leveled off on her grandfather.

"What is the meaning of this?" Samuel Jacoby demanded, his face turning red with anger.

"I bought and paid for this woman. She is mine, and I'll be taking her with me." Pierre stressed his point with his pistol. "Any objections?"

"You cannot take my granddaughter. I won't allow it."

Pierre laughed cruelly. "I don't see you have any choice, old man." He turned the pistol on Spirit of the Mountain.

She saw the pain that twisted her grandfather's face, his hands grasping his chest. "Grandfather," she cried out, trying to get free of the hands that held her.

"Be still, bitch, or I'll see that you join your lover."

Spirit of the Mountain quieted, purpose strong and clear in her mind. She felt the barrel of the gun in her ribs. She reached up and grasped it with her left hand, keeping the Frenchman from pulling it away. "I will see you in hell first."

Pierre's eyes widened as he saw the blade of the knife and her right hand bringing it up into his stomach. Spirit of the Mountain did not hesitate. She drove the long blade up under his ribs as deep as it would go. She heard the click of his pistol, but the meaning did not register with her. She knew only one thing. He would die by her hand if it was the last thing she did on this earth.

Slowly, Pierre sank to the floor, his blood soaking

her white wedding gown as he fell forward against her. Disgusted, she pushed him off her. He landed with a lifeless thud on the polished wood floor.

She stood still, holding the bloody knife in her hand. No one moved. No one said or did anything. Finally, Spirit of the Mountain dropped it onto Pierre's lifeless body. It was done.

Mrs. Ashton screamed, then wilted in a dead faint. Spirit of the Mountain met Nathan's gaze as he struggled to his feet. She ran to her grandfather, who now lay on the floor, Charles by his side.

"Someone get a doctor," she screamed. "Bring the carriage around."

The next few hours were a blur to Spirit of the Mountain. Her grandfather had suffered only a mild stroke, but enough to keep him in bed for a few days. Nathan lost a lot of blood, but the ball had gone through his shoulder cleanly. He, too, would be fine.

It was Spirit of the Mountain who would not be the same. All strength was drained from her. She sat alone in her grandfather's study in the waning light of late afternoon. The smell of leather and cigars comforting her.

The door opened, and Prycilla slipped inside. She was up to something, a content sort of smirk upon her smiling lips.

"What is it, Prycilla?"

"I wanted to know what you would like me to do?"

Spirit of the Mountain was tired. She didn't want to play at any more games. "To do?"

"Well." Prycilla sat, then smoothed out the wrinkles in her skirt, something she never failed to do. "I couldn't help but overhear you and Joseph speaking before the wedding. I know the authorities will be here in the morning to determine exactly what happened at the chapel. I was wondering if I shouldn't tell them about your past?"

At that moment, it all mattered very little to Spirit of the Mountain. "Do what you feel is best."

This didn't seem to be what Prycilla was after. "But it will cause a great scandal, Samantha. Surely you don't want that?"

"It seems there will be a great scandal regardless of what you say." Having a madman interrupt your wedding and then killing him did warrant gossip.

"You want me to tell what I know?"

"I want you to do what you feel is right."

A dark blush crept over Prycilla's neck and face. Anger twisted her features. "You are truly a fool. A scandal will ruin your chances of marrying into the Ashton family."

Irritation finally won through Spirit of the Mountain's numbness. She really disliked this woman, and she was tired of pretending otherwise. "You are the fool, Prycilla. What did you think to gain by coming to me? Money? Is that your purpose? Did you really think I would allow you to blackmail me?"

"If you were in your right mind, you would pay to keep such talk silent. I cannot figure you out. What manner of witch are you?"

This question made Spirit of the Mountain laugh. "Me? The witch? You have been trying to kill me. If there is a witch among us, it is you."

The blood drained from Prycilla's face, which became as white as a fine linen sheet. "How did you know?"

"I've known from the very first time you tried to poison my tea."

Prycilla looked doubtful. "You couldn't have known. Look at you. You are getting weaker every day."

"Think what you will, but my ill health is not related to your efforts."

Charles stepped into the room. His face showed he had heard their entire conversation. "Whatever possessed you to do such a thing, Prycilla? Are you really so evil?"

Prycilla stuttered, her hands reaching out to him. He swatted them away, as he would an irritating fly.

"Charles, I did it for us."

"You did it for yourself," he sneered, his look as venomous as his words. "You are an evil woman, but I allowed the notion I loved you to keep me from doing anything about it."

"Please, Charles, you cannot mean—"

"I can, and I do. Get out of this house. Get out of my life. I never want to set eyes on you again."

"No," Prycilla cried, tears filling her eyes. "She is the one who should get out." Her finger pointed to Spirit of the Mountain. "She is the one who has destroyed what we had, the love we shared. Do not do this, Charles."

"Get out."

When Prycilla did not move, Charles took her arm and shoved her toward the door. "Get out!"

She turned one last time, her eyes pleading. When Charles turned away, Prycilla looked at Spirit of the

Mountain and said nastily, "You will pay for this."

"Oh, Prycilla." Spirit of the Mountain actually felt sorry for her. "You did all this for nothing."

"What do you mean, for nothing? This was all supposed to be ours, not yours."

"That is what I mean. This will all be Charles's. If only you had been patient and waited."

For the first time, the woman had no retort. She slammed the door behind her. When the echo stilled, silence filled the room.

Finally, Spirit of the Mountain walked over to Charles. "I am so sorry, Charles. You shouldn't have heard our conversation."

"Would you have told me what she had done?"

"No."

"Then I am glad I did hear. I've been a fool, the greatest fool on earth."

Spirit of the Mountain placed a comforting hand upon his arm. "When our hearts love, even if our minds do not agree, we are helpless just the same to the hearts' greater power."

Charles turned to look at his cousin. "What did you mean that this will all be mine? You are the heir, Samantha."

Spirit of the Mountain was so tired she hadn't realized what she had said. "It seems my grandfather shall outlive me, Charles. The Jacoby estate will be yours soon. It was not meant to be mine."

"I don't understand," he replied. Then his face reflected horror at his next thought.

"No," she assured him. "Prycilla's plot was not successful."

"Then what—"

"It is something I cannot explain, Charles. It is something you would not understand."

"Surely, there is something we can do."

"Nothing."

Spirit of the Mountain left Charles in the study and sought the solace of her rooms. She needed to rest, to gather her strength to answer the questions morning would bring.

Chapter Twenty-six

Three clergymen sat across from Spirit of the Mountain, their hats clutched in hand, their black clothes as somber as their expressions. The plushness of the sitting room seemed in drastic contrast to their simple dress. The flowered tapestry settee loudly outlined the stiff-backed men crowded on it.

Spirit of the Mountain understood one of the men was the clergyman who had performed the aborted wedding ceremony, but which she couldn't have said. She remembered little of what had happened the day before, except Pierre's appearance and death.

Nathan stood beside the chair she sat in, his hand resting on the back of it. She felt comforted to know he was close. Charles and Joseph had taken seats to her right. She had insisted her grandfather remain in bed, as the doctor advised. He relented after the three men assured him they would be there, should she need them. Spirit of the Mountain felt secure.

"I am sorry, gentlemen. I do not understand what it is you want from me."

"Your grandfather and Joseph came to me and asked that I marry you two." It was Mr. Lewis who spoke, the man she had failed to recognize. The others merely sat, waiting. Mr. Lewis's eyes moved from her to Joseph, then back.

"I felt joy in doing this for a man I have known for many years, a man who has benefited my parish greatly. But now my heart is heavy with sorrow. What we want, Miss Jacoby, is the truth. Why was that man in my church?"

Charles stepped forward to answer. "He was a madman. That was quite obvious to us all."

"Yes." The pastor's voice remained soft, with a sort of singsong tone in its calmness. "He was a madman to come into a house of God and shoot a man in cold blood, then threaten others. What I need to know is why this man was intent on taking you, Miss Jacoby. Did you know this man?"

"Yes, his name was Pierre." Spirit of the Mountain realized she knew him only as Pierre.

"Pierre Charbeneau," Nathan said. "He was a trapper. The man was guilty of horrendous acts and most certainly deserved to die."

One of the pastor's eyebrows shot up. "It is not our right to determine if the man deserved to die, Mr. Walker. His guilt was meant for God to judge, not men such as yourself."

Nathan's anger was clear in his stance and his

voice. "My only regret, Mr. Lewis, is I wasn't the one to send him to his grave."

"But you weren't, Mr. Walker. It was Miss Jacoby. And I must confess I am concerned for her."

"In what way are you concerned for me?" Spirit of the Mountain asked.

This question drew the dark eyes back to her. Spirit of the Mountain was aware there was more to the man than his appearance projected. Beneath the sympathetic words lurked accusation.

"I witnessed you kill a man yesterday. This deed seems to bear no weight in your heart. There were no tears or hysterics for the gravest of acts that can be committed before God. I have yet to see any regret or despair. I see only a coldness that brings great trouble to my mind."

"Samantha would be dead had Pierre's pistol not misfired." Charles's voice was loud and filled with annoyance. "What sort of remorse must she feel for killing such a man? I think my cousin has answered enough of your questions. I must ask you to leave now."

Charles tried his best to hustle the group of men out, but the pastor resisted. "Is that what those filthy savages taught you, Samantha? To kill without conscience?"

Spirit of the Mountain was not surprised by his comment, suspecting all along there was something more to his questions.

But Charles grew extremely red in the face. His eyes were nearly bulging from their sockets in his fury. "I have asked you to leave, Mr. Lewis. I shall not be so courteous if I must do so again."

"Are you not curious about your cousin's past, Charles? Does it not concern you she has told no one where she has come from?"

"Samantha has recently come from the wilderness. It is all I need to know."

The persistent man pushed past Charles and went to stand in front of Samantha. "Was it your Indian family"—he paused, as if to think on a point—"Cherokee, wasn't it? Was it your Cherokee family who taught you to kill, to put a knife into a man's belly without so much as a remorseful thought?"

Charles grabbed the man by the scruff of the neck and forcefully hauled him to the door.

Spirit of the Mountain held up her hand. "I will answer his questions, Charles. I have nothing to hide from him or the others."

Mr. Lewis straightened his jacket and returned to his seat. The other two men, who were prepared to leave, followed his lead and also sat down again.

"Yes, Mr. Lewis, my adopted family was Cherokee."

"So you admit that you have been living with the Indians."

"I have never denied it."

His look was confused. "But you have kept this fact from everyone. Was it shame for what you have become?"

Spirit of the Mountain tried to keep the fire from her voice, to keep her feelings from the row of men who watched her so closely. "I feel no shame for my past. I am proud to call myself Cherokee."

"Then why be so secretive?"

Joseph cleared his throat to get Mr. Lewis's attention. "I knew about Samantha's past with the Cherokee. She told me. I believe, sir, it was no one else's business."

"It wasn't my business that I was about to marry you to a woman who has practiced heathen ways?"

"It wasn't her decision. Samantha's never wanted to deny her heritage." Nathan's voice was sympathetic, his gaze, when he turned to Spirit of the Mountain, apologetic. "We—Samuel and I—insisted she keep her past a secret. We thought it would be easier. We believed no one would understand what she'd been through."

Mr. Lewis stood. "What I understand, sir, is that she lived willingly with the Indians, that she bears no shame for what she has done."

Spirit of the Mountain faced Mr. Lewis with no hesitation, her head raised proudly, her gaze never faltering from his hateful one. "What is it that I have done?"

"You have blasphemed God with your fornication among savages, heathens who promote chaos and murder."

"Fornication?" This did not register in her mind.

"Yes, you willingly went to the bed of a red man. You even bore him a child out of this sinful union. You have flaunted this fact before God, even going as far as to proclaim your love for this heathen."

Shock pounded through Spirit of the Mountain's mind, then over her body. Waves of indignant anger and grief culminated in a point of explosion. Spirit of the Mountain stood, but words were hard to find in the turmoil of her heart. "You speak of a man who was my husband, a man I loved with all my heart and soul."

"You must repent, Samantha. You must ask God's forgiveness for your multitude of sins. You must repent and come back into the loving arms of Christianity. Leave behind your evil past. Deny the sinful woman you were. Come forth and be reborn."

"I do not need God's forgiveness. I have done nothing I am ashamed of. I have not sinned. I went to Red Hawk as a loving and faithful wife. Do not twist what was beautiful into something vile for your own demented mind to feed on."

"You do not know what you are saying, child. You must repent!"

"Get out." Spirit of the Mountain could take no more of this man's venom.

"Repent or you will know the wrath of God."

"Get out!"

Joseph and Charles each took one of Mr. Lewis's arm. Nathan was right behind them.

"Can't you see the error in your ways? Didn't God take your child because of your sins?" Mr. Lewis said.

This ripped her heart open. Spirit of the Mountain nearly crumbled beneath the assault.

"God took your child from you so he would not know a life of evil. You must ask God's forgiveness so you may be with your child in heaven, Samantha. Do you not want to be with your child when you die?"

Spirit of the Mountain quickly crossed to where Mr. Lewis stood. This was the second man to attack her dead child in the name of righteousness, and she could not—she would not—allow him to continue. "You are the one who should beg God's forgiveness. You are a man without enough love and kindness in your heart to speak of the dead in such an ugly way."

"I shall give you time to reflect on what you have done, my child. You stand accused of heresy and fornication. You must answer to these charges. In two days' time I will expect you to appear before a tribunal of clergymen to repent your past regressions and ask forgiveness."

"And if I do not?"

"Then you will burn in hell, Miss Jacoby."

"Whatever happened to guilt being God's judgment, Mr. Lewis, not being for men such as yourself to undertake?"

"I am a servant of God. His will is mine."

"No," she replied sadly. "I believe you are but a man who has gravely misunderstood his purpose in life."

Spirit of the Mountain turned and left the room, the pastor's cries of salvation and redemption trailing behind her, echoing in her mind even after she closed the door to her room. She wanted to cry, to release the anger that surged inside her. But no tears came. She was past tears.

Red looked up, pausing as he chewed on an old shoe Lillian had found for him to play with. Then Lillian came from the bedroom. "Is there anything I can get you, miss?"

"No, thank you, Lillian. I am fine."

Nathan entered Spirit of the Mountain's room. Charles and Joseph were right behind him. Lillian scooped up Red and hurried past them. "I'd best take Red for his walk, miss."

Lillian shut the door quietly behind her. Spirit of the Mountain gently caressed Nathan's cheek, then hesitantly touched the sling in which his arm was bound. "You look so tired, Nathan. Perhaps you should lie down. The doctor said not to do much for a few days."

Nathan closed his eyes, the slight burning in them telling him she was right. It amazed him that she would think of his own well-being at this time. He opened his eyes to see only concern in hers.

"You shouldn't be worrying over me," he whispered, taking her hand in his. He led her over to a chair and made her sit. "You must concentrate on the problem at hand."

"I see no need to give warrant to the man's ravings. I know in my heart what is right."

"But he can ruin your life, Samantha." Charles's face reflected the seriousness of his words.

Spirit of the Mountain smiled, all of them witness to her confidence. "It is easier to live with what lies in my heart than to worry over what lies in the hearts of others."

"But it isn't just yourself you must consider, Sam," Nathan said.

"Nathan is right," Charles added. "You must consider your grandfather."

Spirit of the Mountain understood what they wanted her to do. "You want me to repent, to ask forgiveness of my sins?" She stood and looked directly at Nathan. "You think I should do this for my sake as well as my grandfather's?"

"Yes," he whispered hoarsely. "It is the only way."

"No." She backed away from him. "You cannot ask this of me. You, of all people, know I cannot do this."

"You must."

"I cannot."

Charles took her by the shoulders and faced her to him. "If you know the truth deep in your heart, what does it matter what you do to appease these men?"

"If you truly understood, you would not ask this of me."

"If I understood what? You lived with the Cherokee to survive. You learned to be like them. You did what you had to. There is no sin in that. But now you must do what you must do to survive here."

"I did not live with the Cherokee to survive. I did not learn to be like them."

A sense of deja vu struck Nathan.

Spirit of the Mountain looked longingly at Nathan, wanting him, needing him, to stand by her. "You know that I am Cherokee. You know I am not Samantha Jacoby, but Spirit of the Mountain."

"This is nonsense," Charles said.

Nathan wanted to deny her claim, as he had all the other times. He tried to say the words, but none came. She was right. He knew so now. He had come to accept that her spirit was dying, but even then he had not fathomed the full truth of who she was. Who she was determined what decisions she made in life. For the first time, he truly understood. He truly believed.

Spirit of the Mountain had been right about so many things. Nathan was the man he was, not despite the time he spent with the Huron, but because of the Huron, just as she was a Cherokee, heart and soul.

"You are Spirit of the Mountain of the *Shaconage* Cherokee."

She smiled, tears darkening her eyes.

Charles sat, his shoulders slumped in defeat. "You're right. I don't understand."

"Who was this Pierre Charbeneau? Why did he follow you to Boston, Samantha?" Joseph asked.

Spirit of the Mountain felt Joseph had the right to know. So did Charles. "The village of my adopted people was attacked by the Shawnee. I was taken captive. They traded me for guns and ammunition. It was Pierre who bought me."

"That is why he said you were his? He bought you from the Shawnee?"

"Yes. Nathan helped me to escape, but Pierre followed."

"Dear God," Joseph mumbled, his eyes wide with horror.

"Nathan. Charles. I would like a moment in private with Joseph, please."

When the two men left them to their privacy, Joseph took her hand and kissed it. "I know you have been through much, Samantha. I can only imagine how much."

"But I have not gone through this alone, Joseph. Nathan has risked his life many times for my sake."

"Then I owe him a great deal."

Her heart ached for what she had to do. "Joseph, you are the kindest, most gentle of men. You have shown compassion and understanding for things you know nothing of."

"I love you, Samantha. What is in your past does not matter. We shall face the tribunal together. Together we shall end their false accusations and go on with our lives."

"It is too much to ask. I cannot marry you, Joseph."

"Please, Samantha. None of this matters."

She pulled away from him, unable to bear his love. "You are right. None of this matters. But there is one thing that does. I can never love you as you love me. You deserve better, Joseph. I am ashamed I have not been more honest with you."

"You have kept nothing from me. I know you do not return my love. Not now, anyway. In time—"

"There is no time for me. And I have kept something from you. I love Nathan with all my heart and soul. I cannot love you. Not now. Not ever."

Joseph sighed. "You have not kept this from me. That you love Nathan has been very clear from the first moment we met."

"Then why?"

"Why would I marry you when you are in love with another man? Because I cannot think of my life without you."

"I am so sorry, Joseph."

"I am not sorry to have known you, Samantha. I shall be there for you when you face the tribunal. I will stand by you even if it is as a friend."

A tightness in her throat made it difficult to speak. "Thank you," was all she could manage.

Chapter Twenty-seven

"Grandfather." Spirit of the Mountain rushed up the stairs to Samuel's side. His stance was wobbly as he leaned against Charles for support. Together they descended to the entry, where Nathan waited.

"You didn't think I'd lie about in bed while those hypocritical bastards wagged their pious fingers at you, did you?"

"But you are not strong enough to be up," Spirit of the Mountain scolded gently, helping Samuel to a chair.

"Damnation, child. I'll not let you face them alone."

"I am not alone."

Nathan, Charles, and Joseph would be by her side, but it was comforting knowing her grandfather would be there. And from the determined look on his face, she knew he would go.

"Charles." Samuel pointed impatiently at the door. "Go see what's taking them so long to bring the carriage about."

Charles nodded and left.

"Oh, dear. Samantha, would you mind getting my laudanum? I might need it."

Samuel watched his granddaughter go up the stairs, knowing she wouldn't have thought to ask a servant to get the medicine. "I wanted a moment alone, Nathan."

"What is on your mind, sir?"

"Samantha seems quite pale. Don't you think?" He heard Nathan suck in air. "What ails her, son?"

"I tried to explain it to you, Samuel. You wouldn't believe what I had to say."

"Are you still harping on this spirit nonsense? I would have thought you'd come to your senses by now."

"She is going to die, Samuel. Isn't that what matters?"

Samuel looked away. "If she knows this and believes it is because her spirit is dying, why doesn't she return to the mountains with you? She loves you. What is holding her back?"

"You are, sir."

"Me?"

"She promised to stay with you. She will."

"She would not be so foolish. There is nothing wrong, so there is no need for her to go. Samantha knows this, and so do I."

Nathan saw no point in arguing. He let it be.

Fela Dawson Scott

"Help me up, Nathan. Let's go set these sons of bitches right."

Nathan gave Samuel a helping hand. "There will be no setting them right, Samuel."

This remark stopped Samuel as they walked toward the front door. "What do you mean by that?"

"Nothing Samantha says will change what they believe. She has known that from the beginning."

"Then why is she going?"

"Because she is not afraid to face them and their prejudices."

Samuel seemed to puff up. "She's a Jacoby all right."

"She isn't facing the tribunal as Samantha Jacoby, but as Spirit of the Mountain."

"She's my granddaughter. A Jacoby. Period."

Nathan knew Samuel didn't want to hear differently. He didn't even know why he went on to explain. "I thought of your granddaughter as Samantha Jacoby, a white woman. I didn't believe she could be Spirit of the Mountain, the Cherokee woman she claimed to be. I was wrong. You are wrong."

Samuel pushed Nathan away and walked on his own. "Samantha is my granddaughter. Her past with the Indians is something she will forget."

"It is not something I will forget, Grandfather." Spirit of the Mountain stood at the top of the stairs, then walked down to stand by her grandfather.

Samuel's look was sympathetic, but pride dominated his features. "I know you loved them, child. But they are a part of your past. Let them go, and get on with your future."

"I cannot let go of who I am."

"Why?" Samuel demanded. "Why do you remain so faithful to the Cherokee? They are not your flesh and blood. I am your family."

Spirit of the Mountain didn't know how to make him understand. "Flesh, bone, and blood are merely the housing in which my soul rests. In death, it all withers and rots away, but my soul will live on. My soul and my heart belong to the Cherokee. It is what I am."

"You cannot believe this."

She could hear the agony in her grandfather's words. "I do believe this, Grandfather. I cannot bring dishonor to the memory of my adopted family by denying my love of them. Do not ask this of me again."

A long trestle table sat just below the altar, and eight members of the clergy were lined up behind it. A large, plain cross hung on the wall above them, as if in attendance with the tribunal.

Spirit of the Mountain studied the cross, then the faces watching her. She knew this tableau was meant to intimidate her as she waited for the men to begin. They had even made her sit alone, with her chair positioned so her loved ones must sit in the pews behind her. Instead, she felt comforted by the men who waited with her, only a few feet away, their love her fortitude.

"Miss Jacoby, serious charges have been brought against you," Mr. Lewis said at last. "We hope you understand the consequences of your answers to our questions here today."

Spirit of the Mountain remained quiet for a moment, drawing the last of her strength from deep within her. She concentrated on her Spirit Sister, visualizing her sister in nature as she was in life, cunning and strong. "Mr. Lewis," she said calmly, "I understand fully what you are about."

"If I might ask a question of my own," Samuel Jacoby interrupted.

"Certainly, Mr. Jacoby."

"Who has brought charges against my granddaughter?"

Mr. Lewis conferred with the other clergymen, then spoke for them all. "Miss Ryan came to us with concerns about Miss Jacoby's unholy ways."

Charles laughed. "You cannot take what Prycilla says seriously, Mr. Lewis. I broke our engagement because she tried to poison Samantha. Surely you do not believe her vicious lies?"

"Lies or not," Mr. Lewis said, "Miss Jacoby has admitted many of these accusations were true. She has but to comply with our demands, and we will ask no more questions."

"But then," Nathan said, his voice quiet, yet edged with menace, "the damage is done. Isn't it, Mr. Lewis?"

"Quite the contrary, Mr. Walker. Samantha's soul will be saved."

"I am not in need of saving, Mr. Lewis."

"From where I sit you are drowning in your need for redemption."

Spirit of the Mountain stood. "If you wish to ask me questions, ask. Otherwise, I shall be on my way."

"Sit, Miss Jacoby. We do have questions."

She sat. Her back remained straight, her chin high. Spirit of the Mountain would not allow them to see her distress.

"It is true that you have lived these past years with a Cherokee tribe?"

"Yes."

"How many years did you live with them, miss?"

"Since I was twelve."

Mr. Lewis seemed impatient, his fingers drummed on the table where he sat. "And how many years is that?"

"Eight."

He seemed to contemplate this answer. "I don't suppose that at the young age of twelve one can know the difference between right and wrong. I assume your mother and father were dead?"

"Yes. I lived alone in the mountains for over a year after my father died. He died about a year after my mother."

"So," Mr. Lewis said, standing and pacing the floor. "You were alone in the wilderness, with no place to go but to the Cherokee village?"

"I was alone, yes." Spirit of the Mountain knew where he was leading. "But I went to live with the Cherokee by my own choice."

"How can you consider to remain alone in a savage wilderness fraught with danger and hardship a choice?"

"The wilderness was my home. I saw no hardship or danger."

"Regardless, at the age of twelve you went to live with the Cherokee. You learned the Cherokee way?"

Spirit of the Mountain closed her eyes a moment,

to relieve the weariness and burning. She was exhausted, but she held strong. "I became Spirit of the Mountain, adopted daughter of Chaser of Dreams, shaman of the tribe."

"You claim you loved your adopted family. Was this a child's fancy in a difficult, if not impossible, time?"

"No, I loved my family because they loved me. I became a part of their family, a part of their lives."

"They were heathen savages. How can you speak of such things?"

"They were human beings. They were my family. I loved them dearly."

Mr. Lewis sat once again. "Did you love the man who took you to his bed, Miss Jacoby? Did you love what he did to you in the darkness of night?"

This was beyond her comprehension—their insinuations, their insults. "I loved my husband."

"In the eyes of God he was not your husband!"

"In the eyes of God I was his wife."

Nathan crossed the distance between Mr. Lewis and himself, his anger out of control. He grabbed the pastor and pulled him up with his one good arm so they were nearly nose to nose. "You are an abomination."

"And you, Mr. Walker, have brought this misguided child into our midst. Yet I believe your intentions were not so honorable."

Mr. Lewis twisted free of Nathan's hold and pointed his bony finger in Spirit of the Mountain's direction. "You have fornicated with the savage red man, and now you blatantly lie down with this man, professing your love for him as well."

Spirit of the Mountain rushed between Nathan and Mr. Lewis, fearing for the pastor's safety. The look on Nathan's face alone could kill, let alone what would happen if he got his hands on the other man again.

"You are a whore of the devil, Miss Jacoby. You claim a love for savages. You even dare to grieve for a child spawned from the unholy act of fornication."

Once again, he crushed her heart with his cruel words, hitting the deepest hurt that lay inside her, and she couldn't help saying, "You are the one who is evil."

As Mr. Lewis grabbed her hand, she heard a guttural growl come from Nathan.

"Take your hands from her."

The pastor seemed not to hear Nathan's warning. "Dear God, take this woman into your heart. Forgive her her lustful fornications of the past. Forgive her her youthful desire for a family's love, her misguided beliefs of her proper place in life."

Spirit of the Mountain pulled her hand free, feeling dirty from the pastor's touch. Before she could think, the same hand came up and slapped him hard across the face.

Like a good Christian, he turned the other cheek. And to her horror, she slapped it as well. She felt the floor sway, and she steadied herself on Nathan's arm. "Take me away from this, Nathan."

"Walk away from me now, Miss Jacoby, and you are walking away from God."

"God walks with me, Mr. Lewis. He is always with me."

"And what God are you speaking of, miss? My God

or the one those heathen savages worship?"

"My God is your God. He is one and the same. A God for all," she whispered, the blackness at the edge of her vision slipping closer.

"What manner of evil are you to dare say such a thing?"

Spirit of the Mountain shook free of the blackness and faced the tribunal. "You cloak yourselves in your pious ways, spewing condemnation from your ignorant lips. Like rats feeding upon garbage, you grow fat from your hatred of others. Your bigotry stems from gossip and rumor. You have not witnessed the wilderness, nor its Indian children. You know nothing of my life with the Cherokee, nor my love of them. You damn them and me with your blindness. It is you I feel sorry for. You are the ones who should seek God's forgiveness, not I."

She could not fight the darkness any longer. It took her, and she collapsed.

Chapter Twenty-eight

The first faint murmers—merely noises, not words—made no sense to Spirit of the Mountain. Slowly, the noises started to penetrate her mind, bringing her awake. She opened her eyes, the effort seeming to drain her.

She was in her own rooms. That much she could determine because the lacy canopy above her was familiar. Spirit of the Mountain turned her head to see who belonged to the voice she could not recognize. A man stood at the doorway, deep in conversation with Nathan. Nathan's voice told her he was not happy.

"I don't know what is wrong with her, Charles," the stranger said.

Nathan threw his hands up in the air in exasperation. "I've told you there is nothing that a doctor can do for her."

Charles entered the room and put a hand on Nathan's shoulder. "Nathan, we've got to do something."

"I would suggest bleeding Samantha," the doctor said.

Panic bolted through her. "No," she cried out weakly.

Nathan was immediately by her side, taking her hand in his. He rubbed it with a soothing touch. "You are awake," he whispered.

"Yes," she said, licking her lips. "Could I please have a drink of water?"

"Of course." Nathan rushed to the table and poured her a drink; then he helped her to sit so she could sip it.

"Nathan." She pulled his head close so she could whisper in his ear. "Do not let him do this bleeding. Do not allow him to cut me and drain what strength I have left."

He brushed her tangled hair back from her face. "I would never let him touch you, my sweet."

"It will do no good."

"Ssshhh, I know."

Charles came to stand beside Nathan. "The doctor knows what is best, Samantha. You must let him try to heal you."

"No."

The doctor came up behind Charles. "I must insist."

"No," she said determinedly. "Do not let this man touch me."

"Nathan, surely—"

Nathan cut Charles off. "Get him out of here."

If he'd ever considered defying Nathan, Charles looked as if he might at that point. But instead, he turned to the doctor and shrugged his shoulders.

"Are you mad?" the doctor said, standing his ground. When he got no response from either of the men, he spoke to Samantha. "You are dying, Miss Jacoby. You cannot expect me to stand by and do nothing."

"I am well aware I am dying, sir. It is my choice, and I must ask that you comply."

"I shall speak with your grandfather.".

"He will not change my mind."

The doctor all but stomped from the room, slamming the door behind him.

"Please, Samantha," Charles said, "you must try to get well."

"Dear Charles," she mumbled weakly. The effort of arguing with the doctor had been too much for her waning strength. "There is nothing the doctor nor I can do now."

"There must be something," Charles cried out.

Spirit of the Mountain saw the pain that twisted Nathan's handsome features. She reached out to smooth the lines from his face.

"Let me take you home, Sam. It is the only way."

Charles's attention moved to Nathan. "What do you mean?"

"She must go home to the mountains." Nathan's voice trembled. "The mountains are her medicine. They can give her life."

Charles's look was incredulous. "You are dying because you are homesick?"

"It isn't quite so simple, Charles," Nathan said. "But in a manner of speaking, yes. A wild animal that is captured and caged can long so strongly for freedom it will die."

"But Samantha is not a wild animal, Nathan."

Nathan closed his eyes. "Yes, she is, Charles. Her spirit is wild; the catamount gives Sam her strength. It is dying, and so will Sam."

A quiet peace came into Samantha's eyes, and Nathan knew he had finally given her what she needed. He thought he might die from sadness. "I am so sorry, my love. I have killed you with my ignorance. My stubbornness and misguided principles brought you here."

"We must take her home, Nathan." Charles's statement was simple, matter-of-fact.

"But she will not go home," Nathan said.

"Samantha, why won't you return to the wilderness? If it is what you need to survive, then go. Leave now. You must."

"I cannot." Her voice was so weak, so slight, Nathan had to lean closer to hear her. Samantha's eyes begged for him to explain. She could not.

"Sam has told her grandfather she will stay with him. She will honor this promise to the end."

"This is ridiculous. Come, Nathan. We will take her home."

Samuel Jacoby walked into the room, stopping his nephew from his purpose. "What is this, Charles?

You are not taking Samantha anywhere. Can you not see she is too ill to travel?"

"Uncle Samuel, we must."

"Why must we?"

The doctor followed Samuel into the room and returned to Samantha's bedside.

"Now," Samuel said with as much authority as he could muster in his condition, "we will leave the doctor to his business."

Neither Charles nor Nathan moved, but Nathan said, "She does not wish the doctor's help."

Samuel wobbled a few more steps, closing the distance between him and Nathan with the help of his cane. He lifted the wooden object and pointed it at him.

"You, sir, have no say in this matter. Leave this room. Leave my granddaughter to those who can help her.

Nathan made no effort to get out of Samuel's way, despite the threatening swing of the cane. "I will not let him touch her."

"Then I shall have you thrown out, Nathan. I'll not let you kill my granddaughter."

Nathan tried to control the anger that shook him and the overwhelming grief he felt at that moment. "It is your own stubbornness that is killing her, Samuel. Let her go. Let her live!"

"Are you still dwelling on the preposterous notion Samantha is dying because she needs to be in the mountains? You are a great fool, Nathan. I would have thought better of you."

Spirit of the Mountain laid her hand on Nathan's arm, keeping him from leaving her side.

Tears blurred her vision, and she could no longer see him. She touched his face, laying her palm to the warmth of his cheek. "I love you, Nathan."

Samuel wedged himself between Nathan and Spirit of the Mountain, breaking their hold. "You must let the doctor treat you, my dear. He can help you."

"No," she cried, her tears flowing freely. "Let me die in peace, Grandfather."

"Please, I beg you. Release Samantha from her promise. Let me take her home," Nathan said.

"If she wishes to go home, there is nothing stopping her."

Nathan cried out in outrage. "What must I do?"

Samuel sat on the edge of the bed. "Do you want to go home, Samantha? Is that what you wish?"

She drew in a deep breath. "It does not matter what I wish, Grandfather. I will not leave you."

His victorious look was like a punch in Nathan's gut. "You old fool. She would die before breaking her promise to you. Release her from the demands of her honor. Let her go home. Tell her it is what you wish."

"But—" Tears coursed over the deep wrinkles that lined Samuel's cheeks. He still held to his last hopes of keeping his granddaughter. "But she is home. She is where she belongs."

"She is dying." Nathan's voice was desperate. "What is more important, Samuel? Having her home or having her alive?"

Unable to decide, Samuel remained wordless as his face twisted with sorrow.

"For God's sake, set her free."

"Is this true, Samantha? Do you stay because of me?"

"Yes." She smiled. "I love you, Grandfather. I want only for you to be happy."

"But, if you stay, will you leave me soon?"

"Yes, I will leave you soon."

"Why?" Samuel asked, understanding slowly. "Why must you die?"

Spirit of the Mountain placed her hand over his, which felt leathery against the softness of her skin. "I cannot fight the spirit that is dying inside me, Grandfather. As hard as I have tried, I cannot win this battle."

"If—" Samuel had to clear his throat before he could continue. "If we take you back to your mountains, would you get better?"

"You would take me home?"

"I lost my son because of my stubbornness. I'll not lose you, too, Samantha."

The doctor stepped forward. "Neither of you are strong enough to travel. It is suicide."

"Charles," Samuel bellowed. "See the doctor to the door. We have no more need of his services."

"My pleasure." Charles smiled widely and took the doctor by the arm when he did not move on his own.

"Thank you, Samuel." Nathan offered his hand, and the older man took it.

"Tell me, my boy. Do you love her?"

"With all my heart and soul. She is my life."

"Are we going home, Nathan?" Spirit of the Mountain waited anxiously to hear his reply, to hear the man she loved confirm what she feared to believe.

"Yes, Samantha—" He stopped. "Spirit of the Mountain. I will take you home to *Shaconage*. I promise we shall never leave again."

Just hearing the words made her heart lighter, her soul stronger. The spirit within her came to life with the promise of going home.

Epilogue

Spirit of the Mountain held the letter to her heart. The words in the letter had been memorized and the paper worn after many readings. By the time she had received Charles's letter, many months had passed since he had written it. He was already married—the letter gave her the wonderful news he had fallen in love again. This time, he had assured her, the woman was beautiful, kind, and generous, much like the cousin he missed so dearly.

Joseph had left for England. Spirit of the Mountain hoped he would find happiness and love as well. He deserved to. Charles had no word of Prycilla, other than that she had left Boston. After all the woman had done, Spirit of the Mountain couldn't help but feel sorry for her.

Gently, Spirit of the Mountain rubbed her swollen

belly, the child she carried kicking her from within. He was anxious to be out in the world, and she was anxious to hold him close, to hear the beat of his heart and feel him suckle her breast. By the time her letter made its way to Boston in reply, her son would be born.

If only her grandfather were alive to know he would have a great-grandchild. Sadly, Spirit of the Mountain pulled herself up from the chair, the task taking longer because of the extra burden she carried. Her hand rested on her lower back as she placed the letter aside and left the cabin.

She walked a short distance to the place where her mother and father were buried. Nathan had reclaimed the small cemetery from the forest that had overtaken it in her long absence. A newer headstone stood to one side. The hand-carved piece of wood marked where her grandfather rested.

"The baby will be born soon, Grandfather."

Her mind traveled back to her homecoming. The event had been made more special because she had been able to share it with her family. They had helped her care for the personal possessions of her Cherokee family, giving them a traditional burial to guide their souls to the Great Spirit above.

Among the remains of her adopted family's lodge, Samuel had found a totem in the image of the cougar. Spirit of the Mountain's Indian father had started carving it before his death. Lovingly, Samuel had finished it for her.

It had been a long, hard journey for Samuel Jacoby, one he hadn't been able to make again. Spirit of the Mountain's gaze moved to the totem, tied onto the cross, a symbol of understanding, the meshing of two cultures. Tears came to her eyes; grief was still fresh in her heart. Had he traded his life for hers? This question seemed to dog her, leaving her no peace of mind.

Nathan came up behind Spirit of the Mountain and slid his arms around her, his hands feeling the roundness where their child lay. Red, now full grown, nudged her hand with his wet nose, reminding her that he, too, was there for her.

Nathan didn't speak for a long moment. "He died a happy man, love."

"But he did not die in his home. I took him away from it, and he could not get back."

Nathan sighed, knowing how this fact had troubled Spirit of the Mountain since their return. "You were willing to give up your life for Samuel's happiness. When he realized this, his decision to leave behind all he valued was easy. Your grandfather discovered that everything he had thought important paled when compared to having you share his last days on earth. It didn't matter whether he died here or in Boston. What mattered was that he died with you at his side."

"How is it I loved him so much in the short time we had together?"

"I don't know," Nathan replied, his arms holding her even closer. "Perhaps you both knew that you had only a little time together, that you must live a lifetime of love in a span of a few short months."

"We did do that."

"I love you," Nathan whispered, his breath soft, tickling her ear.

Just then, the baby moved inside Spirit of the Mountain. She turned and looked up into the vivid green of Nathan's eyes. "We love you, Nathan Walker, now and always."

SPECIAL SNEAK PREVIEW FOLLOWS!

Madeline Baker writing as Amanda Ashley

Cursed by the darkness, he searches through the ages for the redeeming light, the one woman who can save him. A creature of moonlight and fancy, she fears the handsome stranger whose eyes promise endless ecstasy even while his mouth whispers dark secrets. They are two people longing for fulfillment, yearning for a love like no other. Alone, they will face a desolate destiny. Together, they will share undying passion, defy eternity, and embrace the night.

Don't miss *Embrace The Night!* Coming in August 1995 to bookstores and newsstands everywhere.

He walked the streets for hours after he left the orphanage, his thoughts filled with Sara, her fragile beauty, her sweet innocence, her unwavering trust. She had accepted him into her life without question, and the knowledge cut him to the quick. He did not like deceiving her, hiding the dark secret of what he was, nor did he like to think about how badly she would be hurt when his nighttime visits ceased, as they surely must.

He had loved her from the moment he first saw her, but always from a distance, worshiping her as the moon might worship the sun, basking in her heat, her light, but wisely staying away lest he be burned.

And foolishly, he had strayed too close. He had soothed her tears, held her in his arms, and now he was paying the price. He was burning, like a moth drawn to a flame. Burning with need. With desire. With an unholy lust, not for her body, but for the very essence of her life.

It sickened him that he should want her that way, that he could even consider such a despicable thing. And yet he could think of little else. Ah, to hold her in his arms, to feel his body become one with hers as he drank of her sweetness . . . .

For a moment, he closed his eyes and let himself imagine it, and then he swore a long vile oath filled with pain and longing.

Hands clenched, he turned down a dark street, his self-anger turning to loathing, and the loathing to rage. He felt the need to kill, to strike out, to make someone else suffer as he was suffering.

Pity the poor mortal who next crossed his path, he thought. Then he gave himself over to the hunger pounding through him.

She woke covered with perspiration, Gabriel's name on her lips. Shivering, she drew the covers up to her chin.

It had only been a dream. Only a dream.

She spoke the words aloud, finding comfort in the sound of her own voice. A distant bell chimed the hour. Four o'clock.

Gradually, her breathing returned to normal. Only a dream, she said again, but it had been so real. She had felt the cold breath of the night, smelled the rank odor of fear rising from the body of the faceless man cowering in the shadows. She had sensed a deep anger, a wild uncontrollable evil personified by a being in a flowing black cloak. Even now, she could feel his anguish, his loneliness, the alienation that cut him off from the rest of humanity.

It had all been so clear in the dream, but now it made no sense. No sense at all.

With a slight shake of her head, she snuggled deeper under the covers and closed her eyes.

It was just a dream, nothing more.

Sunk in the depths of despair, Gabriel prowled the deserted abbey. What had happened to his self-control? Not for centuries had he taken enough blood to kill, only enough to assuage the pain of the hunger, to ease his unholy thirst.

A low groan rose in his throat. Sara had happened. He wanted her and he couldn't have her. Somehow, his desire and his frustration had gotten tangled up with his lust for blood.

It couldn't happen again. It had taken him centuries to learn to control the hunger, to give himself the illusion that he was more man than monster.

Had he been able, he would have prayed for forgiveness, but he had forfeited the right to divine intervention long ago.

"Where will we go tonight?"

Gabriel stared at her. She'd been waiting for him again, clothed in her new dress, her eyes bright with anticipation. Her goodness drew him, soothed him, calmed his dark side even as her beauty, her innocence, teased his desire.

He stared at the pulse throbbing in her throat. "Go?"

Sara nodded.

With an effort, he lifted his gaze to her face. "Where would you like to go?"

"I don't suppose you have a horse?"

"A horse?"

"I've always wanted to ride."

He bowed from the waist. "Whatever you wish, milady," he said. "I'll not be gone long."

It was like having found a magic wand, Sara mused as she waited for him to return. She had only to voice her desire, and he produced it.

Twenty minutes later, she was seated before him on a prancing black stallion. It was a beautiful animal, tall and muscular, with a flowing mane and tail.

She leaned forward to stroke the stallion's neck. His coat felt like velvet beneath her hand. "What's his name?"

"Necromancer," Gabriel replied, pride and affection evident in his tone.

"Necromancer? What does it mean?"

"One who communicates with the spirits of the dead."

Sara glanced at him over her shoulder. "That seems an odd name for a horse."

"Odd, perhaps," Gabriel replied cryptically, "but fitting."

"Fitting? In what way?"

"Do you want to ride, Sara, or spend the night asking foolish questions?"

She pouted prettily for a moment and then grinned at him. "Ride!"

A word from Gabriel and they were cantering

through the dark night, heading into the country-side.

"Faster," Sara urged.

"You're not afraid?"

"Not with you."

"You should be afraid, Sara Jayne," he muttered under his breath, "especially with me."

He squeezed the stallion's flanks with his knees and the horse shot forward, his powerful hooves skimming across the ground.

Sara shrieked with delight as they raced through the darkness. This was power, she thought, the surging body of the horse, the man's strong arm wrapped securely around her waist. The wind whipped through her hair, stinging her cheeks and making her eyes water, but she only threw back her head and laughed.

"Faster!" she cried, reveling in the sense of freedom that surged within her.

Hedges and trees and sleeping farmhouses passed by in a blur. Once, they jumped a four-foot hedge, and she felt as if she were flying. Sounds and scents blended together: the chirping of crickets, the bark of a dog, the smell of damp earth and lathered horse-flesh, and over all the touch of Gabriel's breath upon her cheek, the steadying strength of his arm around her waist.

Gabriel let the horse run until the animal's sides were heaving and covered with foamy lather, and then he drew back on the reins, gently but firmly, and the stallion slowed, then stopped.

"That was wonderful!" Sara exclaimed.

She turned to face him, and in the bright light of

the moon, he saw that her cheeks were flushed, her lips parted, her eyes shining like the sun.

How beautiful she was! His Sara, so full of life. What cruel fate had decreed that she should be bound to a wheelchair? She was a vivacious girl on the brink of womanhood. She should be clothed in silks and satins, surrounded by gallant young men.

Dismounting, he lifted her from the back of the horse. Carrying her across the damp grass, he sat down on a large boulder, settling her in his lap.

"Thank you, Gabriel," she murmured.

"It was my pleasure, milady."

"Hardly that," she replied with a saucy grin. "I'm sure ladies don't ride pell-mell through the dark astride a big black devil horse."

"No," he said, his gray eyes glinting with amusement, "they don't."

"Have you known many ladies?"

"A few." He stroked her cheek with his forefinger, his touch as light as thistledown.

"And were they accomplished and beautiful?"

Gabriel nodded. "But none so beautiful as you."

She basked in his words, in the silent affirmation she read in his eyes.

"Who are you, Gabriel?" she asked, her voice soft and dreamy. "Are you man or magician?"

"Neither."

"But still my angel?"

"Always, *cara*."

With a sigh, she rested her head against his shoulder and closed her eyes. How wonderful, to sit here in the dark of night with his arms around her. She could almost forget that she was crippled. Almost.

She lost all track of time as she sat there, secure in his arms. She heard the chirp of crickets, the sighing of the wind through the trees, the pounding of Gabriel's heart beneath her cheek.

Her breath caught in her throat as she felt the touch of his hand in her hair and then the brush of his lips.

Abruptly, he stood up. Before she quite knew what was happening, she was on the horse's back and Gabriel was swinging up behind her. He moved with the lithe grace of a cat vaulting a fence.

She sensed a change in him, a tension she didn't understand. A moment later, his arm was locked around her waist and they were riding through the night.

She leaned back against him, braced against the solid wall of his chest. She felt his arm tighten around her, felt his breath on her cheek.

Pleasure surged through her at his touch and she placed her hand over his forearm, drawing his arm more securely around her, tacitly telling him that she enjoyed his nearness.

She thought she heard a gasp, as if he was in pain, but she shook the notion aside, telling herself it was probably just the wind crying through the trees.

Too soon, they were back at the orphanage.

"You'll come tomorrow?" she asked as he settled her in her bed, covering her as if she were a child.

"Tomorrow," he promised. "Sleep well, *cara*."

"Dream of me," she murmured.

With a nod, he turned away. Dream of her, he thought. If only he could!

* * *

"Where would you like to go tonight?" Gabriel asked the following evening.

"I don't care, so long as it's with you."

Moments later, he was carrying her along a pathway in the park across from the orphanage.

Sara marveled that he held her so effortlessly, that it felt so right to be carried in his arms. She rested her head on his shoulder, content. A faint breeze played hide and seek with the leaves of the trees. A lover's moon hung low in the sky. The air was fragrant with night blooming flowers, but it was Gabriel's scent that rose all around her—warm and musky, reminiscent of aged wine and expensive cologne.

He moved lightly along the pathway, his footsteps making hardly a sound. When they came to a stone bench near a quiet pool, he sat down, placing her on the bench beside him.

It was a lovely place, a fairy place. Elegant ferns, tall and lacy, grew in wild profusion near the pool. In the distance, she heard the questioning hoot of an owl.

"What did you do all day?" she asked, turning to look at him.

Gabriel shrugged. "Nothing to speak of. And you?"

"I read to the children. Sister Mary Josepha has been giving me more and more responsibility."

"And does that make you happy?"

"Yes. I've grown very fond of my little charges. They so need to be loved. To be touched. I had never realized how important it was, to be held, until—" A faint flush stained her cheeks. "Until you held me. There's such comfort in the touch of a human hand."

Gabriel grunted softly. Human, indeed, he thought bleakly.

Sara smiled. "They seem to like me, the children. I don't know why."

But he knew why. She had so much love to give, and no outlet for it.

"I hate to think of all the time I wasted wallowing in self-pity," Sara remarked. "I spent so much time sitting in my room, sulking because I couldn't walk, when I could have been helping the children, loving them." She glanced up at Gabriel. "They're so easy to love."

"So are you." He had not meant to speak the words aloud, but they slipped out. "I mean, it must be easy for the children to love you. You have so much to give."

She smiled, but it was a sad kind of smile. "Perhaps that's because no one else wants it."

"Sara—"

"It's all right. Maybe that's why I was put here, to comfort the little lost lambs that no one else wants."

I want you. The words thundered in his mind, in his heart, in his soul.

Abruptly, he stood up and moved away from the bench. He couldn't sit beside her, feel her warmth, hear the blood humming in her veins, sense the sadness dragging at her heart, and not touch her, take her.

He stared into the depths of the dark pool, the water as black as the emptiness of his soul. He'd been alone for so long, yearning for someone who would share his life, needing someone to see him for what he was and love him anyway.

A low groan rose in his throat as the centuries of loneliness wrapped around him.

"Gabriel?" Her voice called out to him, soft, warm, caring.

With a cry, he whirled around and knelt at her feet. Hesitantly, he took her hands in his.

"Sara, can you pretend I'm one of the children? Can you hold me, and comfort me, just for tonight?"

"I don't understand."

"Don't ask questions, *cara*. Please just hold me. Touch me."

She gazed down at him, into the fathomless depths of his dark gray eyes, and the loneliness she saw there pierced her heart. Tears stung her eyes as she reached for him.

He buried his face in her lap, ashamed of the need that he could no longer deny. And then he felt her hand stroke his hair, light as a summer breeze. Ah, the touch of a human hand, warm, fragile, pulsing with life.

Time ceased to have meaning as he knelt there, his head cradled in her lap, her hand moving in his hair, caressing his nape, feathering across his cheek. No wonder the children loved her. There was tranquility in her touch, serenity in her hand. A sense of peace settled over him, stilling his hunger. He felt the tension drain out of him, to be replaced with a nearly forgotten sense of calm. It was a feeling as close to forgiveness as he would ever know.

After a time, he lifted his head. Slightly embarrassed, he gazed up at her, but there was no censure in her eyes, no disdain, only a wealth of understanding.

"Why are you so alone, my angel?" she asked quietly.

"I have always been alone," he replied, and even now, when he was nearer to peace of spirit than he had been for centuries, he was aware of the vast gulf that separated him, not only from Sara, but from all of humanity as well.

Gently, she cupped his cheek with her hand. "Is there no one to love you then?"

"No one."

"I would love you, Gabriel."

"No!"

Stricken by the force of his denial, she let her hand fall into her lap. "Is the thought of my love so revolting?"

"No, don't ever think that." He sat back on his heels, wishing that he could sit at her feet forever, that he could spend the rest of his existence worshiping her beauty, the generosity of her spirit. "I'm not worthy of you, *cara*. I would not have you waste your love on me."

"Why, Gabriel? What have you done that you feel unworthy of love?"

Filled with guilt of a thousand lifetimes, he closed his eyes and his mind filled with an image of blood. Rivers of blood. Oceans of death. Centuries of killing, of bloodletting. Damned. The Dark Gift had given him eternal life—and eternal damnation.

Thinking to frighten her away, he let her look deep into his eyes, knowing that what she saw within his soul would speak more eloquently than words.

He clenched his hands, waiting for the compas-

391

sion in her eyes to turn to revulsion. But it didn't happen.

She gazed down at his upturned face for an endless moment, and then he felt the touch of her hand in his hair.

"My poor angel," she whispered. "Can't you tell me what it is that haunts you so?"

He shook his head, unable to speak past the lump in his throat.

"Gabriel." His name, nothing more, and then she leaned forward and kissed him.

It was no more than a feathering of her lips across his, but it exploded through him like concentrated sunlight. Hotter than a midsummer day, brighter than lightning, it burned through him and for a moment he felt whole again. Clean again.

Humbled to the core of his being, he bowed his head so she couldn't see his tears.

"I will love you, Gabriel," she said, still stroking his hair. "I can't help myself."

"Sara—"

"You don't have to love me back," she said quickly. "I just wanted you to know that you're not alone anymore."

A long shuddering sigh coursed through him, and then he took her hands in his, holding them tightly, feeling the heat of her blood, the pulse of her heart. Gently, he kissed her fingertips, and then, gaining his feet, he swung her into his arms.

"It's late," he said, his voice thick with the tide of emotions roiling within him. "We should go before you catch a chill."

"You're not angry?"

"No, *cara*."

How could he be angry with her? She was light and life, hope and innocence. He was tempted to fall to his knees and beg her forgiveness for his whole miserable existence.

But he couldn't burden her with the knowledge of what he was. He couldn't tarnish her love with the truth.

It was near dawn when they reached the orphanage. Once he had her settled in bed, he knelt beside her. "Thank you, Sara."

She turned on her side, a slight smile lifting the corners of her mouth as she took his hand in hers. "For what?"

"For your sweetness. For your words of love. I'll treasure them always."

"Gabriel." The smile faded from her lips. "You're not trying to tell me good-bye, are you?"

He stared down at their joined hands: hers small and pale and fragile, pulsing with the energy of life; his large and cold, indelibly stained with blood and death.

If he had a shred of honor left, he would tell her good-bye and never see her again.

But then, even when he had been a mortal man, he'd always had trouble doing the honorable thing when it conflicted with something he wanted. And he wanted—no, needed—Sara. Needed her as he'd never needed anything else in his accursed life. And perhaps, in a way, she needed him. And even if it wasn't so, it eased his conscience to think it true.

"Gabriel?"

"No, *cara*, I'm not planning to tell you good-bye. Not now. Not ever."

The sweet relief in her eyes stabbed him to the heart. And he, cold, selfish monster that he was, was glad of it. Right or wrong, he couldn't let her go.

"Till tomorrow then?" she said, smiling once more.

"Till tomorrow, *cara mia*," he murmured. And for all the tomorrows of your life.

WIND RIDER
Connie Mason

Romantic Times Storyteller Of The Year

A white man by birth, Wind Rider has given his heart to
the Indians who raised him. Grown to a mighty warrior, he
lives to protect his people from the invasion of settlers who
will take their land. But who will defend him from the
exasperating Irish beauty whose soft, sensuous touch sears
his very soul?

An indentured servant desperate to escape her cruel master,
Hannah McLin will do anything to be free—even trust a
Cheyenne brave. Amid the splendor of the untamed
wilderness, she won't allow herself to admit her attraction
to his hard-muscled body. She can't yield to the bold,
passionate longing in his silver eyes. But the closer they come
to the safety of civilization, the hotter Hannah burns to
succumb to the fiery caresses of the man called Wind Rider.

___3692-4 $4.99 US/$5.99 CAN

DANCE of the FLAME

ELAINE BARBIERI

**Elaine Barbieri's romances are
"powerful...fascinating...storytelling at its best!"
—*Romantic Times***

Exiled to a barren wasteland, Sera will do anything to regain the kingdom that is her birthright. But the hard-eyed warrior she saves from death is the last companion she wants for the long journey to her homeland.

To the world he is known as Death's Shadow—as much a beast of battle as the mighty warhorse he rides. But to the flame-haired healer, his forceful arms offer a warm haven, and he swears his throbbing strength will bring her nothing but pleasure.

Sera and Tolin hold in their hands the fate of two feuding houses with an ancient history of bloodshed and betrayal. But no matter what the age-old prophecy foretells, the sparks between them will not be denied, even if their fiery union consumes them both.

___3793-9 $5.99 US/$6.99 CAN

An Angel's Touch

Time Heals
SUSAN COLLIER

Tired of her nagging relatives, Maeve Fredrickson asks for the impossible: to be a thousand miles and a hundred years away from them. Then a heavenly being grants her wish, and she awakes in frontier Montana.

Saved from the wilderness by a handsome widower, Maeve loses her heart to her rescuer—and her temper over the antics of his three less-than-angelic children. As her angel prods her to fight for Seth, Maeve can only pray for the strength to claim a love made in paradise.

_52030-3 $4.99 US/$5.99 CAN

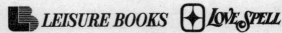